Homeward Bound

Richard Irvin

Homeward Bound

Richard Smith

Matador
9 Priory Business Park,
Wistow Road, Kibworth Beauchamp,
Leicestershire, LE8 0RX
Tel: 0116 279 2299
Email: books@troubador.co.uk
Web: www.troubador.co.uk/matador
Twitter: @matadorbooks

ISBN 978 1838591 595

British Library Cataloguing in Publication Data.
A catalogue record for this book is available from the British Library.

Printed and bound by CPI Group (UK) Ltd, Croydon, CR0 4YY
Typeset in 12pt Adobe Jenson Pro by Troubador Publishing Ltd, Leicester, UK

Matador is an imprint of Troubador Publishing Ltd

*To everyone who gave me time, space,
inspiration and encouragement to write, especially
Arthur Packer, Derek O'Reilly and Douglas Hill,
who sadly will never know how important they were.*

Chapter 1

There were two things George Turnbull treasured above all else. One, his piano – upright, of no particular repute, King's Head not Royal Albert Hall, but much played and well loved.

"This is our luxury accommodation. The Churchill Suite."

"Lovely and roomy." Toby nodded, turning to his wife for affirmation.

"We allow our residents to keep their most precious mementos," the sales pitch continued. "Picture of a loved one to put on the dressing table, favourite clock. So long as it's not too large."

The second was his record collection, several thousand vinyl LPs, EPs and singles, and almost as many CDs.

"We find these suites are very popular, especially with our well-to-do guests."

"Ah. That's something that might be a problem. You see, George isn't really that 'well-to-do'. That's true, isn't it, darling?" Toby paused, turning to Bridget. She frowned, narrowed her eyes and glowered. "My wife and I will be selling his house in London. Even so, I'm afraid we may not be quite in the right – how should I say – ballpark? For the Churchill Suite."

"No matter." Mrs Williams carefully straightened a badge on her lapel. Worn like an ornamental brooch, it sported a designer logo, her name and the words, 'Proprietor, Lastdays Rest Home'. "Perhaps Mr Turnbull would like to see one of our Mornington Rooms." She barely glanced at George as she spoke. "Follow me. They're just down the corridor. An acceptably affordable option, we like to think."

There was a third thing, George now realised. To piano and records, add his cuttings. He'd kept every review, from his first performance pictured in the *Swindon Advertiser*, complete with ration-book outfit and National Service cropped hair, to his last at the Pavilion Ballroom, Strathpeffer, where his hair had been shorn not by clippers but by time. Except they weren't really cuttings. He'd kept the whole newspaper. The front-page banner headlines weren't international issues, more 'Council Debates Road Closure', 'Stray Dog Causes Travel Chaos', 'Garden Blaze Destroys Shed'. And they weren't so much reviews as gig listings and 'Also Playing'. Yet he had them all. This monument to the past was in the same room as his music, a wall of yellowing paper, stacked in date order. 'A fire waiting to happen,' Toby called them.

Bridget put her hand gently on George's arm. "Let's move on to the Mornington Rooms. Don't you think so, Dad?"

"If you want to, Bridget."

It was the first time anyone had addressed George directly for some while, though in truth, he'd hardly been listening. For he'd suddenly realised there was a fourth treasure. Hunter. How could he have left him out? An ageing Labradoodle, struggling with a failed pancreas and the effects of a drug overdose, it was a miracle he was still alive. He'd been Evelyn's dog, but Hunter surely had to fit into the rankings. Was he less important than the cuttings? And was the piano really more important than the records?

"Are you feeling alright, Dad?"

"Just thinking."

"What about?"

"Come on, let's get moving or we'll run out of time to sort anything out." Toby swayed impatiently as he spoke.

"I was thinking about my music. Actually." George ignored his son-in-law.

"Lovely." Mrs Williams strode off down the corridor like a tour guide on speed. "Was Mr Turnbull a musician? Left here for the Mornington Rooms."

Without looking back to check if anyone was following, she made a sharp turn, narrowly avoiding a parked commode. The others duly followed in silent procession: first Toby, mid-fifties, short, greying, appearance by-passed by fashion; then Bridget, younger in age, dress and manner, hair coloured red – too red according to Tara, her teenage daughter. George followed, tall, pale and reluctant, sporting a new knitted jumper, half of an outfit Bridget had bought specially to help 'bring him out of himself', the other half having been rejected in favour of decades-old slacks. All that was missing was a band playing 'The Conga' and any sense of celebration.

Mrs Williams stopped at a sign overhead. 'Mornington Wing'. "We have thirty-two Mornington Rooms, and as luck would have it, since yesterday, one vacancy. Once the room's been cleared."

Toby nodded. "Naturally."

"Yes, very sad. But not really a surprise. Dear Ruby." Mrs Williams paused for a moment, shaking her head. "Anyway, this wing is named after Gladys Mornington, one of our first guests. Ninety-three when she passed away. She loved music. And you say Mr Turnbull is musical? He'll be very welcome at Christmas. We have a sing-a-long in the communal room."

"He *used* to be a musician, yes," Toby emphasised.

"You never lose it," George murmured to himself but audibly enough for everyone to hear.

"He played in bands, supported some of the biggest acts from the sixties until he retired. Didn't you, Dad?" Bridget's tone was part proud, part defensive. George looked away, letting pass his daughter's announcement that he'd retired. She carried on. "You should see his record collection!"

"Wonderful. We love people with such rich histories."

George could sense a 'but' approaching. He wasn't normally wrong when it came to anticipating what people were about to say. Seventy-nine years on this planet taught you most things you needed to know about people.

"I love music myself." Mrs Williams' smile didn't falter. "But of course, we can't accept personal collections here. We have to consider *all* our residents."

Toby nodded vehemently, stern-faced. "Absolutely. Wouldn't expect it. We can probably help him download some tunes to an iPod."

"iPod? I haven't got a bloody iPod."

"Language, *please*, George." Mrs Williams spoke as if addressing a class of under fives.

"And don't bloody 'George' me, *Mrs* Williams."

Toby stepped between them. "Dad, please!"

"And I'm not your dad. Bridget, get me out of here. Please. Now."

"If your father-in-law continues to behave in this manner, I regret we won't be able to welcome him into our family. We are a respectable establishment with a reputation to uphold." Mrs Williams' back stiffened as she spoke.

"Bugger your reputation."

"Well, really! I think you should leave."

George didn't need a second invitation. "Good! I didn't want to bloody be here in the first place."

"Dad!" Bridget hesitated, watching her father march off before giving chase, leaving Toby making apologetic noises in their wake.

For a man his age, who'd spent the last few months on a succession of repeat prescriptions, George was remarkably nimble. A burst of acceleration took him past a nurse escorting two inmates on Zimmers, then around a corner and into a low, dimly lit corridor. Plastered walls, fading magnolia paint discoloured by shaky hands and scarred by daily collisions with trolleys of meals and medication, were broken up only by anonymous, closed doors. Without looking back, George took two abrupt right turns, then a left, each manoeuvre luring him further into the maze and leaving him breathless. But at least it succeeded in shaking off his daughter. Not that he really wanted to, just he needed a few seconds to himself before she found him and the inevitability of confrontation and climb-down.

He reached a crossroads with three more identikit corridors, the corners of each chipped by wheelchair rims George guessed had been made by residents whose departure to the Garden of Remembrance had long since been forgotten.

A single photograph broke the monotony of magnolia. Beaming at him in faded colour was the cast of a pantomime in full stage make-up and costume. He leaned in to read the label: 'St Martin's School Year 2 Christmas Show 1989'. On their faces, smiles of innocence, hope and expectation. And reflecting back from the glass, George saw his own face, tarnished by experience and disappointment.

"Have you come to my party?"

The voice was weak and wavering, barely escaping from a skeletal figure, skin creased and ivory coloured, attempting to back a wheelchair through a closed door.

"I don't think so. But can I help?" George stepped across and pushed at the door. It swung open into a small hall that matched the corridors for bleakness. Worn armchairs were lined up around the sides. These walls were light brown, not magnolia. In the corner, a shelf supported a fish bowl, green slime on the glass and two motionless goldfish, colour now faded by age and neglect, facing a solitary strand of plastic weed. Across the room were two windows without curtains and to their frames had been Blu-Tacked a pair of partially inflated balloons. Along one wall, a row of A4 sheets of paper was hanging limply, taped together to form a banner, declaring in red felt tip, 'Happy 81st Wedding Anniversary Bernard'.

"I'm Bernard, you know."

"Pleased to meet you, Bernard." There was no reason for George to carry over his distaste for Lastdays with someone who looked unlikely to survive to his eighty-second anniversary – or indeed to the next weekend.

Bernard narrowed his eyes, the creases on his brow deepening further. "Do I know you?"

"I don't think so."

"Don't remember you if I do. Don't remember much of anything."

Bernard's voice dropped unhappily away.

"And is your wife here too?"

"My wife?"

"You must remember your wife. After eighty-one years!" It was meant as part-joke, part-compliment that they'd lasted for so long.

Bernard obviously didn't see it that way. "Of course I remember my wife. I'm not stupid, you know."

"No, sorry. I didn't mean that at all."

"Though I do forget things sometimes. And I don't hear as well as I used to."

"Sorry, I didn't mean to offend you." George was saved by the arrival of a nurse – young, blonde, cheery, barely out of her teens, as yet untarnished by her worn surroundings. Dressed in the same uniform as Mrs Williams, she also wore a Lastdays-branded badge, but instead of a name, someone had scrawled in blue felt pen, 'Trainee.'

"There we are, Bernard. We were wondering what had happened to you."

"I've been here all the time." Bernard sounded defeated rather than defiant.

"I was asking him where his wife was. Eighty-one years. That's quite something."

"Sadly she's not here."

"Oh. I do hope I'm not intruding." George wondered if he'd stumbled on something serious – and on the very occasion of their eighty-first anniversary. What would eighty-one years be? Titanium? Was there even a name invented for so many years of marriage? And what if something terrible had happened, today of all days?

"Who's not here?" Bernard demanded.

"Lillian," Trainee responded, in a voice George would have reserved for competing with a low-flying jumbo jet.

"Didn't think she would be."

George frowned, uncomprehending.

"She's at the hospital." Trainee said this in a normal voice as it was directed at George, then returned to ear perforation levels for Bernard. "Not allowed out, is she?"

"Is Bernard completely deaf?"

"Not completely, but you still have to shout at him, silly old sausage. He doesn't understand very much these days."

"And what happened to his wife?"

"Poor Lillian." Trainee dropped her voice again, reaching a level that not only suggested she was breaking a confidence but also had George straining to hear. "So sad. She started to get difficult, you know. We did our best to keep her, but in the end, Mrs Williams had her, you know..."

"That's terrible."

"Yes. Two weeks ago. Just after I got here. We were so sad."

"What a shame."

"So close to their anniversary, too. Apparently, they'd hardly spent a night apart in all that time."

Bernard had fallen silent, staring into his lap. Trainee lifted her voice again and directed a reprise at him.

"Eighty-one years together, you and your Lillian. And hardly a night apart in all that time. Isn't that true, Bernard?"

"Eighty years too long. Old nag."

"Now, now, Bernard, don't be like that."

"Should have got shot of her when I was still young enough to make use of it."

George grimaced at the unwelcome revelation, though from Trainee's reaction, she seemed to find it funny.

Bernard looked up at her. "How old am I?"

"Ninety-nine next birthday."

"Am I? What am I doing still here? I should have snuffed it years ago."

"We've got a lot of life in us yet, haven't we?" Trainee patted him sympathetically, an action that might once have ruffled a thick mop of hair but was now more like polishing his head. "So how long have we known Bernard?"

George knew this question was to him as the volume had returned to normal. "*I* don't know him, actually." He pointedly emphasised he was an 'I'.

Trainee didn't react to his correction. "So what brings us to Lastdays?"

"My son-in-law. He's never liked me."

"Don't let them put you in this shit-hole." Bernard jerked his head away from Trainee's hand.

"Oh, Bernard, what are we going to do with you, you rascal?"

"Don't listen to them. They take everything away from you. Your possessions. Your freedom. Your life…" His voice trailed off.

"Bernard. We know that's not true. We've got a nice room, a television. We've even allowed you to keep Lillian's lava lamp." She turned to George. "Of course, we can't turn it on. It's so old, it gets very hot. We're very keen on health and safety here."

"I used to have model ships," Bernard said to no one in particular.

"I'm sure they were wonderful." If Trainee hadn't meant to sound patronising, she failed.

"People always admired my collection. I had whole fleets."

"Now where would we have put those? Your room would have been overflowing, wouldn't it? And we couldn't have that, could we?"

"I knew where every one came from. They were all numbered and named." Bernard fell silent again.

"I must go." George turned to leave.

"We hope we'll see you again, as part of our little family."

"I'm not sure I'll be welcome."

She laid her hand gently on George's. "Everyone's welcome at Lastdays."

"I was an engineer, a skilled craftsman." Bernard sat forward. "Won awards for my work." He slumped back into his chair, his shoulders sagging.

"I think Bernard needs a rest. He always starts talking nonsense when he's tired."

"Really? He sounds to me like the only one who's made any sense since I've been here." George jerked his hand free, determined this time to leave.

"Well, we hope we'll see you again."

"I hope not." He didn't look back but headed towards the warren of corridors, feeling both a sense of relief at leaving and guilt at abandoning Bernard.

"How old am I?" he heard from behind. He didn't look back, but hurried on, turning a corner and, pushing open a door labelled 'Fire Exit', stepped into a gravelled courtyard, where a plaster Venus dribbled water into a weed-choked pond.

"So there you are." Bridget emerged from a door on the opposite side.

"I expect you hoped I'd be locked up here forever."

"Dad, please don't be like this."

"Like what?"

"So difficult. And swearing at Mrs Williams."

"Swearing? If she can't stand a bit of Anglo-Saxon…" He turned away from her.

Bridget's tone softened a little. "I think you'll find 'bugger' is Middle English."

George turned back, revealing a reluctant half-smile on his face. "I knew a university education would be a dangerous thing. You're wasted on him, you know."

He gestured behind her, towards Toby who was now striding into the courtyard from a third door, Mrs Williams having apparently de-materialised.

"What the bloody hell are you playing at?" he growled through clenched teeth when he caught up with them.

George cupped his ear. "Pardon? I can't quite hear you over the musical tones of trickling water and the sound of people waiting to die."

"Don't be so bloody sarcastic."

"Tut tut, my boy."

"And I'm not your boy, as *you* were quick to remind *me*."

George considered saying 'Touché', but that might have sounded conciliatory, which was the last thing he was feeling. "I'm leaving."

"There's no point in staying. Mrs Williams has withdrawn the offer."

Bridget flashed a warning look that Toby missed. George didn't.

"Offer? *What* offer?" George turned on his daughter. "Bridget, what's been going on behind my back?"

"Dad, can we please go back to the car?"

"Or were you expecting to leave me here? Did you book me a space in the communal graveyard while you were at it?"

Toby grunted, turned and stomped off in the direction he'd come. In an act of defiant independence, George headed back towards the door he'd used, only to find it locked from the inside.

"This way, Dad." Bridget's resigned tone was matched by an apologetic gesture, pointing at Toby, striding away from them. Together, they followed.

By the time they reached the car park, the conga had become a straggling crocodile, with Toby still pacing out in front, Bridget in his slipstream and George reluctantly behind, not because he didn't want to leave quickly but because he was now having a job keeping up. Considering he'd been having trouble with his breathing for some time, he'd done well so far. But the heavy cold that'd turned to pneumonia before Christmas was catching up on him. And his hands were shaking, something he noticed happening from time to time.

It all would have been OK if Evelyn had still been around. 'Tell me if we're ever any trouble to you,' she'd confidently instructed their daughter a couple of years back. 'The last thing we want to be is a burden.' Bridget had laughed and said that would never happen. Now Evelyn had passed away and he didn't need telling that he *had* become a burden. After the funeral, Bridget had persuaded him to spend a short while with her, Toby and Tara. To help him come to terms with his bereavement, she'd said. It'd seemed a good idea at the time. But the short while had stretched to twenty weeks. From the way Toby was carrying on, George knew he'd overstayed the welcome by at least nineteen. Yet how was he ever going to get away and still keep his records? Not to mention his piano, his papers, Hunter.

Chapter 2

"How'd it go, then, Dad?" Tara looked up from *Teen Tips.*

"Don't ask." Toby dropped into the driver's seat and slammed the door shut.

"How'd it go, then?" Tara repeated as her mum slid in beside her at the back.

"Not a great success, darling. Your dad's a bit frustrated."

"You can say that again. And I wish he'd get a bloody move on. We've another four to get to." Toby thrust the key in the ignition.

"Four? I thought you promised Gramps a cream tea by the beach."

"We will, dear, if we get time."

"There won't be any time if he doesn't get a move on. What's he doing now?" They watched as George stopped to lean against a crumbling, rotted wooden sign, its pale, faded lettering welcoming visitors to Lastdays and introducing the rest home's 'proud supporters'.

"That's appropriate, don't you think, Mum? The sign. Falling apart. Past its best."

Toby drummed his fingers on the steering wheel. "Look, he's sitting on it. I think he's doing this on purpose. If he breaks it, he can pay Mrs Williams for a replacement."

"I'm more worried about how frail he's looking." Bridget was tapping her knuckles against her lips.

Tara screwed up her face. "Why's he have to go into a home at all?"

"Just look at him." Toby's drumming became more agitated.

"Your dad's worried about your grandfather's health."

"Not just his health," Toby muttered.

"Dad thinks he's becoming a bit... forgetful."

"I like him living with us."

"How would you know, you're always in your bedroom." Toby's fists were now pummelling the steering wheel. "This'll get him moving." He turned the ignition key and the car burst into life.

Bridget leaned forward to restrain him. "Please, give him time."

"He's pretending to read the bloody sign now."

"Have you read what it says?" Tara pointed at it through her window.

Bridget shook her head. "Not now, darling."

"But read it."

"Later. He's coming now." Bridget sat back. "Can we let this drop, please?"

Tara didn't. "You still haven't said why you need to put him in here."

"It's not going to be here," Toby growled.

"Why's he have to go anywhere?"

Bridget turned to her daughter. "You remember when he left the gas hob on when we were all out?"

"So?"

"Twice." Toby threw his arms in the air. "Could he walk any slower? He's doing this just to annoy me, I know he is."

"Please be patient, dear."

It was the first time in months that Tara had heard her mother use an affectionate term towards her husband. It was lost on Toby.

"Look at him. Just look at him. Do you honestly think he can look after himself?"

Bridget turned her attention back to her daughter. "Your dad's worried something dreadful might happen to your grandfather if he's left alone." She spoke without conviction.

"He'll be a risk to himself." Toby was still talking in capital letters. "He completely depended on your grandmother. He sits around all day. Never does anything. Never says anything. Except talking to himself. And have you noticed how his head and hands tremble? How can anyone think he'll manage on his own?" He tapped the side of his head. "Things happen to your brain as you get older."

"So why can't he stay with us?"

"Neither your mother nor I can nursemaid him. And I don't suppose you're offering." Toby had sat back now, arms clasped behind his head.

"And where would he go?" Bridget stared anxiously out of the window at her dad. "The house isn't really big enough for the three of us."

"It need only be two of you when I go to uni."

Toby flashed a look at Tara in the rear-view mirror. "Don't be bringing that up again, young lady. You know what I've said. The decision is made."

Bridget tapped Tara's elbow as a warning. Tara either missed it or ignored it.

"So what's wrong with a Grampy flat? You could build one over the garage. Or in the garage? You always leave the car on the drive."

Toby gave the wheel another violent thump. "Oh, get a bloody move on, man."

Bridget tightened her grip on Tara's elbow. "We can't have him. It'd be bad for him. He can't live his life through us and he can't live alone. Sheltered accommodation will help him find a new life."

Tara brushed her mum's hand away. "Mmm. And then what about Hunter? If you put Gramps in a home?"

"It's not staying with us, that's for sure." Toby revved up the engine.

* * *

George stared into the bare trees that surrounded the car park, the last few leaves quivering in the breeze, clinging hopelessly to the boughs. What was left for him? A pointless existence dependent on others, where every memory lapse was a sign of dementia, every ache the onset of something terminal – at least that seemed to be how Bridget and Toby saw it. Why had he agreed to stay with them? It was for the best, Bridget had said when they'd invited him, but it hadn't been fun for any of them, he knew that. That's why he'd done his best to be inconspicuous, invisible, letting them get on with their lives, with no intervention from him. And what thanks did he get? It was hard keeping quiet, keeping out of conversations and arguments, not expressing an opinion or taking sides. Or not letting on that while they thought he'd been dozing, he'd noticed things, not least Toby's hushed conversations on his mobile that didn't sound like work.

'We've Gotta Get Out Of This Place' – a song he'd loved since the sixties – was playing in his head now, the imagined pounding rhythm and urgent vocals pulsating through him, his feet tapping, his body pumping, his lips silently mouthing the lyrics. The revving of Toby's car jerked him back into reality. Easing himself up, he stumbled towards the car. He could see them all talking and didn't need to be able to lip-read to know it would be about him.

Tara wound her window down. "Come on, Gramps. Dad says he's going without you."

"Tara," Bridget hissed.

"Only joking."

"Keep it to yourself."

"Who's Mrs Grumpy, then?"

Seeing Bridget and Tara at each other's throats gave George no satisfaction. He didn't want to be dragging his granddaughter into the argument. After all, his grudge was with Toby and Bridget. He heaved himself into the front passenger seat and swung his legs around with great difficulty.

"They ought to make cars a decent size."

"For Christ's sake, it's a Peugeot 607. It's big enough for a bloody tank regiment."

George fumbled with the safety belt and succeeded only in firing his seat backwards.

"Ouch!" Tara had been resting her feet on the seat back and the motion jarred her knees up to her chin.

Bridget took a deep breath. "I've told you before not to sit like that."

"Where am I supposed to put my feet, then?"

"Not on the back of the seat."

"There's no room." Tara thumped her feet sulkily on the floor.

"Christ, what's the matter with you all?" Toby reached across and clicked George's belt together and jerked his seat forward again.

George thought of complaining *he* was short of space now, but decided to say nothing.

Tara picked up *Teen Tips* and started reading. George could feel her feet resting on the seat back once more, but the expected rebuke never came. Without looking up, she murmured, "Is this what they call an uneasy silence?" It was George who broke it, and only after they had been travelling for some fifteen minutes.

"Will someone tell me where we're going?" He might have asked if they were going home, but he wasn't sure he knew what 'home' meant anymore.

Toby tightened his grip on the steering wheel, his eyes fixed on an imaginary hazard on the long, clear road ahead. It was left to Bridget to answer.

"We thought it would be a good idea to look at..." she hesitated, "one more."

"I thought Dad said four."

In the rear-view mirror, George caught Bridget's face contorting.

Toby broke his silence. "Keep your thoughts to yourself, young lady."

George heaved a heavy sigh and looked out the side window, the sunlight flashing through the hedgerows like Morse code. S.O.S they seemed to read.

"Wasn't this meant to be a family day trip to the countryside? Not a route march through waiting rooms for the dying." George's tone sounded resigned to failure, his hostility left behind with his dignity when he'd struggled across the car park. He sat back, determined not to speak again, watching the countryside zip past, seeing nothing.

* * *

Twenty minutes passed before he became aware that the car was slowing down. 'You have reached your destination,' the satnav's voice chirruped. His eyes followed the line of a tall, forbidding brick wall before they turned into a courtyard dominated by the concreted façade of a Victorian building. He guessed that, in its heyday, it might have been an imposing seaside villa, a retreat for the rich, before being tarnished by the indigent, unwashed and uneducated taking temporary respite from the city, courtesy of third class rail travel. Today, fire escapes, handrails and ramps were testimony to its conversion to Tulips Rest Home and modern health and safety requirements. "Looks like a bleedin' workhouse," he murmured under his breath.

"Dad!"

"Well."

Toby stepped out of the car.

George sat tight. "I'm not coming."

"Dad!"

"You two go. I'll stay here. Keep Tara company. We don't often get the chance to talk."

"She doesn't need your company. And you need to see."

"I don't. Unless you've booked me in already."

"Dad, please."

"We'll be alright, won't we?" George strained to look at Tara in the rear-view mirror. "You can read me my horoscope, can't you."

Bridget left them to it, and chased after her husband.

George watched until they were out of sight. "This is nice. Just like the old days, don't you think?" There was no response from the back seat, so he kept going. "I'm sorry I'm not much company at the moment." He hadn't felt much like talking to anyone since the funeral.

Tara said nothing and kept reading. When she was younger and they were together for weekend visits or day trips, she'd always had an opinion and never shied from letting everyone hear it. How George missed those days.

"Come on, then. Tell me my future." He twisted the rear-view mirror so he could see his granddaughter better without having to turn round. Her eyes fixed on her magazine, he analysed her. Elfin-like, auburn hair, newly cropped, she looked so grown up and not the grandchild he remembered playing in the garden, being pushed on the swings, building sandcastles on the beach, skimming pebbles across the sea, being treated to sweets and ice cream despite Bridget's protests about healthy eating. "November 30th. St. Andrew's Day. Sagittarius."

Tara closed *Teen Tips* and slapped her hand on the cover. It was a gesture George recognised from when Bridget was a teenager and about to sound off. Like mother, like daughter.

"You've got to tell them." She was looking straight into his reflection.

"Tell them what?"

"You know."

"That your mum only buys Rich Tea biscuits and I like chocolate Hobnobs?"

"You know what I mean."

"Or the only music I hear is on some local radio station, twittering away in the kitchen. And all there is to read is the free bloody *Basingstoke Tribune* and your mother's gardening magazine."

Tara tutted and repeated, "You know."

"No. Tell me."

"That you don't want to move into one of these homes."

"I should think that's bleedin' obvious, pardon my French."

"Why? What's wrong with them?"

"You've not been inside."

"But if you're living on your own, what will you do with yourself?"

"Things."

"Things?"

"Things I still want to do." George caught her expression of surprise. "Don't pull that face. I may be old, but I haven't given up just yet. Despite your mother saying I've retired. The fires still burn, you know. And don't ask me what. You'll know when I've done them."

"So you've got to tell them."

George folded his arms to show he was taking no notice. "Did you read that sign outside the last place?"

Tara nodded.

"You saw that it was sponsored by funeral directors and an estate agent."

Tara nodded again.

"One to get shot of the body and another to sell off the house. What did your mother say about that?"

"I don't think she saw it."

"I don't suppose your father missed it." George grunted. "And do you know what passes as entertainment in there? I'll tell you. Watching school Christmas pantomimes. I saw the evidence hanging in a corridor. Had ten years of them when your mother was a child. The memory still gives me nightmares. I'd rather die than spend the rest of what's left of my life watching someone else's little darlings."

Tara shook her head. "Gramps. Tell. Them."

"I can't." He was having second thoughts on missing hearing his granddaughter voicing her opinions.

"Why not?"

What could he answer? That he was scared they were right, that he needed to be cared for, that he really wasn't safe to be left on his own? Or maybe this was a sign that his time was done. That he'd have to face up to the reality. That what he hadn't achieved he was never going to achieve. "You tell them for me."

"Me?"

"Yes. They'll listen to you."

"Oh, no." Tara shook her head decisively. "It's not for me. Only you can speak for yourself."

"You can help."

Tara shook her head again. "I can't. I really can't." She opened *Teen Tips* and resumed reading.

George twisted the mirror back round and stared out the front of the car. It was starting to drizzle. She was right of course. How could he expect an eighteen-year-old to argue the case for a seventy-nine-year-old? The fact that he was asking for her help almost proved the case for the prosecution. He couldn't cope with the real world anymore.

They sat in silence for a while, Tara flicking through her magazine, George staring through the windscreen that was beginning to steam up.

"What are you reading?"

Tara reached forward and showed him the magazine, twisting it as she handed it to him so as to reveal only the opposite page to the one she'd been looking at. 'Vegan needn't mean unhealthy,' the headline read. "You're not one of those, are you?" He looked worried.

"Why shouldn't I be? Lots of people are. It is the twenty-first century."

"It's not natural. We're meant to eat meat."

"I don't think it's natural to keep animals cooped up in tiny spaces, now you're asking."

"Well I just don't like fads. Never have. Never will." He turned the page over impatiently. There, in bold, was a different heading: 'Should I have sex with my boyfriend?' Tara stretched to reclaim the magazine but he shifted it just too far from her. He'd read the first line, 'My boyfriend and I have been going out together for almost nine months and have only reached third base', before she was able to snatch it back.

"Thanks," she said as she turned it over again and clasped it in her lap.

"Can anyone read that?"

"Why?"

"When I was a boy, I was reading about fighter pilots, not that kind of stuff."

"It's different today."

"And at your age it was National Service, not 'third base.'"

"Did you talk to your parents about, you know what?"

"Certainly not. Do you?"

She took a deep breath, then shuffled across the car seat and leaned forward. George turned and they were almost nose-to-nose. "If you won't talk to my parents about you, will you talk to them about me?"

George tilted his head, his eyes narrowing. "You're not in any trouble, are you?"

"Sort of."

"Boy trouble?"

"You could say that."

"Not...?"

"God, no. Nothing like that."

"What then? Don't tell me. Your dad doesn't like your boyfriend."

"How do you know?"

"Evelyn – your nan – was like that with *her* dad. She said they were always having rows about boys not being good enough for her. Unsuitable was the word he used. Though with me, I suppose they were right."

"It's not that."

"So tell me."

"It's about uni."

George resisted the temptation to correct 'uni' to 'university'. "You are still going, aren't you? Your mother and father are very proud of you, even if they don't say it."

"That's the problem."

"How's it a problem?"

"Mark. You know, my boyfriend. He's already at the uni I'm going to in London."

"Careful, he'll expect you to cook his meals." George was never much good when things looked like they might get serious. Resorting to a joke usually lightened the atmosphere. Not this time.

"And he says I should move in with him. He says it'll save on rent."

"Is he Scottish?" There he went again, trying to lighten the mood; and again, no response.

"I don't want to. Not yet, anyway."

George blanched at the thought Tara might be about to reveal what bases she'd reached. Another joke would maybe deflect from unwanted information, but for once, he couldn't think of one. "Ah," was all he could muster.

"Anyway, Dad says I can't. Bet you agree with him."

Here was a dilemma. Did he lie to Tara, or admit to agreeing with Toby for what would be an unlikely first time? He'd never got on with Toby, blaming him for the break-up of Bridget's first marriage. Best say nothing and answer with a question. "What did your mum say?"

"She won't say anything. Just asked me more questions."

Like daughter, like father. "You must do what's right for you."

"I've been trying uni halls."

"And?"

"There's a waiting list. I might have left it too late."

"What will you do, then?"

"I'm thinking of a flat share."

"So what did you want me to talk to your parents about?"

"Dad says a flat share in London's not safe. You've lived there forever. Tell him he's wrong and I'll be alright. Otherwise it'll mean travelling up every day. Which is what he says I'll have to do."

"That's not going to work, is it?"

"He says it's that or he won't pay anything towards maintenance costs."

"Ah." George thought she was going to ask him for money. But she added nothing and, in the silence that followed, sat back in her seat again. Arms behind her head, looking up at the car roof, she reminded him so much of Evelyn.

"You know, your grandmother used to sit like that."

"I'm so sorry, Gramps."

"So am I. So am I. If time's supposed to heal, I wish it would hurry up. It's getting worse, not better."

"Seems like we're both stuck with my parents."

George slumped forward, longing for the impossible, for things to be as they used to be. To go home. He pictured the empty hall, post piled up on the doormat; airline tickets in the drawer under the telephone; chocolate Hobnobs going soft in the cupboard over the kitchen sink; piles of records he'd been sorting in his special room, gathering dust; Evelyn's amaryllis flowering to no one in the dining room. Then, abruptly, he sat up.

"I've had an idea. Why not come and share my house in London?" It was a spur of the moment thing and said without any thought to what living with a teenager might mean.

Chapter 3

"Can I give you a hand with that?"

"No thanks, Mr Turnbull. We can manage, can't we, Tara?"

George watched anxiously as the corner of a large metal box scraped along the wallpaper. Evelyn would never have stood for it. The first thing she would do whenever she came home was inspect the house. Anything out of place carried the threat of a major incident. She could sense a smeared kitchen worktop from the front door, a towel off its rack without going near the bathroom. It was as if she had the house under constant surveillance. Spilling anything on a carpet would be punishable by death or worse. George didn't dare think what she'd have made of Mark and Tara scuffing the walls. "Are you sure?" he asked.

"Sure." Mark sounded confident.

A corner was scraped leaving a sliver of paper coiled and dangling.

"Don't worry, Gramps – it's only a wall."

George waited until they'd passed through, then rubbed the paper flat again, though it wouldn't stay down. In his head two voices raged. In the red corner, one argued that she was right, that it was only a wall – a small sacrifice in exchange for company. In the blue corner came the counter, that he was making a terrible mistake suggesting Tara move in with him. Here, for the first time, was his chance to live life the way he chose, without compromise or scrutiny.

"Sorry, Mr Turnbull. Careful, Tara."

"*Me* careful? You're the one who's meant to be steering."

Mark thumped the box down on the landing. "Well do it yourself, then."

"You two, don't start arguing." George looked at them both. Tara, energetic, opinionated; Mark, awkward and gangly, sallow, hands that looked like they'd never done a decent day's work. What had he let himself in for? "I should see if Hunter's alright in the garden. I'll make us a drink while I'm down there. Tea?"

"Yes, please, Gramps."

"Coffee for me, please, Mr Turnbull. No milk. Not too strong. Two sugars. Sorry."

George wasn't sure whether Mark's apology was to him for the complicated drinks' order or to Tara for the argument. He didn't wait to find out, heading straight for the tranquillity of the kitchen, not even reacting when he heard the box being lifted again with more scraping and recriminations, whispered this time. Best shut himself away until it was all done.

* * *

"Has he gone?" Mark asked as they rounded the final landing and arrived in Tara's room.

"Hope so. Anywhere will do."

"Drop in three, two, one, drop."

Tara took it literally and her end thumped to the floor. Mark winced, closing his eyes. They waited in anticipation of a lump of plaster falling off the ceiling below, followed by the stomp of George's feet pounding back up the stairs. But there was neither. Mark eased his end down, and sat on the bed.

"Not bad." He bounced up and down, then lay back. "Here, try."

Tara sat down on the edge next to him and almost at once felt two hands cup round her breasts and attempt to pull her down. She threw back her shoulders and jabbed both elbows to push him off.

"Ow! That hurt."

"You deserved it. I'll do it again if you don't get off me."

"He's miles away. And we'd hear him coming."

She felt his hand loosen and uncup.

"So how old was your mum then, when she married the first time?" He sounded defiant.

"Eighteen." She felt his hands advance again. "No!" She thrust just one elbow back this time, but using all her strength. He jerked away.

"Oww! That *really* hurt."

"It was meant to. And I'm not my mum and she divorced him. So not now, and that's final." Truth was, she wasn't altogether sure when. She wasn't even sure how the whole arrangement was going to work. All the while Mark had been at uni, they'd led largely separate lives and only ever met for occasional weekends, and then he stayed with his parents in Newbury, an hour away on the bus. Their relationship had remained, if not Benedictine standard, certainly just a few gropes and kisses beyond platonic. Being free of her parents seemed to have given Mark new ideas. Yet her ideal man had always been the fit, athletic type, all bronzed and rippling muscles. And here she was, close friends – she wouldn't call it anything stronger – with a tall, gangly, pallid, long-haired wannabe rock star. She'd stuck with him because he sometimes made her laugh and because her dad disliked him intensely. And no one else seemed interested in her. But if this was how he was going to be from now on, she'd have to think again.

With the lack of promise, let alone action, Mark leapt to his feet. "Right." He said it with an air of a man trying to conceal his disappointment. "Let's get the rest of the stuff up before he notices we've wrecked his house."

By the time they'd emptied the van into her new room, there was still no sign of George. Mark surveyed the pyramid of boxes casting a long shadow over the deep shag carpet. "Good luck finding your bed."

"I wonder what Nan would have made of all this."

"Do you think anyone's ever slept in here?"

"I know she liked to keep everything neat and tidy."

He surveyed the havoc they'd wreaked. "Lucky she's not here."

"I think you'd better keep that thought to yourself."

"So now what?"

Tara could see Mark had no appetite to empty the boxes, and she wasn't altogether sure she wanted him to see her most personal possessions. "We've forgotten about Gramps. He was making us drinks."

"I hope he's not dead on the kitchen floor."

"Charming." She led the way down the three flights of stairs, noticing for the first time the trail of scuffs and scars in the wallpaper and muddy footprints on the carpet, evidence of the last hour's efforts. She was nearly at the bottom when she realised Mark wasn't following but lingering by a door on the first floor landing behind her.

"What's in here?"

"Nothing. Leave it."

Mark gently nudged the door open with his shoulder as if to avoid any forensic evidence of his curiosity.

"Please don't go in there. It always used to be out of bounds." Tara anxiously fingered a wound in the banister rail. "Come on. Let's make peace with Gramps."

She heard a door hinge squeak and looked back. Mark had disappeared.

"Where've you gone? Mark?" Her call was muted. Raising her voice might be overheard by her grandfather, with Mark being caught in the act of trespassing. She retraced her steps, hissing between her teeth, "Mark, come on out of there."

"Fuck. Come and see this."

Checking Gramps hadn't reappeared to overhear Mark's profanity or see him entering space that might be private, she followed.

"We shouldn't be in here," she whispered.

"Look at all this."

"He won't like it."

She heard the sound of shuffling and then a series of noises like things tumbling.

"Fuck."

For a second time, Tara checked George wasn't within earshot, then closed the door behind her, plunging them into complete darkness.

"What d'ya do that for? I can't see where I'm going. Turn a light on, will you?" There was more shuffling and things falling.

She pulled out her mobile phone and flicked on its torch. It wasn't exactly the Blackpool Illuminations but it revealed the room, crisscrossed, floor to ceiling, with shelves, all lined with records and CDs, denying any natural light. And across the floor, more of the same, a Giant's Causeway of piled vinyl and silver discs.

"Wow."

"I said you'd be impressed."

"Actually you said 'fuck'. Twice. And I'm not impressed." She edged her way round the corner of a row of shelves where she found a standard lamp. Clicking it on revealed Mark fingering through a toppled stack of seven-inch single records. She'd seen some like them in a cardboard box in a friend's garage but never looked at them. Or seen so many. Without looking up, Mark waved one at her.

"These are old-fashioned records."

"I know."

"My dad had some but gave them away."

"We shouldn't be in here."

"Didn't you know about all these? You must have seen them when you visited your grandparents."

"Only when I was small. Dad never liked coming. And I was always told I wasn't allowed in here. Did you knock that lot over?"

"Not all of them."

"Well pick them up again, then let's get out before Gramps finds us."

"There wouldn't have been so many if you hadn't made it go dark." He paused, then gasped. "Look at this one." He held up a record sleeve with a photograph of two figures, one with a crew cut, the other appearing to be wearing a mop, standing on a rough path and looking guiltily over their shoulders.

Tara took it from his outstretched hand and scrutinised it. "So? Two hippies from the sixties. What about it?" She didn't need to act her tone of disinterest.

"What's written on it?"

"We haven't got time for stupid games." Her voice was becoming impatient.

"Look at it."

"'Homeward Bound'. Simon and Garfunkel. So?"

"No! *Look* at it." It was Mark's turn to sound impatient. "It's signed, see?" He jabbed a finger at some scrawled handwriting on the record's sleeve, just below the guy with the crew cut.

"'Shame about the grammar'. What's that meant to mean?"

"No idea. But look at the next line. A signature." He grabbed the record from her and pointed again.

"I can see that. 'Paul'. So?" She didn't care. All she wanted to do was get out of the room.

"Paul must be Paul Simon. You must know who he is. *Bridge Over Troubled Water?*"

"*You're* studying music. Not me. Come on, let's get out of here."

"It's old. Probably worth money. I wonder how your grandfather got it."

"Everyone's got signed things. I've got a signed One Direction CD, even if it is signed by the one no one remembers. Everyone has them." Tara took the Simon and Garfunkel record back and placed it carefully on top of a row of neatly stacked LPs.

"Sam the Sham and the Pharaohs. Del Shannon. Sonny and Cher. Status Quo." Mark was still sifting through more of the records he'd spewed across the floor, announcing each one as if he were a herald and these were guests at a banquet. "The Sonics, The Shadows, Strawbs, Sonny Boy Williamson, Howlin' Wolf, Frank Wilson…"

"I wondered where they'd gone. Sonny Boy Williamson, Howlin' Wolf and Frank Wilson should be with the W's, not the S's." The voice came, not from Tara but from George, who was now standing in the doorway. "May I ask what you two are doing in here? This is my private room. Not one you have any right to be in."

"I'm sorry, Gramps." Tara looked guiltily across to her grandfather and edged herself away from the record piles and towards the door.

Mark stood up.

"Sorry, Mr Turnbull. I saw the shelves and had to look."

"They've withstood living with my late wife and Tara's mum, so I do hope you're not going to make a habit of trampling over them."

"I didn't knock them *all* over."

"That's as maybe. They were in neat piles and only on the floor as I'd been sorting them out…" His voice trailed off.

Tara imagined him thinking of what had interrupted his sorting and the nightmare of her grandmother's last weeks.

George took a deep breath before he could continue. "… and I didn't expect them all to be splayed over the floor as if a herd of rampant wildebeest had stampeded through."

"I didn't think wildebeest stampeded, Gramps."

Tara's intervention seemed to deflect George's ire. "That's as maybe. But please be careful. Many of those records are over fifty years old. Not as old as me, but as fragile. And more precious." He stepped past Tara and picked up a 45 that had lost its sleeve in the turbulence Mark had caused. "Shirelles. 'Will You Love Me Tomorrow.'" He ran his fingers lightly across the grooves, as if fondly caressing a lover's face. "So small, and yet locked inside, an orchestra, singers, music. Forever. Just waiting for me to play. Magnificent." He spoke softly, as much to himself as the intruders into his personal space.

Mark glanced at Tara with a look that suggested he thought George was mad. "Can we help you put them back?"

"Kind of you to offer, young man, but they've got to be in the right order and in the right sleeves, so best I do it myself. And I'd prefer you not to come in here again without my say so."

"We won't, Gramps, I promise."

"That's good. Now, how about those drinks? The first ones I made will be cold but I'll remake them if anyone wants."

"Yes, please." Mark now seemed keen to escape the scene of the toppled record piles. "You coming, T?" He seized his opportunity and Tara's hand, pulling her towards the door. For a moment, she resisted.

"What's that, Gramps?" She was pointing at an Oscar-shaped trophy serving as a bookend, holding up a row of LPs.

"Oh, that. It's an award."

"Award?"

"Yes, for Best Music in a film."

"Yours?"

"Don't sound so incredulous."

"Sorry, I didn't mean…"

"Royalty gave it to me. A big do in Park Lane. Shook her hand and all. You should have seen me. I looked a real sight in my penguin suit and brogues. I even had to wear a bow tie. I wanted a revolving one that lit up but your gran wouldn't let me. She said it'd be stupid. She was right, of course."

"Shall we go?" Mark tugged at Tara's hand again and this time dragged her out. George didn't follow immediately, instead kneeling down to recover the sleeve for the Shirelles and reunite them.

* * *

On the stairs and alone again with Tara, Mark tried again.

"So?"

"So what?"

"How about it?"

"What?"

"It."

"Why do you think of nothing else?"

"You said it'd be OK when you'd got away from your parents."

"Later."

"You promised."

"I *said*, later."

"When later?"

"What are you two whispering about?" George had emerged from his room and was watching them from the top of the stairs.

"You, of course, Gramps."

"Well, I hope it's nothing too dull. There's plenty of good dirt to dish."

"Not now. Mark's going."

Mark frowned.

If George noticed, he ignored it. "No time for your coffee, then? Never mind. Another day. Thanks for helping my granddaughter, young man." As he reached the foot of the stairs, Tara was holding open the front door.

"Tomorrow, then." Mark's intonation left it open for Tara to say, 'No, tonight.'

"I'll call you." Tara gave him a peck on the cheek, showed him out and closed the door on him faster than she'd intended. She followed her grandfather to the kitchen.

George looked at her searchingly. "That was a bit sudden, wasn't it? Specially after the way he'd been helping."

Tara shrugged. "Didn't want Hunter escaping into the road."

"If I don't need to make new drinks, would you empty the cold ones and put them in the dishwasher?"

Tara obliged. "Urgh, dishwasher's full. Can you smell it? How long's it been left like this?" She pinched her nose. "Where do you keep the dishwasher tablets?"

"I don't know. Try under the sink."

Tara opened a cupboard and pulled out a box. "Is it these?"

"What's it say on the box?"

"Dual action. Concentrated cleaning liquid with built-in stain removers."

"Show me."

Tara presented a capsule to him. He shook his head. "Not sure. What do you use at home?"

"Mum usually does it."

"Isn't there anything else under there?"

Tara rummaged through neatly stacked shelves, toppling a dustpan and brush, disinfectant bottle, shoe polish and pack of wild birdseed. They all crashed out, cascading across the floor.

"Careful."

"I can't see anything that looks like dishwasher tablets." She cleared the floor, stuffing everything back into the cupboard, ramming the door shut to prevent any sudden re-emergence.

"Use this." George handed her a bottle of Fairy Liquid.

"I don't think that's right."

"I use it for washing up in the sink. Can't do any harm in a dishwasher, surely?"

Tara shrugged. "How much?"

George leaned over the opened drawer of the dishwasher and pointed at a small tray. "I'd fill it up to the top." He peered over Tara's shoulder as she followed his instructions. "That should do it."

Tara closed the dishwasher door and they both watched as Fairy Liquid dribbled out the bottom.

"Ah, well. Turn it on and no one will notice. Never saw the point of a dishwasher for two people in the first place." He rubbed his foot across the floor as if to dry the liquid but succeeded only in smearing it over a wider area. "So if I take Hunter for a quick walk, would you see if there's anything you can rustle us up to eat?"

Tara kept a straight face but tensed at the thought he might be expecting her to do all the work round the house.

George continued. "Then what are we going to do this evening?"

"Is it alright if I use your piano?"

"I didn't know you played."

"I don't. I had lessons when I was younger but gave them up. I was thinking I should start again."

"Be my guest. When is it you start college?"

"Uni, it's called now. Next week."

"Tell me again what you're studying. It's History, isn't it?"

"Modern History and Politics. The last fifty years."

"The last fifty years? That's not history. That's my life."

"That's what it's called."

"I lived through all that. Lived it, saw it."

"It's history now, Gramps."

"Well, ask me if you need to know anything. From the horse's mouth, as it were."

"It's probably different from what you remember. It'll be things like politics, film and photography, world leaders, terrorism, women and gender…"

"Excuse me! That's not different. I was there. The IRA. Nelson Mandela. Girls burning their bras. Happy days." George nodded to himself, avoiding Tara's doubtful expression. "And there was music through all of it. Everything had a song. So," he was stabbing his index finger at her as he grew more excited, "before your lecturers fill your head with all the stuff they've probably only read about, you need to hear it like it was sung about at the time. 'Eve of Destruction', 'Free Nelson Mandela', 'War', 'Different Drum'… there's so many." He was about to launch into a song but instead started coughing. "Sorry," he spluttered, doubling over, before straightening and breaking into a triumphant smile. "I know. That's what we can do tonight. You should have a musical induction. A history of the last fifty years through my records. That's once I've picked up the ones your boyfriend knocked over."

"I'm sorry about that."

"After tea. And after I've gone through the post. I've a mountain still to go through."

She was tempted to say she didn't mind missing out. There were bags to unpack and the room to sort, and it seemed unlikely that Sam the Sham and the Pharaohs, Del Shannon and Sonny Boy Williamson would provide a suitable introduction to the history and politics of the last fifty years. Yet he seemed so keen. It felt rude to say no. "That'll be great. Thanks." She turned and escaped up the stairs, two at a time.

* * *

George retrieved Hunter's lead, curled up beside the pile of envelopes on a worktop. He was excited by the idea of playing his favourite music to her, about how music spanned the generations. The thought of it made his stomach churn. It was unmistakably a yearning, a longing to create, to be heard, to perform. He knew he wasn't so much a has-been as a never-was. It was a relief when *Top of the Pops* was cancelled on TV as it meant he couldn't be jealous of the so-called stars caterwauling – all a quarter his age and half his ability. But surely it wasn't too late for him. He still had tunes in his head – good tunes, catchy tunes. He would prove to them all how he wasn't too old, that age was no barrier, that he could still get the recognition that had always eluded him. What he didn't know was how, let alone how it would work with his granddaughter around the house. He was even less sure what to do about the letter burning a hole in his pocket, that was sure to rake up troubles he'd hoped were long since past.

Chapter 4

With Hunter walked and tea eaten, George left Tara to the washing up and retreated to his music room. It was always to his records that he returned when he felt in need of sanctuary. But there was no escaping the contents of the letter he pulled from his pocket.

> *Dear George,*
>   *I've only just heard about the sad death of Evelyn. It must have been a great shock to you. She was like a mum to me.*

The longhand was spidery and meticulous – like a doctor's – but legible.

> *I would specially like something to remember her by. I'm back in England again, so I can drop by sometime soon.*
>   *Peace.*
>   *Robin*

Who would have believed it? Coming back after all this time. And still using that sign-off. Peace? The only thing Robin ever brought was trouble. George knew he'd have to face up to it, sooner or later. Breathing a heavy sigh, he tucked the letter back in his pocket. Later.

More immediate was the mess Mark had made of his room. Surveying the carnage, he stepped over the records splayed across the floor and edged towards a sixties' rocking chair. It had been a wedding present from his grandmother. Now it was positioned within easy reach of his record deck, amplifier, CD player, tape deck, graphic equaliser and a box that he described as making music sound like it was in 3D. Only he seemed to understand what 3D sound was, and Evelyn always put her finger across his lips if he tried to explain.

Facing the seat were two tall black loudspeakers, angled to give the best balance of sound. Just in front was a footstool where George now perched. Reaching out to the fallen records, he began to collect them, checking there was no damage, restoring them to their correct sleeves. It was the rule of the room, just as replacing the lid on the toothpaste and putting down the toilet seat were rules of the rest of the house. And he was secretly looking forward to returning everything to its proper order, reminding himself of records he'd forgotten or not played for ages, then listening to them as if for the first time, or reliving memories.

There was a strict procedure to follow. Having reunited records with sleeves, he would always create little piles in a circumference around him. Then he'd sort them into strict alphabetical order according to group names or surnames. So Sly and the Family Stone before Small Faces before Smith. Next, they must be shuffled by first name. So Aaron Smith before Jimmy Smith before Patti Smith before Whistling Jack Smith. And within each artist, the order each record was released. So Patti Smith 'Hey Joe' (1974), 'Piss in a River' (1976), 'Gloria' (1978), 'Because the Night' (later in 1978). He said it was essential or he'd not find anything. Evelyn had called it autistic.

Normally he'd also create a single, separate, random pile. This would be the ones he would play to himself before restoring them to their rightful, alphabetical place. On this occasion, he was also stacking a second set – those he planned to play to Tara. He wasn't sure why he'd offered to do this. Apart from taking up floor space from the alphabetical piles, it was impossible to teach someone to like music, though there was no doubting some kind of induction for her was necessary. And while it had *seemed* simple enough to find songs that told the story of the twentieth century, it was proving to be more difficult than he'd thought. How would he explain what made Elvis Presley so provocative? Did 'Leap Up and Down (Wave Your Knickers in the Air)' by St. Cecilia count as encouraging emancipation? And should he play to his granddaughter Rusty Warren's 1961 feminist anthem 'Bounce Your Boobies'? Perhaps he would stick to anti-war songs.

The piles had grown and he was able to see floor between the carpet of loose records when Tara knocked on the door.

"OK to come in?"

"Of course. I'm over here."

Tara wove her way round the shelves to find George settling into his rocking chair. He beckoned her to sit on the footstool.

"It's cold in here. How do you manage?"

"It suits me. Or I put on another jumper." He didn't add that when he was standing up, rocking to the rhythm or playing air guitar, he never felt cold.

Tara was looking round the room. "How many have you got?" She was gaping as she surveyed the boxes and shelves filling all but enough space to squeeze between them.

"Who knows?" George gave a shrug of feigned disinterest and pride.

"Thousands? Tens of thousands?"

"Of which? LPs or singles?"

"What's the difference?"

"The big ones are LPs. Long players. The singles are the small ones like the ones your boyfriend knocked over. Seven-inchers. Forty-fives. And EPs are 45s too." He sensed her glazing over.

"I can't believe I've never seen them before. How did you get so many?"

"They just sort of grew."

"Did Nanny Evelyn like records?"

"Not as much as me. And not as loud as I like them. So I made her up tapes she'd listen to in the kitchen."

"How did you meet Nan? Mum's never really told me. It is alright to ask, isn't it? Tell me if it's not."

It was almost the first time anyone had asked that question or indeed mentioned Evelyn's name since the funeral – and even then it'd only been in sympathetic tones about how her passing had been mercifully quick. And George could find nothing merciful about dying, no matter how short the illness.

"Her parents ran a shop. I used to go there from time to time. She worked there after she left school."

"Were you still at school?"

"Heavens no. I was quite a bit older."

"What were you doing? Your job, I mean. When you met her."

"In an office. Working my way up. That's how it was in those days."

"And the music?"

"I played in a group at night. Small things, amateur. We called them hops. And bops."

"Was Nan in your group?"

"Oh no. Groups were boys. Three guitarists and a drummer. I was bass but piano was really my instrument. She loved music, though, your nan. She had a lovely voice, too."

"Who was the group's singer?"

"We shared it around."

"Why not Nan?"

"There weren't many girl singers around then. Not in my day. Nobody wanted them. Girls bought the records and made up the audience. They screamed. Boys played."

"Didn't Nan mind? If she liked singing, why couldn't she be in your band?"

"That's how it was. Music was boys' stuff. Girls got married and had families." He saw her frown. "I suppose it sounds funny now."

"And they just let it happen?"

"Things were different. That's all."

"We wouldn't stand for it now."

"I don't suppose you would."

"Were you any good?"

"That's a cruel question." He spoke with a pretend look of hurt. "Were you planning on moving out tonight?"

"But *were* you any good? Did you make any records?"

"See those over there?" He pointed towards two large and battered cardboard boxes gathering dust beneath a set of CD racks. Tara leaned forward to stand up and inspect them, but George waved at her to stay. "It's a long story." He wanted to tell her. About the disappointments. The sacrifices. Things he'd never told anyone. Not even Evelyn. "But not now." He closed his eyes. "Let's do your music induction some other time."

"I haven't upset you, have I?"

"No, no."

"I'm sorry if I have."

"It's not that. I just suddenly feel very tired. If you don't mind, it's been a long day."

* * *

Even before Tara had left the room, George had closed his eyes and started rocking in his chair. His peace was momentarily disturbed by something warm nuzzling his hand. "Why are you in here, Hunter? You know you're not allowed." He looked down to see a pair of obedient brown doe eyes staring back at him. "Oh, alright. If that apology for a boyfriend of Tara's can barge in here, I won't keep you out." George patted his lap and Hunter jumped up, curling himself round before settling. "It's just you and me now, old boy." George laid his arms across the dog's warm body. It was strangely comforting. "You miss her too, don't you?" As he gently rocked the chair, his thoughts drifted back to the first time he met Evelyn. Evelyn Little she was then. He remembered so clearly the speech her father had given at the wedding.

"It's all my fault we've got George as a son-in-law," he'd said, barely looking at the sheaf of notes he'd prepared for the biggest event in their family's life. "It was my dad's shop and his before that and they'd hardly changed a thing over the years. I wanted to bring us into the sixties. I'd seen electric signs in other shops and wanted one for us. Evelyn's mum wasn't keen, said it'd be a waste of money. I laughed at her and bought it all the same and it brought us at least one customer. Our new son-in-law, George. Who's laughing now?" The Reception gave him a rousing round of applause.

George could still see the neon glow of 'Little's Grocery, Big Reputation' that had enticed him into a shop he'd previously passed without noticing. It'd been a Thursday evening and he was on his way from his office to a rehearsal. And there was

Evelyn, emptying broken biscuits into a jar, head down, her face hidden behind long mousy hair. And she was singing to herself, quietly, under her breath.

George knew the tune well. 'I Almost Lost My Mind'. A rhythm and blues song from the American South, he'd not heard it since his National Service. How did this young girl know it – let alone sing with such feeling?

"Can I have half a pound of sugar, please?" He waved a ten-shilling note. "And can I ask how you know Ivory Joe Hunter?"

The young girl stopped what she was doing and produced a bag of sugar from beneath the counter.

"Who's Ivory Joe Hunter?"

"It's his song you're singing."

From the tiny window to her face behind her hair, George could see her blush.

"Dad doesn't like me singing. I didn't think anyone would hear."

"It's an R&B standard. How do you know it?"

"Pat Boone. He's the most."

George's heart sank. He'd always hated Pat Boone as a crooner from the fifties who took the rhythm and blues out of R&B. But now she tossed her head back, he could see she had an earnest, welcoming face.

"Isn't he a bit too old for you?"

"I guess. I like Bryan Hyland and Bobby Vee better. And Cliff of course."

"Of course." He didn't mean it.

"Do you like them too?" She stared intently at him before allowing her hair to fall back over her face.

"Cliff Richard's rock'n'roll's OK. Bobby Vee's a bit too soft for me. More Fats Domino, Howlin' Wolf, Chuck Berry, Elvis." He looked for signs of approval or recognition. When there were none, he changed tack. "What about The Beatles? Everyone likes them."

She shrugged. "They're OK."

He took a deep breath. "I've got my own group. The Beat Boys. If you like The Beatles, you'll love us. I reckon they copied us." Again, he looked for a reaction. Again, there was none, at least as far as he could tell. "We're playing tomorrow night at the British Legion Hall. Wanna come?"

Being this forward was right out of character. He was more at home hiding behind his music, confident with his piano and guitar, not with people. Certainly not one-to-one. It was how he had stayed single all these years. But this girl wasn't a threat like most other girls he fancied.

"We'll even do 'I Almost Lost My Mind' for you." He saw her glance towards the bacon slicer where her father was tormenting a leg of streaky. He followed the look and knew at once the outcome of his moment of courage.

"I'd better not. My dad wouldn't approve."

He might have asked her to check, or even steeled himself to ask her dad himself. But what would it show? That she was just letting him down gently. He was timid enough without needing confirmation that he couldn't even get a date with a girl who wouldn't turn the head of anyone else.

"Some other time, then." He handed over the ten-shilling note, picked up the sugar and accepted the change without making further eye contact. Not that there was any risk of that, her face having retreated fully behind the curtain of hair.

For a few months he didn't go back to the shop, but was eventually driven in by an empty larder and a wet evening. To his surprise, the same girl looked quite different, more confident, her hair styled, wearing make-up. And she remembered him.

"Hello again. Haven't seen you in here for a while."

"No, been busy."

"What can I do for you?"

"A quarter of Cheddar, please."

"Coming up." She placed a block of cheese on a slab and estimated a quarter of a pound, slicing it off with a cheese wire. "I'm Evelyn, by the way. How's the group?"

"We're still performing. Hope to get a record deal soon. And I'm George."

"Like George Harrison?"

"He's lead guitar. I'm bass. And piano."

She smiled. George fell in love. She continued weighing cheese.

"Anything else?"

George studied her fingers as she caressed greaseproof paper around his Cheddar. "No, I think that'll be all." He determined to offer no sign of how he felt, nor risk being let down.

"You were right about The Beatles," she said as she smoothed the edges of the packet, making neat hospital corners. "That Ringo's fab. Even bought the LP."

He watched her every movement, entranced. "So have I. What do you think of 'Roll Over Beethoven'? First track, side two."

"It's good." She exchanged the cheese for a handful of coins. "Great at parties."

George tried to imagine her at a party. Dancing with him. "It's an old R&B song. Chuck Berry original. We do it in our act."

He wanted to ask her if she still liked Pat Boone and tell her he'd been performing 'I Almost Lost My Mind' ever since they'd last spoken. He wanted even more to ask her to come and watch.

"Wothcha, Frank." Evelyn's eyes were on a new arrival.

"Hello, luv."

"What can I do for you?"

"Kiss over the counter?"

"Later!"

"She's a little darlin', ain't she?" The last was directed at George, who searched for a riposte but ended up with just a nod. "Thanks for the cheese," he called out to Evelyn.

"Bye then, George. See you again, I hope." Evelyn gave a little wave, before turning her attention back to Frank. George gave a wave back, wondering if he'd missed his chance. But he became a regular, popping in more and more frequently. He started buying ham on the hock, not because he specially liked it, but because he'd have to wait while she sliced it and weighed it. And buying sweets meant she had to reach the jars down from high shelves and bag them up, giving him more time to look and talk. He even took to knocking on the side door after the shop had closed to ask for emergency supplies – eggs, milk, candles, anything he could think of. And funnily enough, it was always Evelyn who opened the door, never her mum or dad.

It was one evening when he saw her chatting to a young man in Army Cadet uniform that he knew he had to act, and act fast, or lose her. He couldn't invite her to watch the Beat Boys. He'd been having trouble with them – 'artistic differences lead to break-up', the headlines would have screamed had anyone troubled to discover them in the first place. He'd become a regular at a folk club and jammed a few times, but it was all very loose and certainly not something you'd take a girl to if you wanted to impress her. So it had to be the pictures.

And this time it wasn't straight rejection. It was, "Maybe, when it's a film I want to see."

And when she wanted to see a film, it was The Beatles' *A Hard Day's Night*.

He'd already been and it wasn't his idea of a film worth seeing, but he took her anyway. And he kept the tickets, tucking them into the pocket of his best trousers on the way to the stalls, transferring them to a tin box hidden under his bed when he got home. He still had the box, stashed somewhere beneath his cuttings. He'd kept them because he'd stolen a first kiss in the doorway of the Methodist Mission Hall on the way home. Now they just brought back a bitter reminder of the sacrifice they had led to. But who could say it hadn't been worth it?

From that point on, they were inseparable, even though Evelyn turned heads wherever they went, now she'd become a real looker. There was a phrase from the past. And it reminded him that he was here and Evelyn wasn't. Who could have expected that? Not George. Which made her death such a shock and why it had hit him so hard.

Old age had inevitably brought with it a greying and thinning of hair, of wrinkles becoming furrows. But it had also brought an end to temptation (anything realistic, anyway), ambition, competition and serious disagreement. Instead, there had been a contentment that he'd not experienced before. They'd found themselves rubbing along, even starting to do things they previously hadn't had the time for.

When her parents had retired, Evelyn kept the shop and he'd given up office work to run it with her. Open long hours, seven days a week, meant there was never a time when they could go away together, even before Bridget was born. They were successful for a while until a self-service chain store opened up round the corner. In the face of cheap prices and Green Shield Stamps, the 'Big Reputation' counted for nothing. So they sold up and he went back to an office nine to five. But there was still no time. He was always standing in for musicians on tours and in studios, or having rehearsals and playing gigs with his new band, eating away at any leave he was entitled to. Even after he retired from the day job, passing on his rubber stamp and collecting the obligatory long-service carriage clock, there were still occasional gigs in piano bars. Only as these dried up did he and Evelyn settle into a quiet life and begin to do things together. Nothing too adventurous, mind. The occasional short break in the Lake District or Cornwall, stretching to a week in Ireland three summers back and eight days in Portugal for their forty-eighth anniversary nineteen months ago. And while they were away, they even began to make friends – mutual friends – something that hadn't happened much before.

A sign that things were really changing was when Evelyn persuaded George to book their first ever trip to America. For all his love of the blues and rock'n'roll, he'd never visited the States. Although he'd been under the weather for the best part of a year, they made a decision it was now or never. He was counting down the days when it was Evelyn, without warning, who was taken ill. Maybe she had known and kept it to herself so as not to worry him. It would have been typical of her. Stoicism in the face of her own fear. By the time she opened up, it was too late. She was referred to hospital, treatments were started but she deteriorated mind-numbingly quickly. Her funeral was on the same day and ten minutes before their flight to JFK.

So instead of the Big Apple, he found himself in Basingstoke, with his daughter and son-in-law. And now back home with his granddaughter and vacuous boyfriend, and seemingly set for trouble.

Chapter 5

"Is everything alright?"

"Yes, why shouldn't it be?"

Bridget sounded anxious. "I've been ringing Tara's mobile all afternoon but it's going straight to message."

George shifted the phone from his left ear to the right where it sounded clearer. "Nothing's wrong as far as I know."

"So why's she not answered?"

"You'll have to ask her."

"Will you put her on?"

"I'll have to get her. She's downstairs, playing the piano."

"Really? You must be a good influence on her."

George wasn't so sure. Yes, he'd said it was OK for her to use it, but he hadn't counted on how the sound would vibrate through the floorboards, nor her being a beginner. One-fingered anthems, punctuated by clumsily executed scales, had destroyed his enjoyment of a particularly sensitive passage on Elton John's *Blue Moves* album. If he'd had a plan for her living with him, this wouldn't have been in it. And what if she was in there when he wanted to play it? He might need to pin a timetable on the door.

"Tara." He called from his record room's doorway. There was no let-up from the piano. "Bridget? You still there, Bridget?" he shouted down the phone.

"I can hear you, Dad," Bridget's voice squawked from the phone.

"Sorry, I wasn't sure you were still there. I'll have to go down and get her."

"How's it going with the two of you?"

"Fine." George stumbled on the first step. "Hang on."

"You OK?"

"Fine, just nearly lost my balance."

"Don't do that." Bridget paused. When there was no sound of her father tumbling, she continued her interrogation. "So Tara, has she been behaving herself?"

"Of course. Though she has put the heating up."

"She does that at home."

"I'll have to watch my electricity bill." He stepped over Tara's coat and shoes at the foot of the stairs. "And I hope she's not going to leave her stuff strewn all over the place."

"She does that at home, too."

"Yes, I remember." George grunted as he stepped into the living room. "Tara, it's your mum." The piano stopped.

Tara turned away from the keyboard. "What does she want?"

"Ask her." George handed her the phone, then watched her as she scampered out to the kitchen.

* * *

"Hello, Mum, why are you ringing?"

"Hello, darling. You've not been answering my calls." Bridget's voice was a mix of anxiety and annoyance.

"It's been on silent." Tara had switched it over to avoid having to speak to Mark.

"I was worried."

"Mum!"

"And I've texted you."

"I'm here now."

"Only because I rang your grandfather. I thought something might have happened."

"It's only been a few hours." Tara drew a deep breath. "You're not expecting me to call you every five minutes, are you? I *am* eighteen, you know."

"Don't be silly. I was just worried when you didn't answer or call back."

"You didn't speak to me every five minutes when I was at home."

Calling Basingstoke 'home' was a slip of the tongue – London was going to be home now – but it might have been a masterstroke, as Bridget seemed to relax.

"So is Dad… your grandfather OK?"

"Seems a lot better."

"And you. How are you getting on?"

"You just spoke to him. What did he say?"

"So everything's alright?"

"Why do you keep asking that?"

"What did you have for tea?"

"Mum. I'm eighteen. I can look after myself."

"And Dad, what did he have?"

"I don't know. Am I his carer or something?"

"No. Yes. Sort of. You know."

"Beans on toast if you must know. We had it together."

"On a Sunday? Beans on toast?"

"It's all there was."

"Couldn't you have gone out and got something better?"

"We were OK."

"But beans? On a Sunday?"

"Mum! Please."

"And Hunter? You have remembered his special diet."

"He lived with us in Basingstoke for months. I'm not stupid."

There was a pause and some rustling at the other end before Bridget spoke again. "Sorry, that's your dad. What's your grandfather doing now?"

"Can't you hear?" Tara held the phone above her head for a few moments.

"I can't hear anything."

Tara stepped out of the kitchen and into the hall. "Now?"

"Sounds like a piano."

"It is."

"He said you'd been playing it. It's good if you're going to take it up again."

"He's going mental on it." Tara stepped back into the comparative quiet of the kitchen.

"Perhaps you've inspired him. He hasn't played since, you know… Perhaps he's starting to get out of himself a bit."

"Well, I hope he stops soon. I want to go to bed."

"What's stopping you?"

"It'll be rattling the windows. People can probably hear it in the street."

"I'm sure he won't make a habit of it."

"It wouldn't have happened at all if you hadn't called."

Bridget paused again. "So is everything alright?"

"I've told you, yes."

"OK, then. I'll ring off. Love you."

"Love you, too."

"Oh, Dad asks if the wifi works."

"Sort of. Who did it?"

"Your dad organised it."

"It's not that good a signal."

Tara heard her mum calling back to Toby and there was a scuffling on the line and everything went quiet. A few moments later, Bridget was back. "He says he'll get them back to check it."

"It's not that bad."

"What's your grandfather think of it?"

"Of what?"

"The wifi."

"Why should he think anything? He's old. How would he know about wifi?"

There was more muffled conversation in the background before Bridget answered. "Your dad thinks he told him we were doing it. But we're not sure he took it in. Best not say anything."

"If you say so."

"He's probably not noticed it anyway. Where did they put it?"

"It's all in my room."

There was another gap while Bridget was obviously conferring again. "Your dad says that should be OK. But let me know if he does say anything."

"If you say so."

"And call me if you need anything, won't you."

"Goodnight, Mum."

"Goodnight."

* * *

With the phone returned to its base on the hall table, Bridget took a deep breath before going back into the living room. She knew Toby would be waiting to moan at her. He'd told her enough times not to worry about Tara and especially not to phone. She was greeted by a smirk and a 'told you so' expression.

"I needed to know," she said as she returned to the ironing board abandoned to make Tara's call.

"She's eighteen, for God's sake."

"That's what she said. Minus the God bit." She took one of Toby's shirts from the laundry basket, shook it before hooking it in place on the ironing board, and started work on it, perhaps a little too firmly.

Toby had his nose in a work file. "And are they OK?"

"So you were wondering too."

"Only because you just spoke to her. What was wrong with your old man now? Is he any worse?"

"Nothing's wrong. He'd just started playing the piano really loudly."

Toby looked up. "That's not a good sign. It's nearly midnight. Even if he is losing his marbles, he still can't do that with other people in the house."

"He's not losing his marbles. And it's not midnight, it's just gone ten. And Tara's OK about it." Bridget realised, while she'd been thinking about Tara and her dad, she'd held the iron still on the shirt, leaving a small, light scorch mark. Luckily it was the back. She checked that Toby hadn't noticed the smell, twisted it round and started on the front. He was meanwhile busily collecting together some papers from the carpet beside him. "But Tara's already turned the heating up."

"I told you they wouldn't get on."

"It's nothing much. And early days."

"It can only get worse. We should be prepared for her to turn up on the doorstep wanting to come home, and that's why…" Toby paused to wave some papers in Bridget's direction, "… I got these."

"What are they?"

"Brochures."

"Brochures?"

"Just new stuff about homes. And downloads from the internet."

"I thought we'd agreed to forget the idea."

"You know his health will only get worse."

"You've hardly stopped reminding me." Bridget's tone was agitated.

"And he's never lived alone before and it's too late to start."

"Tara's there."

"Forward planning, that's all." He waved the papers. "Judging by the cranky way he's behaving tonight, not a minute too soon."

"Tara didn't say he was cranky."

"What, playing the piano near midnight?"

Bridget let the time shift pass. "You've said yourself he needs to get out of himself."

"Unless he's planning to resume his rock star ambitions, we shouldn't dump the care home options. And we don't want another Uncle Joss. Do we?"

* * *

Joss, Toby's eighty-two-year-old uncle, had been a writer. Hopeless round the house, he'd relied totally on Lena, his wife. Except they divorced. In recent years, Joss's health had deteriorated. He was becoming more forgetful and absent-minded. And solitary. His closest family was emigrating to Spain and they tried to persuade him to go with them, but he refused. Before they left, they offered to help find him sheltered accommodation, but he'd have none of it. Instead, he became more obstinate and difficult, cutting himself off from everyone, living a solitary existence, allowing no one into his house. A tea towel catching fire in his kitchen changed all that. Neighbours had raised the alarm when they heard Joss's screams for help. The damage wasn't great, thanks to the fire brigade, but five minutes later the whole place would have gone up, Joss with it. Contacted as the nearest relative, Toby saw inside for the first time in years. It was unrecognisable from the home that Lena had kept pristine. Joss had done nothing; it looked like he never cleaned it, tidied it, maintained it. Doors were off their hinges, walls were cracked, ceiling tiles lay where they had fallen, brambles that had overtaken the garden had forced their way through the patio doors into the living room. Handwritten manuscripts were piled on chairs and tables, newspapers and magazines were piled up against walls, takeaway flyers left where they had fallen. His bed was unmade, food not cleared away, dishes unwashed. Toby could see the place was rat infested. How Joss had survived was a miracle and it was clear something now had to be done. With no response from the Costas, and as Joss would only open the front door to Toby, the 'something' fell to Toby and Bridget. Except Toby's job was all-consuming and Tara was having trouble at school. Given the urgent necessity of finding Uncle Joss care, they took the only option that wasn't a hospital bed. Even now the memory haunted Bridget. A care home, miles from anywhere, on Salisbury Plain. Army tanks on manoeuvres rolled past the front door, nights were lit up by flashes of gunfire with accompanying crashes and booms. Inside, there was silence except for the television. The smell of yesterday's lunch and embrocation lingered everywhere. Luckily Uncle Joss had become too confused to realise. But now and again, he did. Then he would rant angrily about how much he hated the place, how his seat next to the radiator was too hot, how things kept going missing, how he was shouted at by the nurses for forgetting things, and how he wanted to go back home.

Except this *was* home now, his house sold and savings spent to pay for the care. Bridget would never forget the final visit. They'd been summoned by the owners to discuss Joss's declining health and behaviour. With Toby away on work, Bridget had gone alone. She'd arrived prepared with her own list of concerns – they were Joss's complaints really – only to be greeted by an empty chair in front of the radiator and two cardboard boxes of possessions in the hall. Joss had passed away unexpectedly and peacefully in the night, they told her, and the room was already being cleaned for a new resident. No, no one deserved that treatment. Especially, Bridget had promised herself, not her dad.

***

With the similarities between Joss and George so stark, Bridget found herself, against her better judgement, taking the papers that Toby was still dangling towards her, having hung the shirt on a hanger, making sure the scorched back was facing away. But not before grumbling, "Do you want me to read these or finish all this ironing of yours?"

"I thought women could do two things at the same time."

Top of the pile was an expensive-looking, glossy pamphlet, with a picture of a double-storey, seventies redbrick building on its cover. She turned the pages and within seconds let out a snort of derision.

"'Tastefully and individually decorated bedrooms'? Have you looked at the picture – it's just a bed and a chair in one room." She read on. "'Our food is appetising, of the highest standard and there is plenty of it.'"

"There's a menu." Toby gestured her to turn the page.

"'Brekky'? 'Morning coffee and bickies'? Is this a rest home or a nursery?"

"They're just trying to make it personal. And the food doesn't seem so bad."

"What, 'fish fingers and beans'? 'Sponge cake'? 'Jelly'? Dad's still got his own teeth, you know."

"It's just a sample."

"If they've printed it in a brochure, they must think it's good – and if that's the best they can manage…" She paused as she carried on reading. "*And* they've spelt tomatoes without an e."

"Hardly grounds for ruling them out."

"Hardly the basis for ruling them in."

"Look at some of the others before you say anything."

"Why do we need them at all? Tara's there with him and, if he's in any trouble, he's got that mobile we gave him at Christmas."

"That he fumbled with for two minutes, said he couldn't use and put back in the box? That'll be handy in a crisis."

"Maybe not yet. I'll ask Tara to try again with him. Once they've been together a bit longer." Bridget let the brochures drop and stood, remembering the phone that had threatened to ruin Christmas Day. He'd said he didn't need it and that it was too complicated. All day it had remained on the floor by the Christmas tree, a constant reminder of an uneasy *impasse*, sucking what little joy there had been from an occasion already scarred by the emptiness Evelyn's absence created. It was only overcome when Bridget encouraged her dad to reflect on how phones had changed. He needed little encouragement to reminisce and gleefully explained to a disbelieving Tara about home phone 'party lines'.

"Party what?" Tara had asked.

"Long before there were mobile phones, you needed a cable to connect your phone. Sometimes one cable went to lots of phones, in different houses," George had tried to explain.

"How did that work? Didn't you all hear each other's calls?"

"Exactly. But it was cheaper than having just your own. It did mean sometimes picking up and overhearing a call already going on. Which was annoying if you wanted to ring someone. Mostly you put the phone straight down. If it was urgent, you'd interrupt and tell them to cut it short."

"What, while they were talking?"

"It was the only way. And sometimes, when you picked it up, what they were saying sounded interesting, so you listened in for a little while."

"What, spying on them? You? Really?"

George flapped his hands apologetically. "If you picked the phone up and someone was in full flow, wouldn't you? Could be quite exciting, especially if there was an argument going on. You'd have to hold your breath so they didn't know you were there. It was awful if you wanted to sneeze. You had to stifle it or they'd know you were there. There was one girl in particular..."

"You mean there was more than one?"

"Several. You didn't know who they were. Or where. But there was this one. Lisa, her name was. She was always having long chats, always with chaps, not usually the same ones. I think she was leading them all on. You'd be amazed at the things I heard."

Tara was shaking her head in disbelief. "Weren't you embarrassed?"

"Yes. No. Not really. She didn't know. And it was better than the wireless. I managed to work some of the things she said into songs."

"Did you ever find out who she was?"

"Never. Though I think she listened in to me too. I'm sure I heard her breathing."

By the time George had finished telling this story, the Christmas sherry was being replenished and the mobile, back in its box, had been secreted away and was never mentioned again.

Bridget was wondering whether George would ever get round to trying the phone, when Toby's voice brought her back into the present.

"Look at the others, will you?" He was sounding impatient.

"Sorry, I was thinking. About Dad." Bridget gathered the papers up again and skimmed through them. Words like 'restful', 'peaceful' and 'tranquil' seemed to appear in them all. She thought of her dad thumping out rock'n'roll on his piano late at night. "They all look like hospices. And look at this." She held a page up to him and pointed at a line. "See?"

"No."

"It's meant to say they are compliant with regulations. Except it doesn't." She prodded the paper again. "Typo."

Toby leaned forward and read where Bridget was indicating.

"Oh, I see. 'Complaint' not 'compliant'." He rolled his eyes, not amused. "Please be serious."

"I am serious. Maybe they're more used to writing about complaints."

"Anyway, that's my shortlist, and unless you have any objections that aren't based on GCSE English and proofreading..."

"Have you thought about how we'll be able to afford them?"

"His house. That'll cover it."

"He'll never agree."

"Uncle Joss? Do you really want to wait until it's too late? So unless you have any objections, I'll make appointments to see some of them."

Bridget let out a reluctant sigh. She leafed through the pages printed from the internet. "These don't say where they are."

"Look on the back."

Bridget turned over one of the sheets and raised her eyebrows when she saw they'd been printed both sides. The home printer barely printed on one side, if at all. She'd been asking him to fix it for months. He'd obviously been planning this at work.

"Bradford? Leicester? Manchester? How will we visit him up there? And when are we supposed to have time to check them out to see if they're any good?"

"I've got a work appointment in Leeds on Tuesday week. I told you."

"I don't think you did."

"I did."

"I don't remember."

"Anyway, it'll work out well as I can recce them while I'm up there. I've a couple of days owing. Stay over. I'll get it back on expenses."

"Really?" Bridget narrowed her eyes and scrutinised her husband, looking for a glimmer of compassion or understanding of how she felt.

"And if there are any that are half decent, we can talk about what we do next."

She looked again at the papers, hoping to find something positive.

"What *are* these – holiday reviews? The one in Leicester says, 'Beautiful open areas and a bistro so you can chat and while away the hours in comfort and contentment. We offer a range of rooms and can accommodate couples if required.'"

"That'll come in handy if the old boy strikes lucky."

"Don't make fun of my dad."

Toby shrugged unapologetically. She slapped the papers down on the ironing board. "I'm not happy about any of this. And who's Sonia?"

"Sonia?"

Bridget was looking at the back of the final sheet of paper. "This email to you with a list of homes. It says it's from Sonia."

"Oh, Sonia. No one. Sonia Hardcastle. She's in Finance. A high-flyer by all accounts."

Bridget didn't react to his pun, intended or not. She wondered when she'd learnt this skill of not reacting to him. She didn't used to. Was that control or complacency?

Toby continued. "She's been really helpful finding places for us. She had to find a place for her dad, so she had all the contacts."

"I'd rather my dad wasn't the subject of office conversation. Thank her for her trouble, wasted as it is. I'll finish the ironing tomorrow. I'm going to bed."

Chapter 6

The piano Tara and Bridget had heard George pumping during their phone conversation was played in semi-darkness. Once Tara had relocated to the kitchen, George had turned off the living room light and gone round lighting candles. A mellow glow was how he'd always set a creative mood. And if he were going to revive his career, he'd need to get some practice in. Once settled at the piano, he wriggled and stretched his fingers. They felt stiff after so long being inactive. He hovered them over the keyboard, but didn't lower them. Bridget used to be like this at the seaside, standing by the edge of the sea, frightened to test the water, saying it would be too cold, working up the courage to take the plunge. He felt the same. Dare he risk finding out the magic had gone? Hands still poised, he contemplated closing the lid and going back to his records. Then, taking a deep breath, he dived in to tunes he hadn't thought about, let alone played, for far too long. And it felt good, relieving him of months of suppressed pain and anger. Rusty, yes, but nothing could take away the relief that his music was unchained at last. Candles on the piano guttered with the vibration from his energy. A framed photograph between them shook, then fell, its fall barely softened by the carpet. He looked down to see Evelyn in her wedding dress, smiling in faded black and white, glass cracked across her face. "Sorry, luv," he apologised. He left the picture and carried on his playing, now letting his fingers interpret not hits from a distant decade but the new tunes in his head.

After a few false starts, he completed a verse. "That's good," he told himself, before reaching out to a cassette tape recorder he'd bought in 1972. "I wonder if you're still going." It'd been state of the art back then and he'd used it ever since to record his improvised ideas, always with the aim of transcribing them later. Sometimes he did. More often he didn't. There was always a gig or something more important to do. Dozens of cassettes were stashed in a box on a windowsill hidden behind his LP racks – tunes never heard, inspiration untapped. But he was going to unleash them now. Or something new. He'd show them. There'd be no more talk of care homes when people heard what he could do. He could see the headline: 'OLD-TIMER TOPS THE CHARTS'. The thought thrilled him even as one of the candles flickered and died.

Pressing the record button, the cassette whirred into action. "Miraculous." He realised he wasn't talking to himself anymore. Hunter had prised open the door and was sitting beside him. His ears cocked as George spoke again. "I don't suppose they make anything these days that'll last like this, eh, boy?" He ruffled Hunter's fur, stretched his fingers and began again. He'd completed three choruses and two verses before stopping.

"Nah. That's no good."

The inspiration was ebbing away. Even Hunter seemed to have lost interest and gone to sleep. He switched off the recorder, then returned to the keyboard to play a melody that he knew too well.

"That's nice. Do I know it?"

The mood was destroyed by Tara's voice and the chandelier in the centre of the room bursting into light. George stopped, blinked and looked up to see his granddaughter standing in the doorway, one hand on the light switch.

"You made me jump."

"Sorry." Tara sounded apologetic, but made no move to turn the light back off. Hunter, woken up, sprung over to her. She knelt and stroked him behind the ears. He rolled over, inviting her to tickle his tummy.

George began playing again. "I used to sing this to your mum when she was a baby. One-handed, while rocking her in the other. When she wouldn't sleep. Which was most nights."

"It's nice. Would you have played it to me? I think I know it."

George grunted and stopped, resting his forearms on the keyboard. "Everything alright with your mum?"

"She was just checking on me."

"It shows she cares."

"I told her that you're unreasonable, that I can't stay here another minute!"

George gave her a half-hearted smile.

She continued. "I should stop disturbing you." She stood up and ledged herself on the corner of the piano. "What happened to the picture?" She was looking at Evelyn smiling at her through the cracked glass.

"Don't touch it. I'll clear it up later."

"OK. I think I'm going to get myself a drink before going to bed. Shall I take Hunter back to the kitchen?"

"You can leave him."

"Do you want anything?"

"I don't think so." Tara turned, but before she could leave George tutted, then said, "There is just one thing."

"That sounds ominous."

"Not really. But while I'm thinking about it, can we just set a few ground rules?"

"Ground rules?" The question seemed to catch Tara by surprise. "OK, alright, if you like. Shall I pull up a chair?"

"It's nothing much. Just a couple of things. I know I've got some funny little ways, so it's best I make them clear."

"Go on, then." She repositioned herself against the piano.

"One. I like my own space. Please don't interrupt me if I'm in here creating music. Especially while I'm playing."

"Did I scare you when I turned on the light? I'm sorry."

"Not exactly. But I like to be able to concentrate."

"I won't do it again. Promise."

"Two. Please, no one in my record room or bedroom unless invited. Boyfriend especially."

Tara shook her head. "I know. I really am sorry about that."

"That's why I'm making things clear, so we both know where we are." He knew he was sounding disagreeable but these things had to be said.

"Is that it?"

"I'd prefer it if you didn't lean on the piano. That's what they do in bars."

Tara stepped back. "Sorry."

"And please try to keep the noise down when I've gone to bed."

"Do you mean me on the piano?"

"Not just the piano. I was thinking radio or whatever you used back at your parents'. But now you mention it, yes. I'm pleased you're giving it a go but maybe not at night."

"Sorry. It didn't seem that late to me."

"Just for future reference."

"I'll try."

"Number three, or maybe it's four. Whichever, please don't leave your coat and shoes on the floor in the hall. I know you've only just moved in but that's what the utility room is for. And something I noticed at your mum and dad's – fiddling with the thermostat. If you're thinking of doing it, please don't."

"Mum always has it set too cold."

"I've got it at a temperature that's comfortable to me and I'd like it to stay like that."

"Is that it?"

George nodded. "I didn't mean to sound grumpy."

"You're not. At least not very." Tara gave him a hug. "And I'm really pleased you're letting me stay."

"And while you're here…"

Tara let go. "Yes?"

"Will that boyfriend of yours be coming and going?"

"Mark? I don't know."

"Is he going to be the one?"

"I don't know that, either. Why do you ask?"

"No reason." George wondered if he should say what he was thinking – or the conditions Toby had laid down to him before agreeing she could move in.

"I hope you're not going to lecture me." It was said with a smile but George recognised the warning signs.

"No, no." Better he change tack. "Just if you're ever going to be out late, would you let me know? I'll worry if I don't know where you are."

Tara looked relieved. "Are you trying to nanny me? Do you want me to wear a tag round my ankle?"

"Now you're talking." They both laughed and George decided to save his idea of a piano-playing timetable for another time, maybe even offering to teach her.

"I'll write my mobile number down for you." She waved her phone at him. "But you're not going to be calling me like Mum does, please."

"Deal."

Tara offered her palm and they slapped hands.

"If that's all, can I have a ground rule?"

"Go on."

"Not to go on about Mark."

"I didn't think I had."

"You haven't, but Mum and Dad did, all the time."

"OK."

"And will you promise not to keep telling me how you lived through the history I'm doing as coursework?"

"I didn't know I did."

"And that you won't comment on what I wear and my make-up?"

"Like your dad does?"

Tara nodded. "All the time. It really annoys me."

"It annoyed *me*. It's *your* life. You must live it your way. That includes what you wear and how you look." He wasn't quite sure he meant it, but it made up for his grumpiness. "So, ground rules are agreed?"

"Agreed." They shook hands, then Tara hugged him again. "We're going to get on alright, aren't we?"

"I really hope so." What could possibly go wrong?

Chapter 7

"Hello, George. Good to see you after all this time."

George stared blankly at the figure on his doorstep.

"Are you going to leave me standing out here all day? I've been ringing the bell. I was beginning to think no one was in."

George still said nothing, eyeing the short, greying figure.

"You do recognise me, don't you? Aged a bit, lost a bit of hair. Robin. Robin Brandon." He thrust forward a hand to shake.

Still George didn't respond.

"I know it's been a long time. Didn't you get my letter?"

At last George spoke. "Yes, I got your letter."

"Then can I come in?"

George stepped aside slowly, unenthusiastically, wishing he'd ignored the doorbell and that Tara wasn't out taking Hunter for a walk.

* * *

Robin had been known in the family as Uncle Robin, though it came with a saying, 'Robin by name, robbing by nature.' Or 'robbin' bastard' for short. He wasn't even really an uncle. He was married to Grace, Evelyn's cousin. A *dis*grace, her mum would say. When they wed, Robin was out of work and Grace five months pregnant. It was a simple, not to say cheap, wedding. After a week's honeymoon in Blackpool, the newly-weds moved into the flat over the family shop with George and Evelyn, who were now managing it. Space was cramped but it was the least they felt they should do – an act of kindness that was not to be reciprocated.

Initially it was only to be a temporary arrangement. But Grace miscarried and they stayed. Robin said he just needed time to get back on his feet. But he didn't show any signs of doing it, nor of making any attempt to try – 'a wrong 'un,' Evelyn would say. George asked for no rent, just that Robin helped out in the shop. Except he hardly ever did. There was always a reason: not feeling well, needing to be with Grace, having to talk to someone about a job that never materialised. On the occasions he put in an appearance, a gang of his mates would hang around outside. Robin would join them when he thought no one was looking. Then things started to go missing – cigarettes mainly, but also magazines and boxes of chocolates. At first, Evelyn put it down to George, giving in to kids who were always asking for freebies. She said he was too soft and that if the finances were left to him they'd have started out as a charity and ended up in the poor house. George denied it, while the losses continued. When the shop's takings also seemed to dip, Evelyn began a surveillance operation. It was as meticulous as everything else she did. The CIA probably took lessons from her. Within days, Robin was found with his fingers in the till. Given time, all might have been forgiven, but Grace couldn't face the shame. So they moved out the same day. Along with George's antique carriage clock and some items of Evelyn's mum's jewellery. No one really knew where the couple had gone. Cards duly appeared for Christmas and birthdays, with a Scarborough postmark and occasionally an address on the envelope that was always different from the one before. Otherwise, they disappeared from family life. Until Grace died.

Run over last Thursday by an open-top bus while attempting to negotiate a zebra crossing.

That's how it had been announced in the Births, Deaths and Marriages section of the *Scarborough Evening News*. The funeral was held at the council crematorium, the wake in a pub outside the crematorium's main gates. A joyless affair, lifted only temporarily by George taking to the piano in the Snug Bar, at least until Evelyn stopped him. After that, all communication with Robin stopped. Until now.

* * *

George ushered Robin into the living room.

"Still got the piano, then? You still play?"

"What did you expect?"

Robin shrugged as he took off his jacket, draping it over the arm of the sofa, and sat down.

"Make yourself at home." George was still standing. "What did you come for?"

"You got my letter? Evelyn. Such a shock. I only just found out and wanted to give you my condolences in person."

"Well, now you have and I'm grateful." George edged back towards the door.

Robin didn't move. "That amaryllis is dead." He nodded to a pot on the windowsill, then pointed at the broken frame on the floor. "And what happened to the picture?"

"If you'll excuse me, I have things to do."

Robin still didn't move. "Don't let me interrupt you. You still using that old thing?" He pointed at the cassette deck.

"Maybe."

"I reckon I could help you."

"So what are you really here for?" George sighed and sat down.

"I told you, my condolences." Robin looked around. "I'm really sorry about Evelyn, I really am. Far too early."

George turned away. What was far too early was this kind of conversation.

"So, how are you coping? Don't you rattle around in this place on your own, just you and your granddaughter – what's her name?"

"Tara." A fleeting thought crossed George's mind as to how Robin knew Tara was living with him. Probably two pairs of her shoes strewn across the hallway. "Anyway, I'm very happy, thank you."

"If you ever think about selling up, let me know. Would make at least three flats. Could fetch a couple of million. More probably."

"When I'm dead. I'm not moving otherwise."

"You still got your records?" Robin looked round. "You must have thousands by now. Very collectable these days."

"I haven't got time for this. Please get to the point, will you? Have you become a dealer or something?"

"Nah. I get by with a bit of this, bit of that. Ducking and diving. Looking for the next thing."

"If you've come here to borrow money…"

"If you've got a few million to spare." He gave a fake-looking smile.

"What then?" George steeled himself for Robin to ask for the keepsake he'd written about in his letter. If he dared,

George was ready to list the clock and the jewellery missing from all those years ago. Though Robin would probably deny it.

"Now you ask, like I said, if you're still playing, I might be able to do you a favour."

"A favour?"

"Listen, my friend, I still have contacts."

"Oh, yes?" George's face was as disbelieving as his tone.

"You know how it is."

"How what is?"

"I've a contact who runs a studio. He records people's demos. Some have become famous."

"Like who?"

"Don't know their names. But I know they got famous. And he's got the kit." Robin pointed at the cassette player again. "He can't be worse than using that thing."

"I only use it for ideas."

"There you are, then. He'll make you a proper recording. No disrespect, but at your age what have you got to lose? Let me introduce you, at least."

"What's in it for you?"

"My friend, you're so suspicious."

"Too right."

"Look, you come up with something decent, I can help you and – who knows? Sky's the limit. I can see it now." Robin made speech marks with his fingers. "'Overnight sensation.'" He laughed.

George hesitated. Evelyn would have shown him the door already. What if Bridget found out about this conversation? But recording, in a studio. After all these years. Toby had touched the one nerve, was offering the one hope that could make him go against all common sense and reason. Prophet bearing false witness or gift horse in the mouth? After all, it had been a long time and people change. Would it do any harm to check it out?

He sucked his teeth. "Maybe."

Chapter 8

"So how was it?" Mark thumped two coffee mugs on the table as he sat down. After the way he'd been dismissed from George's house the day before, it could only have been a gesture of defiance, but he succeeded simply in slopping cappuccino over his hands and froth down his jacket.

Tara watched his punctured dignity without reaction. When she'd left her mobile on silent, she'd made up her mind not to call him for a couple of days. She needed time to think things over. Uni would offer opportunities, new experiences, new friends. She'd escaped her parents, maybe it was time to make clean breaks all round. To stay with Mark looked like commitment. She needed to be able to reconcile with herself if that was what she really wanted or if their time was up. So to bump into him while she was walking Hunter rather messed up her plan. She might yet have carried on without stopping to talk, but it was starting to drizzle. So she accepted Mark's invitation for a coffee.

The High Street that once boasted a hardware shop, hairdresser, two general stores, fishmonger, greengrocer and a police station was now a row of coffeehouse chains. CuppaCoffee was the sole remaining independent and advertised itself as dog, mum and child friendly. It was there that Mark and Tara sat, in the company of unleashed pets browsing for titbits, screaming children running between tables while ignoring their mothers' threats to sit still, and new-borns gurgling from discreetly covered breasts in dark corners. Meetings were being held over papers, computers and lattés, and couples hid themselves from one another behind copies of the *Metro*. Everyone seemed oblivious of everyone else. Guy Fawkes and Robert Catesby could have sat over a mochaccino and no one would have noticed. If she were going to break up with Mark, at least it would pass off anonymously.

"How is it?" Mark asked again as he sat down.

"How is what? And don't do that. You trying to kill him?" Tara was looking disapprovingly at how Mark was inviting Hunter to lick the coffee off his fingers. "Special diet. Remember?" She yanked the lead to distance the dog from the temptation of dropped chocolate muffin crumbs beneath his chair.

"Sorry."

She felt him scrutinising her. Could he tell she was on the verge of dumping him? She was determined to reveal nothing. "If you mean Gramps, he spent the morning winding clocks. There's a clock in every room, feels like. Sometimes more. And he went from one to another, religiously winding them all."

"Sounds fun."

"And collecting up candles and tea lights. He has them all over the place. He scraped out little fragments of wax from ones that were used up and put them into a little jug."

"Why?"

"He says he collects them so he can put the bits on to other candles. To make them last longer and not waste wax. I think he was going to ask me to help."

"What, wind clocks or collect wax?"

"Yeah, right." Tara gave a disdainful snort. "Anyway, that's when I offered to take out Hunter." She looked down at the dog lying contentedly at her feet, avoiding Mark's gaze as he was still staring at her. She wished she'd put proper make-up on.

There were an uncomfortable few moments that felt like minutes while neither spoke, before he leaned forward. "I'm sorry about the way I was."

"So you should be." She offered no sign of forgiveness.

"So are you going to tell me about it?"

"I just did."

"Not this morning. Last night."

Tara shrugged.

Mark reached towards Hunter. "How are you doing, mate?"

Tara tugged at the lead. "He's doing alright, thank you. Better than me."

"I've said I'm sorry."

At last, she looked at him. "You'd better mean it."

"I mean it."

After a pause, she broke rank. Talking to Mark was better than bottling it up. "Well, to tell the truth, it was all a bit odd."

"How odd?"

"Strange. First, my mother phoned."

"I had that on my first night."

"Not just once. Loads of times. And texts. To see if I was alright."

"It'll be a bit weird for her, with you moved out."

"She shouldn't treat me like I'm still a child."

Thoughts of interfering parents seemed to relieve the tension. "So what happened with you and your granddad?" Mark hunched himself forward, closer to Tara as he spoke.

"Like I said, it was all a bit strange."

"Odd, you said."

Tara threw herself back. "Do you want me to tell you or not?"

"Did he moan about what had happened with his records?"

"No. Well, not much."

"So what did you do?"

She skipped the bit about ground rules or being asked if Mark was 'the one'. Instead she jumped to what had happened after their pact. "I was going to go to bed. I'd just given him a hug when he started talking about his past. People he said he'd met when he was a musician."

"Like who?"

"Oh, loads. David Bowie, Fleetwood Mac. Others."

"*The* David Bowie?" Mark sat bolt upright, excited at the thought.

"I don't know. Yes. I suppose so."

"When did he play with Bowie?"

"I don't know."

"Was it before he was famous? Ziggy Stardust? Tin Machine? You must have asked."

"Am I telling you about David Bowie or my evening?" She flashed him a warning look.

"Sorry. Carry on about your evening."

"After he told me about David Bowie and all the other people I'd never heard of, he started again on the piano."

"Must have tolerant neighbours."

Tara nodded in agreement. "But he's really good, you know. He played some songs he thought I'd know…"

"Did you?"

"Not many. Then he started stuff from old family Christmases. It turned into a bit of a sing-a-long."

"Blimey. Not just tolerant neighbours. Long-suffering. Or deaf."

Tara let this interruption pass. "In full voice too. Both of us. Then, nothing."

"Nothing?"

"He just stopped. Changed completely. Stopped singing, stopped playing, stopped talking. Just went silent."

"Too many memories? It's not that long since the funeral."

"I thought he was going to cry. By now, I really wanted to go to bed but I couldn't just walk out on him. It was quite awkward."

"Just being there must have helped. An empty house would've been terrible for him." He reached out to her hand. "It was right you spent the night with him. Without me, I mean."

"Do you want to hear what happened next or not?"

"I thought you said nothing happened."

"He didn't *say* anything. He started playing again. Something different. Nothing I knew. When he stopped, he said it was new."

"New?"

"That's what he said."

"Thought he'd retired ages ago."

"So did I. But seems he's kept writing. And recording. Special stuff, he said. Film music."

"What, *Evita*? *Frozen*? I haven't heard his name at the Oscars."

"Will you stop mocking and listen or I won't carry on." She waited a few seconds, then assumed it was safe to continue. "He called it production music. Music that gets used in training films. Or sometimes theme tunes on TV – you know, *News at Ten*, *Mastermind*, *Escape to the Country*."

"He wrote those?"

"Not them exactly. Tunes like them. Every time one of his gets used, he gets paid. He says it's how he's stayed independent after he stopped working."

"Why isn't he famous, then?"

"How would I know? Perhaps he was happy being undiscovered, working away in the background."

"He didn't tell you which tunes he'd written?"

"I didn't ask."

"Or where he'd played, or if he recorded with Bowie?"

"I think Hunter needs to go." She looked down at the dog, his eyes closed, gently resting his head on her toes. "Come on, boy."

"Sorry. What did he talk about?"

Hunter didn't stir. Tara exhaled heavily. "He mentioned the odd gig, session work, hotel bars."

"Sounds pretty dull."

"But he wouldn't stop talking. I didn't think I'd ever get away." Maybe it was *her* punishment for not agreeing to spend the evening with Mark. She was thankful Mark didn't say as much.

"That's what old people do. I suppose they've got so many memories and don't know when to stop. Did he talk about your gran?"

"A bit. Asked me about helping clear some of her stuff out. Said he couldn't bear to do it by himself."

"And will you?"

"I said I would. It won't be for a while though. I think he needs a bit of time to think about what he wants to get rid of."

"Then what happened?"

"I was trying to think of a way to get up to bed without upsetting him, when without any warning he asked if I minded if we stopped as he was tired. I certainly was. But while I went to bed, ten minutes later, from that room with all his records, music. Loud. And I *mean* loud. Was like the house was vibrating."

"Like what?"

"A mix. Some I knew."

"Like what? Classical? Depressing stuff?"

"Not like that at all. Most sounded like it was way before my time. And then came the tune from that home insurance advert – you know, the one with the cartoon dog."

Mark nodded, though Tara couldn't tell if he did.

"Didn't know if he was playing to himself or to me. It was ages before it all stopped."

"I thought you said he was tired."

Tara nodded. "If hadn't got up to go to the toilet, I think he'd have carried on all night. You joked about the neighbours. I don't know if *I'm* going to be able to stand it."

"Wonder if he does it every night."

"Christ, I hope not." Two feral children ran close to their table, the heel of a size one junior shoe landing on Hunter's front right paw. He yelped but didn't bark. "I think we should go."

"Are we friends again?"

Tara nodded, warily. "If you promise not to push me."

"I promise."

"And that you won't throw coffee over the table." She leaned forward with a napkin and wiped the coffee dribble from his chin. Mark leaned forward too, and kissed her. She let it linger for a few seconds, then sat back.

Mark sat back, resting his hands behind his head. "You haven't asked me how my music is going."

"How's your music going?"

"Kind of you to ask. As it happens, I finished some new stuff. Last night."

"At least something good came of it."

"Do you want to hear it?" He handed her a memory stick. "It's on there."

Mark's music was – how did Tara describe it to her parents? Individual. His uni course encouraged experimentation, and Mark had embraced the concept wholeheartedly. How did *he* describe it? 'Old-lampin, ghetto-grittin, steelo dealo pimped-out mamma-jamma scratch.' And that was just for starters.

"I'll listen in the morning."

"Thanks." He put the tip of his finger into his mouth and scratched it with his teeth, as if deliberating. "One thing…"

"Uh-oh, what's coming now?" She wondered if Mark might be asking her to help. She wasn't going to suggest it but people always said how good a voice she had. Secretly, she liked the idea of being a singer.

"I was wondering. Do you think your grandfather's got any records in that room of his he'd let me sample?"

"Oh."

"Will you ask him?"

She hid her disappointment. "After you knocked everything over?"

"Will you at least ask him?"

"You've seen how protective he is about them."

"You can get round him. Spoil him. Do something so he can't say no."

"Like what?"

"Buy him something special? Let him tell you about all his favourite music."

"God, no."

"Then cook him something he likes. Didn't you say his big weakness is a fry-up? You could do one and ask him about sampling at the same time."

Tara leaned back and gritted her teeth. First her grandfather acting like a warden. Now Mark putting more demands on her. "I might. I don't see why I should." This isn't what she thought independent living would be like. Something was going to have to change.

Chapter 9

"Gramps…" Tara delivered this single word in what Evelyn would have called a wheedle. She was standing at George's shoulder clasping a spoon filled with hot rice pudding, the steam watering his eyes. He'd already gorged on two eggs, bacon, sausages, beans, tomatoes, mushrooms, fried bread, brown sauce and two slices. His favourite breakfast, an irresistible treat, even if it had been served nine hours late, at teatime. A fry-up at any time was not to be sniffed at. It was topped by being able to dip the bread crusts into the egg and mop up the sauce with the fried bread. He had been barred from this pleasure since 1967. Aptly, 'The Last Time' by the Rolling Stones had been playing on the radio and Evelyn was eight months pregnant. 'Must you do that? It's a disgusting habit,' she'd complained, and he'd not been able to listen to that song without remembering. He'd been about to relate the story to Tara when she began her appeal. "You know your records…"

He cut her short. "This is the best meal I've had in ages. I hope you're going to make a habit of it."

"Thanks. But Gramps…"

George sensed a request coming. "Yes, I know my records. Especially now I'm having to put back the ones you and that boy of yours knocked over."

With rice pudding at risk of escaping from the spoon and descending on to George's lap, Tara took decisive action. She filled his bowl and went for it.

"Mark wondered if there was anything he could sample."

"Sample?"

"Use in his music."

"Music? What does he do?"

"Modern stuff. Different from yours."

"If it's different, why's he interested in mine?"

"To take bits of old tunes and put them into his music."

"I know what sampling is. I'm not that ancient. Don't agree with it, mind."

"Don't agree?"

"It's stealing someone else's creativity."

"What, like Elvis Presley? Didn't he steal from black Americans?"

"How do you know about Elvis Presley?"

"GCSE History."

George remembered his promise not to complain about his life referred to as history. "Different thing altogether."

"How's it different? He copied other people's music."

George could see himself being outflanked, but was determined to stand his ground. "Elvis didn't copy. He gave it his own interpretation."

"That's what Mark wants to do."

George recognised imminent defeat. "You're as bad as your mother. Can't face losing an argument."

He expected Tara to say she hadn't lost, but instead she seized on her advantage. "So can he? Use your records. He'll say please."

"What's wrong with using *your* voice."

Tara shrugged, sidestepping the question. "He wants to sample. And he's very sorry about going into your room without asking."

George was going to tell her about copyright laws, but the look in her eyes reminded him so much of Evelyn. How he missed her.

Tara went for victory. "Please. Pretty please."

George sighed. "Maybe."

Tara jumped up and hugged him round the neck.

"Thanks, Gramps."

"Careful. You'll strangle me." Secretly, her energy and warmth made him feel good. "But I need you to do something for me." He had to warn Bridget about Robin, and the letter was burning a hole in his pocket. A full stomach was relaxing him, making him feel the late breakfast didn't herald anything quite as bad as he first imagined.

Tara let him go and went back to serving herself pudding. "How's the rice?"

"Perfect. Just as I like it."

"Glad you like it. So, I can tell Mark it's OK?" She grabbed her bowl. "I'm going back upstairs, if that's OK."

George nodded, sensing the moment for the letter was passing. "But I do need to show you something."

"Of course." She was already past the kitchen door.

"I'll bring it to you when I've finished this," he called after her, his voice building to a crescendo as she reached the stairs. "And tell him there are some conditions to sampling." By the time she was halfway up, he was shouting. Even then he wasn't at all sure she heard. With a sigh, he returned his attention to the bowl of rice and, once it was gone, scraped the inside of the saucepan.

* * *

Twenty minutes later, George made his way upstairs. For a moment, he lingered outside Tara's room, listening to her singing along to music. In his day it would have been a transistor radio. He guessed this was from her computer, an invention he'd never owned nor saw any need to know about. He knocked gingerly on the door.

"Come in, Gramps. I hope I wasn't singing too loudly."

"Sing as loud as you like. I would never stop anyone singing. It's a human right. Even if they can't hold a tune in a bucket. And you can. You've got a lovely voice."

"It's too soft. And squeaky."

"It's not. It's a wonderful voice. What were you singing?"

"Sean Kingston. Was Number One with it when I was in Year Three or Four."

"Hold on a minute."

Tara watched, bemused, as George disappeared from her room. Within a few seconds, music vibrated through the floor. She followed its trail to where George was standing over his record deck. "That's the same song," she shouted over the vocals, "but it's not Sean Kingston."

"'Stand By Me'. Ben E King. From the 1960s, then again in the seventies by John Lennon before your bloke sampled it in the eighties. Not a bad version, I agree." He waved a CD cover to prove to Tara that he owned it.

"Aha – sampling. See? One up to me!" She sounded triumphant.

"OK, Miss Clever Clogs. What about this one?" He ran his fingers along a line of singles, pulled one out, gently slid it from its protective sleeve and, placing it on the turntable, carefully dropped the stylus into the groove.

Tara listened, then nodded. "That sounds like Beyoncé. 'Hold Up.'"

"Andy Williams. Then The Beat in the eighties. 'Can't Get Used to Losing You' is its real title. Beyoncé just sampled it like you want to do. I've got them all if you want to hear." He lifted the tone arm back off the record. "But that boyfriend of yours..."

"Mark."

"... Mark needs to get permission to sample. Legally, that is. I hope you haven't promised too much. He *can* have the songs *I've* written, if they're any use. But he can't just steal someone else's song without asking. Which usually means paying."

"Even Beyoncé? 'Hold Up'?"

"She would have got permission, yes."

"I didn't mean that. You've got Beyoncé's album with 'Hold Up'?"

"Double vinyl." He reached across to a shelf behind and pulled out the record and held it up.

"Wow! I'm impressed."

"I know where everything is. Can find it in an instant."

Tara shook her head. "Not impressed that you can find it. That you've got it."

"Do I have to stop loving music because I'm old and decrepit?"

"I don't mean that."

"I didn't stop loving music when the sixties ended. The decade, or mine. Nothing's new. Things get changed, sometimes improved." He paused before adding ruefully, "But not often." He sighed. "Enough of that. How's you and Mick?"

"Mark. Why do you ask? Have Mum and Dad been on to you?"

"No. Just wondered. What made you think they had?" He might have added, 'What have you done that they should be worried about?'

She shook her head. "No reason. Mark and me are fine."

"What about his musical tastes?"

"How do you know his musical tastes?"

"Is that what I heard from your bedroom? When you came back from walking Hunter."

"Sorry. He gave me his latest stuff to listen to. He calls it his old-lampin', ghetto-grittin', steelo dealo pimped-out mamma-jamma scratch."

"Heaven forfend!"

"You didn't like it?"

"Do you?"

"It's OK. He's getting better. New ideas. And that's why he really wants to sample your music." She waved her finger as inspiration struck. "Tell you what, why don't you come to one of his gigs at uni? You'll see what he does and how he uses samples. Maybe you'll even like what he does."

"I doubt it."

"Why do you doubt it? You've not heard it."

"What I heard from your room's enough."

"Go on, give it a try." The wheedle in her voice was back. "What's there to lose?"

'My hearing, my sanity,' George thought about answering, offering instead, "My heart's really into old stuff. Rock'n'roll, blues, bit of R&B. That's what I used to play. In small halls, big theatres. Never top of the bill but people liked us. Stop me if I've told you all this before." Tara nodded while George continued without pausing. "Then there was folk rock as it was called." He looked away, remembering a song in his head. "That was in small clubs. Much more intimate and free. Improvised. Exciting times." He skipped the hotels and bars that so demoralised him in later years, where the requirement had been to be anodyne, quiet, virtually unnoticed, simply covering up the sound of cutlery and chewing.

"You were good, weren't you? Mum says."

He turned away, replacing the Beyoncé album to avoid answering to Tara's face. "I played with the best, I know that. Gigs, studios, tour support to big American names, that kind of thing. In the early days there was Eddie Cochran, Gene Vincent, John Lee Hooker... and I played the same bill as Eric Clapton, the Yardbirds. Listen to this."

He whisked a Yardbirds single from a pile and put it on the turntable. The speakers thumped to the bass.

"You could dab to this." Tara started to fling her arms in the air.

"Dab?" George braved the question, fearing 'dab' might be a euphemism for something he really didn't want to know about.

"Dabbing. Like this." She dropped her head into one arm and stabbed with the other. "It's a dance."

"You call that a dance? God, what is the world coming to?" He took the record off.

She kept going, exaggerating her movements for a couple of silent beats. "It's what us millennials do, Gramps," she said breathlessly when she stopped.

George shook his head in disbelief.

"You still haven't said about you." She watched as her grandfather put the Yardbirds carefully back into their sleeve and on to the pile. "Did you have any hits?"

George sighed. "I played session on a couple. You'll not have heard of them."

"What about your band?"

"Group we called them, back then."

"Did you have lots of fans? Groupies throwing themselves at you?" She chuckled at the thought.

"Not really my cup of tea. Too old maybe, even then. We were support, not the star turn."

"Is that why you bought so many records?"

"Now, there's one I really like." He grabbed a CD from behind Tara and put it into the CD deck. "Amy Studt. So under-rated. Finding new music like this…"

He waved the CD case and Tara took it from him as he kept talking.

"… it's so exciting and keeps me interested. And I've never stopped finding music I like, so I've kept buying it."

Tara tutted. "2003 this came out." She handed the case back to him. "That's not new. I wasn't hardly born in 2003."

"You can mock. To me, it feels like only yesterday. And it's still one of my favourites."

"What would you say's your favourite of all time?"

George sucked his lips for a moment. "Impossible to say. I've too many to have just one. Depends on my mood, how I'm feeling…"

She looked around the room. "How do you choose which ones to play? It seems like you've got every record ever made."

"Nothing like it."

"Bet you wish you had."

"You'd win." He ran his fingers along a line of albums while he considered what it would be like to have every piece of recorded music at his fingertips. "I could own them all and still not have enough."

"You can now, on the internet."

"Not the same."

"How do you know? You haven't got a computer."

"It's not for me, that interwebthing."

"What about Amazon? Ask Alexa. It's all there."

"I don't have an Amazon or an Alexa." George rolled his eyes and gave the CD tray a firm shove. It clicked shut, LEDs flashing. He picked up the remote and pointed it at the player. "That's for you youngsters. Not me."

"So are you still buying music?"

"I was. Before… you know." Instead of pressing 'play', he let the remote fall to his side, his mind flashing back to a time before the funeral. He took a deep breath. "But all the shops are closing down – and of course I've been held prisoner with your mum and dad for I know not how long."

"You can buy online."

He sighed. "Sorry, I'm not interested in," he wiggled his fingers in the air in mock punctuation, "'online'. I want to see the sleeves, hold them, smell them, before I buy them."

"Maybe as well as sampling, you'll let Mark show you how to find music online."

"I don't think so." He was shaking his head as he put down the remote and started to pat his trousers. "What I wanted to ask…" He scrabbled inside a pocket, producing a crumpled envelope. "Do you think you could show this to your mum?"

Tara took it. Inside was Robin's letter that he knew would upset Bridget. But she had to know. He just hoped it wouldn't wreck his plans.

Chapter 10

Toby read the letter from Robin without comment, then handed it back to Bridget.

"Did you know anything about this?" Bridget looked accusingly at him. "He's got a nerve. Something to remember her by, indeed." She turned to Tara. "Did your grandfather say if he'd had a visit already?"

"He didn't mention it."

"You'd know if he had as all the furniture would be gone. I just hope he's not planning on dropping in here."

Toby shrugged. "Come on, it's been a long time and he *is* part of the family. I know he made mistakes, but I always kind of liked him."

"Shows what a bad judge of character you are."

"I married you."

"Children, children." Tara had already been anxious about becoming a go-between for Gramps with this letter. Being reminded of what it was like to be around her bickering parents only confirmed her fears, though she was shocked to see it seemed to have notched up another level. "Gramps just asked me to show it to you, to let you know."

"Don't worry, love." Bridget's tone suggested anything but love. "I'll decide what I'm going to do if he shows up here," adding as an afterthought, "though if he knows what's good for him, he won't." Bridget screwed up the letter and let it drop to the floor. "In the meantime, how *is* Dad?"

"Up and down. Seems OK."

"Has he talked about clearing out Mum's things?"

"I don't think he's ready yet."

Bridget exchanged glances with Toby, and Tara couldn't miss the look back that suggested she was trespassing on an open sore. "Does he get out much?" Bridget asked.

"He seems to be in that room of records all the time. Except when he's walking Hunter."

Toby gave a look that Tara recognised as 'I told you so', and that Bridget ignored. "We'll arrange something for him to do. Maybe ask him if he wants to play canasta. He and Mum used to have friends they played with now and again. I'll get on to them, see if we can't get him out one evening."

"I suggested he went to one of Mark's gigs."

"Really?" Toby sounded incredulous. "And did he say he would?"

"Not exactly."

"I'm not surprised." Toby was shaking his head.

"Thanks for trying though, darling." Bridget gave her daughter an encouraging smile.

"While you're at it, would you take these back with you and show them to him?" Toby pointed at his stash of care home details.

Bridget acted as if her husband hadn't spoken. "And how about Mark? Does he get on with your grandfather?"

"Mark's fine. He's got so much coursework he hardly ever comes round. And I've not had much time to see him either, what with all the coursework I've got."

For the first time, Bridget and Toby exchanged glances that were not hostile.

"Well, if you've got any other ideas to get your granddad out of himself, let me know. I know you're not his carer, but anything you can do will help."

Half an hour of small talk passed before Tara left, brochures in hand. Toby and Bridget stood at the door, Bridget waving, both watching as their daughter disappeared back into her own life, leaving them with theirs.

* * *

For Tara to say she hadn't seen much of Mark was not exactly true. In fact, it would have bent the needle on a lie detector. Since the café reconciliation, she had tried to put the reservations about him behind her. They had spent most daylight hours entwined, kept apart only by lectures. Still no sex yet, but it was just a matter of time, though he now seemed prepared to wait for her to say when. Question was, where? His place was uncompromisingly student digs – shared, male, poky. He didn't have a car and alfresco was out of the question. But if Gramps might start going out of an evening to play canasta, that would leave the house empty for just the two of them.

"Are you listening?" Mark sounded irritated. He had been telling Tara all about his plans for his music as they were walking from the bus stop towards George's house, about the new files on the hard drive he was carrying in his other hand, how he was going to work on them, put them online, get people interested. She hadn't even commented on how he'd decorated it in felt pen, spelling out the words, Mark'n'Tara.

"Sorry, I was thinking about something else."

Mark pulled his hand away. "Well, if you don't want to know..."

"I do. Really." Tara felt relief that he hadn't asked her *what* she'd been thinking about. So they walked in silence, rescued by their arrival at the front door. They'd come hoping to sample some of George's records and use Tara's computer. Toby had bought it for her last Christmas, complete with a vast memory and seemingly every available program and plug-in. It'd been a surprise as all she really needed was basic Word and internet. But it'd given her an excuse to spend more time in her bedroom away from everyone – and there were times when she wondered if that hadn't been why her dad had given it to her in the first place. But it was perfect for Mark and she'd agreed he could use it to create his music from the noises in his head. It also made her feel good to be with someone so creative.

"Hi, Gramps," Tara called out to George as they passed his special room. She peered in to see him with a pile of records on his knee. She called again, loud enough to be heard over a Simon and Garfunkel CD blasting out through the loudspeakers. "What you up to?"

"Sorting. Tidying. Cleaning. Always something to do. Some of these haven't had any attention for half a century or more."

"Don't mention the sampling yet," Mark whispered to her.

"Mark's come round to work on his music. Do you want to hear..." She didn't finish. Mark had put his hand over her mouth and dragged her away. George was still caressing the records on his knee and seemed not to notice. Not that Tara saw it that way.

"What do you think you were doing?" she hissed once she'd closed her bedroom door behind them. "In front of Gramps. This is my home. You've no right."

"Well, don't you go telling him about my music. It's private."

"Private? You've been saying you're going to put it online."

The revelation that maybe Tara *had* been listening on the walk didn't appear to make him feel better. In fact, he seemed angry now. "If you were creative, you'd understand. Putting it online's different."

"You mean, where no one will hear it?"

"Oh, fuck off. If that's all you think about my work…"

Mark turned to leave, and would have gone if Tara hadn't reached out to grab and stop him. They stumbled towards her bed.

And so it was, as her grandfather sorted his London American label 45s while listening to Simon and Garfunkel's *Bridge Over Troubled Water* album, Mark reached fourth base; but it was ruined because he was angry all the way through.

And as they sat up afterwards, Tara was hoping for something along the lines of 'that was great' or 'you were fantastic' or 'what an amazing body you've got'. What Mark actually said was, "Did you mean that about my music?"

"Mean what?"

"That no one will hear it?"

"It was a joke."

"Oh."

"Your music's brilliant."

And to prove she meant it, they did it again. Accompanied through the floor by Paul Simon and Art Garfunkel wailing 'Keep the Customer Satisfied'. And this time Mark wasn't angry. And this time he said it was fantastic. And she said he was too. And she meant it.

And George found his very rare copy of Smiley Lewis's 'Shame, Shame, Shame' that he'd lost for years, and listened to it three times before falling asleep in his chair.

Chapter 11

Bridget was deadheading roses in the front garden, her secateurs decapitating each stem with uncharacteristic venom, her mind less on pruning than on Toby. Upstairs and packing his bags, he was preparing to leave two days earlier than planned for the client meeting in the Midlands. He said he'd forgotten about a company away weekend and team building. His description was of a low-key and casual event, but he was spending more time than usual selecting what he would be wearing. He even rejected a shirt for an ironing burn. 'Will Sonia from Finance be there?' she'd asked. Toby had shrugged and answered with a dismissive, 'How would I know?'

The sound of a car screeching round the corner interrupted her thoughts. A BMW Z4 two-seater convertible, roof down, stopped by the garden gate. She knew immediately who the intruder was, even though she'd not seen him since the eighties.

"Hello, darlin.'"

"Don't *darlin'* me, Robin Brandon." Bridget struck her best 'repel all borders' pose.

"Hello, Tobes. Mighty pleased to see you." Robin was looking at the open front door where Toby had appeared.

"Hiya, Robin. You're the first person outside the Turnbull bloodline we've had visit us for ages."

Bridget didn't relent on her pose. "Lucky I saw this little shit arriving or he'd have pissed on our lawn or stolen the front door." She didn't comment that as much as she hated *darlin'*, she knew Toby hated *Tobes*.

"Water under the bridge, Bridge. Eh, Tobes?" Robin sounded pleased with his pun.

"And I wish you'd drowned in it."

"Hold on, Bridget. Give the man a chance."

"No. *You* hold on, *Tobes*." Bridget's mimicking of the reviled nickname was evidence she wasn't ready for reconciliation. "He had his chance. Thirty years ago. Before you lecture me, *you* remember that this lowlife stole from our... *my* family. Do you expect me to welcome him back with open arms?"

"We can at least be a bit civil. Maybe even show some forgiveness."

"Only if we screw down the furniture."

"Don't mind her, Robin. Come on in."

"Over my dead body. And he'd probably find a buyer for that."

Robin looked amused rather than offended. "I take it I'm not altogether welcome."

"And you're no quicker on the uptake, either."

"Excuse her, Robin. Maybe it'd have been better if you'd called first. Bridget's not one for surprise visits."

Bridget thought of saying something about rotten surprises, but let it pass.

"I was in the area. And I'd lost your number or I'd have called."

"Maybe later. When things have calmed down a bit here."

Bridget still said nothing, though her face suggested calming down might not be an option.

"OK, I'll go. Can I use your khazi first? I've been in the car for more than three hours."

"Use the gutter. Where you came from."

Toby ignored his wife's return to the proceedings. "Yeah, come on in."

Robin eased out of his car and made his way up the garden path. Bridget stood, unmoved, arms folded, face creased, watching every step he took, waiting until he was past her before hissing, "Put a padlock on the toilet seat."

* * *

Once inside, Toby reached out and shook Robin's hand.

"Sorry about all that. Bridget's still edgy about her old man."

"No problem, my friend, no problem. I saw him the other day."

"Did you? Did he say anything about the wifi? Or his records?"

"He said he's still writing songs."

"As if."

"I know."

"As you're here, you'll need these again." Toby fumbled in his pocket and handed over a set of keys. "Tara's having wifi trouble."

"No worries. I'll go back when they're all out. Which way?"

"Round the corner, third door on the left. You haven't really lost my number?"

"Of course not. Just being diplomatic. You still wanting to use my pad?"

"I'll know after this weekend. Getting ready for it now. Don't say a word."

"Of course not." Robin was halfway up the stairs. "'Secrets' is my middle name. Give her one for me."

"Just one?" Toby laughed. "That's it, third on the left."

* * *

Bridget didn't appear to have moved when they re-emerged.

Robin raised his arms. "Want to frisk me?"

"Fuck off."

"I'll take that as a sign of trust."

"If it's all you've taken, that'll be a first."

Robin pulled a face that said 'couldn't care less' then shook Toby's hand, and winked. "Thanks for the number, Tobes. I'll give you a bell."

"And don't you go near my father." Bridget turned and stormed back inside, pausing only to spit at Toby, "Traitor."

She hadn't added to it by the time Toby left for team building and Sonia.

Chapter 12

"Hi, I'm Mark and these are my songs." That was how Mark introduced himself as he arrived centre stage.

George wasn't quite sure what he was doing there. Tara had persuaded him because she said he really should experience Mark's music live. He, having boasted that he was up to date with music and open to new sounds, could barely refuse. But there had been opportunities to renege, so why had he not taken them?

At first, it didn't seem like it would be that bad. Recognisable songs had been playing through the PA when they'd first arrived. The floor had been filled by dancers, girls mainly, gyrating in a way that seemed more extreme than he remembered, but he certainly knew the songs. Some covers, some originals, all familiar.

"I played with them," he shouted into Tara's left ear as a song by the Small Faces exceeded a decibel level higher than his voice, which meant the remark went unnoticed. They were standing close to what passed as a stage, once a raised wooden platform at the front of the old University Reference Library. Where once would have sat the librarian as guardian of the knowledge and maintainer of order and silence, stood banks of loudspeakers and amplifiers. Lights were suspended from the arched ceiling, the university crest and grand decorative mouldings festooned with baubles and fairylights. Shelves, once filled with books, were now covered in dust or masked behind draped black curtains. George wondered where all the *Encyclopedia Britannicas* had gone – once the treasure of every library and source of all knowledge. He remembered helping Bridget on a school project on the Second World War. Reading through her essay, he'd been startled to read,

Adolf Hitler was Chancellor of Germany, charged with the responsibility of bringing prosperity back to his country.

"Where did you get this from?" he'd demanded.

"The library. From an encyclopedia," she'd defended herself. He later discovered she'd used a 1936 edition. Later editions would have revised their description somewhat, but eleven-year-old Bridget had found an old set on the shelves and been blissfully unaware. He would have told Tara about this had he been able. But the Small Faces saved her from this as well.

Mark's arrival on the platform was without fanfare or pizzazz and, without acknowledging the room, he simply ambled into position, plugging in his Mark'n'Tara drive, donning a pair of headphones, flicking switches and pressing buttons before disappearing behind a bank of keyboards and computer screens. All that was visible now were his eyes and a peaked baseball cap that, to George's mind, was round the wrong way. From the speakers came a low hum that first vibrated then developed into a high-pitched whine. None of this prepared George for what was to follow. Looped screams, accompanied by deep bass and random jangles, boomed across the room. The lights shook, one of the black drapes slipped to the floor. It was not 'music' by any definition George was familiar with. He instinctively put his hands over his ears and imagined inmates of Guantanamo Bay facing similar barrages of torturous noise. The gyrating dancers continued for a few moments until they sensed no respite from the cacophony, then succumbed to the inevitable and headed to the bar. Yet in the opposite direction, a handful of girls headed towards the stage to cluster at Mark's feet, accompanied by blokes carrying plastic pint glasses, slopping beer over the once pristine oak floor. There was now a firm divide: Mark loyalists congregated at the front, the remainder – and majority – around the sides and at the bar, attempting to talk or numbed into watching. Between them, a vast space of floor, occasionally populated by the curious or the brave, but never for long.

Mark continued, oblivious to all around him. The bar was doing a roaring trade, four or five deep, service limited only by the inability of bar staff and customers to make themselves heard. Of those at his feet, some chose to sit or kneel on the floor, all violently nodding their heads to a rhythm that was not evident in the music, oblivious to the rivers of warm lager flowing around them.

In his day, George's audiences had seats, usually in rows, though if it were a hop, they'd be set around the sides, with a glitter ball suspended over the dance floor, splaying light, glamour, romance. He'd played in theatres, cinemas, pubs and ballrooms, even in rooms over department stores where the only drinks were fizzy pop. Or later, in clubs, where the audience stood, crammed together, jostling for space, the air thick with sweat, tobacco or weed. Nothing like this.

At the bar, none of the drinkers seemed to be taking any notice of Mark. George could see some wearing earbuds, maybe on their mobiles or listening to music of their own choosing. Yet if Mark paused, which he did occasionally, there was wild whooping and frenzied clapping from everyone, even from those with earbuds.

But the pauses were few and short, seemingly more to give Mark time to reset his computer than signify the end of a song and the start of a new one. He might take a swig from a bottle of water but offered no introductions or explanations as to what he was playing. Except once he muttered 'thank you', and allowed himself a brief glimpse of Tara, who was sitting cross-legged, directly in front of a loudspeaker. There was no recognition, no smile, no joy. And on starting up again, his gaze became determinedly fixed on the keyboard, avoiding eye contact with the audience, face serious and grim. It was relentless. George could stand it no longer. He strode across the empty centre of the hall and through swing doors at the back.

He faced a stairway, cold and dim. As he made his way down, the music seemed to follow him, echoing off faded white concrete walls and metal handrails. It wasn't until he reached the ground floor, and another set of double doors had slammed shut behind him, that the sound was masked. He found himself in the entrance foyer and comparative silence, aside from residual ringing in his ears.

"Hello, old-timer. You lost?" The question was asked by a security guard who was doubling as box office. A book of raffle tickets and a red cash tin were on a table in front of him.

"Not a busy one for you, then?"

"Nights with that kind of shit never are."

"Not a fan, I assume?"

"You must be havin' a laugh. Crap. All of it."

"Is that a piano?" George nodded to under the stairs and in the direction of a sheet over an object unmistakably upright and piano-shaped.

"A heavily disguised unicorn." Security chuckled at his own joke.

"May I?"

"Be my guest."

"Fats Domino. 1957."

The security guard nodded. "Great record."

"You know it?"

"My old man brought me up on that stuff. Real music. Not the crap up there." His finger gestured towards Mark's noise that was still finding a way to seep relentlessly from the main hall.

George was already at the piano, sheet ripped off and dumped on the floor, keyboard lid open. With a brief bend of the knuckles, he launched into 'Be My Guest'. His fingers felt stiff, the piano was out of tune, middle C didn't play and when he launched into the vocals, he began with a cough. It made no difference. It was music. And not just to his ears.

"Encore!" Security was standing at his side and applauding.

George struck up the opening of 'Twist and Shout'. George took lead vocal, Security repeated each line, full pelt. But when George launched into a second verse, there was no answering refrain. A group of students had eased through glass doors into the foyer and, while Security was tearing off a strip of tickets from his book, they dropped a handful of coins into his tin.

George, having lost his backing, persevered solo.

Instead of heading up the stairs, the new arrivals hung around the foyer, watching in amusement. To George, it felt like the old days.

"Join in," he called. "Go 'Aaahhhh' after me."

It never ceased to surprise George how young people still knew the songs of more than fifty years back. As one, the students, whose combined age probably didn't reach his, joined in with an ascending scale of "Aaahhhh, Aaahhhh, Aaahhhh, Aaahhhh."

He thumped the final few notes, hearing it in his head as if augmented by guitars and drums. By now, his audience, swelled by a further seven or eight, had clustered round the piano, cheering, clapping, baying for more.

"Sorry, folks." They were interrupted by Security. "We'll have to leave it at that. Health and Safety. This is a fire exit and we mustn't block it."

"One more," George begged and ran his fingers up the keyboard.

"Yes, more," echoed the impromptu audience.

"Sorry, but regulations is regulations. If someone came in now and saw this, I'd be out of a job. So if you young people would make your way up to the hall…" He gestured at George. "Sorry an' that. Don't worry about the piano cover. I can put it back."

George played a few final notes that decayed enough for him to catch what sounded like, "He was good," and, "That's one way to beat Alzheimer's," before reluctantly lowering the piano's lid.

"So there you are." Tara swung into the foyer through the double doors.

"He with you?" Security seemed relieved to see her. "Thought he'd wandered in from the old folks' home across the road."

"He is. Come on, Gramps. What were you doing down here?"

"Tell you what, he's a real live wire. He should be playing up there, not the shit making that racket."

George was grateful Tara didn't react. He didn't want to be competing with her boyfriend.

"Let's go. Gramps?"

George nodded. It would have been a dream to have kept playing, better still to swap places with Mark upstairs on stage. Another time, maybe. It was enough to have made a friend of Security and proof that his was real music. His longing to be heard, to be noticed and acknowledged may have been dimmed and suffocated over the years, but at least this showed he still had it and people seemed to like it. He just had to convince everyone else.

Chapter 13

"You ready?"

"What's it look like?" George was standing in the doorway, coat on, plastic bag in one hand, door keys in the other.

"Shoes?" Robin was looking at the slippers on George's feet.

"Oh. Sorry. I'll go and put some on." George hadn't been this excited since he couldn't remember when. "Hold these." He handed Robin the bag and keys. "Just keen to get going. Silly me."

"What are these for?" Robin called after him, holding a cassette he'd pulled from the bag.

George looked up from lacing up his best brown brogues. "Why not? Just in case."

"No one uses cassettes anymore. What's on them?"

"Ideas. Rough recordings. Old stuff and some new."

"You won't be needing them." Robin kept hold of the bag anyway, ushering George out and pulling the front door shut, slipping the keys into his pocket.

"Right. Let's go." George hoped he sounded confident. He didn't feel it. Robin had made a phone call the day before, demanding, 'Studio. Yes or no? I need an answer.' Since Robin first suggested it, he hadn't been able to get it out of his mind. Should he change his name when his CD was released? George sounded old-fashioned. Single names were in vogue, he'd noticed. Maybe just Turnbull. Or simply GT. His stomach turned with anticipation at the thought of being Record of the Week on Radio 2; of his face on the front of the local paper – maybe even the *Daily Mail*; of his name at last in the *Guinness Book of Hit Singles*. His stomach had turned again at the thought that he was relying on Robin. Was he being what Evelyn used to call a 'silly old fool'? If only she could be there to advise him. Instead, he'd sat in his room and listened to The Who's 'Won't Get Fooled Again' three times, at ear-splitting volume, joining in with the chorus each time, before deciding. Even if he was being fooled, what was there left to lose? So he agreed, then spent the next twenty-four hours working on what he would record. But the more he'd practised, the less confident he'd become.

He stood now by the front gate, wishing it was all over. "Which is your car?"

"This one." Lights flashed on a BMW convertible and the doors clicked unlocked.

George eyed the car and looked back at Robin. "I thought you said you were skint?"

"It's not what you know. Speaking of which, you haven't forgotten?"

"Of course not." George fumbled out an envelope from inside his coat. "You won't tell Bridget, will you?"

"Tell Bridget? Why would I? Our secret. Anyway, haven't seen her in years."

George watched as Robin fingered through £5 and £10 notes inside the envelope, then tucked the envelope into his coat pocket.

"Right, get in and let's get going."

Music boomed inside the car while Robin drove and George sat silent and tense. There'd been no mention of money until he'd agreed to go, and when Robin demanded £850 in advance, he thought of calling it all off. But a studio. After all these years, he was getting somewhere at last. It seemed a lot of money but no one else needed to know. And it was only Evelyn's New York holiday savings that she'd kept in a vase in the bedroom, so it was going to waste anyway. It wasn't as if it was going to Robin, George justified to himself. There would be upfront costs for recording and mixing, then producing CDs, designing cover artwork. He hoped they might even be able to make a vinyl record. And all before any publicity and distribution. With the contacts Robin had promised, there was always the hope of it being more than a one-off session – a starting point, leading to a proper recording deal. What if Robin *was* skimming off the top? It'd be worth it. Bridget wouldn't have approved of any of it, of course. But she'd understand when he was famous.

* * *

The studio was a disappointment. George expected a cavernous space in an old church or a converted stable, or at least the upper floor of a block in Soho. This was a dingy basement in East Ham. Entrance was through a door at the back of a hardware shop, stacked high with plastic bins, light bulbs and mops. It didn't feel very rock'n'roll. George wondered if he was being taken hostage. He didn't reckon much to his chances of Toby paying any ransom.

Greeting them was a short, stocky man, Robin's age and who, in George's eyes, would have looked more at home on a used car forecourt. Toby did the introductions. "George, this is Ron. Ron, George." They shook hands, Ron thrusting out his hand, skin rough, fingers stubby, almost crushing George's. Was this the owner, George thought, hoping that a younger, techy-looking sound engineer would soon emerge. Not that there was anywhere to emerge from. The studio complex appeared to be the room they were standing in. It smelt of damp. The only sign of recording equipment was a microphone stand on a table next to a laptop. Metal crates and coils of tangled cable lined the bubbled plaster walls, broken only by a draining board with kettle, a box of teabags and bag of white sugar beside a sink stacked precariously with mugs and plates. There was barely room for the three of them, which Robin seemed to acknowledge. "You don't need me getting in the way, so I'll leave you two to it."

"My cassettes?" George called after him.

"You won't be needing them," Robin answered without stopping. "I'll be back in about an hour or so."

To George, an hour didn't seem much. Rumour had it that The Beatles took 700 to record *Sgt. Pepper*. Although his ambitions were set somewhat lower, he still wanted to create his own masterpiece.

"Pleased to meet you, George, after all this time." Ron was at the sink, filling a kettle. "Robin's told me all about you. Tea or coffee?"

Water would have done, but from the state of the sink George opted for a drink that had been boiled. "Tea, please."

"Black OK? There's no milk."

George nodded, adding, "So where is everything?"

"I'll show you. Here, take this." He handed George a chipped mug with a faded photograph and bearing the slogan 'West Ham, Cup Winners 1980'.

"Looks like it's seen some action." George raised the mug before sipping the tea. He'd not asked for sugar but it tasted as if it had been laced with at least two tablespoonfuls from its previous user.

"You a supporter? I can get you tickets for home games if you're interested. Let me know how many you want. And if it's football memorabilia you're after," Ron opened a door that George hoped might have been the studio, "take a look at this lot." Ron pulled down a lever. Neon lights flickered on, revealing the back of what looked like a warehouse, stacked with boxes and crates. "Those over there," he gestured vaguely to a corner, "are football. Mugs, pictures, scarves. All the Premier League clubs."

"Incredible." George hoped he sounded interested.

"And the rest is general stock. Kitchen stuff, electrics, furniture, antiques, you name it. If you want it, it's probably in here somewhere. If I've not got it, you don't need it." He laughed at his own joke.

"A veritable Aladdin's cave." George tried not to reveal he'd rather Ron saved his enthusiasm for sound recording.

"This isn't the half of it. The rest is in my lock-up. Where we spend most of our time."

"We?" George still harboured hope an engineer would appear.

"I couldn't do it all on my own. We do auctions, house clearances, car boots, street markets. It's lucky I'm around today. Here." Ron handed George a business card. 'Ron Toogood and Friends, Antiques and Replica's of distinction', it read.

George decided against commenting on the unnecessary apostrophe but couldn't let pass the lack of reference to a studio. "Do you do much sound recording?" He was still hoping this would not be a wasted journey. Even before he thought of the £850.

"Now and again. Not much call for it, really." Ron seemed oblivious to what this was doing to George.

"But you *do* have a studio."

"Of course. You're standing in it." Ron wafted a hand in the direction of the sink.

"What sound mixer do you have?"

"Mixer?" Ron laughed. "It's here." He tapped the laptop.

"A computer?"

"It's all we need these days."

"And a recorder? CD duplication?"

"CDs? No one does CDs anymore. It's all downloads."

"What about vinyl? I'm told it's back in vogue."

"We do a few. Coloured and rainbow splattered. Look great. Sound shit."

"Will mine be on vinyl?"

Ron shook his head. "Nah. We just use it for oldies. Collectables. Bootlegs – though don't tell anyone."

George tried to hide his disappointment. "So where do I play?"

"Over there." Ron pointed at one of the metal crates. "I'll set it up when you've finished your tea."

"I thought Robin said there was a *real* piano."

"You wait 'til you hear it. It may be a synthesiser but you won't know the difference."

"I will. It never *feels* the same as a real piano."

"You'll soon get the hang of it. Finish your drink and we can get cracking. Don't want to waste any more time."

Chapter 14

"I hate driving in London." Bridget announced this to Tara after a cyclist had prodded a one-finger salute at her.

"You were a bit close."

"Well anyway, as I was saying, I sent him off with a flea in his ear and that's been the last we've seen of him."

She had been talking about Uncle Robin ever since collecting Tara from uni. Her visit had come out of the blue. 'Just a quick visit,' she'd said on the phone, to help go through wardrobes and cupboards, and sort through Evelyn's things. Except Tara hadn't heard George agreeing to it yet. He'd been absorbed with his piano, endlessly churning out tunes she'd never heard before. At times, he'd been agitated, slamming down the piano lid and storming out the room, before going back to start again a while later. But she made no mention of this to her mum, nor that each time he came back from walking Hunter, he'd started asking if Uncle Robin or someone called Ron had called. She might have, but her mum already seemed very tense and was acting strangely. There must be something and she didn't want to worry her with her grandfather's behaviour. It wasn't until they'd pulled up outside George's house that her mum revealed what.

"I think your father's up to something."

"Up to something?"

Bridget hesitated, then sighed. "Having an affair."

"Oh."

"Is that all you can say? I tell you your father's having an affair, and all you can say is 'Oh'?"

"What am I supposed to say? Who with?"

"Something. Anything. Not, 'Oh.'" She switched the engine off and grabbed the keys out of the ignition.

"How long's it been going on?"

"Did you know about it?" She made it sound like an accusation more than a question.

"Of course not. I haven't spoken to him."

"That's alright, then."

"How do you know?"

"Things. The way he talks, acting funny, arguing."

"You're always arguing."

"Not like this. I know there's something. He's late home from work more than ever and was away all last weekend. I just can't stop thinking about it. I need something to take my mind off it."

That explained the unexpected visit.

"Are you two going to sit in there all afternoon or are you coming inside?" George was standing on the pavement in his slippers, halfway between garden gate and car, and the house door was open, Hunter enthusiastically wagging his tail on the doorstep. "I've made some tea."

"We'd better go in," Bridget said.

"Does he know?" Tara nodded towards George. "About Dad?"

"God, no. And don't tell him. Just let him think I've come to do the wardrobes."

George was relieved when Bridget said her unexpected visit was to clear wardrobes, especially as he'd been dreading sorting through them. He'd already come across a cupboard full of candles, mementos of family occasions; permanent reminders, like diary entries.

There were other hidden treasures, too, scattered in odd places around the house. He discovered she'd been secreting away china cups and saucers. And thimbles. He'd seen her browsing them on bric-a-brac stalls and in antique shops, and even seen her buy the occasional one, but he'd had no idea how many there were, all hidden at the back of cupboards and behind books on shelves. While he'd openly top up his record and CD habit – though he hadn't always confessed how much he'd paid each time – she had kept these collections hidden. This was a side of his wife he hadn't known about, even after all those years together. Finding out now, not able to ask her why, was so painful. Contemplating what else might be lurking inside her wardrobes was off the scale. So it was still something of a relief to find that Bridget's unexpected arrival was nothing to do with Robin and would take away the responsibility of going through the house and making more unwelcome discoveries.

Bridget and Tara started almost straight away. And while they were at work in his bedroom, he shut himself into the music room. Halfway through Chuck Berry's 'Roll Over Beethoven' he realised he was remembering jiving to it with Evelyn and imagining her in one of the dresses that Tara might now be looking at, maybe even trying on or screwing up into a bin bag. He took the record off and sat looking at its label before slowly dropping it into its sleeve.

There was a knock at the door and it swung open.

"Am I disturbing you?" It was Mark.

"Not really." In fact George was relieved by the distraction.

"Who was that song by?"

"Chuck Berry. Why?"

"I'm working on my music on Tara's computer and thought I might sample that riff." He was looking round the room. A single shaft of daylight, peeping between rows of LPs, spotlit racks of records opposite and unsorted piles on the floor. Before George had a chance to run through the rules of copyright, Mark followed up with a question. "Can I ask you how many records you've got?"

"You can ask. I can't tell you. I don't know. I don't count them. I play them."

"How do you know what you've got? Have you got more than one of any?"

"I expect so. I sometimes do forget. I didn't used to but nowadays…"

"They must be worth a bit."

George sighed. It was what everyone said. "So they say, whoever 'they' are."

"What's the most valuable one you've got?"

"They're all valuable to me. I bought them to enjoy and listen to." He was always irritated by people wanting to put a monetary value on them, even though he was proud that his collection was coveted. Some sort of justification for what Evelyn had variously dismissed as his addiction and profligacy. "Most are just a few pounds, if that. Some might be £50, £100 maybe. Who knows?" Then he added defiantly, "But there's no way I'm parting with any of them, so to me they're not worth anything, money-wise. Beyond value, really."

"Anything you haven't got? That you wished you had?"

"Oh, loads. I could live forever and not find some of the really rare stuff. And there's probably millions I haven't even heard. It's never ending."

"You can buy rare stuff online. And find out how much yours are worth. There are web pages devoted to old records. Have you ever tried?"

"What's all this trying to get me on a computer? First Tara, now you."

"Thought you'd be interested, that's all. Sorry."

"I'm too old to start learning to use a computer. It's for you young people. Anyway, I like browsing in shops. It's the hunt, the chase, the excitement of finding something new, taking it home and playing it. Holding it. Reading the sleeve. Though these days, thanks to your blessed computers, the hunt now is finding a shop that's still open."

"That's what I mean. Honestly, Mr T, let me show you how online works."

George might have launched into another rant but he was interrupted by excited squeals from Tara in his bedroom next door. Followed by laughter and more shrieks. What of Evelyn's was being discovered in the wardrobe? Anything that distracted him from more of this would be welcome relief. And it might prove to be an opportunity to talk to Mark, to give him some help with his music. So he nodded nonchalant agreement and followed him up to Tara's room. It was the first time George had set foot in it since that first night after Tara had moved in. She'd made it her own, with little bottles of perfume and make-up on the fireplace and on tables. But it was remarkably tidy, unlike the mess her mother used to create when she was a teenager.

The computer was already humming on the dressing table, surrounded by electronic gadgets and a piano keyboard that Mark had been working with. George sat in front of it and ran his fingers across it, but there was no sound, just soundwaves and bars across the computer screen.

Mark pointed at the computer screen. "This is my studio."

To George it looked like a more sophisticated version of what Ron had been using. He was still waiting anxiously to hear back about the session. They'd run out of time before he'd done more than a few practice runs but Ron had said he'd send over a copy of the best takes. That was before a power failure. A fuse in the warehouse, apparently. They'd had to make their way up from the basement in pitch black and, when they reached the light, Ron had said he'd try and cobble together what they'd done and let Robin know when it was ready. There had been talk of a second session – well, George had suggested one – but nothing had been arranged. Since then, there had been no news. But Mark was still explaining.

"So what I do here is integrate sounds, make textures." He tapped the keyboard and the computer screen came to life.

"Why can't I hear anything?"

Mark lifted up a pair of headphones. "I use these. I can hear much more detail and I hate people listening in while I do it. You know what I mean?"

George didn't. He remembered playing his piano in the folk clubs, jamming, joining in with everyone else. That's how they shared ideas, learnt, got better. So many great nights. And so much better than sitting at a screen on your own. No wonder music was dying.

"Can I offer you a suggestion?"

Mark shrugged as if knowing it would be offered whether he wanted it or not.

"You know your concert the other night."

"Concert? Oh, the uni gig. Did you enjoy it? Tara said you both had to leave early as she had a headache."

"You saw how everyone was dancing? At the start." George decided against adding, 'before you came on'.

"Yeah, they always do that to the deejay."

"They all seemed like a nice bunch of people. Having a great time." In his mind was the group around the piano, singing 'Twist and Shout' with him. "Have you thought about maybe doing some old stuff? That people know?"

Mark was staring blankly, uncomprehending. George feared the only way was to be blunt. "If you want to fill the floor, people taking notice of you and not talking at the bar, you need to get everyone on your side. And the best way to do that is play stuff they know. Once they're hooked, then you slip in new ones. But people always like what they know. You must have been at concerts when it's all going well and then they say, 'Now we're going to play songs from our new album.' Nothing's more certain to kill the atmosphere. Give the audience what they want. And what they want is something they're familiar with."

"I think my audience knows my stuff. It's what they come to hear."

"But you'd get more of them. If people know the songs already, don't you think those people at the bar might stop and listen? Catch their ears, get them on your side before you slide in your own material. Win them over first. Then you can convert them."

Mark started to say something, but held back. George imagined a dig at his own lack of success, or being questioned on his credibility to criticise and give advice. That's why he needed to get those recordings with Ron into the world. Until then, he'd have to continue with a history lesson. "Look at The Beatles. Wonderful songwriters. But how did they start? Covers. Other people's songs their audiences knew. And the Rolling Stones. Covers too, even though Mick Jagger and Keith Richards knew how to turn out a tune." He was on the verge of quoting hits for Cliff Richard and Gene Pitney, singers of the old school, who had hits with Rolling Stones' songs while the Stones themselves were recording covers. But Mark could hold back no longer.

"Sorry to disagree, Mr T. That's the old days. What I want to do is experiment. Be different. And write what people *think* they know, make them want to listen to *me*."

"Yes, but…"

"Not be a tribute band. Regurgitating and copying is not what I'm about. It'll be *my* music. The occasional sample maybe, but I want to perform my own sounds. Not someone else's." He turned back to the computer. "Anyway, I was going to show you online music."

"Have you *tried* some of the old tunes? You can always use my piano downstairs."

"Tell the truth, I don't use a piano keyboard much. It's all programmed in the computer."

"That's not music."

"Don't want to sound rude and all that, Mr T, but it is to my generation."

George remembered saying much the same to Evelyn's parents. And Bridget saying the same thing about punk. Argument was futile. Mark would just have to learn the hard way.

"See here." Mark leaned across to the computer mouse. With a couple of clicks, he changed the screen from a soundmixing desk to a blank page with a giant banner. George had heard the word 'Google'. "So let's search for a song. What was it you were playing in your room just now?"

"Chuck Berry. 'Roll Over Beethoven.'"

Mark began typing the title, then tapped a key a couple of times until a list appeared. George leaned forward to read it.

"Shall I make the text bigger for you?"

"I can see well enough. I may be old but I'm not blind." But the text was small and he was pleased when Mark doubled its size anyway. There was every artist George knew had recorded the song, and a few others he'd never heard of.

"Impressive, I'll give you that."

"It'll do artists, albums…"

"OK then, try it on Ivory Joe Hunter. That'll stop it in its tracks."

Seconds and a few clicks later, there was a complete list of Ivory Joe's recordings. George was a bit taken aback.

"Can you buy all of these?"

"Some, not all."

Another click or two, and there was a list of records for sale. George saw £300 against one he had two copies of. He also saw one he didn't have and had long wished he did. Mark now typed 'most valuable vinyl records'. Up came a list.

"Got any of those?"

"The Beatles, yes, all of them. Several of some of them. Sex Pistols, yes, EMI and Virgin. Frank Wilson, yes. What else?" George leant in closer. "Leafhound? How's that LP in there? No one liked them when I bought it, what, fifty years ago."

"They do now. It's sold for £8,000." Mark tapped a few more keys. "Wow, There's a Beatles' LP here sold for £750,000. The Sex Pistols for £12,000. And I've never heard of Frank Wilson and that's sold for £25,000. And you've got them all?" Mark's voice was a mix of excitement and disbelief.

"I guess so. Shall I play you Frank Wilson? Good if you like Northern soul." He doubted Mark had ever heard of Northern soul.

"I think you should get your records insured."

George shook his head. "No one knows about them."

"What if the house burns down? Tara tells me you like candles."

"Does she now? I like lots of things. What else can your interweb do?"

Mark sighed. "Well, if you type in 'live' there's loads of old film and video. TV clips, programmes you might remember and want to watch again." He saw George shaking his head again. "You interested in live gigs? Festivals? Or if you don't want them, there's even people's personal videos. Bands and singers no one's ever heard of. There's even some of me, live, that people recorded on their iPhones."

"Tea, anyone?" Bridget was calling from downstairs. They must have taken a break from the wardrobes.

"We'd better go." George stood up, then hesitated. "Just look up one last one for me, will you? Phaedra."

"How do you spell it? Is it a song?"

"P-h-a-e-d-r-a. It's a band – 1960s – we called it a group then."

"Have I ever heard anything by them?"

"I doubt it. We weren't very successful."

"We? Was that you?"

"It was. Ages back. I'd been the Beat Boys but we broke up. Then I helped form a new group. Beat with a bit of psychedelic. Phaedra and the Phaeries we were called. Phaedra was the singer – I was back-up vocals, piano and bass guitar. Mostly piano."

"And you had records out?"

"Just one. A single."

Before the page loaded, Bridget called again, this time more urgently. "It's getting cold."

"Don't worry, Mr T, you can always look things up for yourself. You see how easy it is. Just keep tapping the mouse or 'Return' – the one with the squiggly arrow. Or back space – this other arrow – if you get stuck." He gestured at the keys, though George was focused on the screen, hoping to see Phaedra pop up. "Don't worry. I'll write you a list of instructions and tell Tara to leave the computer on for you. You should have a go. Surprise yourself."

"I doubt I will." George was still staring at the blank screen but his mind had wandered to what he was going to see when he got downstairs. He was dreading finding black bin bags of memories in the hall.

* * *

They made it to the kitchen without finding any signs of a clearout.

Bridget eyed them suspiciously. "We thought you'd got lost."

George looked round but nothing seemed to have changed. "Well done, you two," he said. "And don't tell me *what* you've done. I'd rather not know. Here." He opened up a cupboard door, revealing a row of chocolate biscuits. "Have these on me."

"Oh, thanks, Gramps." Tara seized on them.

George looked down on Hunter, sitting in perfect begging pose. "Careful, no crumbs."

"I know." Tara's response was world-weary, as if tiring of being lectured.

"Just reminding you." He ruffled Hunter's head affectionately.

"So what have you two been doing?" Bridget asked.

"I've been showing your dad the internet," Mark proudly announced.

Bridget almost choked on her Earl Grey.

"We've been looking at records for sale," he continued.

"Not before time. Well done, Mark, for persuading him. I'm always telling him he's got too many." Bridget sounded positively buoyant.

Mark grimaced as George stiffened. "Not exactly. We looked at what his are selling for and I showed him how he can buy ones he's missing."

"Good Lord! He doesn't need any more." Bridget frowned at her dad.

"But you'll never guess what some are worth." Mark seemed to think this was helping.

"Oxfam will be grateful. Not the rest of us when we have to clear out the space."

"Mum!" Tara sounded shocked.

"I'm not selling anything." George was irritated that his daughter was talking like he wasn't there, let alone thought he might ever contemplate selling his records. Did she really know so little about him? Or had Toby been on to her? Yet secretly, he had been impressed by this interwebthing. He made up his mind to explore it, but he'd have to do it secretly so no one would know. He'd wait until everyone was gone and the house was empty.

Chapter 15

George got his chance to explore the internet sooner than expected. Bridget drove off home while Tara and Mark fancied a curry. He screwed up his face when they asked if he wanted to join them. It was a gap in his food education that stemmed from his mum only ever cooking 'Beef in Rice' from packet ready meals, followed by Angel Delight. He took a dislike to both and had steadfastly refused to try either since.

Once he had the house to himself, he settled down to listening to records. He started with 'Twist and Shout' from the first Beatles album – it was still in his head from the other night, linking naturally to playing Rolling Stones covers and the Cliff Richard and Gene Pitney songs he'd not mentioned. One seemed to lead to another, segued by musical links or memories, dragging out LPs and singles that hadn't felt a stylus for months, maybe years. But the pleasure ground to a halt when he couldn't find one – an LP by the Yardbirds with Sonny Boy Williamson. There was nothing more certain to destroy the magic of the moment than an absentee record. It didn't matter that he had it on a CD. He wanted to play the vinyl. And even though there were thousands of other records he could play instead, until the missing one was found, it felt disloyal to listen to anything else. Evelyn used to call it obsessive. But it made no difference. It had to be found.

After fifteen minutes of searching, he began to waver. He'd created small piles of albums as he sorted through and many of those had now enticed him into being played. But a thought crossed his mind. It was one he didn't welcome, initially dismissed, but it wouldn't shake off. He'd talked about the Yardbirds to Tara. Mark had said how valuable his records were. He needed to check Tara's room. Just to be sure.

* * *

The last time he'd intruded without permission into someone's private space was when he was a teenager. He'd never been allowed into his parents' bedroom and never dared until he reached a certain age when such taboos had to be explored. One afternoon, he'd stolen in, browsed around and wondered why his parents were so secretive. Their room was unremarkable and rather dull – painted green, with thick curtains, eiderdown, wicker chairs and chest of drawers, also green.

But his eyes became drawn to the bedside table where there stood a postcard-sized print in a passe-partout frame. Of a woman on a bed, wearing no clothes, staring into a mirror. It was only her back, but it was a naked, lady's back. He knew it now to be from a painting. The Rokeby Venus by Velázquez. He'd since seen it in the National Gallery. But at that moment, it was as exciting as it was shocking to find it beside his father's bed.

And there was more. Behind it stood a table lamp. In the form of a woman. Her long hair was draped behind the nape of her neck, arms stretched out behind her head. The stand of the lamp protruded from between her bare buttocks. The effect was to thrust her breasts forward. And they were uncovered. On full display. He gasped, his eyes gorging on the revelation. He'd never been this close to images of naked women, only ever glimpsing them in art galleries before being rushed on to a landscape or still life. His childhood cultural diet had consisted of Gainsborough and Constable, yet all the while, these forbidden images had been here, hidden from his gaze. He gulped, not daring to touch them in case it should trigger an alarm.

After what might have been minutes, a pile of books caught his eye, protruding from under the bed. He bent down to inspect what his father had been reading: five copies of *Reader's Digest* and two overdue library books. But there was a greater discovery to be made. Concealed within one *Reader's Digest* was a very different magazine, smaller and thinner and printed in black and white. Yet it had a tantalising title. *Two Eves.* Curious, George opened it.

Inside the front cover was what looked like a primitive set of spectacles, made of card. Coloured plastic was inserted where the glass should be, red on one side, blue on the other. There were instructions on the back cover. He was to put the spectacles on, hold the 'illustrations' (as the pictures were called) under 'the maximum possible light', and wait a few seconds, after which 'stereoscopic images would appear and be seen to best effect'. And the stereoscopic images were not paintings or statues. Real photographs. Of two women, both evidently called Eve.

And neither wearing anything.

Just moments after the revelation of nudity in a picture frame and table lamp, here it was in virtual reality. He'd not seen a real naked woman before (if you didn't count accidentally walking in on his mum in the bath). Now he was about to view two of them, not only completely nude but also in 3D.

He didn't hesitate. Pressing the card glasses to his nose, he fumbled on the table lamp to get maximum possible effect. But barely had his eyes adjusted to the stereoscopic image when he heard the scuffling of a key in a lock, the front door opening and his mum's voice echoing round the hall and up the stairs.

"Hello, love. I'm home. Where are you?"

"I'm upstairs, doing my homework."

Sliding the magazines back under the bed, he made a dash for the door.

"I've got something to show you," she called back and he heard the creaking of the bottom stair. There was a total of fourteen steps, before two turns that would give her full view of the landing and bedroom doors. He knew he had seconds to make it out of the room or be discovered. Moving at the speed of light, escape was almost complete when he saw that not only had he left the table lamp on, but also the 3D glasses had slipped out of *Two Eves* and were lying in full view on the floor. He raced back in. Switching off the light left no time to replace the glasses, so he snatched them up and headed back to the door. He was just angling himself to hide the glasses and appear like he was coming from his own room as she rounded the final corner.

From later experience as a parent, he was now sure his mum would have detected something amiss. At the time, she appeared not to. She was clutching a set of photographs she'd just collected from the chemist's – this was a time when a roll of film might stay in the camera for a year or more, so when they were eventually processed they were like ancient history. Quite what made them so interesting he couldn't remember now. What he would never forget was the lingering dread of discovery that he knew wouldn't go away until he was able to return the glasses.

He lived with that nightmare for two days before he felt the coast was clear and that it was safe enough to retrace his steps.

Even though everyone was out, he tiptoed back into his parents' private space and eased out the pile of magazines from beneath the bed. It was the same as before, the *Reader's Digests* and library books. But there was a difference. *Two Eves* had gone.

He kept the glasses, hidden under his mattress, in a perpetual state of guilt and trepidation. For a few days, he didn't feel able to make eye contact with his father, and he had a feeling his father was avoiding his gaze in return. But nothing was said and he never set foot in their room again, nor anywhere else that was out of bounds. He did tell a friend about it a few months later though and went to find the 3D glasses to prove it, but when he lifted his mattress they had gone.

It was why, looking inside Tara's bedroom, as he was now doing nearly seventy years on, made him feel distinctly uncomfortable. There were wardrobes, drawers and unopened removal boxes; a desk with books and neatly stapled papers; her mobile phone lying on a mouse mat, charging up; and her computer, its screen displaying colours like the oil on a psychedelic projector. He cursed his own suspicions and determined to make this quick and leave no trace. Holding his breath, he started on the drawers beneath the computer, sliding them open to inspect their contents, hoping against hope not to find any records. But as he did, the swirling patterns on the computer were replaced by a close-up picture of Tara, wide-eyed, poking her tongue out and looking accusingly at him. What had he done? Had he left an indelible stain that would give away that he had been in here?

"Can I help?"

George would have gushed guilt if he hadn't been so shocked at how Tara was standing right by him and he hadn't heard her come in.

"Don't do that – you nearly gave me a heart attack."

He was grateful Tara let pass the fact he was complaining when he was the intruder.

"Sorry. Did you like my screen-saver?" She pointed at her picture before leaning over and rattling her fingers across the keyboard.

"How many fingers have you got?"

Tara laughed as the screen came to life. "So what were you looking for?"

He couldn't tell her about his suspicions over the missing record. And she seemed not to have noticed one of the drawers of her table had not been completely closed. So he concocted a lie.

"I was just looking to see if I'm on your computer." It wasn't entirely untrue as, ever since his introduction to the 'interweb', he had wanted to know if he had left any mark on history. Then he added, "But I shouldn't have come into your room when you weren't here."

"No, Gramps, we said you could use it any time."

"Trouble is, I can't."

"Let me help. What were you looking for? You type it in here." She pointed at a box in the centre.

"Yardbirds."

"The people you played with."

"Not with. They were top of the bill, we were at the bottom. Small print."

She had already typed in Yardbirds, and the page filled with rows of text. "Then click on any of these and you'll get what you want. Easy."

"Not so sure about that."

"See?" She clicked on one of the list and pointed at what appeared. "One sold for £40 only last week."

George pulled a face that so used to annoy Evelyn, like the people on *Antiques Roadshow* who feigned surprise at a valuation while secretly disappointed it wasn't higher.

"Now you try." Tara slid sideways to leave George space to type. "Go on. Have a go."

George tentatively typed in a few names, starting with the obvious, none of which was selling for much.

"You've got it. Can I leave you to it? Mark'll be wondering where I am. I only came back for this." She unplugged her phone, waving it at George.

"Hang on, look at this." George had typed in an album title he knew he had three copies of. He'd picked them up for almost nothing when doing a gig in Sheffield. Still shrink-wrapped. And here was the same one, for sale at £6,000.

Tara leaned across to look at the screen. "Wow."

"And I've got three."

"Why did you buy three?"

"They didn't cost anything like that much."

"But three?" Tara sounded like she was tempted to side with her mum about having too many.

"I liked the album."

"Hmm. Well, you'd better think about getting them insured. Maybe make a list of the valuable ones. Or put a sticker on their sleeves."

George couldn't tell her he hated the idea of compiling a list of his records. It made it seem like a hobby, and that's what teenagers have, not people of his age. And stickers were worse – a desecration.

"Anyway," Tara slipped her mobile into her jacket pocket, "keep going for as long as you like. You can't damage anything. If you get stuck, Mark and me'll be back soon. I didn't say, change of plan. We're just going for a drink and a takeaway."

With that, she was gone. How did young people move so fast – at least, when they wanted to? He waited until he heard the front door slam, then typed in what he was dying to find out about – 'Little Lisa', the title of Phaedra and the Phaeries' one and only single. Within seconds, up it came. A solitary copy for sale at £25. If Tara had still been there he would have joked it was probably the only one anyone had bought. But how much would that make the two boxes of unsold copies hidden behind the shelves in his record room? He wouldn't have told her of the disappointment of it not being a hit, of a third box of unsold copies he'd dropped into a council tip, having spent an afternoon skimming copies across the lake on Hampstead Heath. Nor would he have told her that the disappointment had never left him.

He vaguely remembered the night they'd first performed the song at the Bag O'Nails pub in London. There were maybe a hundred people there and they went wild for it. If only they had all bought it. He used to rely on Evelyn to explain why they couldn't. Picturing them now, dancing and singing and baying for more, he recalled someone with an 8mm film camera. What was it Mark had said? That people often put old films on the internet? It would have been poor quality and surely long since consigned to landfill. But it was worth looking, long shot or not. He typed in 'Phaedra' and 'Bag O'Nails'. 'Do you mean "Bad Tonsils"?' the computer asked. He checked his spelling and gave it another go. Plenty of references to the venue but nothing about Phaedra and the Phaeries. Undeterred, he tried a few more combinations. Still nothing showed.

"One more," he said out loud, this time trying, 'Phaedra' and 'live'.

Unlikely as it seemed, a new list appeared: 'Live Phaedra: live shows'. He gasped. The interweb really did have everything, just as Mark and Tara had been telling him. Without hesitating, hands shaking in excitement, he clicked the mouse. He wasn't sure why the computer asked if he was over eighteen, which seemed curiously unnecessary, but he tapped on 'yes' anyway and waited. The screen went blank before bursting into psychedelic colours displaying a bold banner, 'LIVE PHAEDRA', followed by rows of tiny boxes with what appeared to be faces in them, all too small to be seen clearly. Were these people who knew the Bag O'Nails? Or were they people like him, looking at this page. Was his face amongst them? He tapped the keyboard and the screen went blank again. It took longer than previously for anything to reappear. When it did, it was still the 'LIVE PHAEDRA' banner across the top, but with an added headline below: 'Welcome to Romantiques room'. Nothing else. George's finger was poised over the 'back' arrow when the screen came to life. In it appeared a video image, not grainy black and white film of a pub stage and five hairy men playing an R&B anthem to Lisa. It was a clear picture in full colour. Of a girl. The first, most striking thing about her was her size. The second was that she was completely naked.

He stared, transfixed, the revelation almost as stark and certainly as unexpected as the one in his parents' bedroom. He'd never really cared much for big breasts. But looking at those in front of him, that this woman was fondling and caressing, he could see an attraction. As she lifted one to her lips and began, incredibly, to kiss her own nipple, he wondered when he'd last seen so much female flesh. Or indeed ever, since Evelyn had always preferred to keep the lights off, at least after Bridget was born. Romantique – he assumed that was her name – wore no make-up, and her long, blonde hair was tied back and draped over one shoulder. Evelyn used to do this when she said it was in need of a wash. In fact, the figure now wiggling her finger in a 'come closer' gesture couldn't have looked less sexy if she'd been on a checkout at Lidl. Yet here she was, uninvited and in front of him. At least his dad had kept his pictures stashed, hidden in his bedroom. As he watched, Romantique leant forward. "Hello, Major." She was talking. Was it to him? And if he could hear and see her, could she see and hear him? Was she spying on him the way he had listened in to conversations on the phone party line?

He checked behind him that Tara hadn't secretly crept back into the room, and when he turned again to the screen the girl was gone, bold text replacing her, declaring 'Model now in private show'.

He watched as the screen filled again with tiny images of other people. 'Keep tapping,' Mark's voice echoed in his head, though he wasn't sure which arrow to tap as there were so many on the keyboard. A new video image appeared. The words 'Lovelyanas Room' appeared, followed by a screen with a different girl, her white skin tanned, long blonde hair framing her face and draped round breasts that were covered by a black and white speckled bra. She was smiling, her mouth outlined by dark red lipstick. On one shoulder, a tattoo – of a face maybe. To the side of her was a rectangle into which white text kept appearing, looking much like the screen of Tara's mobile when George had watched her texting. At the top it read, '196 Guests in Lovelyanas Room' and appearing below were what George assumed to be messages to Lovelyana. KingL – George guessed it was a pseudonym – wrote 'Your gorgeus', to which he nodded agreement even if he didn't approve of the spelling. When Nigel69 wrote, 'There are 21 letters in the alphabet. Oh, I forgot U R A Q T', it even made him smile. If all the messages were this amusing, he might stay watching. Then W@nk@r began typing, 'I wanna bury my head in your…'

"I don't need this," George said out loud and, rather than waiting to find out where W@nk@r had in mind, he stabbed a key, then kept stabbing. Another face appeared, then another, each time a different naked girl, each with an exotic name, all equally beautiful, all in a variety of revealing poses. Who were they all? Was every girl in the world doing this? He recoiled when it struck him that the next name up might be Tara, punching at all the arrows on the keyboard to banish the thought. For a moment the screen went blank and he hoped he might be back looking at record prices. Instead, the screen blinked the words 'Welcome to Sexy Dominos room' and another picture slowly emerged. This girl was different. Older, and what Debenhams would have called 'Outsize'. But still naked. Is this what models posing for Velázquez or sitting in Renoir's studios would have been like? True, they had been framed by billowing, vibrantly coloured curtains, plumped cushions and opulence. Sexy Domino was sitting on a metal chair against chipped, varnished wood panelling. But she was no less voluptuous. He stared at her like he had stared at his dad's stereoscopic *Two Eves*. The text box alongside her was empty except for a heading, 'One guest in Sexy Domino's room'. They were alone. She wasn't talking but he could hear tinny rap music playing.

"Hello," he said. "Can you hear me? How are you?" He paused for a response, then carried on. "Where do you live? Are you in London?"

Did Sexy Domino just nod to him?

"If you can hear me, what's that music playing? I'm a rock musician, you know."

If she could hear him, she didn't reply, but instead leant forward. The music changed, from rap to rock. Was that for him? He felt a quiver of excitement.

"I like that tune. What is it?"

No response. Another try.

"Aren't you cold?"

Sexy Domino stretched forward again and appeared to be typing. George waited. Beneath her picture popped up in bold red text, '330 token nude show with toy'. She sat back, opened her thighs, picked up what looked like a wine bottle and pressed a remote control. The camera began slowly to zoom in.

"God, please, no," George gasped. He thumped the keyboard once more, but instead of the picture changing, it merely froze, leaving an image he remembered from a book he'd bought for Evelyn to show ten-year-old Bridget. There was only one course of action. He pulled the plug out of the wall, the computer stopped humming and he beat a hasty retreat to his room.

Lying on his bed, he cursed himself for wasting good music-composing time. Yet he also felt a sense of loss. Not for Sexy Domino. She was from a world he didn't recognise or no longer understood. But for the friendships he had lost, the daily human contact that had been part of his life for so long. Banter, debate, laughs. Now there was only ever talk about illness and family conflict. How he missed meeting people day to day, having conversations that came naturally. He knew he wanted that back. He just didn't know who with or where.

Chapter 16

Bridget arrived back home from her dad's just as daylight was fading. The house was empty and there was no message from Toby about whether he would be back from work at the normal time or late. The day had been long, and rummaging through her mother's possessions had been more draining than she'd expected. Too tired to make herself anything to eat, she poured some hot water in a mug, mixed in a spoon of drinking chocolate and took it up to bed.

When she awoke, the mug was on the bedside table, the hot chocolate cold and the room dark. She remembered the inviting look of the pillows, resting her head on them, but nothing more.

It was voices from outside that had brought her back to consciousness.

"Told you it'd be alright. She's not home."

"If you're sure. I'm still OK to drive."

"Those birds. We could've pulled them."

"Didn't fancy yours much."

"Whatever did they see in those other blokes?"

"Can't have been the looks."

"Must have been their money."

"Weren't good enough for us anyway."

Raucous laughter followed. Bridget had edged her way along the bed to the window and was watching as Toby and Robin stumbled up the drive to the front door.

"You can have the spare room." Toby was aiming his key in the direction of the lock.

"Sure she won't mind?"

"She's still at the old man's. And it's my house. I'll invite in whomsoever I like." Toby's voice was as slurred as it was unnecessarily loud. "She'll never know."

"Let me help you." Robin grasped Toby's hand and tried to steady it. Still the key failed to connect.

"Maybe we'll have to go back and spend the night in the pub."

"And the girls."

"Bingo!" The key was in the lock and the front door swung open. The two fell into the hall.

"Good job we weren't carrying anything."

"Like clocks."

"Or records."

There was more giggling as they hauled themselves off the floor towards the stairs.

"Where do you think you're going?"

The hall light flickered on, revealing Bridget on the landing, one hand on the light switch, the other grasping the mug of cold hot chocolate.

"Oh, hello, darling," Toby said with a slurred guffaw.

Robin offered his support. "Nice to see you, again, Bridge. Though Tobes didn't think you were in."

"Don't think you're staying. Either of you." Bridget's voice was taut and sharp.

"Come on, Bridge. Be reasonable," Toby whined.

"Leave. Now. Both of you."

Toby put his arm out to calm Robin's giggles, stopping him from edging further into the house. His tone changed, now menacing, though his diction was still slurred. "This is my house too, you know. If I want to come in, I will."

"Out!" Bridget had walked defiantly down the stairs towards them and was pointing to the front door. Toby grabbed at her arm, pulling her to one side and spilling the cold hot chocolate. She let out a cry. "Ow! Let go, you're hurting."

He didn't. She swung a foot round to kick him, but with no shoes it hurt her more than him. She tried a punch, but his grasp was too strong and she couldn't turn.

"Let go of me."

"Only if you don't fight me."

"I said, let go of me."

Toby relaxed his grip and pushed her away, more chocolate drink slopping on to the carpet. As she fell back into the stairs, she threw the cup at them. It was wild and wide of the mark, but still close enough to spray them both.

Toby lurched forward, before Robin restrained him, tugging his jacket from behind. "C'mon, Tobes, leave it." Together they staggered into the living room.

"Make sure you're gone before I get up in the morning," Bridget yelled, failing to disguise the tremor in her voice, before marching upstairs and turning off the light.

* * *

The evening turned out quite differently for George. When an aroma of curry wafted into his room, he followed it to discover Mark and Tara unpacking their takeaway. He hoped he was appearing nonchalant, and if he were displaying guilt on the intrusion into Tara's room – not to mention Romantique's, Lovelyana's or Sexy Domino's – neither seemed to notice.

"Fancy a vegetable samosa?"

It felt wrong to refuse, a seventy-year abstention from curry ending with a shared takeaway. "I can't think why I haven't had this before. What is it?"

"It's a bhindi bhaji," Mark answered.

"And that?"

"Chana masala."

"And that?" George was pointing at the Peshwari naan. Tara and Mark exchanged glances. "Sorry, am I eating your tea?"

"It's OK, Gramps. We've enough for three. Just surprised you don't know what they are."

He told them about the childhood experience of packet curry and a lifelong aversion. "I never thought food could taste this good." He tipped a pile of sag aloo on top of a mountain of Bombay potato.

Tara seized the moment. "If you like this, how about this?" From under the takeaway bag, she pulled out a leaflet and offered it to George.

"Luncheon club for the over sixties?" George eyed her suspiciously. He took it and opened it warily. "Ridgeway Community Centre? Has your mum been on to you?"

"No." Tara paused, then grimaced. "Actually, yes."

"I thought you were looking through wardrobes, not plotting together."

"We weren't plotting anything. Just she asked me to look some things out for you. From the library. I'd forgotten about them until she reminded me this afternoon." Tara produced more from under the bag. "And Dad handed me these last time I was down in Basingstoke."

George tilted the leaflet he was holding to the light and at an angle. He still didn't have glasses and, although these days he sometimes had trouble reading, he was never going to admit it. Not needing glasses was one small victory over age that he wasn't willing to concede. Luncheon clubs were about to join the list. "Ridgeway *Luncheon* Club. *Lunch*eon? When did anyone ever eat *Lunch*eon?" He looked up to check that Tara was following his distaste for a word he considered archaic, then read on. "'We provide a delicious variety of foods from Afro-Caribbean to Continental cuisine.'" He stopped at another word he disliked. "Cuisine? Oo-oo, la di da. And anyway, I don't like Afro-Caribbean and Continental, cuisine or not."

"You just said you'd never tried Indian and now you like it."

George skimmed down the page. "'We provide a range of activities for older people to take part in each day from...'" He stopped.

"Go on. From what?"

"I'm not doing any of these."

"Let me see." Tara reached out to retrieve the leaflet but George drew it closer and began to list the centre's activities with rising volume and increasing incredulity.

"'Social dancing. Gardening. Cake decorating.' Your mother seriously wanted me to see this?" He didn't wait for an answer but read on. "Line dancing? Yoga? Tai Chi? Is she trying to kill me?"

Tara waved one of the other papers. "Aromatherapy?"

"Sounds smelly."

"Massage? You'd like that."

"It'd just be plain embarrassing. Who at my age has a massage?"

"I'm sure lots of people do. Relax you, ease the tension in your muscles."

"I haven't got any tension." He suddenly felt like he was his own grandfather. He remembered how his parents would talk about old people becoming cussed. Was he turning into that sort of person? He looked down to avoid any accidental connection with Tara's gaze. Was that really his stomach, extending over his trousers? He'd have disowned his body long ago if there had been a choice. "Anyway, they'll struggle to find muscles to massage." The self-deprecation gave him the courage to look up.

Tara smiled indulgently. "It'd give you the chance to meet new people, new friends."

"Is that your mother talking?"

"Or maybe you should meet those people you used to play canasta with."

"That *is* your mother talking."

Truth was, while he'd felt lonely in front of Sexy Domino, the prospect of meeting real people frightened him. He'd never been good at small talk and had lost count of the times he'd started an anecdote and realised no one was listening, even before they'd walked away. He couldn't face that anymore. No, for all Tara and Bridget's good intentions, being forced to meet people wasn't for him. He'd just have to make do with Hunter, who demanded nothing. And his music.

He put the leaflet down and nodded to the ones Tara was holding. "Just leave them on the table. I'll look at them later."

Tara let the papers fall away, hesitating just before laying them on to the table. George noticed. It was a sure sign there was more to come.

"There's just one thing, Gramps."

He'd been right.

"You've booked me on a mountaineering course?"

"Parachuting."

They both laughed.

Tara continued. "Actually, Mark's parents *have* promised Mark a sky dive for his birthday."

"They've obviously got life insurance on him."

More laughter, including a weak smile from Mark who had used the lack of involvement in conversation to fill his plate before George took it all.

Tara tore off a piece of naan. "They said they'd buy me one for my birthday if I wanted one."

"I hope you said 'no'. Crazy idea. I'd tell them what I think of such foolhardy ideas if I ever saw them."

"Funny you should say that. You can. This weekend."

"How?"

"They've invited us all over for Sunday roast."

"Oh." The dread of having to make conversation engulfed him again.

"You, Mum, Dad."

"Oh." This last was in response to the thought that Toby would be there too.

"It was Mark's idea. Please say you'll come."

George sighed. He didn't want to upset his granddaughter and he'd not had a decent roast beef and Yorkshires for ages. He nodded reluctantly.

"Alright. On one condition."

"What's that?"

"It's for lunch and not luncheon!"

Chapter 17

"Is everything alright?" George twisted round so he could face his daughter sitting in the back of the car. The sun was low and streamed into his eyes beneath the service station canopy so he needed to squint to see her. It had been obvious since the start of the journey that something was up. Now Toby was concentrating on refuelling and Tara and Mark were in the shop, it felt safe to ask.

"Alright?"

"Yes. You and Toby."

At first, George thought it was the driving that was upsetting Toby, a long journey to his house to pick them all up, then back to Mark's parents' for lunch. But the tension between Toby and Bridget was so strained it had to be more than that.

Bridget avoided George's gaze and waited for Toby to replace the petrol cap and stride to the shop before answering. "It's not Toby. Well, it is, but it's more to do with Robin."

"Robin?" George was grateful Bridget's eyes were following her husband rather than looking at him or she would have seen the alarm on his face.

"After I left you the other night, he turned up at my house. With Toby. Drunk, both of them."

"What happened?"

"Nothing much."

"Did Robin say anything?"

"Like what? He was too drunk anyway. And he'd left before I got up the next morning."

"And Toby?"

"We've hardly spoken. He's been in the spare room ever since." She let out a deep breath. "We're not going to be much fun today. We really shouldn't have come. We're only here because I promised Tara."

"Does she know?"

Bridget shook her head. "Somehow we've got to give a united front to the Ramsays." She sighed again. "United. What a joke."

If George had been in the back, he'd have put his arm around his daughter like he used to do when she was small. Instead he peered through the shaft of sunlight, not knowing what to say.

"We've got two Double Deckers, two Kit Kats and a Mars bar. Who wants what?" Tara had wrenched open the back door and was waving a handful of chocolate bars. She stopped when she saw her mum. "What's up? Mum?"

George finally found some words. "Your mum's not feeling very well."

"Oh, Mum, I'm sorry." Tara slid in beside her mother and gave her the cuddle George had wanted to give.

Bridget looked up and gave Tara a watery smile. "I'll be OK."

The driver's door swung open. Without looking back, Toby threw himself into his seat. "I don't know what you lot have been talking about," he growled, "but tell your boyfriend to get in. I want to get moving."

Toby seemed to take his agitation out on the car, his driving aggressive and making no allowance for George cramped in the front seat and the rest of them squeezed into the back, or for other road users. He careened corners and jumped lights, cursing at every delay and motorist who dared block his acceleration.

"Irritable vowel syndrome," Bridget muttered under her breath, the only words she spoke for the remainder of the journey and which only led to Toby driving even more erratically. The result was arriving at the Ramsays' early, with queasy passengers and unprepared hosts. After polite, if awkward conversation and an early introduction to the Ramsays' drinks cabinet, Mark, his mum, Phyllis, and Bridget retired to the kitchen, leaving George, Toby and Tara with Gerald, Mark's father.

"Another sherry?" Gerald was hovering over George, brandishing what was recognisably a good demi-sec. George held up his glass by way of answer, a reward for enduring the journey they'd had.

"Say when." Gerald tipped the bottle, waiting for an instruction to stop refilling.

George waited until the glass was close to overflowing. "When."

"Toby?"

"Don't mind if I do." Toby's manner seemed more relaxed now Bridget was out of the room.

Tara looked up from her phone. "Don't forget you're driving us back, Dad."

Toby glowered at her. "Don't lecture me, young lady. I know my limits."

Tara turned back to her texts.

George was on the verge of supporting his granddaughter, but before he could speak Toby had begun asking Gerald about work. Instead, he gulped a mouthful of sherry, then tuned out. Why had he agreed to come? There was so much he wanted to do at home, he had nothing in common with the Ramsays and now he was going to have to act as peacekeeper within his own family. Resorting to a well-tried tactic for distracting himself from unpleasant truths, honed through years of unrequited optimism and disappointment, he began reciting to himself UK A-sides and B-sides of sixties' singles, in chronological order. He completed The Beatles, from 'My Bonnie' backed by *The Saints* to 'Let It Be' and 'You Know My Name', ruling out anything after they broke up, then moved on to Elvis Presley. He'd reached 1965's 'Do The Clam' but was struggling to remember the B-side when he tuned back into Toby.

"I've got a client who's always changing his mind."

"Tell me about it," was Gerald's reply.

Toby duly obliged, relating an anecdote of anodyne pointlessness. George's rolled eyes and expression of barely concealed boredom were missed by both Gerald and Toby but not by Tara who had temporarily looked up from her mobile. Their eyes locked in recognition of shared disbelief that people could be so dull, exchanging secretive, conspiratorial glances across generations, then smiling before looking away to avoid discovery. As Tara returned to her texts, into George's head came a melody. It came from nowhere but it was insistent, tuneful, catchy, a sure-fire hit. He was just creating the verse when Phyllis arrived bearing plates.

"Sorry about the delay. Lunch is served," she announced. "Follow me, please."

Gerald jumped up and opened a pair of pine doors, revealing a second half of the room, set up for dining. While Phyllis laid the plates out, Gerald indicated to George where he should sit, before walking round the table, filling glasses from a carafe of deep red wine. George downed his sherry and settled himself in readiness for lunch.

It was obvious the Ramsays had made an effort. There was a lingering smell of Pledge and air freshener, and the table settings probably only saw the light at weddings, funerals and Christmas. Mark, Bridget and Phyllis formed a chain from the kitchen, delivering a succession of serving dishes. George couldn't remember the last time he'd had a meal when it wasn't already piled up on the plate or eaten out of a saucepan.

While he waited for everyone to settle at the table, George began a new list. Favourite meals. Number one was indisputably a fry-up, but close behind was Sunday roast. Beef, Yorkshire pudding, vegetables, roast potatoes, thick gravy. A tradition that wouldn't ever be topped.

"Right, serve yourselves, will you," Phyllis announced.

George licked his lips in anticipation and lifted the lid of the nearest serving dish. What he hadn't counted on was Gerald and Phyllis Ramsay being vegetarian. He could never fathom what possessed seemingly sensible people to give up meat. Maybe their parents had been hippies in the sixties, something else he never understood. By the time the Swinging Sixties had become the Spliffin' Sixties, he'd felt too old to join what he called 'kaftan culture'. Whatever the Ramsays' family history, it still didn't justify a Sunday lunch of lentil and walnut roast, no matter how surprisingly tasty it turned out to be. It just wasn't what he'd been looking forward to. The only consolation was Gerald's wine, both in quality and the frequency with which his glass continued to be topped up. Which was happening again as George chased a pea between two carrots and a broccoli stem.

"Don't you think you've had enough, Dad?" Bridget said softly to her father.

Gerald hesitated, but Tara came to his aid. "He's alright, Mum. It's not as if he's driving." She shot an accusatory glance at her dad, who'd already had a refill and whose eyes were on George.

"Mind you don't spill it, George. Gerald, watch him. His hands are like a drunk's at the best of times." Toby made a shaking gesture that mocked his father-in-law.

Almost on cue, George's hands began to tremble. Wine slopped over the lip of the glass and dripped down the stem.

"Watch out!" Toby barked. This served only to agitate George into tilting the glass, with the result that a wave of wine splashed across Phyllis's special occasion white lace tablecloth. To cover his embarrassment, he put down the glass and grabbed his napkin to staunch the flow. In the confusion that followed, with Tara, Bridget and Mark all reaching across the table to mop up the spilt wine with whatever came to hand, Gerald's glass of wine was toppled, along with the gravy boat.

Phyllis bravely reassured them with a calm 'never mind', but it was clear that this tablecloth would see no further active service.

George was surveying the carnage before him. He felt he should apologise. What he actually said was, "What a waste of good wine."

* * *

The main course having gone badly also delayed what remained of the lunch. The jam roly-poly, specially made by Phyllis after Tara's tip-off that it was George's favourite pud, was abandoned as the custard had gone lumpy. Respite was sought in the lounge, everyone taking extra care not to spill coffee or drop After Eight shards on the carpet. Conversation was stilted and about politics or business or the latest TV blockbuster, none of which George found capable of contributing to. Instead, he took to observing his daughter and Toby. There was no eye contact between husband and wife. They spoke only to contradict one another. It couldn't all be down to Robin turning up. He'd seen it before with her first husband. What was it about her that she couldn't keep a marriage alive? He and Evelyn had lasted for so long, yet here was Bridget struggling to keep any kind of relationship. Was something the matter with her? Maybe it was *his* fault. Maybe all those missed nights when he'd been rehearsing, doing session work, playing in bars, had taken their toll on his only daughter. Absentee dad. And what for? Boxes of unsold copies of 'Little Lisa' stacked up in his record room, and a lifetime of unfulfilled ambition.

"I understand you have a dog, George. Mark's been telling us all about it." Gerald's voice betrayed a search for something uncontroversial to bring George back into the conversation.

"Yes... what's his name?" Phyllis nudged Mark for support.

"Hunter," Mark prompted.

"Such a shame you couldn't bring Hunter with you."

George, Tara, Mark and Bridget all turned accusingly to Toby.

"Don't look at me. You're the ones who complain about the car being too small. Anyway, that mutt is nothing but a walking disaster. Putting it down would be a relief for it."

"He's a he, not an it," George grumbled under his breath.

"He can't be that bad." Phyllis sounded quite taken aback.

"Please excuse my husband," Bridget looked directly at Phyllis as she spoke, avoiding Toby's look. "He's always exaggerating."

Toby was shaking his head in dramatic disagreement, though his gesture was either missed or ignored.

Bridget continued, undeterred. "Hunter's quite old though, isn't he, Dad? Poor thing has serious pancreas problems. Dad took him to a festival. You know, like Reading, but not. And Hunter only went and sniffed out a paper bag full of drugs. He ate the lot. Nearly killed him."

"He went on to write some cracking psychedelic tunes." Toby won the laugh he'd been seeking.

"Snoop Dogg?" Gerald added. Phyllis tutted.

George was saying nothing because, in his mind, he was re-living that day. 'Family day, dog friendly', the festival had been billed. It had a sixties theme and one of the tents was going to be non-stop sixties music from local bands. George needed no second invitation when – out of the blue – he was asked to join a specially formed tribute act made up of pensioners. They settled on the name Sounds of the Sixties, which suited the repertoire even if it exceeded George's age.

It had been his idea to take Hunter. He thought it'd make everyone laugh, make the group memorable. They were going to open with an Animals medley and had lined up an encore of Cat Stevens' 'I Love My Dog'. He was sure it would bring the house down. Get them noticed. Maybe leading to proper gigs, even a record deal. Strictly, Hunter was Evelyn's dog and she didn't like the idea, but despite her reservations he won the day.

It had all started well enough. Everyone was good-natured and Hunter was petted, patted and hugged. George kept him under close control and strictly enforced the 'no treats' rule to make sure nothing would inflame the pancreatitis. It was all good publicity for the group's set later in the day and the weather was perfect. Nothing could go wrong. Except just before they were due on stage and the organisers were briefing the group, George's grip on the lead slackened and Hunter slipped free. It wasn't for long, but it was enough. When Hunter was rediscovered, he was staggering and disorientated. The festival may have been family friendly but it had not been drug free. The dog had nosed out and gorged on someone's stash, making up for years on a dull diet of prescription food.

"How much was the vet's bill, Dad?" George became aware Bridget was still explaining. "Dad?"

"Too much."

"He pulled through, but he's not the same as he was. Very quiet. Used to chase around and bark all the time. Now seems frightened of everything. What with his age and dodgy pancreas, he's on borrowed time. Isn't he, Dad?"

But George had moved from remembering the festival to telling Evelyn. Hunter was too sick to be moved from the vet, so George had to go home without him. It was one of the worst rows they ever had. Evelyn called him irresponsible, that he wasn't fit to be left alone with anyone or anything, of caring more for his music than life. She didn't stop at Hunter. She dragged up his failings as a father. To cap it all, he missed the gig. Sounds of the Sixties played without him while he was at the vets, so he never got on stage. 'Who needs keyboards anyway?' they'd said as he apologised for his absence. When they took pub bookings on the strength of the festival performance, they remained a four piece without keyboards, and a last stab at fame passed him by. At least that was how it had seemed until Ron came on the scene. And even that felt like it was slipping away the longer he was stuck here making pointless small talk.

"Hunter, that's a great name for a dog. What is it?" Gerald asked.

George hesitated, giving the impression he knew about breeds of dogs.

Gerald continued. "One of those big hunters? Irish Setter, Golden Retriever, Bloodhound?"

"Gerald. This is the Turnbulls we're talking about," Toby scoffed with a dismissive roll of the eyes. "It's a Labradoodle. Tiny. Gets under your feet all the time. Number of times I've nearly trodden on him. 'Prey' would be a better name. Or 'Bloody Annoying.'"

"That's not fair." Tara defended her grandparents' pet.

"But why Hunter?" Phyllis persisted.

"I think it's to do with Gramps' music, isn't it, Gramps? Ivory Hunter or somebody. He's got records by him. He's got records by almost everybody, haven't you, Gramps? And he's played with loads of famous people."

George didn't respond. What was it Frank Sinatra had sung about regrets, he asked himself? He'd always hated the song, but it had a point. Of course there were things he wished had gone differently. But the bad times led to good times and you can't change anything anyway. Just his conscience kept resurrecting memories. Guilt he hoped would have long been despatched was still festering. Yet despite everything, Bridget and Tara had made it. Grown up. Making their own way in life. Making their own decisions, making their own mistakes. Building their own regrets. And what had he contributed, really contributed? Could he have done more? *Should* he have done more? How was he supposed to feel? Proud? Proud of what? He certainly couldn't think of anything he'd really achieved that would justify pride. And what was he to them? What was the point of his existence? To them? To himself? There was only one conclusion. He *had* to make it with his music. Just to show everybody.

"Gramps. Gramps." Tara was tugging his arm. "Mr Ramsay's talking to you."

"Oh, sorry. What did you say?"

"I was asking about your music." Gerald was leaning forward and sounding genuinely interested. "Mark has told us so much, we'd like to hear more."

George jerked out of his melancholy. "Sorry. I was somewhere else. My music. I've got a room full of records. If that's what you mean."

"Tell us about bands you played with. I couldn't remember who you'd said." Tara clasped his hand to encourage him.

"Yes, who did you play with? Anyone I'd know?" Phyllis waited expectantly.

"Go on, Gramps, tell us about it," Tara urged.

Mark joined in. "Yes, Mr Turnbull. I've only heard it from Tara."

George shook his head. "It's nothing worth telling, really it's not." He wasn't normally slow with tales of his musical connections, but after the wine, the gravy and the introspection, he wasn't ready to talk to anyone, let alone talk about the past. It'd all be different when Ron had come up trumps and he'd made it big.

"No, really, I want to know. How did you get into playing?" Gerald persisted.

Phyllis interrupted any further questions from her husband. "Never mind, darling. If he doesn't want to…" She stood up. "More tea or coffee, anyone?"

George realised he was losing the opportunity to talk about himself to people who actually seemed to want to hear. "If you really want to know."

"Of course we do." Gerald was smiling indulgently.

"Well, I played in clubs mainly, small places."

"Clubs? How interesting." Phyllis delayed making drinks and was beaming and nodding vehemently to encourage him. Perhaps a little too vehemently.

"We also played halls and bigger places. That's when I got to know people on the same bill – the Creation, the Artwoods, the Yardbirds…" He had hoped that Gerald and Phyllis would have been of an age to have heard of at least the Yardbirds, impressed maybe. But there wasn't even a glimmer of recognition.

"Mum and Dad are more into classical music," Mark offered.

"Not entirely. I think I've heard of the Yardbirds. Didn't they sing 'Mr Tambourine Man'? You know, the Dylan song."

"That was the Byrds. This was the Yardbirds. With Eric Clapton." Surely everyone had heard of Eric Clapton.

Before anyone could gasp that he'd met what he'd argue was one of the world's greatest guitarists, Toby intervened. "If you're not careful, he'll be telling us what hits they had, what record label they were on…"

"Did *you* have hits?" Phyllis asked.

Always the same question. And the answer inevitably implied failure. But Phyllis was still beaming and nodding. If he didn't give her an answer she might get a migraine.

"We were Record of the Week. On Radio City." This was true and saved lying about the hits.

"Was that a pirate station, like Radio Caroline?" Gerald asked. "We could never get a decent reception."

George put on an American deejay accent. "This is Radio City on 197 metres Medium Wave. It's time now to introduce our Record of the Week, the fabulous Phaedra and the Phaeries singing about Little Lisa."

"Is that what you were called? Phaedra and the Phaeries?" Gerald exchanged a dubious glance with his wife.

George nodded.

"I never heard it, I'm afraid," Phyllis apologised.

"It nearly bubbled under the charts." George had resumed in his own voice. "It would have done much better if we'd had a bit of luck."

This would have been Evelyn's cue, stepping in to explain about Radio City's transmitter going off air and, by the time it was fixed, there was a new Record of the Week. Or the record pressing plant strike. He was sure the baying crowd in the Bag O'Nails would have gone out and bought it, but by the time the strike was over and copies made it into the shops, the moment had passed. But if *he* tried to explain all this, it'd just sound like excuses.

Bridget made an attempt to fill the void. "You were invited to join a famous group, weren't you, Dad?"

"That sounds exciting." Phyllis added her encouragement.

"Go on, Dad. It's a lovely story."

"Yes, go on," Gerald urged.

"Well… I applied for an audition to join a band. I saw it in a music paper. *Melody Maker* it was called."

"I think everyone's heard this story," Toby muttered in a low voice.

"Shh, Toby. I want to hear." Phyllis waved him down but kept her eyes fixed on George.

"I was courting Evelyn, Bridget's mum. She wanted to see a film and when I asked if she would let me take her, she said yes. I was so excited. We hadn't been out alone together before."

"Different times," Gerald nodded, looking towards Mark and Tara.

"You can say that again." George seemed emboldened by Gerald's comment, or maybe it was the wine. "I remember the ladies' underwear department in Marks and Spencer was the most exciting thing I used to do as a teenager. And my mum would smother my eyes if we walked past the drapers when they were about to dress a naked mannequin."

Tara stepped in before he could remember anything else. "You were saying about your first date?"

"Yes, so it was arranged. I was going to pick her up and take her to the film. It was The Beatles. *Hard Day's Night*. Evelyn wasn't much of a fan but had become one."

"And?" Tara prompted him again.

"A letter arrived at my flat. Handwritten. Wasn't very easy to read but I could make out that it was asking me to come to an audition I'd applied for. It was only the same night as I was taking your gran to the pictures." He was looking at Tara as he spoke.

"Didn't you phone them up to change it?" Phyllis asked.

"If they had a phone, I didn't. No one had phones in those days."

"Not even those party phones you told us about?" Tara chipped in.

"Before them. You used to wait outside a phone box if someone was going to call you. All I had was the time they were expecting me and an address – a house in Wembley."

"Walthamstow. The last time you told it." Toby was rolling his eyes as he spoke.

"Dad, shh. What did you do?" Tara asked.

"Nothing. There was no way of letting them know and I daren't cancel taking your gran to the pictures. I didn't want her to think I wasn't sweet on her. So I didn't go. I wrote to them but they never replied. Never did find out who the audition was for. I think it might have been someone who became big."

George could see expressions of disappointment on everyone's faces at the unsatisfactory end to his story, that they were feeling let down at not having a major name to round it off and rub in the pathos of his missed opportunity.

"I remember reading somewhere," Gerald began tentatively, "that Paul McCartney invited someone to audition to become one of The Beatles and they never showed. Around 1960. The letter turned up at a car boot sale a couple of years ago. Inside an old book. That couldn't have been you, could it, George?"

"Mine would have been later. I always wonder who it might have been. The Who maybe or the Moody Blues."

"The Muppets?" Toby rolled back in his chair in satisfaction. "Dad!"

"Just a joke, Tara, just a joke. Your grandfather can take a bit of ribbing, can't you, George?"

An uneasy silence now descended. George shifted uncomfortably. Why did every story he told have to end like this? Tara rescued him.

"You've got the most amazing collection of records, haven't you, Gramps?"

It didn't help. How he ached for people to be able to acknowledge music he'd recorded, not the records by other people that he just happened to have collected.

"Have you, George?" Gerald prompted for details.

George shrugged an acknowledgement. "I suppose so. Rock'n'roll, blues, old stuff mainly," adding quickly "not classical old, though."

"You should see them." Mark sat forward. "A room rammed with them, racks and racks of them. They're worth tens of thousands of pounds each."

"I'm not sure about that." George refrained from adding about the time Mark had sent them flying across the floor.

"Do you still play?" Phyllis asked George.

"My records? All the time."

"An instrument, I mean."

"A bit, not as much as I used to." 'Not while I'm stuck in places like this,' he nearly added.

"Pianos in bars and God-awful tribute bands," Toby whispered to Gerald whilst fumbling in his trousers, trying to extract his mobile phone that was bleeping. Scrambling from his chair, and without apology, he hurried outside.

Bridget's eyes followed him until he was out of earshot. "I'm sorry about my husband. He's under a lot of pressure at work."

"Tell me about it," Gerald said, nodding, though this time no one did.

Phyllis was more interested in George. "Tell us some more about your group."

"There's not a lot to say. One of the clubs we played was the Playboy Club. Just after it opened. That was quite exciting."

Bridget cupped her palms over Tara's ears. "Not in front of your family, please!"

"It was all pretty harmless. The chefs used to cook us a meal afterwards, though they weren't supposed to. We didn't have much money. We didn't get much, just a few bob between the lot of us, and most of that went on travel and equipment." Not having Toby there to criticise seemed to help bring it all back. "And special effects – when we got more psychedelic we started using lights and smoke. 'Happenings', people were calling them. So it wasn't enough to just stand on stage and sing. We had to make a show of it. Set fire to a curtain once."

"And you still play?" Phyllis asked again.

"You should hear him, he's really good," Tara enthused proudly.

"We've got a piano over there in the corner, George." Gerald stood up and pointed at it. "Hardly used since Mark gave up lessons."

"That's because I make music differently these days, Dad."

Gerald ignored his son. "Why don't you give us a tune, George?"

"Come on, Gramps." Tara took George's hand and pulled him up. He feigned resistance but let her lead him to the piano.

"It's an electric one – here." Gerald stretched past to turn on the switch and lift the keyboard lid, before settling back into his armchair to listen.

George knew there was no turning back now. "I'll try. I don't really like electric pianos. They're fake to me. They don't have the same resistance as a real one." He rolled his fingers up and down the keyboard. "What shall I do?" He thought maybe he should audition one of his new tunes. He'd finished one the day before, a tender ballad that he was going to call 'Missing Evelyn'. Perhaps the wrong mood to do now. "We used to close with this." Memories of the other night at Mark's gig were still fresh, and although there were probably more appropriate songs, he launched into 'Twist and Shout' as he had in the uni foyer. This time though, no one clustered around him. They stayed fixed in their armchairs. The alcohol consumed over lunch didn't prompt any swaying or clapping, though it did have an effect on George's playing. He missed more than the odd note, the piano's volume was set too low and he was singing too loudly. Gerald and Phyllis shifted uncomfortably. Still he ploughed on, reaching a crescendo of rising 'Aaahhhs'.

"Come on then, join in. Aaahhhh…"

He pummelled the keys to give the cue but it made no difference to the sound and only Tara joined in. He stopped abruptly, leaving Tara in mid-Aaahhhh, then sat back. "Well, something like that."

Tara and Mark let out whoops. Phyllis clapped which prompted Gerald to join in. It all felt as appropriate as a stripper at a funeral. There was no call for requests or an encore. The only words spoken were Bridget's. "That's enough, Dad," though as she said it, she was taking more notice of the garden than her father. George followed her eyes to Toby, leaning back in a lawn lounger, relaxed and laughing, immersed in conversation on his mobile phone.

"Did you play any other instrument, George?" Gerald was switching off the power to the piano as he spoke.

"Mainly keyboards. Bit of guitar. In the early days. In the folk clubs." George wiggled his fingers. "They're not as mobile as they used to be."

"I liked folk music as well as classical." Gerald looked across to Phyllis. "We met at a folk club."

"I played in folk clubs. A gang of us used to meet up in Soho. And East London."

"We were in Runcorn, actually, though Soho sounds much more exciting."

"Some of the gang got quite famous. You know Bert Jansch?" George looked for signs of recognition. "Paul Simon? Peggy Seeger?"

Phyllis perked up. "I've heard of the one you just mentioned."

"Peggy Seeger?"

"The other one."

"Paul Simon?"

Phyllis nodded.

"You might even have seen him." George was now relishing being able to name drop on someone they'd heard of. "I think Paul played in Lancashire once. Widnes had a folk scene and I'm sure he played up there. Before he was famous, of course. Wrote a famous song because he missed his girlfriend. Kathy. Lovely girl."

"It would have been before our time." Phyllis shook her head. "Shame."

"I thought he was American." Gerald sounded dubious.

Here was a rich vein that George could mine. He swung round on the piano stool to face everyone properly. "He lived here in the 1960s. We were regulars at a club in Soho – it was under a restaurant. Berwick Street, Greek Street, one of them, never can remember. There was Ewan MacColl, too." They must have heard of Ewan MacColl. "'Dirty Old Town'?"

Phyllis nodded. "Ewan MacColl – isn't he an actor as well?"

"We used to get together every Tuesday, or maybe it was a Wednesday." He didn't get the chance to finish.

"Been having a sing-song?" Toby had interrupted while weaving back to his chair, mobile bulging in his shirt pocket.

Phyllis nodded. "And George has been telling us about his playing career."

"Not much time needed for that, then." Toby was smirking. He spoke as if George had left the room. George sat stony-faced and silent, wishing he could.

Tara stepped in to rescue her grandfather. "He wrote the *News at Ten* theme. And *Mastermind*. Didn't you, Gramps?"

"Not exactly." George hesitated, wondering if he should mention the soap commercials they probably knew from their childhood, or some of the other famous people he'd met or jammed with.

"And he's got an award the Queen presented to him," Tara continued.

Toby tutted. "I don't think so."

"It was a big gala event. A good evening, wasn't it, Dad?" Bridget was pointedly addressing everyone but Toby. "I thoroughly enjoyed it."

"What did you win your award for, George?" Phyllis shifted uncomfortably.

"It was nothing much. Just a public relations film."

"Don't be so modest." Gerald offered George a gesture of encouragement. "It won an award, didn't it? It must have been good."

"If you don't want to tell them, George, allow me." Toby glanced briefly at his father-in-law. "It was about pig farming. An industrial film about pig farming and slaughterhouses in Denmark. And the awards were handed out by Princess Margarita of Romania or someone who was zillionth in line to the throne."

George watched as Gerald and Phyllis exchanged glances.

"It's not funny, Dad. Please stop."

"But it's all true. I wouldn't tell porkies." Toby sat back, satisfied with his pun.

Bridget stepped in at last. "Toby. Enough." She sounded both angry and embarrassed but there was no conviction that her words would carry any weight. There was an awkward shuffling and people avoiding each other's eyes.

Tara stood up. "I think it's time we were going. I've got some work to do for uni tomorrow."

"So soon? That's a shame." Phyllis's tone was betrayed by the way she had also stood up, encouraging her guests to depart.

"And don't worry about taking us, Mum." Tara very pointedly was ignoring her father. "We'll get a minicab."

* * *

"That was a bloody awful idea," Tara whispered to Mark through clenched teeth.

"I'm sorry. I just thought if our parents met…" Mark paused.

Tara checked the front of the minicab. The driver didn't appear to be listening and George seemed to be dozing. It felt safe for her to carry on. "My dad's such a shit. How could he be so rotten? Not just to Gramps, but to Mum. In front of your parents, too."

"Do you think he said that about slaughterhouses because my parents are vegetarian?"

"I should apologise to them."

"Meantime," Mark was fumbling in his pocket, "can I play you this?" He pulled out his mobile. From the tiny speaker came electronic sounds.

"What's that?"

"Some new stuff I've just finished."

"Must you?"

"I put it online before breakfast. I want to know what you think of it."

"Can't it wait? You'll wake Gramps."

"Please."

The sounds were mechanical, electronic and synthesised. Tara grimaced. "Turn it down. You'll wake Gramps."

"I'm not asleep." George didn't move as he spoke.

"Sorry, Gramps. Didn't mean to disturb you."

"It's alright. I was only thinking about this afternoon."

"I'm so sorry about my dad."

"Don't worry. You can't live a life as a musician and not expect to be slaughtered now and again. I was more embarrassed for you and your mum in front of the Ramsays."

"They'll be fine with it, Mr T."

"I hope so."

"So what do you think of my new music?" Mark turned up the volume.

George kept his eyes closed and listened for a few seconds. "Doing away with real instruments is a slippery slope, if you don't mind my saying."

"We've had hits," Mark said defensively.

"What, Top Ten? Number Ones?" George sat up and turned so he could see and hear Mark properly.

"No. Hits. People looking at it on our website. Fourteen since this morning."

George rocked his head back and thought again of 'Little Lisa' and of the sealed boxes in his record room. How many did it *actually* sell? On reflection, probably not even fourteen. "Is that a lot of, what do you call them, hits?"

"It's a start."

George was wide awake now, leaning forward. In Mark's eyes was the unmistakable look of the certainty of youth – that success was not only inevitable but also owed. It wasn't for George to disabuse him. Time would do that soon enough.

"What genre is it?"

Mark tapped his mobile and merciful silence reigned. "It doesn't really have a genre. I knew you wouldn't like it."

"Let's just say it's not to my taste." On another day, George might have asked if that was the best a degree course in music could offer. But criticism always used to put *him* off and the last thing he wanted was to discourage this boy from making music. No matter how little like music it might sound. "Sorry. I didn't mean to be negative. Give it another go."

"Not now." Tara rested her hand on Mark's arm, but he clicked play anyway.

George turned back, sitting upright, arms folded across his lap, eyes closed again, a pose he imagined looked like careful consideration. Except it didn't make the music sound any better. He shifted uneasily. What pose wouldn't betray how he felt? Should he drum his fingers when he really wanted to plug them into his ears? Did he tap his feet when there was no discernable rhythm or tune. He tried nodding his head, furrowing his brow and pursing his lips as if he were seriously considering its merits.

"The speaker on this mobile isn't helping," Mark offered.

"Have you thought about adding something a bit more..." George paused as he sought a word that would cause the least offence, "musical?" Too late, he realised he'd probably settled on the word *most* likely to cause offence. To cover himself, he turned to the driver who had remained tight-lipped. "What do you think of it?"

"It's OK. I've heard worse. Not really my kind of music."

"What *is* your kind?" George asked.

"Rock. Blues. Soul. That's what I like to listen to."

"It's my kind too." George could imagine *his* music playing in the cab. Despite everything, he could sense the tide flowing his way at last.

Chapter 18

George headed straight to his piano once they arrived back from the Ramsays'. But the tune that had been in his head before lunch had gone. So memorable a few hours ago, now lost. And still no message from Robin or Ron. He'd checked the answerphone twice. He clenched his fists before taking out his frustration on the keyboard, pummelling and punishing it as he launched into a thumping, rock'n'roll version of Tchaikovsky's *Nutcracker*.

Tara and Mark had made for the kitchen. While Tara was staring out into the garden, watching Hunter chase dandelion puffballs, Mark was filling the kettle. Through the wall, George was showing no sign of relenting.

"He's still got it, hasn't he? He must have been brilliant back when." Mark rattled the top of the kettle in time to the music.

"I still can't believe my dad could say such things."

"Like your mum says, perhaps he's working too hard."

"Too much alcohol, more like."

"I'll take him some tea."

"No, I'll go." Tara put some chocolate fingers on a saucer and balanced it on top of the tea mug to carry into the dining room. George relented on the keys somewhat as she peered round the door, tea and biscuits perched perilously. Thumping rock was replaced by something more rhythmical.

"This is called boogie-woogie," he called to her without stopping. "Heard of it?"

It was intended as both an education and a challenge.

Tara looked around for somewhere to put the mug and was about to place it on top of the piano but was put off by a warning glance.

"Not there, not there. Some respect for the old lady." The boogie-woogie continued without pause.

She stood the mug on the floor.

"How long have you had her?" she asked, tapping the piano as she spoke.

"About forty years. Bought it when we sold the shop that me and your gran used to run. Needs a bit of tuning now." George stopped at last and exercised his fingers in mid-air. "My hands are not as supple as they used to be. Don't play enough. As you heard earlier."

"It still sounds good."

"Once in the old days we were paid not to play. There was some argument because clubs wanted records not live music. The unions made them pay us anyway, so we showed up with our instruments and collected our money without playing a note while the kids danced to records. Crazy, crazy days. But that passed. They realised you can't beat live music."

"But what about your records?" Tara gestured in the direction of George's music room. "They're all recorded."

"Different. Relaxation. Inspiration." He began playing the opening notes of 'I Almost Lost My Mind'.

On cue, Tara began singing.

George stopped abruptly. "How do you know that song?"

"I haven't heard it for years, let alone sung it."

"But how do you know it?"

"Mum used to sing it to me. Before I went to sleep."

George felt goosebumps. "It was my song to your gran. And I sang it to your mum before *she* went to sleep."

"Go on, keep playing."

George played gently while Tara sung along. "You've got a wonderful voice," he said when they reached the end.

"Can you play 'Let It Be'?"

Without answering, he went straight into it. It was a tune he hadn't played for years and, after he fumbled a few notes, he sighed and stopped. Tara didn't. She kept on, *a cappella*. When she finished, George was shaking his head and staring admiringly at her.

"You are just amazing. Do you know that? Have you sung – in public?"

Tara shook her head. "I hate standing up in front of people."

"What about with whassisname?"

"Mark? He has his own ideas and doesn't want mine. Though he's getting me to do a few bits. Build his soundscape, he says."

"Let me tell you, young lady," he placed his hand on her wrist, "a word from the wise. You should sing. You've got real talent."

"I don't know…"

"I do. If not for you, do it for me. Don't let that boyfriend of yours stand in your way. Let nothing stand in your way." His hand tightened. "I mean that. Nothing."

Before Tara could ask what he meant, there was an urgent call from Mark.

"Tara, Mr T, can you come here?"

Bridget was sitting in the kitchen, staring out into the garden. She didn't look up when George and Tara came in behind her.

"Mum, what are you doing here?"

"She came in the back way." Mark sounded confused and was studying her appearance.

"Your lawn needs cutting, Dad." Bridget didn't acknowledge her father or daughter.

"Whole garden needs sorting. I should train Hunter to eat grass. Or get a goat. But what are you doing here? Nice to see you again, but I wasn't expecting you."

Bridget hadn't expected to be there either. She and Toby didn't speak once they'd left the Ramsays'. As soon as they'd got home, he'd changed his clothes then gone straight out again without explanation. Once he'd left, she opened the back door into the garden and snapped off a few deadheads in an effort to blot out the memory of lunch at Mark's parents'.

Her life changed when she came back in. She heard a phone ring. Not hers, but Toby's mobile, somewhere distant in the house. She tracked it down as it gave its final message bleep in the shirt pocket Toby had been wearing at the Ramsays' and left behind in his rush to leave.

Three missed calls. She didn't recognise the number but it was local. Most likely one of Toby's clients. Calling on a Sunday didn't seem especially odd, what with the long hours, late evenings and urgent deadlines that had been occupying him for the past few weeks. And there had been that urgent call he'd taken after lunch. She needed to know who it was.

The mobile was locked, so having made a note of the caller's number, writing it on what looked like a screwed-up receipt stuck inside the phone case, she headed back downstairs to the home phone, tapped in the number and waited. She resolved to be polite and calm so Toby's client wouldn't know how she was feeling at the moment.

After a few rings, it was picked up, but remained silent. At first, she thought she must have phoned a call centre or someone offering to help on a claim for an accident that had never happened. Twice in the last month someone had rung to follow up a survey done at Malaga airport, and they'd never been to Spain, let alone Malaga airport. Her instinct was to put the phone straight back down, but her hesitation was time enough for a tentative female voice at the other end.

"Hello?"

"Hello. Did you just call Toby Waller?"

"Who's that?"

"It's his wife. He's left his phone at home and I could see you've called three times. So I thought it must be urgent."

There was hesitation at the other end. "No. I must've dialled a wrong number. I'm sorry to have troubled you."

"Do you want to check the number you think you've called?"

"No, I must have made a mistake."

"Three times? Can I ask who I'm talking to?" But the line had already clicked and Bridget found herself talking over a male voice in perfect Queen's English, declaring, 'The other person has cleared.'

A sickening void opened in the pit of her stomach. She'd been denying the obvious for weeks, yet confirmation was no comfort. She rang the number again, but it went straight to voicemail. The void now collapsed and swallowed every part of her being. Not knowing quite why, she began a search of the house. Little things that she'd noticed but not reacted to suddenly took on a new significance. Like a new air freshener Toby had put in the bathroom. When had he ever bought air freshener? And then there was the unexpected present he'd brought back from the company away weekend. He rarely brought her anything back from work trips. But perfume? And one she'd never used? She'd put that down to his paying no attention to what she did most of the time. But it all fitted together now.

She barely needed more evidence to support the obvious, but continued her search anyway, riffling through his coats and jackets in the hall. Urgency and desperation increased with every pocket, but the only discoveries were cough sweets and fluff. If he was having an affair, he was being very careful.

She went to his wardrobe. Pockets still revealed nothing. Sweeping the hangers along in a final act of desperation, a shirt at the end – the one she remembered burning with the iron – fell off. Reaching in to remove it, she noticed a bundle of old, rarely worn fleeces, heaped on the floor beneath. A moth fluttered from them. "Out," she uttered, not sure whether she meant the moths, the fleeces or their owner.

With nothing found, there was no alternative but to phone again. She reached for the receipt where she'd scribbled the number. She saw now it was for a restaurant that she and Toby had used a lot before Tara was born. But not only had they not been there for many years it was also on a day that she remembered he'd said he'd been working late. They had been due to visit one of her friends when he'd phoned in to say he had some urgent work to complete. The receipt detailed three courses, wine, a total of £75.48, two covers.

"Bastard. Fucking bastard."

She completed dialling but this time left a message. "How could you, you… you… cow."

Eyes ablaze with anger, she returned to Toby's wardrobe, tearing down his clothes from hangers and hurling them out to the bedroom floor. Grabbing at the old fleeces revealed beneath a row of cardboard boxes that she didn't recognise. What were they? How come she hadn't seen them before? But what really caught her eye is what lay on top of them.

A shoebox. She pulled from it a bundle of envelopes and cards. Decorated with hearts and kisses. But not drawn by her. Handwritten messages. But not her handwriting. And scented letters. Scented with the same perfume Toby had surprised her with. She let out a small scream and realised there were tears on her cheek.

"What are you doing in there?"

Still holding the letters, she turned to see Toby in the bedroom doorway. He repeated his question. "I said, what are you doing in there?"

She waved the letters at him, in case he hadn't seen she was holding them.

"What have you been doing, going through my things?" He took two steps into the room.

Bridget stood up.

Toby edged further forward, his tone becoming menacing. "I said, what are you doing going through my private things?"

That was the trigger.

"Bastard!" Crushing the letters in her hand, she lunged at him.

He pushed her away and she fell against a mirror on the wall behind. It shuddered as she bounced off it. It was strange how, despite the pain caused by its frame and confrontation with a cheating husband, her immediate concern was that the mirror might fall off the wall.

"Give me those." He pointed at the screwed-up letters in her fist.

She held them up theatrically and began to tear them. "You're nothing but a bastard. A cheating, lying bastard."

"Give me those."

"Cheating, lying bastard."

"Shut up."

"Cheat. Cheat. Cheat."

"Shut. Up. I'm warning you."

"Cheat. Cheat. Fucking, bastard, cheat."

She ripped the paper again and tossed the shards into the air like mock confetti. He lunged forward. He might have been trying to catch a fragment. Or simply cautioning her to stop mocking him. Certainly, his contact with her face wouldn't have counted as a punch by Queensberry Rules, more of a slap by a partially curled hand than a blow from a fist, and there was no follow-through. But it made contact nonetheless. And as it landed, Bridget felt an explosion of pain beneath her left eye.

Toby jumped back. "I didn't mean to do that."

Bridget said nothing. Her first instinct was to put her hand to her nose to see if it was bleeding but she didn't want to show any sign of weakness. If he saw fear, he might do it again. Instead, she turned to look in the mirror. What she saw was not just her eye already puffing up but also Toby's face, reflected and frightened.

"Bridge, I'm sorry. I really didn't mean to do that."

Without a word, she turned and marched for the door. Toby at first looked like he might block her, then stepped aside. He made no attempt to follow as she stormed downstairs, grabbed the car keys and strode out the front door, slamming it behind her.

Her hands were shaking so much she couldn't put the key into the ignition. But once the engine coughed into life, she eased the car forward and round the corner. She knew she was in no condition to drive, so she slipped into the first space, turned off the engine, twisted the rear-view mirror towards her and inspected her eye that was retreating behind the swelling. Had she imagined the last few seconds she would have expected to have cried. But in real life, she didn't. Instead, she kept checking behind to make sure that Toby hadn't followed.

How long she sat there, mulling over the last few hours, she didn't know. She did know that she missed her mum now more than she'd ever thought she could. That was when she knew what to do, restarted the car and pointed it in the direction of her dad.

Chapter 19

"Bastard." That was George's reaction as Bridget, between sobs, explained the bruising round her face. "Sorry, Tara. I know he's your dad. But your mum's my daughter and look what he's done."

"Don't apologise, Gramps. I think he's a bastard, too."

Mark stood there, unwilling spectator, looking as if he should join in and call Toby a bastard as well. It was Bridget who spoke.

"Please don't take it out on your father. If I'd been a better wife…"

"Better wife, Mum? You do everything for him. And he's hit you."

"He's still your father."

"He's still a cheat and a shit. And he's here."

Bridget looked confused. "Who is?"

"Dad." Tara was pointing at the window.

Standing in the garden, peering through the glass, was Toby. He rapped the window, mouthing, 'Let me in.'

"How'd he get here? I brought the car. Don't let him in, please."

George stepped up to the window. "Go away."

"He won't hear you through the double glazing, Gramps."

"He'll notice this." George tugged at a string and the window blind dropped.

"How'd he get here?" Tara echoed her mum.

Before they had a chance to debate likely modes of transport between Basingstoke and London on a Sunday evening, there was a sharp rap on the front door.

"I know you're in there so let me in. Or I'll let myself in."

"Oh, God, he's got the spare key."

George frowned at his daughter. "What key's that?"

Bridget sighed. "We had some spares made. In case something happened to you. Sorry, Dad, but we were worried about you when you came back here."

"Thanks for telling me."

"I'll give you ten seconds to open the door, then I'm coming in to take you home."

"You leave my daughter alone."

"Ten."

"Yes, Dad, go away."

"Nine."

"I'd better go. I don't want to cause any more trouble."

"Eight."

Bridget stood up.

"Seven."

"She's not coming with you." George put his arm across Bridget, gently restraining her. Hunter buried his head under the blanket in his basket.

"Six."

"You hit Mum."

"It was an accident. It won't happen again." A pause, then "Five."

"Again?" George felt a surge of anger pulse through him. "How many times have there been already?"

Another pause. Then, "Four, three."

They heard the sound of a key being inserted into the lock.

"Wait a moment." George let Bridget go.

"What are you going to do, Gramps? You can't let him in."

"Two."

"I don't think you should let him in, Mr T," Mark quavered.

"One."

Before Toby had a chance to turn the key, George swung the door open. Maybe the red wine from lunch or the hurt at being humiliated by Toby made him feel bigger and stronger than he was. Or that his age made him invulnerable, that it was his duty to protect his daughter, granddaughter and the apology for a boyfriend cowering in the kitchen. Had he seen himself in the hall mirror, he might have had second thoughts. Instead, he stood across the doorway, blocking Toby from entering.

"Out of my way, old man."

"You've hit my daughter. You'll have to hit me, too."

"Don't think I won't."

"You're right. I don't think you won't. You. Stooping so low as to threaten a seventy-nine-year-old man. How brave are you?"

George was relieved he delivered this without his voice wavering. His heart was racing now and he didn't know how this was going to end. What if Toby *did* hit him and push his way in? He was no match for a younger man. But he held his ground and stared unflinchingly into Toby's eyes, hoping his doubts weren't showing.

"Yes, bugger off, you bastard." The voice came from behind him. Mark, feeble sallow Mark, had come forward and doubled the human shield. And behind, Hunter, wagging his tail. Inexplicably, the first thought George had from this unexpected show of support from his daughter's boyfriend was he'd promise to help him with his music, even if it meant sacrificing his own ambitions.

"I won't forgive you for this. You wait and see." And with that, Toby turned. George didn't wait to watch him go, firmly pressing the door shut.

"Good riddance," he said, almost treading on Hunter as he headed back to the kitchen. "Now, I had a cup of tea that you made me ages back. Would one of you make a fresh pot, please?"

Chapter 20

"Dad." Bridget gently opened the door of George's record room. She called louder. "Dad." He was in his listening chair, staring at a record. "Daaaad!" Bridget was practically shouting. George jumped, startled by the intrusion.

He spun round and blinked her into focus. "Sorry, didn't hear you, come in."

"What are you doing?"

"Looking at this record. It's very rare. A demo copy of Pink Floyd's 'Apples and Oranges'. I've been wanting to play it for ages and couldn't find it anywhere. Then just now I stumbled across it. Must have misfiled it somehow."

"That's good." She spoke as if her mind were elsewhere. It had been three days since they'd seen off Toby, during which her face had first swollen and now shrunk to reveal a dark shade of blue around her eyes.

"How did you sleep?" he asked.

"Better than the night before. And the night before that." Bridget had taken Tara's room while Tara had moved to the living room sofa. "But I can't keep Tara out of her room for much longer."

"I don't think she'll mind while you sort things out."

"Is that what you do in here? Sort things out?"

"More or less. There's always something to do."

He fell silent, looking across the room at nothing in particular. Bridget looked fondly at her dad. "I miss her too."

He blew out his cheeks. "I remember..." then paused, his shoulders slumping over some distant reminiscence that he kept to himself. "Sorry, what were you saying?"

Bridget moved on quickly. "At least you've still got all these." She waved her arms around at the records. "Every one a memory."

George nodded, sadly. "Just no one to share them with."

"What about all those people you said you played with way back. Where are they?"

"We lost touch over the years."

Bridget hesitated for a moment. "Did you *really* play with those famous people you always talk about?"

"Of course I did. Don't tell me *you* don't believe me. I've told you. I played with them all, played in bands, in my own band."

"Of course I do. It's just..."

"Just what?"

"It's just names and places change sometimes."

"They don't."

"They do."

"Well, maybe I get muddled up with names. There was so much, so many. In such a short time. And it's a long time ago."

Bridget sat down on the footstool. "Did you ever want to be famous like them?"

"They weren't all famous then."

"But after. Were you... jealous?"

"A bit perhaps. Now and again." He thought of telling her about his renewed ambitions, but satisfied himself with, "What's meant to be is meant to be," and let her carry on asking about the past.

"So why them and not you?"

"Lots of reasons. I didn't think I was good enough. At the start. So I never really pushed myself forward. I probably let chances slip. And they don't come twice. Maybe everyone else just had more ambition. Who knows?" He scratched his chin and heaved a great sigh. "Phaedra might have made it. But then..." He looked away.

She finished the sentence for him. "Didn't get the breaks?"

He shrugged. Should he tell her the real reason? When he'd sworn never to?

She reached out and clasped his hand. "As you said, what was meant to be..."

"I was better off than most." He put down the record he'd been holding and eased his way out of his chair. "I played with the best. Really. Great memories." He crossed to the shelves with the S albums and ran his fingers along them, then back, as if searching for something. He pulled out a Paul Simon album. "This was the fellow I'm always talking about. Came to the same folk club I used to go to. You *do* believe me, don't you?"

"Of course."

"This was his first album, before he became famous. I've got a signed one somewhere."

"Must be pretty valuable."

"Three shillings when I bought it, if I remember rightly. Still has the price sticker on it. I'll show it to you." George slipped the unsigned record back, then twice more checked the area where the signed album should have been. "I know I played it just before... you know, your mum." He pulled out a few random LPs to make sure it hadn't slipped to the back. "And nothing's been quite the same in here since that squeeze of Tara's..."

"Mark."

"Yes, Mark. Since he knocked over my records the day Tara moved in." He looked again, trying to remember what he might have done with it, but the record still wasn't there. "I'm sure I had it."

"So how's it going with Tara? Having her here?"

"Aside from having my records tipped over, it's OK. Has its moments."

"Like?"

"I worry when she's late in. Don't really sleep until I hear the front door lock."

"She says you're always asleep in here when she comes in."

"I don't know about that."

"Food, washing, tidying? How's that going?"

"We rub along. We don't really see much of each other and when we do she's always on that phone of hers."

"What about shoes left in the hall? Coats on banisters? Dirty plates in the sink? They used to drive me mad. Or has she become a reformed character?"

"I suppose I wish she wasn't still in her pyjamas in the middle of the day. And she has milk in Earl Grey tea. But is that what you came in to talk about?"

Bridget stood up, as if steeling herself. "I'm going back."

"Really? Toby moved out, then?" He hoped his response betrayed no judgement.

"I don't know. I don't think so. But I have to sort things out with him."

"He punched you." Again, he hoped he sounded clinical, matter of fact.

"He really didn't mean it, I'm sure of that." Bridget's tone too, was calm, measured.

George harrumphed. "How many other times won't he mean it?" He looked directly into her eyes. "You mustn't go back. You really mustn't."

"I'm a grown woman. I'm a mother of a teenage daughter. I can look after myself. And it's my fault as well. I haven't been as good a wife to him as I should have been."

"Rubbish. He's a worthless toad."

"He might be. But I still married him." She pulled a set of car keys from her pocket.

"You're not going now?"

"I've got to. I need to work things out. Sorry it's so sudden. But my mind's made up."

With that, she gave him a hug. He knew he should prevent her from going, say again that she would be best rid of him, that if Toby thought he could get away with it, he'd hit her again, that leopards never change their spots. George also knew there'd be nothing he could say to change her mind.

"Love you, girl."

"Love you, Dad."

Chapter 21

After George had waved Bridget off and watched the car disappear down the road, he closed the door, turned and sat on the stairs. The house felt eerily quiet. He didn't want to disturb it by playing the piano and he didn't feel like playing records while there were missing ones to be found. Their supposed value was nagging at him, too. He could wait until Tara was out and check again on the computer, but after his experience last time he wasn't sure he wanted to.

"I know," he said out loud to himself, then called up the stairs. "I'm going out, Tara. See you later."

"OK, Gramps."

Two bus journeys later, he was back on his old stomping ground. He'd not been to Soho for yonks. Just being back made him feel better, more positive. Except, while the street patterns were just the same, not much else was. The cafés and clubs he'd played back in the sixties had long gone, and whatever had replaced them had gone too. In their place, vapes, street food, poké and matcha bars – whatever they were. Nor were there 'private' shops and 'model shows'. One window declared 'Strip' but it turned out to be a waxing boutique. And no sign of record shops. Even here, where there had once been music for sale on every corner.

A phalanx of Chinese tourists, in rigid formation, faces covered by pollution masks, bustled round a corner straight at him. The only evasive action was to hop into a doorway. This at least had a familiar, worn look. Except, where once you'd have been able to see into a grimy hallway with chipped plaster walls bathed in a soft red light, the way was blocked by a door with a double lock. On one side, a bank of bells testified multiple occupancy. George gasped. One of the labels read 'Domino'. Could it really be her? Was Soho's sleazy reputation intact after all? Had he stumbled on the very building where Sexy Domino was performing inside, even now? What if he rang the bell? Would she let him in? What would she say? What would *he* say?

"'Scuse me." A figure that George recognised instantly as an actor, but couldn't place, reached out and pressed a buzzer. Not any buzzer. Domino's. How had this doyen of television programmes George was unable to recall fallen on such hard times?

The intercom crackled into life. "Domino Post."

"Hi." The anonymous celebrity leaned into the speaker. "Voiceover session, travel agency commercial."

George recognised the voice. He'd always watched *Dr Who* back in the day. This actor used to be on it, he was sure. Maybe even the Doctor himself.

"Third floor. Come on up."

So it was all perfectly innocent. George wasn't sure if he was relieved or disappointed.

The door clicked open, but before the maybe-ex-Time Lord could enter, the step was besieged by the masked Chinese tourists, brandishing scraps of paper, books and bags. Barely smiling and sighing wearily, he signed them all, then, just as quickly, pushed past George, striding into the hallway beyond.

"Excuse *me*," George spluttered at the closing door. But at least he had witnessed first hand what real fame was like. He'd always wondered. The intrusion The Beatles suffered had always felt like it'd been stifling, but adoration on the scale he'd just witnessed seemed rather special. Perhaps he'd ask Ron if he did photo shoots and, when he became famous, he'd come back here and offer to sign them for people.

Stepping back into the street, he glanced at the girls who'd taken off their pollution masks and were giggling excitedly, then walked the opposite way. He was almost immediately rewarded by a dimly lit shop front that, despite its unremarkable window display, seemed to be purveying music. From the type of beats blaring out across the pavement, it seemed unlikely it'd have what he was looking for. His mission was to find a shop that sold oldies, where he could check the prices of the records he owned, maybe even find something new and exciting. It didn't look promising but it was worth a look. He stepped inside.

At the front were cabinets with phones and other electrical appliances he didn't recognise, pausing only to feign interest and casually sidle further into this alien territory. He made out three people browsing, all male, wearing headphones, no one talking. Yet in the murk at the back, a revelation. A bank of turntables for people to audition before they bought. He hadn't seen that since HMV in the late fifties. And racks of albums, in clearly marked sections with names on the dividers. But anticipation turned to disappointment. 'Hard Core' seemed vaguely familiar, but the rest? 'Trip Hop', 'Fusion', 'Planet MU'. He'd boasted to Tara about keeping up to date with music, yet he didn't recognise any of these. It was no better in the racks behind. 'Lobster Theramin'? 'Monkey Town'? 'Osgut Ton'? What were they? Relief came from a corner that was shielded from the music and contained a small box labelled 'Classic Rock'. It was in two sections, one 'Classic Rock A-M', the other 'Classic Rock N-Z'. It took only seconds for George to confirm that no originals by The Beatles and Leafhound were here, nor the lost souls – the Yardbirds with Sonny Boy Williamson and Paul Simon. Worse, the few there were had been sorted under first names, not surnames, a cardinal sin in George's book. He was in the process of moving Van Morrison and Steve Miller from the N-Z section to the A-Ms when, even in the gloom, a tall figure cast a shadow over him.

"I would prefer it if you didn't move all the records about."

George wasn't about to argue with a man a good six inches taller than him. He clearly worked there, though he was dressed in a way that he would expect to be described as 'cool' rather than the traditional dishevelled look of record store owners.

"Can I help you in any way?" The question was asked with an expectation that a man of George's obvious age was beyond help, aside perhaps for an offer of a Zimmer frame.

"Actually, yes."

George's answer seemed to catch the assistant off guard. "How would that be?"

"I was looking for Leafhound." George searched for any sign of recognition. "The Yardbirds? Paul Simon? Originals, of course."

"Who?" It wasn't clear if the assistant was unfamiliar with the genres or the piercing beats from the speaker above them had drowned George out. It didn't matter. George already knew the answer.

"Never mind. I'll try somewhere else."

"There's a shop a hundred metres on the other side." The assistant might have pointed in which direction, but instead stretched across George to restore Stevie Nicks and Steve Miller to the N-Z section.

Back outside, in the comparative silence of roaring motorbikes and car horns, George saw immediately the other shop. He paced down to it and, rather than waste more time browsing, went straight to the counter. The response was more positive.

"We specialise in oldies. Classics and rarities, albums and singles. Our stock's always changing and price depends on condition." He followed George's gaze to a small pile of singles behind him. "Are you interested in those?" He picked one up. "Pink Floyd's 'Apples and Oranges'. Great single. Very hard to find. These are repros, mind. We sell reissues and copies as well as originals. Do you know it?"

"I've got the original."

"Really? If you ever want to sell it..."

"I doubt it." George found himself distracted by a figure he recognised coming from a door on the other side of the shop.

"We'll always give you a best price if you ever do. And you can join our mailing list when you're looking for something to buy. It's always being updated. Just leave us your email or mobile."

George might have retorted he hadn't got an email or mobile but distraction from across the shop had gone past the point of no return. "Thanks," he said, turning towards the front of the shop to intercept the figure he recognised. "Hello, Robin. Fancy seeing you here."

Robin turned in surprise. "Why, hello, George. This is a handy coincidence. I've been trying to reach you."

"This isn't your normal territory. Didn't think you liked music."

"Mate of mine runs it."

"Have you heard from Ron?"

"Should I have?"

"I want to know what's going on with my recordings."

"I thought he was going to phone you."

"Why? What's happened?"

"Maybe he texted. Have you got a mobile?"

"What's going on? Tell me."

"Or emailed."

"Tell me!"

Robin shook his head. "Sorry, my friend. It's not good news, not good news at all."

"How not good?" George braced himself for criticism of his piano playing. "Was I that bad? I told him I didn't like synthesisers."

"It's not that. They've lost what you did last time."

"Lost?"

"Technical fault. The power cut you had. Wiped everything."

"Everything?"

"Everything."

"Nice of Ron to let me know."

"He's been busy."

"Wouldn't have happened if we'd been recording onto tape, not this newfangled computer stuff."

Robin rolled his eyes. "Still, you had a good day, didn't you? Enjoyed yourself."

"It wasn't meant to be a fun day. I went to work. I want my CD. If he's lost it all, I need to get back in there."

"I'm not sure that's possible. Like I said, Ron's very busy."

"You can't just leave it. You promised me."

"I didn't promise you anything."

"I still need to get in there. I've new material too." The chorus of 'Missing Evelyn' had struck up, uninvited, in George's head.

Robin sighed. "I'm not sure I can do anything."

"Have a word."

"I don't think that'll help."

"Please." George hoped he wasn't sounding too pathetic.

"I'll ask Ron to call you."

"When?"

"Or you call him. Gotta go. Be in touch."

* * *

With George out, Tara heaved a sigh. This was the first time in ages she'd had to herself. Her first thought was to the piano. She'd been promising herself she'd put in some much needed practice but somehow there was always something more pressing – a text to answer, an Instagram posting to look at, a web page to browse, Gramps needing help. There could be no excuses this time. Except, as she made her way down from her room, the sun on the stairs picked out dust on the banisters and specks in the carpet. Had anyone done any cleaning since she moved in? The piano would have to wait.

Hoovering the house offered a guilty pleasure. With no one to hear, she became Taylor Swift, letting rip at full throttle, thrusting the pipe back and forth in time to her singing, occasionally posing in front of mirrors, the nozzle her microphone. She only stopped when she reached her grandfather's music room. Here was a dilemma. The forbidden space. She'd promised never to go in. But wasn't this different? Pushing open the door, the state of the open carpet between piles of records answered her question.

"I know you won't mind this once," she explained in a one-sided conversation. "You probably won't even notice."

Picking her way as far round as she dared, she was drawn to a glow of LEDs shining out from an amplifier and CD player that had been left switched on. Her first instinct was to turn them off. Mum was always moaning about wasting electricity. But then

Gramps'd know she'd been in his room. A second thought came to her. What harm would it do to try some CDs? Discover what it was he found so compulsive about this old technology. Yes, there was always the risk he'd come back, find her trespassing. But she'd limit herself to just one. Switching off the hoover, she ran her fingers along the rows of CD spines, looking for Taylor Swift, but stopping when she reached Simon and Garfunkel. He was always talking about them. What would they sound like on his big loudspeakers?

Slipping a silver disc into the player, the silence was filled with strumming guitars and sweet vocals. She surprised herself that she knew some of the songs, harmonising when she could. The lyrics were poetic, personal, angst-ridden – sentiments she recognised. She played the whole album and was about to change it for another when she thought she heard the front door being opened. Replacing everything as she'd found it and grabbing the hoover, she sprinted up to her room, slumping on her bed. From under her pillow, she pulled out a bundle of papers. These were handwritten notes, inspired by the pain she was seeing in her mum and grandfather, composed on buses, in cafés, when she was alone. They'd seemed heartfelt and genuine when she'd written them. Looking at them now, and compared to the lyrics of Paul Simon, they seemed wooden and clumsy. And too personal. But maybe with a bit of effort they could be made to work. Then she'd offer them to Mark. If he ever asked. She resolved to record them anyway. She'd have to tone them down so he wouldn't think they were about him and he'd probably still say they were rubbish. But if she recorded a few lines, maybe he'd use them, even if just cut or distorted to add to a mix.

As the computer booted up, she plugged in a microphone and looked at her notes. She sang a few lines quietly to herself, saw Mark's file upload from his Mark'n'Tara drive and clicked on it. But instead of opening, she saw only the whirring, coloured wheel of death.

Two restarts later, and with nothing working, she phoned Mark. "What have you done to my computer?"

* * *

It was the same question she asked some twenty minutes later when he walked into her room. He'd complained bitterly on the phone that she'd interrupted his uni work, but she guessed he was secretly relieved to get away from it.

"I think you've got a virus," was his prognosis after ten minutes of starting and restarting of his own.

"What do you mean, *I've* got a virus?"

"A virus is all I can think of. Is everything backed up?"

"How is it *my* virus? You're the one who put your sodding music on there."

"I won't bother again, if that's what you think. I'll find someone else's computer to use."

"Well, how else did I get a virus? You uploaded stuff to it."

"Works OK on mine." He restarted the computer yet again. "I'll give it one more go."

Tara was relieved he didn't look like carrying out his threat of abandoning her. She watched him as he jabbed his fingers at the keyboard, bringing something to life. "Shall I make some tea?"

"I'll go." He jumped up. "Let it try what I've just done there. It'll take a few minutes."

* * *

"Tea, Mr T," Mark called as he passed the music room on his way up with a tray of mugs and biscuits. There was no reply, so he knocked gently and poked his head round the door. He could see George with his eyes closed, a CD softly playing. "Tea, Mr T," he said again, enjoying the rhythm of his question. When George didn't respond Mark stepped forward and tapped him on the shoulder. George sat up abruptly.

"Sorry, did I make you jump?" Mark asked.

George opened his eyes blearily. "I was miles away."

"Didn't mean to disturb you. I've made you some tea."

"Thanks. Put it down there." George reached across and turned the volume down and waved the CD case. "Brilliant album this. Do you know it? From the 1960s. Digital remaster."

Mark shook his head. "Biscuit?"

"No thanks. When did you come in? I thought I was alone in the house."

"I haven't been here long. Tara's been here ages, though."

"I didn't hear you. Glad you found the Hobnobs. Hope you didn't leave any crumbs that Hunter might pick up."

"I was very careful."

"I met a thespian today."

"Thespian?"

"Actor. Used to be on TV."

"Really? Anyone I'd know?"

George shook his head. "Can't remember. Was a Dr Who, maybe? They all become a blur at my age."

"So how do you know he was famous?"

"I was standing right next to him. In a doorway. In Soho."

Mark frowned. "OK. I'd better go. Tara's tea's getting cold." He realised George was scrutinising him.

"You haven't been in here, have you?" George asked, his eyes searching for a reaction from Mark.

"No. You said we're not allowed. Why?"

"When I've not been here?"

"No. What's wrong?"

"Nothing much. And you haven't been going through my records?"

"No."

"OK, then." George paused as Mark turned to leave, then added, "It's just I have the feeling something's different."

"Different?"

"I don't know. Probably my age! Never mind."

Without waiting for any further comment, George turned the volume back up. Summarily dismissed, Mark backed out between the shelves. By the time he reached Tara's bedroom door, tea was slopping out over the tray and Hobnobs.

"Tea up. And soggy biscuits."

Tara was at the screen. "It's going now. What did you do?" She was logging on to the internet while waiting for Mark's music files to load.

"Did a virus search, then quarantined and deleted whatever was causing the problem. Don't know where it came from. It couldn't have been my music. I wonder if the drive I used has got something yours doesn't like." He put the tray down beside her.

"You weren't joking about the soggy biscuits." Tara picked one up that folded in half and fell back on to the plate.

"Just call them pre-dunked. But you'll never guess where I found them."

"In the sink?"

"Nope."

"I don't know. Biscuit barrel?"

"Tea caddy. Is your Gramps alright?"

"Why?"

"It's not just the biscuits. He said he met an actor. Thespian he called him. In a doorway. Says it was Dr Who. And he just said he thinks people are going through his records. He's not losing it, is he?"

"Hmm." Tara was not listening but glowering over her computer. "You've been using my computer to help make your music, right?"

"Not since last week."

"What else did you do while you were working on your music files?"

"What else? What do you mean 'what else'?"

"You know."

"I don't, honestly. What?"

She prodded the screen, accusingly.

He leaned forward to where she was pointing.

"You've done your fingernails. I like that colour." Her hands were one of the things he loved most about her and always found it sexy after she had her nails newly painted.

"Don't change the subject. What is *this*?"

She jabbed an accusing finger at the screen, jabbing her fingers at what had just loaded. 'LivePhaedra.com'.

He peered at the blank box on the screen and message: 'Model offline.' "I've no idea. What is it?"

"How dare you. How dare you look at porn? On *my* computer." Tara let him have it, full on. The hands that Mark had found so alluring a few moments earlier were now pummelling him in the chest.

"How dare you. How dare you." She paused for breath.

Mark, caught out by this onslaught, only now put his hands up in defence and cowered back. But Tara simply stepped forward and carried on, pummelling his palm instead, in a gesture more futile than with any intent to hurt. She was crying now. "How could you, how could you?"

As she slowed, Mark leaned forward to put his arms round her, to comfort her.

"Keep your grubby hands off me." She slumped back into the chair.

"Look, Tara, it wasn't me, I really don't know what…" he leaned in towards the screen, "…'LivePhaedra' is. I really, honestly don't."

"Well it wasn't me and someone's looked at it on my computer."

The icy silence that fell between them was broken only by gentle footsteps on the landing followed by the sound of George's bedroom door quietly closing.

"I think that solves that," Tara giggled. "Who would have believed it?"

"Say sorry."

"I can do better than that."

* * *

"I love it when we make up." Mark was talking as he lay on Tara's bed, watching as she slipped on her bra. "Can we have another argument?"

"I do worry about Gramps."

"I think it's quite funny. And you're giving people in the road a great view of you in your underwear."

Tara stepped back and pulled a jumper over her head. "It's not funny if he's starting to get dementia and acting funny. The biscuits. Now the computer." Her voice trailed off.

"You're not his keeper." Mark kept watching as she wriggled into her jeans. "Can I ask you something?"

"What?"

"And I'm not getting dementia."

"Please don't make fun of Gramps."

"I'm not. It's just I'm having a bit of trouble with my music."

"Trouble?" Tara's heart skipped a beat.

"Yeah. Like writer's block. Call it musician's block. Maybe you could help."

Chapter 22

The house felt cold when Bridget let herself in. The curtains were closed and it smelt musty like it did whenever she and Toby came back from holiday. She wasn't sure why she was there. Hoping that everything was a mistake, maybe? For reconciliation with Toby? Or maybe a declaration of war? So she was relieved to find no signs of life.

She inspected every room for signs of change, signs of life, maybe even a message. But the house was deserted.

She deleted three missed calls, none leaving a message. She thought about the time people used to leave messages – invitations to dinner, friends catching up, calls for Tara, Mum wanting news. It all seemed so long ago. She found herself staring at a wedding photograph on a shelf. They all looked so happy, so full of expectation and anticipation.

"This won't do," she cried out loud to no one. And if there was no one, what was there *to* do? She poured herself a glass of wine and opened the post. There was a pile of envelopes but nothing of interest. That there was so much suggested Toby hadn't been back since he'd chased her to London on Sunday. At least she was safe to stay, though she put the chain on the door to make sure. Then with glass in hand, she tiptoed upstairs. She wasn't sure why, but protecting the silence seemed right.

Their bedroom was unchanged, except the confetti of letters she'd torn up had been cleared away. She looked inside the wardrobe. If Toby had moved out, he'd not taken much by way of clothes. She slid the hangers along the rail to check if anything was missing. But what would that prove? That he wasn't coming back? That he had a duplicate wardrobe somewhere else?

Of more interest now was what stood on the wardrobe floor. The shoebox of letters was gone. All that was left were the cardboard boxes that had been hidden under fleeces. She tugged at the closest one. Whatever was inside, it was very heavy. Grasping hold of the edges, she dragged it forward so that it thumped on to the bedroom floor. She clawed her fists and ripped at the top.

Inside were records. Vinyl LPs. Rammed in so it was impossible to slide any out. She tipped the box over but still they wouldn't budge. Kicking at the bottom succeeding only in jarring her toes but not displacing the contents. Grappling with the top of the box proved more effective, using all her strength to rip the side off.

"Gotcha."

She lifted up the top one. Carl Perkins. She didn't recognise the name, but it looked old. "What was he doing with you?" she asked out loud. "And why has he kept you hidden?" Without Toby to give evidence, the record remained tight-lipped.

She dropped Carl Perkins on the floor and lifted up the next. This time, she recognised the name. Jerry Lee Lewis. Dad had played his music to her. Out of respect, she laid this one down more carefully. She could imagine George's anguish if he saw her mistreating records. Under it was the Yardbirds.

Dad had talked about them at the Ramsays'. Would he be interested in seeing these? Stupid question – of course he would. She looked through a few more. All seemed old, some names she recognised, a couple still shrink-wrapped, but nothing that had played a part in her life with Toby. If he'd had them all the years they'd been together, how come he hadn't mentioned them? And why were they under fleeces in his wardrobe, hidden away?

The remaining boxes defeated her – she now could see there were about five more, stretching the full length of the wardrobe and double stacked at the back, but they were too heavy and too awkward to reach. She'd try again another day.

* * *

Bridget said nothing of her discovery a few days later when she came back to London. She was sitting in CuppaCoffee, drinking a cappuccino with Tara. The tables were dirty and music loud. She would have preferred to have gone to the coffee chain shop next door, but Tara called CuppaCoffee her local. At least it was neutral territory and out of earshot of George.

"So how was it?"

"He wasn't there."

"And?"

"I think he's moved out."

"Oh."

"I'm sorry." Bridget placed her hand on her daughter's. "I think it's over. I didn't want this to happen. Not again…"

Tara withdrew her hand as she interrupted. "It's not anything to do with me. And the way he treated you, I'd leave too."

"I'm getting the locks changed. I'll get a spare key. For you."

"Thanks."

"I hope you'll stay friends with him. He's still your dad."

Tara took a deep breath and puffed out her cheeks. "What happened? What went wrong?"

"It'd been difficult for a while."

"Nothing to do with Gramps staying with you?"

Bridget shook her head. "I don't know. Maybe. I don't really want to talk about it."

A child ran screaming past, creating sufficient punctuation for Tara to change the subject.

"I think that child follows me around. It seems to be here whenever I come in. Was I ever that bad?"

"Don't ask."

"Go on, tell me."

Bridget smiled for the first time in days.

"You used to walk around restaurants with your favourite soft toy…"

"Koala Katy?"

"… yes, Koala Katy. You'd say 'hello' to everyone, then introduce them to Koala Katy. They had to say 'hello' back before you moved on to the next table."

"Didn't people mind?"

"Mostly not. And if they did…" Bridget's voice trailed off.

"They did what?"

"Your dad would bring you back." She went quiet, remembering the kicking and screaming and how good he was at calming her down – how good he used to be at being a kind and loving father. Although Tara knew none of this, she recognised her cue to change the subject again.

"Are you going to stay there or coming back to Gramps'?"

"I'm OK to stay there. I've got too, anyway. I've got a job in the school round the corner, so I have to be there."

"I didn't know you'd looked for a job."

"I don't tell you all my secrets. It's only part time in an office, but they seem like a good group of people. Certainly better than moping around an empty house all day." She paused, thinking of how her life seemed to revolve around empty houses – first her father's, now her own – places that had once been so full of life. Memories. How they kept provoking her. She hoped the child would come screaming past again. But he seemed to have gone. She pulled herself back into the present. "How's Mark?"

"He's OK. He texted me this morning to say we've been invited to a weekend in a country house by some of his uni friends."

"Sounds exciting."

Tara shrugged. "We'll see."

"And the music. How's it going? Didn't you say you were getting more involved? Are you writing or singing?"

"Yeah. It's fine."

"Fine? That doesn't sound very positive."

"Well, it is and it isn't. I think Mark is getting too stuck up his own…"

"Arse?"

They both laughed. "I wasn't going to say that, but yes, probably. The other day, he said he was composing sounds to represent a pizza."

"A pizza?"

"A pizza – he played me something and said that's how a pizza would sound if it was music. I had no idea what he was talking about."

Bridget wanted to ask if Tara's voice would make a good topping but thought better of it. Instead, she asked how uni was going, and all thoughts of men were lost to chat like they used to have before everything started going wrong.

It must have been over an hour later before Tara got back to her grandfather's house. Mark and George were making music. She knew this before she had even turned the corner of the road, it was so loud. She followed the sounds through the front door and up the stairs, into her room.

Pounding a keyboard she'd never seen before and that was linked to her computer was George, sitting on the piano stool from the living room. His left hand was playing a blues riff, his right an unrelated series of staccato chords. Next to him, a loudspeaker was emitting thumping electronic sounds, controlled by Mark who was wearing headphones, fingering a mouse and concentrating on a digital mixing desk. On the floor, a pair of microphones was pointing at the ceiling.

"Wow." Tara had her hands over her ears. Her entry was unacknowledged. "Wow!" she said again, this time more loudly. Still they continued. She let out a piercing scream.

Mark ripped off the headphones. "You nearly deafened me."

"How was I any louder than that racket?" She was yelling while George kept playing, seemingly unaware that the jam session had come to an abrupt halt. "Gramps. Gramps! Stop!" She put her hands over George's to stop him.

"Oi, why did you do that? We were having fun."

"Fun? It's not what I'd call it. Where did that come from?" Tara was pointing at the electronic keyboard.

"Saw it online. Your Gramps' suggestion, actually. But you've given me an idea." Mark had put his headphones back on. "Can you scream again for me?"

"No."

"Please – I think I might be on to something."

She gave a heavy sigh.

"Louder."

"That wasn't meant to be a scream. Oh, never mind. If I must…"

And with that, she screamed for him.

"Brilliant. And what did you say before? Say it again. No, sing it again."

"I can't remember what I did."

"Doesn't matter. Anything."

"Tra la la la."

"Be sensible. Make something up."

"Am I role playing? Am I a baguette? Or a lampshade?"

"Anything. Words. Short sentences."

"What were you playing, Gramps?"

George answered in a tune. "I was just making things up," he sang, "anything I liked the sound of."

"That's it. He can do it. You try, Tara."

"I really don't want to do this."

"Do what you talked about with your mum. Short bursts of song. Doesn't need a tune. Just be musical."

"I'll show you." George played the opening notes of a twelve-bar blues and did his best Blind Lemon Jefferson impersonation.

"Well, you woke up this morning,
To go meet your mum.
Well, you woke up this morning,
To go meet your mum.
And when you got to the café
All their croissants had gone."

Mark pulled a face. "Not exactly…"

"Tell you what, I'll leave you to it." George scraped the piano stool back, gave the keyboard a final flourish, then headed out.

"I didn't mean that…"

"Yes you do. It's Tara's voice you need. And about time too. Can't you hear what a lovely voice she's got?"

"Gramps!"

"Sorry. But you two get on with it. I was getting tired anyway."

* * *

Once outside, George hesitated. It was something of an understatement to say he was tired. They'd been jamming – if that was what it was called – for well over an hour and his wrists and shoulders were aching. It had started when Mark appeared to show a first genuine interest in 'real' music. He'd actually asked for help, and when the keyboard and microphones came out George had felt a sense of achievement. Mark seemed more open to ideas as they'd talked about hooks and choruses. Doubts crept in every time he played anything resembling melody and Mark would stop him with, "Just chords. Unrelated. Not a tune." Or, "Play louder, harder, tougher." But it was progress. And although he hated to admit it, ever since the night they'd stood together in the doorway against Toby, he'd started to like the boy.

From the landing, he listened to similar instructions being barked at Tara.

"Just do me short phrases. I don't want a tune."

Perhaps he'd have a word later. How could he not hear how good Tara was? Her voice was strong yet plaintive and appealing. He couldn't make the words out exactly, but what was quite clear was the sensitivity of her delivery. What might Phaedra and the Phaeries have achieved if they'd had someone like her on lead? But Mark kept interrupting like he'd been doing to him. "I said. Not a tune." "Just do me short phrases." "Again, but louder, angrier." Then, "That's it, more, more."

George left them to it. He knew he really ought to get back to his piano and refine 'Missing Evelyn' for when Robin or Ron got back to him. But he'd left the piano stool in Tara's room and, anyway, he really didn't feel in the mood. Instead, he did what he should have done ages back. Picking up the phone, he pressed the 'last caller' button. He expected Robin's voice, but instead it was a female with a clipped, precise tone.

'The number you have called is not recognised. Please check the number and dial again.'

This created a dilemma. What if he did and got the same response? That would just prove he had been wrong to trust Robin. And what if Robin did pick up and had bad news? George couldn't face either. Instead, he dropped the phone back on its cradle and headed to his room to immerse himself in his records. But he didn't play any. Instead, he simply stared at a row of albums, at first barely looking at them, appreciating how they were always there and never let him down. Then, bending down and leaning in, he read the familiar names and titles along the edges, fondly running a finger down ones he loved most. Turning to a shelf of singles, he lifted out a handful, but instead of taking them to his record deck, perched them on his lap, settled back into his chair and flipped through them, checking the titles and hearing voices singing in his head.

"Gramps."

He felt a soft hand on his arm and Tara looking down at him.

"Where did you come from?"

"I've been here for a few moments." Tara took her hand away. "I'd been knocking on your door and when you didn't answer, wondered if everything was alright."

"I didn't hear you, sorry. You finished recording?"

"Ages back. Been having a break."

"I must have nodded off."

George straightened the pile of records that were slipping from his grasp. At his feet was a solitary empty sleeve. He looked around to see where the record had rolled. It was standing upright against some shelves. He gave a little laugh.

"What's funny?"

"That record." He reached down to pick up the sleeve. "It was in the wrong place. All these were F." He lifted the records from his lap to the floor.

"Sorry if that's Mark's accident again."

"But it's funny." George was picking up the escapee and inspecting it to make sure there was no damage from its roll across the floor. "It's by the Quiet Five. Should have been in with the Qs."

"Like I said…"

George wasn't interested in Tara's apology. "It'd rolled to where I keep the Qs. Like it was finding its own way home. And what makes it really funny – look." He held it out towards her.

"The Quiet Five." Tara could see nothing funny.

"Look closely."

She leaned in. "Columbia?"

"That's the record label – the company that manufactured it. Look closer."

She shrugged. "Give up."

George pointed at the label. "The song title. 'Homeward Bound'. The record's lived up to its name. It rolled home."

"Oh. I get it." Tara didn't find it as funny as George, who was still smiling fondly at the recalcitrant disc.

"It was written by – sorry if I've told you this before – by Paul Simon. Bloke I played with. They copied it." He waved the record as he spoke. "It was what all English groups did, copied American songs, hoping to have hits with them. Swinging England it was called."

Tara nodded politely, which gave George licence to reminisce again.

"And the Americans loved us. We were all suits and long hair – long by sixties standards, anyway. They lapped it up over there – they called it the British Invasion."

"Did you invade? Your band? America?"

Before George could answer, Mark had put his head round the door. "There you are. Can we get started again?"

"Sorry, Gramps. Got to go. Oh, nearly forgot what I came in to say. Mark and I are going to a party over the weekend. It'll mean I'm not here. Is that OK?"

"Of course it's OK. Where are you going?"

"One of his friends has a country house."

"I hope it's not haunted."

"Me too. You sure you'll be alright? On your own."

"If you mean your dad, I don't think he'll be back."

"Keep the chain on the door in case."

"I will. You go and enjoy yourself." In George's mind was not Toby. A weekend to himself would mean he could work not just on 'Missing Evelyn' but also on some other new material without interruption.

"Thanks." Tara kissed him on the cheek and chased after Mark.

"And make him let you sing properly," he called as she closed the door on him, but he didn't think she heard.

Chapter 23

Tara spent the next few days worrying about the weekend away with Mark, hoping it wouldn't be as bad as she feared. What to wear? A country house? Was that jeans or a dress? Sandals, shoes? Who was going? How many would be there? She hated large crowds. And what would they be doing? She knew there'd be alcohol. What else? Muddy walks, horse riding, grouse shooting? Drugs, orgies? What if she was the only girl?

She'd laid out her wardrobe on her bed before choosing what to take, making sure she had alternatives to wear over the weekend, plus four pairs of shoes and sufficient toiletries and shampoos. On reflection, there was enough for a fortnight, but better safe than sorry. The first suitcase she tried to pack them into was too small. The second was hard to lift but she was going to look and smell good, whatever happened.

When a minibus arrived to pick her up on the Saturday morning, Mark jumped out, but instead of greeting her, pointed instead at the case.

"What's that?"

"I just threw a few things together, that's all."

"It's only one night." He opened the back doors of the minibus to reveal that everyone else had only the smallest of grips and bags. "It's not going to fit."

"Sorry."

Mark lifted her case and slung it onto the other bags where it immediately shifted and slid back out, bringing with it three smaller cases and a plastic bin bag. "Shit." He lunged forward to slam shut the doors and prevent an avalanche, but the bin bag was ahead of him, getting trapped in the doors and spilling personal possessions into the road. "Don't just stand there, help me, will you." His urgent tone was accompanied by a mobile ringing. "Double shit."

"Everything alright out there?" came a voice from inside the minibus.

"It will be," Tara called back.

"Not if I don't take this call," Mark hissed at her. "Hold these, will you?"

Tara swapped with Mark, ramming her hands against the doors while he fumbled through his pockets. By the time he'd produced his mobile, the ringing had stopped. "If I've lost this, I'll blame you."

"Can we sort out these doors? Then you can start blaming me."

"None of this would have happened if you'd brought a proper-sized bag." He stooped down and scrabbled in the gutter, collecting a toothbrush, deodorant can, sock and pair of men's underpants, then crouched under the doors. "Gently let the doors open just a bit."

Tara released the pressure on her hands and the bag slipped down for Mark to catch. "Right, just let one door open enough for me to sling this bag back in, then slam them both shut. Ready? 3-2-1."

"What's going on out there?" came another cry from inside as the doors banged and the bags inside cascaded against the glass.

"That was entertaining. You must be Tara." The voice came from the steps at the front of the minibus. "I'm Jeff." He looked a stereotypical Australian – big, blonde hair and broad shoulders – and his voice betrayed the same roots.

"Pleased to meet you." Tara went to shake his hand. Instead, he gave her a kiss on the cheek.

"Pleased to meet *you*. Mark's told me all about you."

"All good I hope."

"Probably not good enough. Hop in and I'll introduce you to our little party. You OK, Mark?" Jeff was watching as Mark desperately fingered his mobile.

"Is it just us?" Tara asked.

"I don't know what Mark's said but, yes, just us."

Tara climbed inside, and was relieved to see that of the eight people in the bus, five were girls and all looked respectable. That ruled out some of the fears she had of the weekend, though not the orgy.

"Let me introduce you – there'll be a test at the end," Jeff announced from behind her. "You already know Mark, wherever he is."

"I'm on my mobile," came Mark's voice from outside.

"Well bloody get a move on, mate." Jeff pointed at the faces peering above the seat backs. "That's Col and Jen, Ian and Natasha, Ant and Maya." They all waved in turn. "And up the back is Kim and Emily. Everyone, this is Tara." While everyone chorused in unison, "Hello, Tara," Tara let out a deep breath of relief that the weekend might be OK, masking it with a nervous smile. Jeff noticed it.

"You worried you might be being kidnapped?"

"Nothing like that."

"Or a rave? Nothing like that, either. My stepdad's just away for the weekend. He'll kill me if we do anything to the place. So it'll be all very British."

"How far away are we going?"

"It's not that far. Hasn't Mark told you anything?"

"Just it's a country house."

"That's about it. It's in Oxfordshire. It's not a palace or anything. It's not even a mansion. No maids or servants. You lot abolished slavery a while back if I'm right."

Tara sat down in the nearest empty seat. "And we tried to get shot of our convicts, too, except they keep coming back."

"Touché." He nodded at Mark who was now scrambling on board. "You struck lucky there, mate." Then, raising his voice, he announced, "Right, seat belts on, everyone. There are tinnies at the back. Col, hand 'em round to anyone who wants one, will you?" He settled himself into the driver's seat and adjusted the mirror. "Next stop, my place."

* * *

Saturday passed and Tara's fears about the weekend seemed misplaced. It was alcohol infused but relaxed, friendly and carefree. It was too cold to do much more than wander around the garden. The rest of the afternoon passed with talk about politics, art, trivia, and there were board games involving silly noises, blindfolds and Post-Its, but nothing like she had feared. Team games might have been awkward, there being eleven of them, but it was made easy by Mark disappearing almost as soon as they'd arrived. They'd hardly spoken on the journey. She'd asked him what was so important about the missed phone call and he'd said he'd tell her when no one could overhear. Then he went AWOL. But Tara hardly missed him. She couldn't remember talking and laughing so much in ages. A couple of times she checked her mobile in case there was a message from her mum or Gramps. There wasn't, but that didn't stop her worrying and wishing she could get thoughts of them out of her head. As the day drew on, the company, conversation and alcohol succeeded in doing just that.

* * *

Saturday night was going to be a barbecue, despite the time of year. "We do it in Brisbane all year," Jeff said. But it started to drizzle halfway through the afternoon, so the plan changed to ordering a takeaway. Except being in the country meant Jeff taking orders and driving to the nearest town.

"Wanna come?" he asked Tara.

"No thanks. But have you seen Mark?"

"He's setting up in the conservatory."

"Setting up?"

"Yeah, we're looking forward to you both."

* * *

It took a while for Tara to find Mark. "What's going on?" she rasped when she saw him, cables in hand, behind a set of loudspeakers. Beside them were a keyboard, laptop, microphone and Mark'n'Tara drive.

"It's for tonight."

"You didn't say you were doing a gig. And you've not told me what was going on this morning, either."

"The gig's a last-minute thing. Jeff's idea. The call was from Zak."

"Zak?"

"You know, I told you about him."

"You didn't."

- 217 -

"Oh. I meant to."

"Well you didn't."

"He's the brother of someone in my music group. She wants to use my music in an art installation she's doing."

"She?"

"Chris. You don't know her."

"Should I?" Tara wondered if this girl was a threat. Mark was certainly looking uncomfortable. And did she care?

"Her brother is Zak. He's in the music industry. He heard my music. Says he's interested in it. That call was about getting together. I thought if I missed it, he might lose interest."

"And has he?"

"He's going to call on Monday."

Tara looked at the equipment suspiciously. "Well don't make it too loud. It's only a small conservatory."

"There's another thing. You know I told you I was putting online the music I recorded with you and Gramps?"

"You didn't, but go on." Tara blanched when Mark called her grandfather Gramps. It was her special name for her grandfather. It was one of the first words she'd learnt to say and she didn't care for it being hijacked, even by Mark. *Especially* by Mark. She made a mental note to bring it up with him sooner or later. "And you didn't tell me about Zak, either. Or Chris."

"Oh. Well anyway, I did put it online and it's getting hits and Zak likes it. And I said we'd play it tonight."

"We?"

"It's me mostly, but I think they'll expect you to join in a bit."

"You can count me out."

"Jeff thought it'd be a good idea." He started putting plugs into sockets.

"You can use what you've got on your drives."

"No, I need you." Mark carried on connecting cables.

"You can carry on needing. Because I'm not doing it."

"Please. They're expecting us. I promised them."

"Without telling me?"

"Please."

"And do what? I've no idea what you've been doing."

"Improvise."

"Improvise?" Tara knew she was shrieking but didn't care if the others could hear.

"Like you did in your room when I recorded you. Alongside my sounds."

"That'll be rubbish. I'm not doing it."

"All you'll need to do is just follow me on the keyboard. I'll cue you. Just make it up. You're good at that."

"When I've never heard it before? I'll just look stupid."

"They're friends."

"Maybe your friends. I hardly know them."

"They'll be alright. They know all about you. They've heard you online."

"That's even more embarrassing. Leave me out."

"Really, I need you to say 'yes.'"

"And do what? Go 'la la la'? I wish I hadn't come."

"There's these." Mark reached out to the keyboard bag. "After I talked about music to Gramps…"

Sooner rather than later.

"… I had some ideas." He pulled out sheets of paper. "Look." He held them out for her to read, but didn't let go. There was a mix of single handwritten words and printed lines, looking suspiciously like couplets. "I've created some new tracks and you can do these over them. It'll be easy enough."

"And do what exactly with them? You're not making any sense. How can I do anything if I don't know the music?" She was careful not to say 'tune.'

"Chant. Harmonise. Be creative. Just sing."

"You guys ready?" Before Tara could refuse, Ant had poked his head round the doorframe. "Jeff's back with the food. Then I think we're in here as your eager audience."

"We can't let them down," Mark whispered as they followed him and the curry odour trail.

Tara grabbed the papers without speaking.

* * *

Meal over, they all moved into the conservatory as threatened. Everyone watched as Mark and Tara silently finished connecting keyboard, computer, drives, microphone and speakers. All eyes seemed to be on Tara. There was no backing out now. What had Mark been saying about her? As she leaned forward to adjust the mike stand in front of everyone, she realised her short, loose top was gaping and too revealing. Jeff's eyes seemed glued on her until he realised Tara was looking back at him.

"Can I be your groupie when you're famous?" he asked, then corrected himself. "Roadie. I meant roadie. Can I be your roadie?" He flushed red.

The effect on Tara was to make her more determined to sing well, even if she had no idea what she was going to do. And she didn't let herself down. Mark began by playing four of the tracks put down in Tara's room. She allowed the recordings to dominate, adding occasional words and voice sounds for effect and to give it a live feel. She felt stupid and self-conscious but hoped it didn't show. Each track was greeted with applause and clapping – encouraging, appreciative, positive, but polite. Tara caught Ant checking his watch during the third track and Ian and Natasha exchanged doubtful glances during the fourth.

"And now some new stuff," Mark announced. He took the papers he'd given Tara before supper, shuffled them as if looking for something specific, then turned them over before handing back one she hadn't seen.

"Very new. So new I don't know what it is," she said, trying to joke away her embarrassment. The group waited, smiling patiently in silence and expectation while Tara scanned Mark's words. Each line could have been about the two of them. About lust, desire, confusion, disappointment. She hoped they couldn't read her face while she adjusted to the revelations. She might yet have said she wouldn't do it, but Mark had started to play. His head was down, eyes switching rapidly between keyboard and computer screen. She cleared her throat.

What now throbbed through the speakers began as a rhythm track – a mash-up of George's keyboard and electronic sounds, melded together as surreal and eerie. Mark let it build, tapping his fingers on single keys to create sonic variations before stretching his fingers across the whole keyboard that echoed and filled the room. He let it decay for a moment, then swung round from the computer towards Tara and nodded. It was her cue.

She glanced at the lyrics and took a deep breath. Her voice was effortless, clear and haunted, sometimes breaking with emotion as she reached a word or line that felt especially poignant or revealing. She wove her own simple, heartfelt melody, allowing the ebb and flow of her voice to be led by Mark's variation in pitch and tone. She was tentative, nervous, at least at first, and it was so unlike anything they had done before. Closing her eyes, she became absorbed in it, swaying to her own rhythm, adding words and phrases of her own. It had a magic and she could sense the group feeling it. When she re-opened her eyes, Mark was shaking his head, glaring at her that she wasn't following his lead. When she ignored him, he brought it to an end. Spontaneously, everyone was on their feet, no longer politely clapping, but cheering, standing, baying for more.

Mark clicked a mouse and the speakers boomed with a different mash-up of wails, single words, piano chords and syllables. Piercing his eyes at her, he pointed at his keyboard then at himself, a gesture that could only mean to follow him. But she no longer cared. She was confident, taking control, making the music hers, dominating the floor. Mark was following now, mixing and cross-fading his recorded tracks to complement her. And everyone loved it, swaying, arms waving, lights on mobiles casting a soft light across Tara's face. No one was checking for the time now.

After about four minutes, Mark stepped out from behind the keyboard and waved down the hollering that belied there were only nine people watching. Tara dropped the lyric papers, emotionally drained.

"I'm sorry." Mark spoke when the noise subsided at last. "That's all we've got." He stepped back to the keyboard and was about to speak again, but he was drowned out.

"Shame."

"More."

"Encore."

"How about," it was Jeff speaking, "that you do those last ones again." He was looking at Tara as if he was feeling the pain she'd sung. The rest were whooping again.

"More, more, more," they chanted, clapping in rhythm.

"I can't remember what I sang, but I'll give it a go," Tara whispered to Mark.

"I think we should stop."

But the chanting was relentless and showed no sign of subsiding. And Tara showed no sign of wanting to stop. She collected up Mark's lyrics. And they performed it all a second time. Whether it was the same or not, no one seemed to care. Even when Mark stepped back on to a cable and the microphone and keyboard were temporarily silenced, no one minded as Tara kept going *a capella*. First, Mark's lyrics, then phrases from her own lyrics that she'd memorised, then mixing them into songs she knew. Heartfelt. Plaintive. Beautiful. The crackle from the muted speaker when the cable was reinserted seemed like a deliberately stripped-down rhythm track. Mark was reconnected, but all eyes were on Tara. It was only when she was ready to stop did he play a final note and let it fade away. He sat back and watched as the girls ran to her, hugging her while she bowed her head and lowered the mike, exhausted, emotionally drained, and while the boys stepped forward to applaud as heartily as they dared.

* * *

"I think I really would like to be her groupie," Jeff whispered to Ian as they walked up the stairs to bed much later that night.

Chapter 24

It was well past two in the morning when Tara threw herself on to the bed, drained but elated. Mark was already there, lying on his back, staring at the ceiling. He'd not joined the group when they'd drifted to the lounge, slumping until the wine and conversation were exhausted.

"That went really well, better than I thought," she said, expecting a compliment in return at the very least. "Where did you go?"

"Someone had to put the kit away."

"Went well though, didn't it?"

Mark responded through clenched teeth. "No it fuckin' didn't."

Uncomprehending, Tara wearily turned her head towards him. He didn't move, eyes fixed firmly upwards. "I set the gig up, I had my music ready and you fucking took it over."

Tara looked uneasily around, as if to check no one had crept into the room with them. "I thought we were a team." She was whispering. It may have been an old house, but she didn't trust walls to keep secrets. "What does it say in your drive? Mark'n'Tara?"

Mark made no allowances for secrecy. "It didn't fucking feel like it, not the way you kept taking it over. It's not as if you'd done anything. I did all the work. All you did was add a few screams. Under my direction. And I edited them. I asked you to improvise tonight, not fucking take over!" He was shouting now.

Tara sat up, tiredness forgotten. "I did nothing? Excuse me..." She resisted the temptation to crow over the reaction to her singing, at least while they may have been overheard. She might even have let it all drop, putting it down to alcohol or tiredness, expecting it all to be forgotten in the morning. But Mark still kept going.

"You wouldn't stop. I never got the chance with my other music."

"What other music? You didn't say anything about anything else."

"You didn't ask and you didn't let me. That I'd done when you weren't there, with Gramps."

It was no longer 'sooner or later'. It was now or never. She was standing now. "He's not fucking Gramps to you." The thickness of the walls was forgotten. She was yelling too. "That's my special name and you have no right to use it. And me taking over? It's you trying to take *me* over. And I'm sick of you and your attitude and your so-called music. What about *my* music? It was me they liked. If you don't like what I do, do it by yourself." She picked up the pillows she'd been resting on as she spoke, shaking and beating rather than straightening them. "When we get out of here, I never want to see you again."

Her outburst at least spared those in neighbouring rooms the disturbance of further loud exchanges.

She spent the night sleeping on the floor and they did their best to avoid each other the following day. In fact they barely looked at one another, let alone speak again, for the rest of the weekend.

"Is everything OK?" Jeff asked Tara after breakfast.

"OK?"

"You and Mark. Things seem a bit odd."

"Yeah, we're OK," she lied.

"And are you excited?"

"About what?"

"Hasn't he shown you?"

"Shown me what?"

Jeff pulled out his mobile and flicked through some screens before handing it to her. There she was, on video, on Facebook. With 5,000 hits. "How did that get there?"

"I did it on my mobile. Uploaded it overnight. I think people like you."

* * *

In the days that followed, Jeff sent her texts to keep her up to date with the growing number of hits and Twitter and Instagram posts. When he set up a WhatsApp group between them, conversation broadened, first asking if a scarf left in the minibus had been hers and, if it was, should he bring it round to her (it wasn't), then asking the names of the songs she'd sung (she couldn't say as they didn't have any), before sharing pictures and jokes (which she found funny). By the end of the week, she'd sent back as many messages as she'd received.

She revealed none of this to her grandfather when he asked her how the weekend had gone. It'd been good, she'd said, and that Mark had done an impromptu gig. But she was feeling really positive about herself, more energised than she'd been for ages; free, maybe even cleansed. It was this spirit that promoted her to surprise her grandfather.

"Fancy going to the seaside on Saturday?" she asked him.

"What on earth for?"

"Early birthday present."

"I suppose so. How will we get there?"

"Car. Mum's driving up here."

"Is she coming with us, then?"

"I think she wants to go to the West End, so we can borrow the car while she's shopping. Then she'll stay over and take us down to Basingstoke on Sunday."

"Why do we have to go to bloody Basingstoke?"

"She says she's got a surprise for you when we get there."

"I hate surprises."

"But it's your eightieth."

"What's there to celebrate about that? That I've survived? Against all the odds? I'd rather not be reminded." Talking about age always made him feel grumpy.

"Anyway, she's said we can have the car on Saturday so we can go to the seaside."

"You're not expecting me to drive, are you?"

"Oh, no. Chance for me to practise my driving. Do you want to go? I thought you'd like it."

George heaved a reluctant sigh.

Tara tried not to look hurt. "We don't have to, if you don't want to."

Sensing that the opportunity would be lost if he kept being negative, George shuffled uneasily. "Oh, alright. On one condition."

"What's that?"

"Promise you won't mention my age again."

Tara offered up her palm to her grandfather and they sealed the deal with a high-five.

* * *

"Mind you drive safely," Bridget had said when she dropped off the Peugeot. That had been over an hour ago. Speeding through the countryside, Tara was enjoying the open road, having overcome her nervousness at not driving much since passing her test, feeling good she was spending a 'thank you' day with her grandfather. She'd been living in his house for nearly five months and hardly spent any time with him, and was ashamed it'd taken breaking up with Mark to realise it. Going out early and coming home late or working on her computer wearing earphones left only the occasional mealtimes. Now Mark was history she vowed to change all that.

"I haven't been this way in ages." George was sitting forward in the front passenger's seat, peering through the windscreen, admiring the trees silhouetted against a low sun and clear blue sky.

"I thought you'd like it."

"Just like the old days."

"There's something really beautiful when you get an Indian summer this late in the year, don't you think?" The sun was warm through the windscreen, belying the cold wind that was making the few remaining leaves shimmer and dance.

"Thanks for bringing me out."

"Just hope the rain holds off."

George squinted at the strobing of the sun through the trees. "I love London but watching the countryside speed by really raises the spirits. Uplifting."

"That's the idea."

"You going to tell me about your weekend?"

"There's not much to say."

"How's Mike?"

"Mark. Why do you ask?"

"Nothing. Anything come from when he played his music?"

"Actually, they got me to sing."

"That's great. I bet it went well."

"It did, actually."

"I said you had a lovely voice." George was nodding to himself. "What did they make of Mark's music?"

"Why do you keep asking?"

"I think he might have something, that's all. He's very talented. He's started listening to me and he's taken up some of my suggestions. Like the keyboard. That was my idea. He probably won't do everything I say, but that's how music develops. I hope I'm some help to him. You're lucky to have him. Hold on to him."

Tara said nothing, instead tapping the stalk on the steering wheel so the radio came to life. A phone-in caller was droning on about something inconsequential, punctuating a succession of ums, ahs and you knows, with the occasional distinguishable word. She turned it off again.

"Is he the one? Mark?" George emphasised the name, as if in triumph at getting it right at last.

"The one?"

"You've been courting for some time."

Tara laughed at her grandfather's expression. "We don't call it *courting* anymore."

"Stepping out. Whatever you call it. Is he the one?"

She shrugged. "Can I ask you something?"

"Go ahead. Ask."

"Will you help *me*? With *my* singing?"

"You don't need help. I've always said what a great voice you have."

"It's just I don't know many songs. Good songs, that is. You do."

George nodded. "True, there's not many I don't know. I played requests in hotels for years. Sadly."

"I need to know more."

"Is this with Mark?"

"I don't know, maybe not."

"Nothing wrong, I hope."

Tara said nothing. She didn't want intimate details of the weekend to ruin their day together.

"Well, if there's one bit of advice I can offer," George continued, "it's make the most of your talent. If you don't, no one else will. The world is too full of missed opportunities."

It sounded to Tara like there was a touch of regret in his voice. She'd ask him later. "So you'll help? I don't want to force you or tire you out."

"You won't tire me out. I've never felt so creative."

"Me too."

"Sounds like fun, then. Whatever you want to do. When do you want to start?"

Tara felt her grandfather scrutinising her. "It can't be when we get home tonight. Mum'll be with us."

"Maybe she'll join in."

"I don't think so. And it'll probably be too late anyway. It can't be tomorrow – it's your birthday in case you'd forgotten."

"Singing not allowed on my birthday?"

"You know what I mean. Mum's got it all planned."

George screwed his face up. "I wish she hadn't. Why does she have to take us away to her house? You know I'd be happy if I never saw that place again. I hope she doesn't think we're staying overnight."

Tara patted his hand. "Don't worry. She knows how you feel. She's promised she'll bring us back. I need to get back too."

Jeff had sent a WhatsApp that morning to say he had a spare ticket for a comedy club in the evening, asking if she'd like to go with him. It was hardly the most romantic of invitations but she wasn't about to turn it down. So her grandfather had an ally if her mum tried to get them to stay overnight in Basingstoke.

George reached forward and turned the radio back on, tuning it to an oldies radio station. The Beatles were playing and he began to sing along. When Tara recognised the chorus, she joined in, until distance from London and a dip in the road meant the signal was lost. George sat back and breathed out heavily. "Do you know, I think the last time I was taken out for a day, it was because your mum and dad were trying to put me into a home."

"It's coming up on the right."

He jerked his head round to glare at Tara. "You're not taking me back there, are you?"

As the 'Lastdays' sign emerged from behind a hedge, Tara eased her foot from the accelerator and the car began to slow. George reached for the dashboard. "You're not, tell me you're not."

The car sped up again and Tara laughed. "Of course not."

"That's not funny." George strained his head further round and watched the sign disappear into the distance. "At least they've given the fence a lick of paint." He sat back into the seat and relaxed again. "I wonder how they're getting on in there. Poor old souls."

"It looked awful."

"You should have seen it from the inside. Not just the look of the place. The terrible silence. Everywhere. No music, no joy."

"I can't imagine a place without music. That must be something from your genes." Tara would have hugged him had she not been driving.

As if on cue, the oldies station burst back into life and the singing resumed. By the time they were in sight of the sea, they were in full voice, alternating vocals on 'California Dreamin''. It almost came too soon when Tara announced, "We're here." The car turned a corner and they arrived on the seafront. The wind had deterred most visitors, so parking was not a problem.

"Fancy a walk on the beach?" Tara asked as she stretched across to unbuckle George's seat belt.

George was looking the opposite way. "In a minute. Mind if I...?" He tapped on the window, pointing at a row of shops facing the esplanade.

"Why not? It's your day."

George fumbled his way out of the car and headed across the road. It wasn't the Rock Shop or the Tourist Information Centre that had attracted him, nor Norman's Novelty Souvenirs. They were closed, anyway. It was Charity Books and Records that had enticed him away from the beach. Like the other three, it was shut. Worse than that, it looked abandoned, dirty and gloomy, windows covered in salt and caked sand. On the glass drooped posters for a circus and funfair long-since departed. Behind, pinned to a pegboard, were album sleeves, curled and faded by sunlight, and a line of 45s dangling like washing from a string. George pressed his nose to the door, peering through grime and a metal grill. An 'Open' sign was hanging, lop-sided, suspended from a blob of Blu-Tack, but inside was dark and neglected, a fan of unopened letters splayed across the doormat.

"I think it's closed, Gramps."

"So much for charity." George was disappointed. Browsing a charity shop for records was always a must for adding to his collection. Making a periscope with his hands, he leaned in to see if he was missing anything worth investigating, but it was all too gloomy and messy.

"Beach then," Tara called, already about to cross the road.

They made their way to the promenade, George climbing the steps like a toddler – eager but wobbly. There was no stopping him as he jogged across the tarmac and on to the shingle beach. Cold as it was, there was joy in the scrunching of the pebbles beneath his feet, the chill of the salty air and the alternate crashing and swishing of the waves.

Together they followed the contours of the shingle, dodging any wave that encroached further in.

"This is great," George shouted above the roar of the backwash. "I haven't felt this good for ages."

A crashing wave raced across the stones and meant they had to clamber up the pebbly slope. As the water receded, George stooped and picked up a stone, skimming it across the top of the waves. He watched it skip, once, twice, three times before it sank beneath the surface.

"Three! That's awful. I'm losing my touch."

He tried a second that didn't make it over a breaking wave. A third was faring little better when it was overtaken by another.

"Four, five, six, seven." Tara was counting her skimming triumphantly. "Beat that, Gramps."

"Oi! I'm supposed to be king of the skimmers."

They laughed, skimming in turn, none matching Tara's sevener.

"Back to the promenade?" Tara pointed to the sky, clouds dulling the sun.

"One more." George had found a really flat one that fitted all the criteria of a winning skimmer.

"OK. Seven to beat." Tara secretly hoped he would. He had taught her to skim stones when she was tiny and he'd always come out on top. Somehow, today of all days, it didn't seem right to overturn that record. She watched as he waited for a lull in the waves, crouching low before launching his pebble.

"Two, three, four..." It disappeared behind the swell and did not reappear, but George kept counting, "... five, six. Yes! Seven! An honourable draw, I think."

They shook hands on it and walked back up the beach.

"So, how about you and Mark?"

She kept her head down, in part to negotiate the uneven cobbles beneath her shoes, but also because she didn't want him to catch her eye. "What about us?" She wondered why he kept coming back to the same question. What had he noticed? He'd even got Mark's name right again.

"Has he used any of my music?"

"Used?"

"Samples. From my CDs."

Tara relaxed. At least it wasn't about her relationship with her now ex-boyfriend. "Bits, yes. I think so. And your voice that he recorded in my room."

"And are people listening to them?"

"I think so."

"I hope my contributions helped, maybe made it a bit better."

"Of course they did."

"Luckily I haven't heard any of it. I'd just hope I'm not so far out of touch with modern tastes." He laughed but sounded serious. "If you say he used some of *my* music, and someone likes it, there's still hope for civilisation. Will you be going into a studio? Recording a CD? I might be able to put you in touch with someone."

"No one uses studios or makes CDs anymore."

"Someone must."

"It's all downloads. Or mobile."

George shook his head. "Your generation's missing out on so much. I got to love music belting out across a dance hall. Or the radio. And the jukebox. They were great. Flashing lights, colours. Listening on tiny loudspeakers squawking on computers and those phone things of yours – where will it end? And what happens if you lose your phone? You read about them being snatched in the street all the time. Or your computer breaks down. You've lost it all."

"It's also instant. And we don't need record shops."

"That's a good thing?"

"It means you can be global. When Mark looked at the analytics, he saw that nearly half of our views were in America."

"Really? LA? Memphis? Where they make real music?"

"He thinks *his* is real music. And you said you thought he was talented." Tara surprised herself that she was defending Mark. "And yes, maybe, could be anywhere. And on any device."

"Device?"

"iPad, computer, mobile."

"Pah! If it's on a phone, it's hardly worth bothering about." A seagull swooping overhead let out a piercing shriek, as if making a comment about music on mobiles. It allowed George to modify his tone. "Does that mean someone in LA or Memphis might have heard *my* music?"

"I guess so. Pier?" They had been heading towards it since they'd left the beach, and now it was just a few yards away.

"Why not."

They walked past what would once have been a tollgate at the pier entrance.

"When I was a boy, there'd be a queue here. You needed to hand over a bundle of coins to get on. Those were the days." He stared at the boarded-up ticket office, paint peeling, ironwork rusting. "I used to be scared of falling through the cracks between the planks." He looked down at the white tops of the waves beneath. "Or dropping my money through the gaps. I used to keep it in my fist in case a hole appeared in my pocket and I lost it all. I never did but I always worried."

They both laughed and walked on, Tara pointing to the other side of a glass partition to avoid an icy wind that had picked up. Protected from the gusts, there was a line of deckchairs facing into the low sun. All were taken despite the chill in the air, gathering clouds and threat of drizzle. Their occupants were of George's age, wrapped in uniforms of scarves, macs, coats and blankets, holding Tupperware containers with salad and white bread sandwiches of paste and cheese. Once she might have joked, 'Waiting to die,' but settled on, "Don't think I'd fancy sitting out here like that."

George must have been thinking the same. "Glad I'm not like that. Especially as I think it's starting to rain." He nodded towards the Pavilion. "Shall we waste your mum's inheritance on the slot machines inside?"

"Race you." Tara sped on ahead. She was inside before she realised she was on her own.

* * *

George watched Tara disappear into the Pavilion before stretching his neck back to look to the sky. The clouds may have gathered but it was wonderful to be away. The seaside was the next best thing to the city. But it reminded him too much of his own frailty. While the waves would crash relentlessly and forever, his time was short, no matter how well he felt today. He was already past three score years and ten. How many more had he? How many more days like this would he see? And there was so much still to do. Perhaps he should take Tara into his confidence, ask her to help *him*, not the other way round. Finish 'Missing Evelyn' for him if he wasn't around to do it. Tell her about the studio, get her help in getting Ron to answer. The day before, he'd dug out the business card Ron had given him and braved phoning the studio's number. It rang six times then went to answerphone. He'd left a message, joking about being kidnapped for the weekend by his family and asking them to get in touch once he was back. What if they didn't? Maybe after a day or two he'd ask Mark or Tara to chase for him. The train of thought led him to Mark. It was odd how he'd been dropping round when Tara was out. Not only that, asking for more help, much like Tara had just done. And with his own time running out, would he have enough for two protégés as well as his own music?

With drizzle spattering into his eyes, he looked back along the pier and imagined it as it was in his day, bustling with families, here for their two weeks by the sea. Every holiday included at least one show in the Pavilion for the kids. It was tradition. A matinee, with jugglers, magicians, comedians, maybe a ventriloquist and a couple of music acts. Once it should have been Phaedra and the Phaeries.

The metalwork that some Victorian craftsman had curled and twisted was still there – bright blue now, not the sludge brown of old. Everything else was changed beyond recognition. He made his way into the dry. The box office was now a fortune teller. The stage had gone. Slot machines had replaced the rows of red seating. It was a temple of light, not to performing arts, with neons flashing and dancing. Instead of a band, electronic noises assaulted the ears.

Tara was waiting beside a machine. "I wondered where you'd got to."

"I was thinking."

"Well, have a go at this. Waterfall. You used to play this with me when I was a child."

He nodded as he watched a metal arm rhythmically ease backwards then forwards towards a glistening ridge of ten-pence pieces. Fumbling in his pocket he was satisfied by the recovery of two of his own. He dropped one through a slot and poked the glass in front of the slider, as if directing his coin. It duly landed where he wanted it, but the slider merely pushed it into a pile of other coins that shimmered, poised tantalisingly over a precipice, but did not fall into the winning cup.

"This time." He dropped the second coin. Again he stabbed his finger and again it landed obligingly where he instructed it. "I was good at this. Though it used to be a halfpenny." The slider thrust it forward, depositing it into the mound of coins. "Wait for it." And on cue, they toppled, gushing over the precipice. But only one coin found its way into the winning cup. George scooped it out and held it up triumphantly. "Success!"

He promptly returned it to the machine. This time, not even his magic finger did the trick, instead pushing a different pile of coins close towards a different precipice, but none fell over.

They wandered on and around the arcade, to the accompaniment of staccato voices from the machines.

'Play to win.'

'You're a winner.'

'Wise guy, eh?'

'Place your bets.'

In amongst them, fighting for supremacy, fragments of songs. "I played with this guy." George waved his finger in the direction of the music. "He said I was one of the best he'd heard. Can't think of his name."

Tara was staring intently at the Steeplechase, clenching her fist that her yellow horse might reward her with a ten-pence return on her two-pence investment.

George carried on reminiscing, but he could tell it was getting lost in the blaster gun from a Star Wars machine, Union Pacific railroad sirens, crowing cockerels, an electronic Scottish reel and the rattling of coins into Tara's winning cup accompanied by her whoops of delight. Scooping them out, she turned back to him.

"Sorry, Gramps. What were you saying?"

"Nothing much, really."

They walked on, past electronic roulette wheels and shooting galleries, their flashing lights failing to entice either Tara or George. As they passed a row of gaudy Wheel of Fortune slots, there seemed to be a lull in the sound effects, or maybe they'd just reached a quiet zone.

"Why were you Pharaoh and the Phaeries?"

"Phaedra. There already was a band called Pharaohs. At the start, we were just the Beat Boys. In the folk clubs I was plain George Turnbull. But after The Beatles it all changed. Crazy names – Pinkerton's Assorted Colours, Hullaballoos, Knickerbockers, Leafhound, Tierney's Fugitives… everyone had to have something that sounded weird and wild."

"Simon and Gar-something?"

"Garfunkel." George shook his head. "No. They were quite different." The background sounds ratcheted up a notch or two. "I'll tell you about Paul Simon when it's not so noisy." He cupped his hands over his ears to exaggerate the point, adding as an afterthought, "That's if you're interested."

Tara gestured towards the exit sign.

Familiar sounds now mixed with different ones. An Irish jig merged into bleeps; a scattergun effect blended into a Southern drawl repeating 'Wise guy, eh?' punctuated with explosions.

"God, it's like being in a disco. And this," George was shouting now and waving his hand around in the air again, "it's almost a rap. A psychedelic rap. If there is such a thing. When we get home, tell me to dig out The Beatles *White Album*. There's a track where John Lennon experimented with random sounds. I never liked it, but Mark might like it. Maybe I should give it a second chance, even if I am fifty years late."

Walking on, they followed the signs through the arcade to 'Pavilion Café – best Value on the Pier'. While George was observing the unnecessary use of capital letters on 'Value' and 'Pier', they were distracted by an addition to the psychedelic rap, what sounded like wild celebrations, gushing coins and an electronic voice declaring 'Jackpot, Jackpot' from the Waterfall machine they had not long left behind.

* * *

Outside, the day had changed. The sky had darkened and the chill wind was carrying sleet. They struggled to the end of the pier where they found the café, its ice cream banner swinging in the wind, mildewing curtains in the windows and paint peeling from the doors. And closed.

Nothing more was said as they turned round and headed back, passing the now empty rows of deckchairs. Tara tried to speed up but risked leaving George behind, as he walked, head down, huddled and braced against the wind, gasping for breath.

"Are you alright?" she asked once they'd reached the car. "You're shivering."

"It's nothing. I'm a bit cold, that's all. I've enjoyed it. Really." He was wet and tired and he suddenly felt his age, but it had been worth it. For the moment, everything was just perfect.

Chapter 25

"Happy birthday to you, happy birthday, dear," Tara and Bridget hesitated over whether to sing Gramps or Dad, but finished the tune with gusto, "happy birthday to you."

The two cheered.

George stared at the cake, two candles – one in the shape of an eight, the other a nought. Was he really that old?

"Come on, then," Bridget urged, "before the wax runs onto the icing." George made an exaggerated sigh as if he hadn't got the wind.

"I'm sorry. Yesterday's taken more out of me than I thought."

"You can do it, Gramps." Tara held her mobile up to capture the moment on camera. He breathed in, wheezed, then blew.

Flames flickered, thought about going out, then carried on burning. Tara and Bridget exchanged glances.

"Try again, Dad. Ready on camera, Tara?"

"I'm ready."

"I don't think I can."

"For the camera."

Another sigh. He breathed in and coughed as Bridget, who'd knelt down beside him, blew with him. The candles flickered again and this time went out.

Tara cheered. "That's one for Facebook. Have you got a page, Gramps?"

George grunted. "What's a Facebook?"

"Anyway, happy birthday." From under the table, Tara produced a package. Flat, about thirty centimetres square, it was unmistakably a vinyl record.

George took it and began to pick at the wrapping. "Why on earth do you make presents so impossible to undo?" he moaned. His hands were shaking and the sticky tape stubborn. Again, Tara and Bridget exchanged glances.

"It's a shame Mark couldn't come today," Bridget said to distract from George's fumbling. "And I'm sorry it's not really a party." She offered a hand to help find an edge to the tape. "I'd invited some people over you might know but they couldn't make it either."

George's hands were shaking even more now and still he struggled to get to grips with the paper. Tara leaned over and, in the same movement, ripped the paper right back, revealing what was inside.

George stared at it for a moment then looked up. "Oh. *Simon and Garfunkel's Greatest Hits.*" He hoped it sounded like he was pleased.

"I thought you'd like it. You haven't already got it, have you?"

George read the titles out loud to deflect from not answering. "'Bridge Over Troubled Water', 'I Am a Rock', 'Homeward Bound.'"

Tara continued. "Well, it's new, so even if you have, it'll not be scratched at all."

"I didn't know you could get it on vinyl anymore."

Bridget joined in. "Back in fashion, Dad. Haven't you heard?"

"Of course I have." George wondered why his daughter suddenly felt she'd become an expert in music. "I meant I didn't know albums like this were being re-released." He tried to sound enthusiastic. He'd never been a fan of 'Greatest Hits' albums. They required no effort from either artist or listener. People who bought them were either lazy or ignorant. Half the pleasure of music was discovering it, learning it, growing to love it, not having it handed over on a plate. But nonetheless, he was grateful to his granddaughter. He reached across and gave her a peck on the cheek.

Bridget tapped the table. "I know what I'd almost forgotten."

"That you're going to cut the cake soon? Having blown out the candles, I was hoping to taste it sometime before I'm eighty-one."

"I've a little surprise. Go and look in my bedroom, in the middle of the floor. There are some boxes with old records. Too heavy for me to lift on my own. It's why I wanted you to come down here. I thought you might like to look at them. If there are any you like, we can take them back to London – not that you need any more."

"I can never have too many."

"Any you don't want, I can take them down the charity shop."

George was already unsteadily out of his chair and on his feet. "Where did you say they were?"

"Upstairs. Do you want Tara to help you?"

"Never. I'm better on my own. Where did you get them?"

"No idea. They were Toby's."

George hesitated. "Should I be looking at them if they're his?"

"That's his look-out. They're yours now. If you want them."

Of course George wanted them. He just didn't want to look too eager. "In your bedroom, you say?"

"Yes." She opened the door for him as he stumbled out, watching as he trod gingerly up the stairs.

* * *

Once George was out of sight, Bridget pushed the door to and turned to Tara.

"I still find it funny calling it 'my' bedroom."

"Have you heard from Dad?"

"Nothing. How's your grandfather been?"

"We had a good day yesterday."

"I hope you didn't tire him out too much."

"Do you think he liked his present?"

"The record? I think so. He's never very grateful for presents."

Bridget glanced at the door and lowered her voice. "Have you noticed anything about your grandfather?"

"Like what?"

"Did you see the way his hands were shaking when he couldn't unwrap your present? Is he like that all the time?"

Tara nodded. "I've seen it sometimes."

"What about his breathing?"

"What about it?"

"The way he couldn't blow out the candles."

"He is eighty."

"I still don't think he's really over that cold flu thing he had when he was here. Not properly. Maybe it'd be a good idea if he stayed with me for a while. You can always get the train back tomorrow."

Jeff and the comedy club – Tara's brain screamed the words over and over. "No, he doesn't want to stay. And I have to get back."

"Really? Alright."

Tara was relieved that her mum didn't push the idea.

Bridget continued. "When you're back, please keep an eye on him. I'm still not sure you should have gone out in the cold yesterday."

Tara shrugged. "I think he enjoyed it."

"How wet did he get? He's an old man. Don't forget it, no matter how he acts. And how's his hearing? Have you noticed anything?"

"His hearing?"

"Not catching what you say."

"His music is very loud."

"It always was. I used to have to tell him to turn it down when I was a child. A daughter telling her dad to turn the music down! How ironic was that? It always felt like it was the wrong way round." Bridget laughed at the memory.

Tara rested her head in her hands. "Tell the truth, I have made him jump a few times when he hasn't heard me. And the other day I walked into his room and he didn't know I was there."

"Has Mark noticed anything?"

"Mark?"

"Yes, has he noticed anything when he's in the house?"

"Oh, no, he's not the kind. And his music was always too loud, too." Tara wondered if now was the moment to reveal that Mark was off the radar. Luckily, her mum was still focused on Gramps.

"Well, it all seems worse than when he was staying here."

"Maybe you notice it more because you don't see it so much."

"Maybe you don't notice because you see him all the time."

From upstairs came the sound of shuffling and boxes scraping across the floor.

Satisfied George wasn't about to re-emerge, Bridget leaned forward as if about to confide. "Not hearing is one thing. What I've really been worrying about is sometimes I wonder if he's not really listening. Or not taking things in."

"He's still keen on his records."

"It seems to me like he goes off into a world of his own."

"Maybe he's just not interested."

Bridget was shaking her head. "I'm not so sure. Didn't you notice that faraway look he had when your dad was, you know, sounding off at the Ramsays'? It's as if he's lost the ability to concentrate." She sighed. "How is he in himself?"

"Seems OK."

"I just wonder if he's not getting something."

"Like what?"

Bridget lowered her voice to almost a whisper. "Is he forgetting things?"

"He talks a lot about his music when he was younger. He seemed to know everything about a record that fell off his lap when he had a nap the other afternoon."

"That's another thing – the way he sleeps all the time." Bridget paused to consider the implications of what she was about to say. "I hope it's not Alzheimer's."

"He did put biscuits in the tea caddy."

"Really? God, I hope it's not."

"I'm sure it's OK. He's a bit forgetful, that's all. And lonely. He's been looking at things on my computer."

"What, dating sites?" Bridget said it as a joke.

"Something like that."

"Really?"

"Since Nan died, I don't think he's got any friends."

"I wish you could stay the night."

"He's made up his mind." Tara tried not to sound too keen to get away.

"I don't know. With all the troubles, I feel like I'm neglecting Dad. And you, of course." Bridget looked apologetically at her daughter. "Has he tried anything from those leaflets?"

"Not that I know of. He wasn't keen when I mentioned them."

Bridget looked out the window for a moment, then turned back to her daughter. "So what does he do all day?"

"Plays his piano. He even started playing in the uni foyer at Mark's gig!"

"Oh dear. I worry about him, I really do."

"And he's promised to help me."

"I suppose that's positive."

"And he plays his records of course. And moves them around. He's always saying he can't find things." Tara saw the worried expression on her mum's face. "But he's pretty alert the rest of the time. I don't suppose it's anything."

"I don't know. If he's doing strange things, forgetting things… maybe we should get it checked out. Does he do much around the house? Are you having to do everything?"

Tara shrugged. "It was part of the deal moving in with him."

"What's going to happen when your course finishes?"

Tara shrugged again. "It's years yet."

"What about Christmas? Next summer? Are you going away?"

"No idea."

"I'm wondering if I should try and talk to him again about sheltered accommodation."

"He'll hate it."

"I know, but it's obvious he won't come here and I can't move to London, what with my new job. Someone's got to care for him and it's not fair if it falls on you."

There was more noise from upstairs.

"Better change the subject. You sure you haven't heard from your father?"

"No. Why should I?"

"Nothing."

"You're not thinking of getting back with him, are you?"

"It's been over a month since I last saw him and he hasn't been in touch."

"Do you want him to?"

"We'll have to at some point. About the house, divorce possibly..." Her voice trailed off.

Before Tara could react, the door pushed open to reveal George standing there, holding a bundle of LPs.

"Hello, Gramps. Find anything you liked?"

"I most certainly did."

"Well?"

"I more than liked them." He held up the top one, clasping it with fingers on the three shillings price sticker, pointing at the signature of Paul Simon. "They're mine."

Chapter 26

Bridget's car was slowing down as the traffic lights turned to red. It seemed like every set had been against them the whole journey. "I'm going to need a cup of tea and a breather before I head back," she said, drumming her fingers on the steering wheel.

The birthday celebrations had been muted by George's revelation. He seemed pleased to be reunited with the missing records and for the vindication that they really had been going missing. But for Tara, any joy was drained by the only explanation – that her dad had stolen them and was selling them on the internet. What made it worse was she'd been trying to buy one. It had taken Bridget's special roast to lighten the mood, after which they'd all slumped in front of the television. Her grandfather had been hard to rouse, and by the time the record boxes had been loaded into the car and they were on the road, they were far later leaving for London than anyone expected.

"I've never known it take so long," Tara murmured from the back seat. It wasn't just the traffic that was unnerving her.

She checked the time on her mobile and wondered if it was still worth trying to make the comedy club. Maybe Jeff would have even given up waiting. She tried to text him but her phone obstinately refused to give her a signal.

"Did you see that?" Bridget called out, startling George, who'd been dozing in the front.

"What's the matter?" he mumbled.

"That cyclist. Nearly knocked over by that van. He jumped the lights and the van was going too fast."

"That's London for you."

They travelled on in silence, George with his eyes closed and Bridget sighing every time the traffic ground to a halt. Tara was alternating between staring out the side window, reading the graffiti on the shuttered shop fronts and checking her mobile. She shook it, hoping it might pick up a signal.

"Anything wrong?" Bridget asked, looking in the rear-view mirror at her daughter.

"Just this phone. I really must get a new one." Looking up, she caught sight of a figure in the shadows, walking in the opposite direction, head down, texting. She tapped on the window, hoping he'd see her.

"Anyone you know?"

"Someone from uni. A friend."

George peered round his seat. "Why don't you phone that boyfriend of yours and tell him to put the kettle on?"

"What?"

"I think your grandfather means Mark," Bridget said as at last they turned off the main road into the maze of terraced streets leading to George's house.

Tara frowned. "I know that. What makes you think he'll be at your house?"

"I thought he was always there." Bridget sounded puzzled.

George turned back to face the front. "He will be. He asked me if it was alright if I minded him missing my party. So he could work on his music. Very considerate, I thought."

"Gramps, I wish you'd told me."

"What do you mean, 'wish you'd told me'?"

There was no time for an answer. Nor did Tara have a chance to check her mobile that had sprung into life and was bleeping like Morse code. As the car rounded the corner into George's road, her eyes were drawn to the blue flashing light reflecting off the frosty tarmac and brick terraces lining it.

Bridget gasped. "Oh, no. What's happened?" She brought the car to a stop behind the police car and jumped out. "I think you two had better wait here," she called back.

Tara already had her seat belt off and was on to the pavement. But instead of following her mum to the open door of her grandfather's house, she ran up to a disconsolate figure, hunched over the garden wall of the next-door neighbours'.

"What are you doing here?" Tara demanded.

"I'm so sorry," Mark whined.

"What's happened? Have you been drinking?"

"It's not my fault, T, honest."

"What isn't? What's happened?"

"The house. It's been burgled. They've cleared the place. Worse than that. It's awful."

Tara strode towards the front door. She could see her mum on the first landing, standing next to a uniformed police constable, both staring into George's record room, its door propped open by two large cardboard cartons. "Mum? What's up?"

Bridget didn't speak.

Now alongside of her, Tara followed her mum's gaze. "Oh my God." Where once had been George's hifi and shelves stacked floor to ceiling with records and CDs were now just shelves.

Only a few stray records and covers remained, strewn across the floor as if abandoned in haste. Streetlight beamed through the windows across the empty space. "It's not possible."

"I'm afraid it is." It was the policeman who answered, Bridget still incapable of speech.

"How could this happen?" Tara knelt down to one of the cartons that was wedging the door open. "Is this all they've left?" She opened the top to reveal the neatly packed, unsold copies of Phaedra and the Phaeries' 'Little Lisa'. "How could this have happened?"

"No sign of a break-in," the policeman offered. His radio crackled something incomprehensible. "Luckily this young man arrived and reported a burglary in progress." He was looking towards Mark who was just arriving on the landing. "That may have stopped them before they cleared the whole house."

"Did they get upstairs?" Tara started towards her bedroom. She could see her door propped open by George's Best Music award.

"I shouldn't go up," Mark paused, close to tears. "It's gone. Your computer, my drive. And my music wasn't backed up."

At last Bridget spoke. "Who would do such a thing?"

"It's not my fault, T, Mrs W. Honestly." Mark was standing unsteadily.

"Will you stop saying it's not your fault and tell us what happened," Tara demanded.

"I came round to work on my music."

"Why? When? You had no right." Tara ignored her mum's confused expression.

"This morning. Gramp... your grandfather said it would be alright. I wanted to sample some of his records."

"And?"

"I just couldn't get started. The more I tried, the less I could think. So I went out. I swear I locked the door."

"How long were you out for all this to happen?" Tara waved her arm at the empty music room.

"I was only here, I don't know, less than half an hour. Then one thing led to another…"

"I can smell it." Tara put her hand across her face to shield it from the alcoholic fumes.

"I meant to get back but I couldn't concentrate, and when I did get back, the door was open and I could see people inside."

"Who? Who did you see?"

"I don't know. Shapes. Blokes. I think they saw me."

"Didn't you do anything?"

"I went round the corner and called the police."

"Why didn't you stop them? Lock them in or something."

"I couldn't."

"Why not?" Only now, in the light of the landing, did Tara see a graze on Mark's forehead. He was rubbing the other side of his head, where a bruise was coming up. "Did they do that to you?"

"I'm sorry. I would have chased after them."

"But?"

Mark hesitated. "I tripped over."

"Tripped over?" Tara screwed her face up. "I get it." She was shaking now. "Because you were pissed."

Mark hung his head.

"So pissed you didn't do anything to protect my grandfather's house. You're pathetic, you really are."

Below, they heard the sound of George letting himself in.

"We'd better not let him see this," Bridget said. "Not without warning him first."

Mark tensed. "Oh, no. Is that Gramps? Don't let him go in the kitchen."

"Why not, what's happened?"

Mark didn't answer but turned and lolloped down the stairs, two at a time. Tara and Bridget followed, more slowly.

They found George staring into the kitchen. A trail of muddy footprints led to the back door, hanging open, the chill night air drifting in. Cupboard doors were wrenched off their hinges, contents strewn across the floor. But George's eyes were on the dishwasher. At a figure sprawled in front of it. Limp and lifeless. Hunter.

Chapter 27

Tara watched as the rear lights of the ambulance disappeared round the corner. She turned back to Mark who was sitting on the stairs.

"I'm sorry, T. I promise you, it wasn't my fault. You do believe me, don't you?"

"If you're just going to sit there whimpering, you should go. You shouldn't be here anyway." She swung round on the door handle and stood like a sentry. "Leave, please. Now."

Mark slowly stood and looked like he was about to utter another apology. Tara didn't let him.

"Come on. I've things to do."

Mark shuffled towards the door. "Can we talk about this, please?"

"Not now. Sometime perhaps." She hoped she didn't sound like she was offering him a way back. "Goodnight."

He was barely on the front step before she was pushing shut the door, then double locking it. She felt relief at cutting herself off from the outside world. Yet inside hardly seemed any more secure. The house was cold and she noticed the wallpaper and banisters had been scratched and chipped by whoever had ransacked the place. She pressed down one rip as she had the day she'd moved in. How long ago it seemed now. But there were more important things to be done before she could chase after her mum and Gramps. She clenched her fists, trying to blot out the image of him collapsed on the kitchen floor, his body limp, face white, eyes glazed; then being wheeled into the ambulance.

"Come on, get on with it." She took a deep breath and exhaled, creating a white cloud that drifted across the hall. Looking up to the cartons poking out of her grandfather's once special room, she made her way up the stairs. Carefully, she removed the records inside, creating a neat row of cairns, arranged so the labels 'Little Lisa', 'Phaedra and the Phaeries' faced the same way. "Like Mecca," she uttered to herself.

Picking up the empty carton, she carried it to the kitchen, positioning it carefully next to Hunter. Gently wrapping him in his favourite blanket, she laid him inside. Before closing the lid, she placed beside him a pack of chocolate Hobnobs that had been left on a worktop. "These can't hurt you now," she said to herself. In a solemn, solitary funeral procession, she carried the makeshift coffin to the shed at the end of the garden. "I'll come back and put you to rest properly as soon as I can." She felt a tear that she didn't wipe away, standing for a final look before gently closing the door on him, heaving a heavy sigh, then making her way to the hospital.

* * *

Bridget looked up at the A&E clock. "There must be some news soon."

"How long did they say they'd keep him?"

"They said they're doing some tests, checking him out. They may keep him in overnight for observation. If he's released, we've got to decide what to do with him. I just wish they'd let us know."

"Why would anyone do such a thing? It's just not fair. He's never hurt anyone."

"You're sure Mark had nothing to do with it?" Bridget was scrutinising her daughter's every reaction.

Tara found herself defending her ex. "At least he called the police. If he hadn't been there, it might have been even worse."

"I still find it strange he says he didn't see anything." Bridget sounded dubious.

"It's not him, I know it's not. Why would he? And he's lost his hard drive. It had all his work."

"And he didn't leave the house unlocked or anything?"

"What difference would that make?"

"Ask him again, to be sure."

"You ask. I don't ever want to speak to him again." Tara thought about the comedy club. Where she should be. With Jeff. Not waiting in A&E.

Bridget sighed. "Oh, I don't know. I don't really think it's Mark." She shook her head, then bent her neck back, staring at the ceiling, as if interrogating herself. "I just don't want to think of the alternative."

"Alternative?"

"I'm afraid it might be your father. I keep trying to tell myself it couldn't be but end up back at the same answer. No one else really knew about the records. There was no sign of a break-in. Your father has a key. And he had a grudge against us – well, me – and your grandfather stood up to him. Who else could it be? His way of getting us back."

"Mum, you're not blaming yourself, are you? Because my dad's having an affair and you stood up for yourself?"

"Think about it. The boxes of records in my bedroom. How did they get there?"

"That was before the burglary."

"And then he came back to steal the rest. What other explanation is there?"

* * *

Tara had a chance to challenge her father when a nurse took her mum to see Gramps. She hadn't much charge left on her mobile but she had to know. With no signal inside the hospital, it was outside in the car park that she called him. What reaction she'd get she wasn't sure, especially calling so late at night. What she got was a strange ring tone, then silence.

"Dad?"

After a short delay, Toby spoke. "Hello, I wasn't expecting you to call." His voice sounded anxious and odd.

"Where are you?"

"Let me ring you back."

"Why?"

"I'll call you back."

Tara sat on a wall and waited. It was damp and the air cold, and she was about to go back inside when her mobile rang.

"Sorry about that." He sounded more composed, but still strange. "Is everything alright?"

"Yes. No. Where are you?" Maybe she'd go round if he wasn't too far away. Accuse him to his face and see his reaction.

There was a pause. The line crackled. "Tananger."

"Where?

"Tananger. Norway."

"You joking me?"

"No, why would I?"

"Does Mum know?" Tara couldn't stop blurting out questions.

"No."

"How long have you been there?"

"Since last week. I'm sorry I missed your grandfather's birthday."

It felt hollow after what he'd said a few days ago. But if it was true, that ruled him out of the burglary. Or at least, carrying it out. "Are you there on your own?"

"I can't answer that. Not at the moment."

"So you're not alone."

"I didn't say that."

"So who's with you? Have you got another woman?"

"Can we can talk about this another time?"

"I suppose. Are you going to talk to Mum at all?"

"I don't know what to say to her."

"You mean, after what's happened?" Tara didn't mention the burglary or the discovery of the records in the wardrobe.

"I'm so sorry. I really didn't mean to catch her face. Why would I? She's your mum."

Tara was relieved he sounded like he knew nothing of the events of the night. "When are you back?"

"I can't say. I'll know better in a few days. Look, Skype me when I've got more time."

"Where are you staying up there?"

"In the company's apartment."

"Do you have an address?"

"I'll get it for you. Hang on a moment."

"Can you text me?" There was no response. Looking at her mobile, she saw that her battery had died. Heading back inside, she at least had some news for her mum. And wondered how she'd react to hearing that her husband had run away.

* * *

It was some hours before Tara could tell her mum where Toby was staying. The hospital might have kept George overnight but there were no beds and, anyway, George was insistent he wasn't staying. "Once I'm an inmate they'll keep me here forever," he'd bawled at Bridget. He was hardly any more co-operative when Bridget headed the car in the direction of Basingstoke. It had taken Tara to calm him. "Gramps, we can't go back to yours, not tonight, with the mess it's in, and the police have said they want to check it for forensics." Even then he'd muttered that they wouldn't find anything if they even bothered to show up, but it was token resistance. Within a few minutes of arriving at Bridget's, he was in bed and asleep.

"I called Dad while we were in the hospital," Tara told her mum as they stood in the kitchen over a boiling kettle.

"Really? Did he answer?"

"You'll never guess where he is."

"Tell me. I'm too tired for games."

"Norway."

"Really?" Bridget hadn't the energy to sound surprised.

"So he said."

"Did he say why?"

"Not really. Work."

"That'll be nice for him. He never told me he was going."

"He said to Skype him. Can I use your computer in the morning?"

"Course you can. What did he have to say about what happened tonight?"

"He didn't seem to know about it and I didn't say."

The kettle clicked and Bridget used the distraction of pouring boiling water into cups to help unburden herself. "I'm still afraid he might have been behind the burglary."

"Don't say that."

"He was angry with us, with me. And your grandfather stood up to him. He won't have liked that. And those records in our bedroom."

"But he wouldn't. Surely?"

"I hope not. But I can't help thinking he might."

"Not if he's in Norway."

"He says. How can you be sure that's where he really is? I don't know what to think anymore."

* * *

"Hunter? Dead?"

"It was awful." Tara hadn't been able to shake off the memory of her grandparents' tiny dog sprawled on the kitchen floor. She leaned into the computer screen to look into her father's eyes for any sign that he might know more than he was letting on. He'd looked genuinely upset and angry, but she was surprised to see it was Hunter, who he'd professed to despise, that seemed to distress him most.

Toby shook his head. "He was so placid. He wouldn't have barked. I never liked the creature, but how could they have done that? Bastards."

"Maybe they fed him Hobnobs. Or he had a heart attack. I hope they didn't do it on purpose. Poor old thing." She wondered if a Skype picture was clear enough for her father to see tears in her eyes as she pictured Hunter in the shed. "Have you any idea who might have done it?"

"None." Toby hesitated. "You don't think I had anything to do with it?"

"Did you?"

"Of course I didn't. How could I?" Toby swung the webcam round to the window to show mountains and sun reflecting off a stretch of tranquil ocean. "I've been here for a week and didn't know anything until you just told me. You believe me, don't you?"

"Sorry. I needed to ask, that's all."

"I know I've been a bloody fool."

"Yes." Tara wasn't going to make it easy for her dad even if she was relieved he had an alibi.

"A right bloody fool."

But he was her dad. It wouldn't take long to forgive him, she knew that. Even over Skype. "So when are you coming back?"

"The thing is, the company's been reorganised and I'm being offered a long-term contract here."

"Oh."

"It's a good opportunity, at my age."

"So you're *not* coming back."

"I didn't say that."

"But that's what you mean."

"Of course I'll come back. I want to see you. To explain. I just can't come straight away."

"When?" Suddenly forgiveness seemed like it might be hard after all.

"Look, it's very difficult."

"Too difficult to come back and see me. Is that what you're saying?"

"Of course not." Toby was shifting uncomfortably in his chair.

"So what *are* you saying?"

"It's just a bit tricky. The company needs me here full time. For the moment."

"And Mum? What about her?"

"You'll have to ask her." He looked away, avoiding eye contact with the webcam. "Maybe she'll forgive me and we can start again."

Tara didn't know which part of that sentence surprised her more. Forgiveness or starting again. She waited until he looked back at the camera. His expression was asking if she knew how her mum might react.

"In Norway?"

"It's where I'm going to be for a while."

"Well, if you want to patch things up, you'll not do it using Skype."

"No, I don't suppose I can." Toby paused, then leaned forward. "How is she doing?"

"How do you think?"

Toby puffed out his cheeks, then sighed. "About what went on that afternoon after we went to Mark's parents'. And when I came round to your grandfather's house. I shouldn't have done that. Any of it. I was messed up. And angry. I only came round to apologise to your mum."

"It didn't sound like it."

"No, it didn't."

"And you didn't have a grudge or anything about what happened?"

"Not at all. I admired the way you all – you, your mum, your grandfather, your boyfriend…"

"Please don't call him that. He's Mark. And he's not my boyfriend anymore."

"Oh."

Tara mentally crossed her fingers that her dad wasn't going to ask about Mark.

He didn't. He took a breath then continued. "I admired the way you all stood up to me that night. Not at the time, I admit, but when I'd calmed down."

"And the way you carried on at the Ramsays'?"

"Oh, that. I was angry with your mum, with myself, about everything, and took it out on your grandfather. I know I shouldn't have."

Tara stared at him. Still the thought persisted that he might still have been involved in the burglary. A form of retribution. "And you really had nothing at all to do with what happened yesterday?"

"I'll say it again. Why would I do anything like that?" His voice tailed off.

It was now or never to ask the unanswered question that was still troubling her. "So how about those records in your wardrobe? The ones Mum found?" Tara watched for a reaction. There was one. Surprise.

"What are you trying to say…?"

"I don't know what to think anymore."

Toby sighed again, stiffening himself. Tara watched him closely. If this wasn't a good answer, she wasn't sure what she would do next. She wanted so much to believe in him again.

"I'd bought them in an antiques sale."

"You don't go to antiques sales." So far, not a good answer.

"I did this once."

"How come Mum didn't know?"

Toby took a deep breath. "I was with someone else."

"Oh."

"I saw them, your grandfather was staying with us and was particularly depressed so I bought them. For him. I thought there might be some things he'd like."

"He says they were his already."

Another deep, reluctant sigh. "I don't want to rake up the past."

"But?"

"But I'm afraid it's what I have been saying for some time. I think his memory is going." He was scrutinising Tara's reaction. "Please don't look like that. If it's not his memory, it's something else. I'm really worried for him. You've heard him talk. Some of his stories – about what he did and who with. They just don't add up. And they get more outrageous every time he tells them."

"But he was a real musician."

"Of course. And he made a record and played session for people. All that's true. But he's been embellishing them for years now to the point where I don't think he knows the truth anymore."

"But he says the records were his," Tara repeated, "and I believe him. When did you get them? How much did they cost? When were you going to give them to him?" She felt his story starting to unravel. His unease did nothing to reassure her. She steeled herself for one more question. "Who was with you at the auction?"

"It's too complicated."

"I think I've got to go."

"No, please."

"Bye."

She reached for the mouse to end the session, but in slow motion to give her dad time to come clean.

"Listen. Stop. I couldn't tell your mum but I hid the records because I was with someone from my office."

Tara's hand hovered over the mouse.

Toby continued. "Who I shouldn't have been with. And I didn't actually buy them."

"So you just lied. Goodbye." She still didn't click the mouse.

"The records weren't from an auction. They belonged to a woman I was seeing. Your mum didn't know."

"So you were having an affair. While I was still living at home."

"Absolutely not." He waited for a challenge, but none came this time. "This woman was…"

"Was?"

"OK, is. She'd just broken up with her husband and was clearing his stuff out. She'd heard me talk about your grandfather's collection. She wanted rid of them so I told her I'd give them to him."

"So how come Gramps never got them?"

Toby sucked his lip. "To tell the truth…"

"That's what I was hoping you'd do from the start."

"… although I told her they were for your grandfather, they weren't. They were for your Uncle Robin. I'd not heard from him for ages. Then he got in touch, to say he'd been abroad and was back in England, looking for work and wanting to meet. I told him about your grandmother."

"Is that how Gramps got that letter from him?"

"That's how he knew, yes. And we met up and he told me he was looking for work. I was trying to help him out. He talked about selling antiques online and when Sonia…"

"That's the woman, is it? Sonia?" Tara spat out the name.

Toby nodded without expression. "When she offered me the records, I thought he could use them. Make a bit of money from them. But I never got the chance to hand them over."

"You took your chance with this Sonia woman, though."

Toby looked straight into the camera. "It's complicated."

"I'm sure it is. That's why I'm still not sure I believe you."

"But it's true." Toby waited for another challenge that didn't come. "And even if you can't, please believe I did not break in and steal them from your grandfather's house."

"So that explains all the records in your wardrobe, does it?"

Toby didn't answer but was staring at the screen yet somehow not focusing at her. It was a look she recognised.

"Dad. Why've you stopped? What aren't you telling me?"

A look down that could only be interpreted as shifty was followed by another reluctant sigh. "Actually I did take some records. Not me. Robin."

"When?"

"When he did your wifi."

"He did my wifi?"

"I told you he was looking for work."

"Did Mum know?"

"No."

"And that's when you stole Gramps' records?"

"Robin. And not stole. He said we should get them valued. For insurance."

"And you believed him? How did they end up in your wardrobe?"

"He said he was finished with them. I was meant to put them back in your grandfather's room, but I didn't get round to it, so I stashed them in the wardrobe." Toby was looking away from the camera.

"And?"

"I did give him a set of keys."

Tara let out a shriek. "You did what? You let him let himself into Gramps' house to get the rest? And some."

"It wasn't for that. You'd said the wifi wasn't working properly."

"Don't blame me."

"I'm not. But I gave him the keys to check that everything was working OK. Did he do that, do you know?"

"All I know is he used *your* keys to let himself in and steal everything."

"No. He wouldn't. I'm sure of it."

"It has to be. He'd already taken the ones you had in your wardrobe."

"I've said. They were going back." Toby was looking straight at the camera again. "I know what you're thinking. You think the keys I gave him are how there was no forced entry."

"Too right."

"But you have to believe me. He just wouldn't. And how would he manage all that on his own?" He was shaking his head. "He wouldn't know what to do with them even if he had. It's just not his game."

"It's no game to Gramps. He loved those records."

"He was going to have to downsize, anyway."

"Gramps'd never have agreed to get rid of them."

"Something had to happen. He can't stay in that house forever." His voice tailed off.

"So you thought it a good idea to let Robin come back and steal the lot."

"Absolutely not."

"That's what it looks like."

Toby pulled a face that suggested he was coming to terms with the evidence. "I just can't believe that Robin would ransack the whole house. He ducks and dives. But he's not a thief. Not like that. Didn't anyone see anything? Neighbours?"

"I've managed to get in touch with one. She thought it was removals. That Gramps must have gone into a home or something, so she wasn't suspicious. She did notice a flashy sports car parked in the road but said it had been there before so thought nothing of it."

"Sports car? A convertible?"

"I don't know. Why?"

"No reason. Your Mark see anything?"

"No, and stop calling him 'my' Mark."

"Sorry."

Tara tried to read her dad's expression. There were things going on in his head she could only guess at. "Have you heard from Uncle Robin? Do you know where he is?"

"No idea." Toby shook his head. "We're not that close."

"If he gets in touch, you will tell the police down here, won't you?"

"I don't suppose he will." Toby sat back. "But how's your grandfather through all this?"

"What do you think?"

"I know. It's not fair. What's going to happen to him?"

"He hates being here in Basingstoke. So do I as a matter of fact." Tara skipped the missed date with Jeff and now missing lectures. "I've got to get back to London, tidy the place, bury Hunter, get Gramps back in. It's killing him here. Though I don't know why I'm telling you this."

"It's why I wanted your mum to agree to find a home for him."

"He's got one with me."

"I'm just saying. Something to think about."

"Thanks. Not."

"Look, I've got to go."

"Me too."

"Love you, girl."

"Bye, Dad."

Chapter 28

Two weeks passed before George got his wish to go back home. It had been purgatory at his daughter's, alternating between bed and living room chair. *Bed and bored,* he thought in the few moments he felt like thinking. All the energy that had been surging through him had evaporated, sapped by the burglary, losing his records, losing Hunter and the sterility of the house in Basingstoke. Making it worse, getting wet at the seaside seemed to have made him ill again. At times, he was doubled up with coughing and he could barely walk for being breathless. Bridget had insisted on his seeing a doctor, who had supplied him with a bag of potions that didn't seem to be doing any good. He'd even been offered a wheelchair, which he refused as the certain death of his independence. Yet he felt too feeble to do more than rest. Had Bridget not needed to return to work, he wasn't sure he would ever have escaped.

I'm never, ever going there again, he vowed as he heard the front door of his house shut and his daughter drive away. She'd kissed him goodbye, leaving him alone, sitting in what used to be his music room, shrouded in a blanket. The heating was on full blast but still he felt cold. What was he going to do now he was back? No

Hunter, no records except for the few left behind by the burglars. Even the boxes discovered in Toby's wardrobe had ended up back in Basingstoke after all the fuss of the burglary. There wasn't even going to be Mark to coach. The piano was still downstairs, and he knew he'd promised Tara they could work together, but he just didn't feel up to it. Then there was Ron. He saw now he'd been taken in, that there never had been a last chance of fame. And even if he *did* come back, what was the point? Of anything?

Little Lisa
She's a pleaser
Little Lisa
Such a teaser
Won't you let me please ya, please don't tease me again
Won't you let me please ya, please don't tease me again
Little Lisa...

The song was coming from a 1960s record player. It had been recovered from under the bed in Tara's room, where it had been stashed some thirty years before. The brand name 'Dansette' was caught in a shaft of orange light from a street lamp that would once have been blocked by records entombing the room. As remarkable that the player had been missed by the burglars was that it still worked. A relic from the sixties, it could stack up to seven records, and he'd loaded seven copies of Phaedra and the Phaeries' only single from one of the piles of singles Tara had laid out on the floor.

Won't you let me please ya, please don't tease me again
Won't you let me please ya, please don't tease me again
Won't you let me please ya...

As the song slowly faded, the record arm lifted up and the next record dropped down to play. The stylus clicked into the groove and began again.

Little Lisa
She's a pleaser

A light from behind arced around the room.

"Hello, Gramps." Tara stepped in. "Just come home. May I?" She pointed to the record player and, when George nodded, turned down the volume from almost full to a level she could talk over. "What's this you're playing?"

"My single."

"Oh, sorry." She turned the volume back up, though not to the eardrum-piercing levels that had greeted her, perched herself on the arm of George's chair, and listened. After two minutes and it faded, she turned to him. "It's good."

"Too much like the Rolling Stones' 'Not Fade Away'. And the lyrics are a bit trite."

"I liked it. Should have been a hit."

"Help yourself." George pointed to the cairns of unsold copies.

She straightened his blanket in more of an affectionate gesture than as a necessity. At once, he pulled it back to as it was.

"Mum been gone long?" she asked.

"I don't remember."

"Have you taken all your pills?" He nodded.

She frowned. "I don't think you have or you'd have seen the surprise in the kitchen. You're supposed to be taking them regularly, you know."

"Sorry. I just didn't feel much like it."

"You'll not get better if you don't take the pills the doctor has prescribed."

"Yes, nurse."

Tara gave him a sympathetic smile. "I'll get them."

There was time for one more play of 'Little Lisa' before Tara returned, glass of water and pill packets perched on something flat in a plastic bag. Gently easing it to the floor, and slightly out of breath, she put his medicines to one side. "Close your eyes."

George duly obliged.

"Open them again. Ta-dah! Surprise!"

The pleasure of darkness made his eyelids slow to respond. When they did, he could see Tara waving a copy of *James Last A GoGo*. A record he'd never owned nor ever wanted.

"Oxfam shop. 50p. I've got some more downstairs."

"That's very kind of you." He was sounding unappreciative and particularly frail.

She gave him a cuddle. "Shall I put it on for you?"

"If you like."

"I'm sure the police will have some news soon. They're sure to find your records. And we can get you a proper player and speakers." She tried to sound positive as she slipped the record out of its sleeve. George watched, saying nothing before closing his eyes again. "Aren't you pleased I got these for you?"

George now spoke in a barely audible whisper. "That's not the problem."

"What's not the problem, Gramps?"

George closed his eyes, but didn't answer.

"Please tell me. What's up?"

"They'll be no use to me."

"Why not?" Barely had she finished asking than her mobile rang.

"If you really want to know, I think I'm going deaf." George felt a faint draught of cold air and looked up to see Tara had gone. She hadn't heard. Perhaps it was best that way. What could she do? What could anyone do? There was nothing left for him. He felt too tired, helpless and worthless to carry on.

* * *

"Sorry I've not called you, I've been a bit busy."

"Glad to be back?" Jeff sounded genuinely pleased to hear Tara's voice.

"You bet. And I'm still sorry about the comedy club. I didn't mean to stand you up." Tara was lying back on her bed, head propped on one arm, the other pressing her mobile to her ear.

"No worry. I'm ringing 'cos I've some good news. Really good." Jeff's Australian twang boomed with excitement.

"Go on."

"You know your singing I put on the internet."

"I haven't forgiven you. I'm getting messages every few minutes. Even my course tutor seems more interested in the music than my project."

"That's good, isn't it?"

"Would you believe he said I could defer my course. That's if I'm not too big a star to ever come back."

"Well, there you are, then."

"It's not funny. It's just embarrassing."

"I'm sorry. I should have asked you."

"I wish you had."

"What I was saying, though, is do you know a Zak Chambers?"

"The only Zak I know was talking to Mark."

"The same. He's got on to me through my Facebook page. He wants to meet you."

"Me? It was Mark he was interested in."

"It's you he was asking about."

"Really?"

"Come off it. You were good. You know you were. And he's really keen to see if there's more. Shall I text you his details?"

She felt a growing sense of excitement. Was it hearing from Jeff again or knowing Zak was interested in her? Either way, best not to sound eager. Nothing good ever came of being too enthusiastic, her mum would say. "Alright, then."

"Don't sound so keen! He could make you a star. The next Rita Ora. Katy Perry. Beyoncé."

"I don't think so."

"They had to start somewhere. Make sure you get back to him."

"I will."

* * *

"I have some news for you." Bridget was resting against the sink, peeling off her Marigolds.

Tara was leaning against the fridge, mug of coffee in hand. On return visits like this, she used to do all the talking, telling everything in one go, barely drawing breath. She'd gone to Basingstoke, skipping morning lectures, to confide in her mum about Jeff, and tell her about Zak. Instead, it was Bridget who was doing the talking. About the house, the weather, things she'd seen on television, and all the while busying herself with non-urgent chores like cleaning round the hob and washing down the draining board. Tara could tell it was leading up to something. Now she was about to find out what it was. Though she already knew. She braced herself for the inevitable divorce announcement.

"News?"

"I'm going away."

"What?"

It was obvious to Tara that this was not the reaction Bridget had been expecting.

"Going away."

"Away? Where?"

"North Wales. To a retreat."

"On your own? Or is Dad going with you?"

"God, no. On my own."

"Do you want me to come with you?"

Bridget looked sorrowfully into her daughter's eyes, shaking her head. "I don't think so, no. I just need time to myself. To think. I know it's hard for you at the moment, but I just need space. You don't mind, do you?"

"Of course not. The last few weeks have been awful for you."

"Are you sure?"

"Of course."

"I hope it's the right thing to do."

"You deserve some 'you' time."

"I suppose I do."

"You don't sound very convinced." How odd it felt for Tara to be talking to her mum like she was her mother. How had their relationship switched poles like this?

"I just wasn't expecting any of this."

"So what's it like?"

Bridget reached behind her and handed Tara an iPad. "Here."

Tara flicked through the pages, reading only the headlines, lines like 'Believe in yourself, Recover self-esteem, Regain lost confidence'.

Bridget leaned forward and put her hand on Tara's arm. "You won't tell anyone, will you? They'll only scoff."

"Who would I tell?"

"Your grandfather? I don't know."

"Of course I won't. And he wouldn't scoff anyway."

"I'm sorry. I don't feel like I can trust anyone."

"Oh, thanks."

"You know what I mean. How is he, anyway? Any better?"

Tara grimaced. "No, not really. I'm thinking of going back to the doctor's."

"Oh. Is it really that bad? Tell me." Bridget scrutinised her daughter for clues. "I thought it was starting to clear up. I won't go if you think it's serious."

"Why? When are you going?"

"It's supposed to be next week."

Tara tried not to look surprised at the suddenness of all this. "Supposed to be?"

"I can get a refund if I cancel before the weekend."

"What about your job?"

"I'm taking it as leave."

Tara hoped she wasn't revealing the sense of panic that was rising within her. "It's OK. We'll be alright."

Bridget took her hand away, stiffening her back. "No. I won't go. I should stay here. It was just a spur of the moment thing."

Tara shook her head. "If it means you getting things sorted, you should go."

"I don't have to…"

"No, Mum. You go."

Bridget sighed. "I'm not sure now."

"We'll be OK. How long will you be gone?"

"It's a full week."

"Can we get in touch if we have to?"

Bridget sighed. "They say they prefer not. And that the signal is very poor anyway." She clapped her hands together. "No, that settles it. I won't go."

"Yes you will. Nothing much can happen in a week."

Bridget gave her daughter a hug. "Are you really sure?"

"Really."

"Thank you, darling." Bridget tightened her grip. "I so wish things could go back to how they were."

Tara allowed her mum to engulf her. She felt like a vulnerable child again. Nothing was said, but they both knew they were crying.

And it meant Tara wasn't able to reveal *her* news.

Chapter 29

"You were going to tell me about Paul Simon."

It was another three days before Tara made the emergency appointment at the doctor's. George had said he was alright, but as his cough was showing no signs of improving – the opposite, in fact – and he'd been looking less well almost by the hour, she made the call in secret. When the time came, he said he didn't feel well enough to go. He only agreed when she said she'd get an Uber and go with him to keep him company, though her real motivation was to make sure he actually went into the surgery. In the end, they'd made it and he spent well over the allotted ten minutes in the consultation. When he'd emerged, he was carrying a sheaf of prescriptions but saying nothing.

A wait of twenty-five minutes was predicted by the pharmacy, so they had retired to what had been a launderette but had just re-opened to sell 'great coffee, organic herbal tea infusions, fresh juices, fantastic salami and surprising cheeses', at least according to a sign outside that also boasted, 'a stress-free place, with a relaxing atmosphere like that of a country house'.

As they settled down in chairs more reminiscent of IKEA than Blenheim, Tara asked again.

"Paul Simon?" She thought prompting him to talk about his past might help bring him out of himself. He'd barely spoken since he'd come back from her mum's. He'd not even asked what could be surprising about cheeses as once he might. And it was obvious he wasn't about to reveal anything about what the doctor had said. So she turned to history as a last resort. "You were going to tell me."

"You don't really want to know."

"I do."

"It's not very interesting."

"I am interested."

"Not very much happened."

"Let me hear it."

"I don't feel well enough to tell it properly."

"Try anyway. Please."

"Well, stop me if it gets boring."

"It won't."

George took a deep breath, which turned into a loud cough. Everyone in the café turned and stared. Some put their hands over their mouths. George didn't notice. "I knew Paul when he was living in London. Must have been about 1963, 1964. He was American and had made a couple of records but they'd not been hits. Came over here and played in clubs where I used to go. Places with names like Hole in the Ground and Tinkers Club. Troubadours we used to be called."

"What's a Trewba…?"

"Troubadour. Musician, like an old-fashioned minstrel. Didn't they teach you anything in school?" It was the most animated he'd been since the burglary. Just seeing the doctor seemed to have acted as a pick-me-up.

"What did you do, folk songs, sea shanties?"

"There'd sometimes be a handbill. I can still see it now. 'Songs will be taught every night and song sheets will be distributed to take away,' it used to say."

"Really? You had a sing-a-long? Early karaoke?"

"It wasn't people mimicking stars. We were ourselves. All joining in together." He shook his head in fond memory. "It was brilliant. Paul stood out though. He had his own songs and he was good. More than that. Really, really good. Much better than me, I hate to admit. And he worked hard, too. So while I stayed in London, having a good time, jamming in clubs, messing about with my own band, he went on a solo tour. Right across England."

"What happened when he came back?"

"I didn't see him again. He had a big hit in America and off he went."

"Do you think he remembers you?"

"I doubt it. I don't suppose he missed us. But he wrote that song while he was here. 'Homeward Bound'. Have I ever mentioned it?" Tara nodded. "He wrote it sat on a railway station up north somewhere, depressed as hell. He certainly missed his girlfriend, Katy."

"I thought you'd said her name was Kathy at the Ramsays.'"

"Katy, Kathy, Katarina. All the same. Then he went back to the States, like I said. Became a megastar. And that was that. But they were good times."

Now seemed safe for Tara to ask a question that had been bugging her since that first day in his house. "Can I ask you something?"

"Go on."

"You had a small record that was signed."

"Did I?" He sounded confused.

"One with a cover that had a picture of two people on a road."

"You mean, 'Homeward Bound.'"

"So if he went back to America, how did you get it signed?"

George first frowned, then chuckled. "Signed? That's not signed. That's my writing."

"You wrote on it?"

"Yes."

"So it's not his signature?"

"Of course not."

"Do you remember it?"

"Course I do. 'Shame about the grammar, Paul.'"

"What did it mean?"

"Have you ever heard it?"

"I don't think so."

"When I heard the song, I was really irritated by the lyrics. He sings that he wishes he *was* homeward bound." George broke into song, his voice croaking.

Tara was ahead of him. "I get it. Should be *were*, not was. Subjunctive verb."

George nodded. "Whatever subjunctive is. But I knew it was grammatically wrong. To an English scholar, at least. So I wrote him a note on the sleeve as a joke, always planning to give it to him if I saw him again. Which I didn't."

"So that's not his signature?"

"I've said, no. Whatever made you think that?"

"No reason. But you did have that LP with his autograph. The one with the sticker that you found in Dad's box. That was real, wasn't it?"

"Got it in a junk shop. Antique centre they called it, but junk shop really. Years ago. Big old place, Peacehaven, Sussex. Cold, damp and draughty. I saw it and had to buy it because of the signature, even though I already had my own copy. Three shillings. Price still on the cover. That's how I knew it was mine."

"You remember where you bought all your records?"

"Most of them. It's all part of it."

"So what about Phaedra and the Phaeries? What happened with them?"

"What happened?" He mused for a moment. "We were offered a possible tour in the USA. About the time Paul was being 'discovered'." George made a gesture with his fingers representing inverted commas to suggest his distaste for the word. "The Beatles and other groups from England were becoming really famous. 'British Invasion' it was called. Stop me if I've told you this before."

Tara nodded. It sounded familiar, but since he was opening up she'd no intention of halting him.

"Lots of groups started up, many of them having hits. Herman's Hermits, Hollies, Dave Clark Five. And they toured the world, did America." He paused to think of more. "Zombies, Animals, Freddie and the Dreamers."

"And Phaedra and the Phaeries?" Tara offered.

"Not quite." George waved away a menu but nodded to the invitation for a coffee. Tara pointed at a freshly squeezed orange juice. George continued, unperturbed by the intrusion. "Swinging England. That's what it was called. The world couldn't get enough of it. Especially the Yanks." His pace was slow and he was still short of breath, but the memories seemed to be energising him. "So while the big groups went to all the big places, there was talk of a 'British Invasion' tour of the States. We'd just done a gig in London and there was so much screaming no one could hear us. *We* couldn't hear us. But we got invited to audition for the tour anyway."

A delicate cup on a square saucer was placed in front of him. Tara watched as he tried to poke his finger through the handle that was clearly designed for appearance not function. His shaking hands didn't help. He fumbled for a moment. Had the cup been more than half full, it would have spilt. Thumping it back into the saucer, he muttered something about Fancy Dans, then pointed at her orange juice.

"Why have they given you yours in a jam jar? What's the matter with the world?" He paused to get his breath back. "Where was I? We had the audition in a warehouse in Hackney. There were several groups and we all got a turn. I was one of the oldest – the oldest in our group, certainly. But I had long hair, lied about my age. Don't suppose they cared. And we passed." He stopped now and waited for a reaction.

"The States? That's brilliant. So what happened? Where did you go?"

"I didn't."

He reached down for a second attempt at the cup. This time he grasped the handle more firmly and managed to sip some of the coffee without spilling much.

"Why not? I thought you said you were good."

"We were. Not the biggest of places, Iowa, Wisconsin. But they were opportunities."

"This isn't the same as you told us at the Ramsays'?"

"No, this was different."

"So why didn't you go?"

"Reasons."

"Like what?"

"Reasons."

"Was the tour cancelled?"

He put the cup down firmly and leaned forward. "There's something I've never told anyone." He leaned forward still further until she could feel the warmth of his breath. "You must promise me that if I tell you, you'll never tell anyone else. Not your mum… especially not your mum."

"Of course."

"You must mean it. Promise me."

"I do, honest."

Even now he didn't seem sure. He sat back and made to stand.

"Maybe later. The prescription will be ready."

"More coffee?" Imminent departure was barred by the arrival of an assistant. Her pronounced Eastern European accent made her sound like she was barking an order and George felt unable to refuse. She topped up his cup to roughly halfway.

Tara seized the opportunity. "So now we have a bit longer, won't you tell me what happened after your audition?"

There wasn't really much George could do to escape this time. He seemed almost relieved, and the distraction of holding the cup and drinking helped. He didn't even have to make eye contact with Tara while he spoke. "We passed the audition. We were one of the best. They told us, but I already knew." He took another sip, his eyes now focused not on Tara but events in his memory. "We went straight to a pub to celebrate. I'd never felt so excited in my whole life. We talked about what new songs we'd need to learn, what we would wear, made jokes about who was the better player. We laughed a lot. And imagined what the future might look like. We didn't dare to think we might be as big as The Beatles. But we all had that thought. That dream. By the time I'd got home, I was a few sheets. Or worse."

"Sheets?"

"Sheets to the wind. Drunk." He took a gulp of coffee. "Your nan, Evelyn, was sitting in the dark by the light of a radio, listening to a late night music programme. I remember it like yesterday. There was some guy on the wireless, singing. Jimmy Young. He was very famous. Was for many years after, too. I could tell your nan wasn't happy. There were no mobile phones in those days, to tell people where you were, if you were going to be late. She ignored me at first as if she was really listening to the song. I said that was music for squares, the future was Phaedra and the Phaeries or something like that. When she spoke, all she said was, 'I was worried about you. I didn't know where you were.'"

"And what happened when you told her you'd passed the audition?"

"She didn't know we'd had one."

"Why?"

"I'd not told her."

"You're joking."

"No. I'd kept it a secret. In case we'd failed it. I didn't want her thinking I was a loser."

"But she must have been excited when you told her."

"I didn't tell her."

Tara let out a quizzical laugh. "Now I don't believe you."

"I couldn't tell her."

"Why not? I'd have been jumping up and down, shouting it in the street."

"She had news for me instead." George had now what Tara remembered her grandmother calling a faraway look, his thoughts deeper than even his memory. "I'll never forget it." His voice was quiet, sad, distant. "She said, 'I'm in the family way.' We were going to have a baby. Just when I would have been going to America. I couldn't leave her, could I? Not then. It was my duty. The right thing to do. The *only* thing to do."

"Couldn't you have done some of the gigs, then come back? How long would you have been away?"

"Different times. It's not like today when I could have hopped back for a few days when the baby was due. Even if the tour organisers would have let me. Which they wouldn't have. And planes crashed. Famous people died in plane crashes touring

America. Jim Reeves, Buddy Holly, Patsy Cline, Otis Redding. Your nan would have worried. No. I couldn't go."

George fell silent.

"So what happened?"

"When the organisers heard we were breaking up…"

"But you weren't."

"That's what it looked like to them. So they gave the gig to another band."

"What did the rest of your band say?"

"Nothing. They never spoke to me again. I found out they changed their name and eventually got a record deal in England. Even had a couple of small hits. But they never really made it like we might have done if we'd toured America. Eventually they broke up and joined other bands."

"And Nan never knew?"

"I said we'd split, that the band didn't need a pianist and, as they had a better bass player, we'd agreed to go our separate ways. If she was curious, she never let on." At last he looked up. There might have been a tear in his eye. "Now you have it. My secret."

"That's so sad."

"I hoped the chance might come again, but it didn't. Got close, but no cigar."

"Oh, Gramps." She reached out for his hand and gave it a squeeze.

"I carried on playing when I could. Gigs and sessions kept me busy for years. When they dried up, hotel bars and restaurants. No one listened much but it felt good. And there always were my tunes for commercials and what they call corporates. They made a bit of money. I still get the odd cheque come through. But nothing serious. What really mattered was we got your mum. And now you, of course. You're the real prizes."

"My mum? The baby – it was my mum?"

George nodded. "I thought you'd worked that out."

"Does Mum know?"

He withdrew his hand. "No." He shook his head vehemently. "And she must never know. I wouldn't want her to think she ruined my life. She didn't. It was just different, that's all. But that's what she'll think. And that's why I've kept it secret. No one has ever known. And it must stay secret."

"So why are you telling me now?"

He fell silent for a moment, as if weighing up his answer. "If things had been simpler, who knows where I might have ended up? But I'm the past."

"You can get back to playing when you feel better."

George shook his head. "I don't think so." His voice had become weary again. "I missed my chance. It's your time now. Don't waste it." He made a fist and gently thumped the table in front of her, making his coffee cup rattle in its saucer. Tara looked around at the startled looks of other customers, raising her eyebrows to them in acknowledgement and apology.

"Promise me. Don't waste it," George repeated.

"OK, Gramps. I get it."

"Do you? I hope you do. You've no ties, not like I had. You're clever. You're talented. If you get a chance, grab it." George's fist became a claw gesture with his right hand, tightening it as he spoke as he struggled for breath. "Believe me, it won't come again."

Tara scraped her chair back. "I think the prescription will be ready."

Chapter 30

Tara's mobile bleeped. She hoped it was her mother, saying she'd found a signal and was enjoying the retreat. Mind, she wasn't sure what she was going to text back. She would keep Gramps' confidence about his secret but would she say how worried she was becoming about his health? It didn't matter. It was a text from Jeff. 'Call me,' read the message. Two stabs of her fingers later, Jeff's voice was on the other end.

"It's your friendly Antipodean fixer here," Jeff answered brightly.

"What do you want? I'm not in the mood for jokes."

Jeff's tone switched instantly. "I'm sorry." He sounded genuinely concerned. "What's up?"

"Nothing. Just my grandfather's not well at all."

"I'm sorry."

"It's not your fault. What did you want?"

"I don't know if I'm the bearer of good news or bad, after what you've said. But I've just had a message from Zak. He says you've not been in touch."

"No, sorry. It's been horrible here."

"Well, the news is he's still interested in you. Wants to meet up. So I said I'd fix it."

"Really?"

"Sorry, I thought you'd be pleased."

"I am. It's just not a good time. When?"

"This afternoon."

"Really?"

"He's in town and said he could meet you at uni."

"I'm not sure I can."

"He apologised for the short notice. I think you should try and do it."

"I can't promise anything."

"You've got a lecture in the history block this afternoon, haven't you?"

"Yes. How did you know?"

"Been stalking you." He gave an uneasy laugh. "When's it finish?"

"About 5.30."

"I've got one that finishes the same time, in the science lab. So why don't I come over? I'll say we'll meet him there at a quarter to six. You don't mind me being there, do you? Then, if all goes well, maybe we can go somewhere and celebrate. I can book a table at a little Italian I know."

Tara let out a deep breath. At last he seemed to have worked out that she and Mark were finished. "OK, then. But I might have to get back if Gramps is bad."

"Can't someone else look after him?"

"There's only my mum and she's not even in the country. She's swanned off to Wales."

"Should have told me. I've got a cousin who lives in Cardiff. She could have stayed with her."

"I don't think so." Maybe she would tell him why her mum had gone, though she wasn't convinced she understood herself.

"I think she said she might be going to some place in the middle of nowhere."

"Sounds adventurous, your mum. She going alone?"

"I'll tell you over the Italian."

"It's a date."

And about time too, Tara thought of adding. "See you just before a quarter to."

* * *

Tara stood alone in an empty lecture theatre, packing her books away. There was no sign of either Jeff or Zak. From behind her came a voice.

"Is it alright for me to talk to you?"

Tara spun round to find herself face to face with Mark.

"You already are. What are you doing here?" she asked.

"So it's OK to carry on."

Tara gave a non-committal shrug. "What are you doing here?"

"Zak. Why are you here?"

Tara thought it unwise to mention Jeff just yet. "Same."

"Why's he asked to see you as well as me without telling either of us?" Mark's eyes locked with Tara's as they tried to read each other's mind.

"Does he know we're not together anymore?" she asked.

"Did you tell him?"

"Did you?"

Mark shuffled uneasily. "I've had time to think. I was taking things too much for granted. Getting too familiar with your grandfather's name and…"

"Too right."

"Then all that with the burglary. I know you blame me." He looked back at her for signs of forgiveness.

"I don't. Not really. I was just really upset. His records, Hunter. I still can't get over Hunter." She might have kept going but she found her eyes welling up.

Mark involuntarily stepped forward to comfort her. And his touch, his warmth was familiar and comforting, and she realised how much she missed him. Instead of pushing him away, she let him draw closer.

"I'm sorry," he whispered in her ear. "I've missed you so much." He paused, then gulped, "I love you." Involuntarily, Tara found herself kissing him.

"Steady on, you two. Or we'll need a bucket of water," came a voice from the corner.

They carried on.

"Well, excuse me. If you want me to leave, just say so. I'll just get you a mattress and push off." The voice had an unmistakably Australian twang.

The two separated now.

"Hello, Jeff, what brings you here?" Mark followed Jeff's gaze that was fixed firmly on Tara. "Am I missing something here?"

"No, mate. You carry on. Sorry to have intruded."

Tara looked apologetically back to Jeff but said nothing.

"So what brings you here?" Mark asked again.

Tara glanced across to Jeff. "It's a bit complicated," she said uneasily.

"How complicated?"

"I'm your new agent," Jeff offered, trying to sound bright. "Only taking 50% of your fees."

Mark's eyes were darting between Tara and Jeff. "Have you two been seeing each other?" he demanded.

Jeff answered for the two of them. "Look, mate, Tara's come to meet Zak. What about you?"

"How do you know about Zak?"

"Quite easy. Zak saw Tara on my channel and liked what he saw, so got on to me. Maybe hedging his bets in case he wanted to work with her, not you."

Mark didn't react to the implied insult about his music. "That doesn't explain why he's got us here together, does it?" It was the question that was also bugging Tara.

"Guess we'll have to ask him." Jeff looked at his mobile. "When he gets here. He's late. Have any of us ever met this bloke?" Simultaneously, Mark and Jeff's mobiles bleeped. "Well, there's funny."

"What's funny?" Mark wrestled his mobile from his pocket. "Fuck. That's not funny."

Tara looked at both of them, waiting for an explanation. "What isn't?"

"He's only not coming. Gone off somewhere in a hurry." Mark sounded desperate as well as angry.

"Read on, mate. He says he'll catch up with you tomorrow."

"Tomorrow?" Tara stamped her foot. "Will one of you tell me what's going on?"

Mark answered. "Battle of the Bands. This weekend. It's a talent show. He told me to enter us."

"Us?"

"Straight after he saw the video from the party. Said it takes all kinds of music and we might have a chance. Heats are tomorrow and the finals on Sunday."

"And when were you going to tell me?"

"I was going to. Then I thought you wouldn't come, so I'd do it on my own. Or ask Zak if he knew anyone else I could work with."

"Oh, thanks."

Mark shrugged. "I'm sorry, but what else was I supposed to do?

"But you didn't."

Mark shook his head.

"So he thinks we're still Mark'n' Tara?"

Jeff made a coughing sound. "Not necessarily."

"What's that?" Mark turned angrily to him.

Jeff shrugged. "I might have told him."

"You did what?"

"I thought he ought to know."

"What's it got to do with you?" Mark's eyes were blazing.

Tara looked straight at Jeff. "Did you know Mark was going to be here?"

"Nope. Like I said, looks like Zak's been hedging his bets. If you weren't going to work as a pair I guess he would have wanted Tara to go as a solo."

Mark was still glowering. "How could she, she hasn't got any material."

"Talent, mate, that's what she's got."

"Meaning?"

"Stop it, you two." Tara tucked her books tightly under her arm and prepared to leave. "It makes no difference. I'm not doing it. Solo or duo."

Mark turned his attention back to Tara. "Please, T. It could be a big break. For both of us."

Jeff intervened again. "How sweet! You were happy to go on your own before you got here. Now you're saying you're a team."

"Leave it, Jeff." Tara's tone was sharp. She had seen Mark's angry reaction to Jeff's sarcasm and meant to calm things. Instead, it came out unintentionally harsh.

"Right, then. If you don't need me to sort you out, I'll leave you to it." Jeff didn't move though.

Tara felt helpless, trapped between Mark, vulnerable, desperate and needy; and Jeff, his face betraying hurt and rejection. She had to make a choice. "I'm really sorry, Jeff."

"No worries." Jeff's Australian accent had become more pronounced.

"You're sure?"

"Of course. I can see I'm not wanted. Sort your life and careers out. Both of you. I've better things to do." This time, he turned to leave. "See you later."

Mark watched the lecture theatre door slam. "Thank God he's gone." He turned back to Tara. "Say you'll do it, please. For me."

"How come you hadn't said anything about this before?" Tara demanded.

"You weren't talking to me, that's why."

"And if I'm so unimportant and you were going to get someone in to replace me, why do you need me now?"

"I didn't mean that. You're the only one I want to work with. I won't go if you won't."

She arched her eyebrows. "You haven't even said where it is."

"Birmingham."

"Bloody hell. How are we going to get there?"

"I've booked a car."

"And where would we stay?" She felt the books slipping from beneath her arms.

"If we're going to do it, we should stop arguing and get on with putting together a performance. We only need to work up four songs. We can do it, I know we can."

Tara thought back to how much she'd enjoyed singing at the party. "Four songs? There's no time." Despite her resistance, she knew she was weakening. "And I'm not sure I can leave my grandfather alone for the weekend either."

"I thought he was all action these days."

"Not since the burglary. He's gone downhill. Really badly."

"You've got to do it, T. We can't let Zak down."

"You still haven't said what happens on Saturday night."

"I've booked an Airbnb. I'll have to cancel it if we're not going."

"You think I'm spending the night with you?"

"I'll sleep on the couch. If there is one. Or the floor. Or the bath. Anything."

Tara checked that Jeff had really gone, put down her books and threw her hands behind her head, arching her back to stare at the ceiling before blowing out a deep breath as she turned to look into his big, pleading brown eyes. "I really don't know." Except she did. She knew she was going to go and that the couch, floor or bath wouldn't be needed. "Let me call my grandfather to tell him I'm going to be late, then we'd better get to work."

Chapter 31

George wished Tara good luck, put the phone back on its base and made his way up to his room. He dropped the pharmacy bag and papers on to his eiderdown, placed the glass of water on his bedside table and slumped on to his bed. Around him, pictures, mirrors, furniture, a photograph of Evelyn and Bridget, two piles of unread books, a clock radio and holiday nick-nack memorabilia on top of the chest of drawers that hadn't interested the burglars. All were Evelyn's and all meaningless to him. The only real difference from before she'd gone was the array of tablets in packets and potions in bottles that he seemed to be accumulating. Maybe it was worthy of a lifetime of underachievement. He hoped failure wasn't hereditary, though what had been happening with his family didn't give him much cause for optimism.

He tipped upside down the pharmacy bag, emptying it of the latest set of pills. He waited until they'd all landed, then picked up one of the papers he'd been carrying and that Tara had been given by her parents for him to look through. He'd skimmed them before but, with Tara going away and nothing to do, he thought he should give them another chance. The top one looked suspiciously like the *Basingstoke Tribune*.

It wasn't. Holding it up he could see the title, *Golden Times, the voice of the mature*. He skimmed through it in the expectation there would be nothing of interest. Each page seemed to be fixated with the most depressing editorial. In-depth articles about debt, wills, ageing. A full-page advertisement for a limited edition World War One memorial watch caught his eye, first because of its ugly design and then the thought that time was the one thing *Golden Times* readers no longer had. He gave a grunt that turned into a cough, waiting for it to subside before flicking the remaining pages. He found an article that was in a font size he could read, devoted to hearing aids. He tore it out to read later, folding it and placing it on the bedside table under a box of antibiotics. The next double-page spread was on cancer and rising funeral costs, which he skipped. Was this supposed to be uplifting? He dropped the paper on the floor and picked through the leaflets that had been with it. Maybe there'd be something for when he felt better. *If* he ever felt better.

A bright, postcard-sized brochure was an invitation to send for details of a funeral monthly instalment payment plan. He imagined a headstone: 'George Turnbull, never-never be forgotten'. The incentive to apply was a free pen, worth £10. What use would a pen be when he was beyond the incinerator? He tore the card into four and dropped the pieces on to *Golden Times*.

Brushing aside two packets of tablets with long, depressing sounding names ending in xine and ide, he convulsed again. His cough was causing him more pain than he thought possible. Not just physical. Psychological too. Each one felt like a countdown to his death. His doctor had recognised this, telling him, 'I can keep giving you drugs. But you really need to be looking after yourself better,' listing diet, drinking more water and other stuff George forgot instantly. But the words that struck home were 'looking after' and they wouldn't leave his head. Maybe Toby had been right all along. He knew he had to do something if he wasn't to be found mouldering in his bed by someone wondering why they'd not seen him for a couple of months. He reached out to an envelope that he'd kept hidden under the photograph of Evelyn and Bridget. He'd sent for it after his encounter with Sexy Domino. With Tara away for the weekend, it was his only option.

Chapter 32

It had been easier rehearsing with Mark than Tara had expected. He'd been working on incorporating more conventional melodies into his abstract soundscapes, inspired perhaps by the reaction to her improvisations at the party. The Battle of the Bands was a contest to showcase undiscovered talent and the only restrictions were performers couldn't already be signed to an agent or record label and not be a tribute band. So long as incorporating lines and hooks from songs that she'd heard her grandfather play didn't disqualify them, they stood a chance. Mark's arrangements were certainly original. When she told him about her grandfather's idea of 'psychedelic rap' from the pier, he was inspired and began to work up a few new ideas. And while he was happy developing the arrangements and the tracks, she focused on melodies and lyrics, and wasn't as terrified as she thought she'd be.

That just left Gramps. She really wasn't sure about leaving him behind. Since the burglary, the house had no longer resonated with music but his coughing. The apparent remission after the doctor's appointment had lasted only until he'd revealed his secret, after which he'd deteriorated again. Even as she worked on the songs, she couldn't stop worrying about him.

It was after two in the morning before she arrived back home, having stopped off at the 24/7 to buy him some ready meals for the weekend. She could hear his whooping from the road. What if he was too ill to be left by himself? Something needed to be done but she didn't know what. Maybe after Battle of the Bands. Creeping into the house, she set her alarm for seven and lay on her bed, imagining herself on the bill for Glastonbury. Before she had reached the stage, she was asleep.

* * *

Next morning was a rush. Mark was picking up the hire car and they were meeting at nine. She knocked gently on Gramps' bedroom door, but there was no sound. Second thoughts about leaving swept through her. But it was too late now. And it was only a weekend. Peering into his room, she could see him on his bed, in his clothes, holding an envelope that he must have been intending to open and read before falling asleep.

She tapped him lightly on the shoulder. He grunted and turned away, but didn't wake. She knew she should tell him she was on her way, but it seemed a shame to wake him. And what if he said he didn't want her to go, that he was too ill to be left alone? Or worse, said to go but made her feel guilty? She eased the envelope from his fingers and scribbled she'd be back Sunday evening and her mobile number. She signed it 'luv Tara', then added 'xx' to ease her conscience, before easing it back into its original position between his fingers. He was breathing heavily but didn't stir.

There wasn't time to get nervous or excited. Or back out. In the kitchen, she arranged his meals on a worktop, with Post-Its on each of the tins and packets on how to cook and when. Then it was back to her room where she grabbed her bag – a much smaller one than last time – and was creeping down the stairs when she heard a cry.

"Evelyn. Is that you? Evelyn?"

She put the case down and put her head round her grandfather's bedroom door. He was half sitting up. "It's only me, Gramps."

"Is there something the matter?" He sounded confused.

"I was just putting some things together. For my weekend away." She said it in a way to make him feel like he should know about it.

"Oh," was all he managed in return. He looked her up and down. "You're not going out in those?" He was staring at her torn jeans. "Haven't you something decent to wear?"

"Fashion, Gramps. Fashion."

"What's the fashion in those? They look like they've come from a charity shop. And not a very good one. And is that a vest? You'll freeze to death. Let me lend you a woolly."

"Do you want anything before I go?"

"Can you pass me my water?"

She handed him a glass from his bedside table. "I'll be off in a minute. But back on Sunday afternoon. If you need me, I've written my mobile number on your envelope." She stretched out to pick it up and show him but he snatched it back, slopping water from his glass in the process.

"Mind," he said urgently, rubbing the damp spot on his eiderdown.

"I'll get you some more." He allowed her to take the glass that she filled from the en suite Evelyn had insisted on adding to the room. "I've left you some meals ready in the kitchen, too."

"Can you get me a small cheese sandwich if you're going downstairs," he called across as the glass filled. "And a mug of warm milk. It'll help me sleep."

"What will you do while I'm away?" she asked as she put the water back on the bedside table.

"Nothing much. I might stay in bed tomorrow if I don't feel any better. There's plenty to listen to on the wireless. And I might go for a walk in the park if it's nice on Sunday."

"Make sure you wrap up warm."

"Look who's talking, you with holes in your trousers."

"You know what I mean."

"And who'll do up my buttons and tie up my shoelaces?"

If he meant it as a self-deprecating joke or observation on how roles had changed, for Tara it only served to allow a twinge of doubt to make an unwelcome intervention. "Are you sure it's OK to go? To leave you. On your own."

"Of course it is. You're not my carer, you know." He waved her away. "Now, you get off for your weekend. Don't forget my sandwich and hot milk."

When she returned with a tray of sandwiches, hot milk and a chocolate Hobnob, he was asleep again. She thought of looking at the envelope that he'd plainly not wanted her to see, but not at the risk of disturbing him again. So she placed the tray on the floor and gently tiptoed out.

Chapter 33

When George woke up, he knew what he had to do. He struggled out of bed and stumbled downstairs to the phone, coughing all the way, carrying the envelope Tara had written on. From it he pulled out the brochure.

'Lastdays' was the bold headline. He could see how the brochure had enticed Toby all those months ago. And had it been so bad? He'd been agonising over giving them a second chance for ages. Now was the time to act. His hand shaking, he dialled the number on the back.

"Good morning, Good Days. How can we help?"

"Hello, is that Lastdays?"

"Yes, but no. We're Good Days now. Is there something you'd like us to help you with?"

"Is it possible to come and visit you?" He hadn't really got a plan, just a half-baked notion of checking the place out properly, maybe agreeing to spend the odd day or weekend there, until he felt better. Convalescence, it used to be called.

"When were you thinking?"

"Tomorrow?"

"Can I just ask you a little about the retired person who you're thinking of?"

"It's me."

"Can I just take your name and a few details?"

This was the one thing he had thought about. He didn't want them to know he'd been before or what had happened in case they remembered. "My name is Simon Paul. I'm eighty and I live alone." He was going to make no mention of his current state of health though a burst of coughs and his quavering voice may have acted as a warning sign.

He was put through to a lady with a kindly tone who introduced herself as Joan Tufnell, the new owner of what was now called Good Days Retirement Community. The conversation was chatty, friendly and not the language of a heavy-handed sales spiel he expected. He still expected they would try to persuade him to part with his life savings and a room with no view. But it was worth the risk and he was effusive when she said 'yes' to his uninvited visit without any mention of the short notice.

"How will you be coming? Do you know where we are?" Mrs Tufnell asked as the call came to an end.

"By train."

"Worthing is the nearest station. From Victoria, though I expect you knew that. I think there are four an hour. If you tell me what time train you're getting, I'll pick you up from the station."

"I was thinking about eleven o'clock."

"It's about an hour and a half journey. So I'll check when you're due to arrive and look forward to meeting you then."

By the end of the conversation, George was exhausted. And not feeling well. He'd hardly reached halfway up the stairs when he sank to all fours, stopping every few moments to cough. It didn't seem so long ago he would bound up, two at a time. How had it come to this? At the landing, the level surface made going easier, and once his bed was in sight he sped up a little, hauling himself in, pulling up the covers and closing his eyes.

* * *

When he woke the next day, he wasn't feeling much better. Staying where he was and sleeping through until Tara returned was a tempting option. He resisted it. Trouble was, by the time he'd summoned up the energy to go, he'd left it too late for breakfast. He'd find something to eat on the train. From getting dressed, it was straight out the door, ignoring the winking 'message' light on his phone. If that was Ron, it'd just have to wait until the evening. By the time he arrived at Victoria station, he was already feeling tired but was buoyed by a sense of accomplishment at making it – and with ten minutes to spare. Stopping to get his breath back, he looked around the station. The magic of the railways could never be completely lost, the Victorians had seen to that. Portland stone façade, ironwork and arched roof; they were still magnificent, even though neglected during the twentieth century and violated in the twenty-first. He was almost looking forward to the journey, rolling over the Thames and looking into the back windows of suburban houses.

"Can I help you?" The station concourse was strangely silent and the booming voice of a young man in a yellow high visibility jacket startled him.

"Thank you, yes. Worthing. Train to Worthing. Where do I get a ticket?"

"Sorry, mate. No trains today."

"Four an hour, I was told. I just need a ticket." George had fumbled open his wallet and was producing a £20 note.

"Yeah, but not a train. It's a bus. Outside." HiViz waved vaguely in the direction George had just come from.

"This is a train station, isn't it?" George tried to impose the authority his seniority warranted.

"Not today it's not. Emergency engineering works. Replacement bus service. All day. It says so on the website. You should always check online before you travel."

George might once have argued that he didn't have 'online' and knew nothing about replacement buses. Instead, he stood there, confused and helpless. His hand holding the £20 note began to shake.

"You OK, mate?" HiViz turned and yelled to a lone figure in the distance. "Chandra, there's an old-timer here looking for the replacement buses. Can you show him?"

It took a few minutes for the entire conversation with HiViz to be rerun with Chandra before she guided George to a ticket office. Still clasping the £20, he was shocked to find the fare was more. "I got change from ten shillings in my day," he moaned, although it was unlikely the cashier was the slightest bit interested or had any idea what a shilling was, let alone ten of them. He proffered several more notes in exchange for a ticket and offered Chandra some of the loose coins he'd received back as reward for shepherding him to a coach outside. She politely refused, smiling and wishing him a good day while helping him up the steps into the coach.

As he squeezed into a seat with almost no separation from the one in front, he wondered if this was not going to be such a good day after all. He loathed coach travel as much as he'd loved trains. Cramped and uncomfortable, with no refreshment bar or toilet, he wasn't sure how he would manage the next ninety minutes. Except after the driver tapped his microphone twice and mumbled, "One, two. Welcome aboard this bus to Worthing. Journey time is around three hours."

* * *

The coach's progress was slow and the roads congested, even on a Sunday, and the time dragged. A *Private Eye* had been left on the seat and he flicked through it. It didn't look much different from the days he reserved a copy at his newsagents, now closed down. But the print seemed smaller and the movement of the coach – sluggish as it was – made him feel nauseous. With nothing else to do, he alternated between watching South London pass by and closing his eyes. Once or twice he stuck his leg into the aisle to delay a noisy small boy who persisted in running up and down, but the child simply hurdled it, then ran back around hoping for more obstacles.

Just as he started to relax, he jerked upright with a mild panic attack. What did Mrs Tufnell look like? How would he recognise her? How would she recognise him? And worse, if this coach was going to take so much longer than the train he said he was catching, surely she'd give up and go back to Good Days? It was then he realised he'd left behind the brown envelope with the Good Days' leaflet inside and Tara's phone number written on the outside. He was doomed to be helpless and stranded in Worthing.

Trying to distract himself from the certain disaster awaiting him, he stared out the window again. The last time he'd been on a bus going south out of London, Bridget must have been about seven. He'd been reading her Enid Blyton's *Five Go To Billycock Hill* at bedtime, half a chapter a night, before kissing her goodnight and switching off the light. They must have reached chapter five when he was offered a gig at a hotel in suburban Croydon. During the sixties, he'd been a regular playing as a session man at the Croydon ABC, working alongside big names like Billy Fury, Del Shannon and Chuck Berry. It was how he'd met one of the guys he'd formed the Beat Boys with, and then Phaedra and the Phaeries. By the seventies, the ABC had been destroyed, its giant 2,000-seater auditorium split into three small cinema screens. The hotel gig, some ten years later, was just outside the town centre and more modest, playing piano to diners. The incentive had been the hotel's reputation for big name guests. George had hoped he might get discovered, the same way he'd hoped *every* booking might lead to discovery.

Travelling there meant leaving work bang on five thirty, catching a train to Croydon and then a thirty-minute bus ride and ten-minute walk. Getting home was even worse. After three weeks of playing to unappreciative audiences and picking up a measly hourly wage plus meagre tips and a free meal, his dream of discovery was no nearer fulfilment. Tiredness grew as optimism faded and he began increasingly to play to the other notoriety of the hotel – its reputation for being haunted. No one ever seemed to notice what he played anyway, so he began adding ghost songs to his set – 'Spooky', 'Voodoo Woman', 'I Put a Spell On You', 'Ghost Riders in the Sky' – then made up ghost lyrics to others. 'Fools Rush In' became 'Ghouls Rush In', 'Crying' became 'Dying' and he performed 'I Almost Lost My Mind' as 'Is Haunted All the Time'. It was when he was requested to sing Frank Sinatra's 'Lady is a Tramp' for a newly engaged couple and changed it to 'Lady is a Vampire' that a complaint was made. He was dismissed on the spot. It was a relief in a way, and meant he could return to bedtime reading duties. Except he found Bridget had finished the Enid Blyton by herself. Worse, she told him icily that being read to was for babies, and she didn't need him anymore.

Now the tables were turned. He needed her and she was in purdah somewhere. He put the *Private Eye* over his head to stem the rising sense of loss and despair and was soon asleep.

He knew he'd arrived in Worthing when he was gently shaken by the driver.

"We're here, mate."

Bleary-eyed, he stumbled down the steps of the coach on to the pavement.

"Mr Paul?"

George turned to see a grey-haired lady that Evelyn would have described as portly, walking up behind him. He hesitated at the unfamiliar name before answering. "Yes. How did you know it was me?"

"There was no one else left on the bus."

"Have you been waiting long?"

"About five minutes."

"How did you know we were going to be so late?"

"It's about on time. I'd checked and found out it was a coach today. It often is. Didn't you hear my phone message? Never mind. Did you have a good journey?"

It was safer not to admit he'd not known about the coach. And anyway, he hated the ritual of describing journeys at the start of a visit. Toby would insist on listing the red traffic lights, near prangs and 'bloody Sunday drivers' for the first ten minutes of any visit to him and Evelyn. So he simply mumbled that it was OK.

"Let me introduce myself properly. I'm Joan Tufnell, owner and manager of Good Days." She held out her hand so they could shake hands.

"I like the name." George didn't let on that he'd visited before or that he was using an alias.

Mrs Tufnell ushered him towards her car. "Actually, it used to have a different name that was a bit depressing. So I changed it when I took over. Good Days. Actually Good Days Retirement Community, but I don't want it to sound too pompous. I really want it to be somewhere people want to be." She smiled. "It's about a fifteen-minute drive from here. I hope the long coach journey didn't wear you out too much." The description of her plans continued as she drove. "It was quite a bit rundown when I took it over, so you'll see there are still changes taking place. And we've not finished yet. I've lots of plans. Exciting times. We're so very lucky as it's all being funded by a bequest from a local businessman. He was a multi-millionaire and wanted this as his lasting legacy." She may have intended to outline what the plans were, but was interrupted by George suddenly breaking into a coughing fit. Instead she limited herself to, "Nearly there," and they continued in silence while George struggled to contain further convulsions.

They passed a newly painted 'Good Days Retirement Community' sign and turned into the drive. George remembered it from his first visit. Narrow, shrub- and tree-lined, it was one residents normally saw once and only from this direction, with the return journey inside a black limo and wooden casket. But while it had been overgrown last time, the undergrowth had been trimmed back. He saw between the trees what looked like an old lodge or stable shrouded in scaffolding and then the main buildings. Some looked brighter than before. More scaffolding cloaked another part, but the end block still looked like an abandoned barracks. He felt a sudden surge of doubt about his mission. Mrs Tufnell must have felt it too because she tapped the steering wheel and gestured at the building work.

"There's still a lot to do. As you can see. It's got to be special to live in. As a first-time visitor, any thoughts you have as you look round, please tell me. By the way, how do you prefer to be known? Mr Paul or Simon?"

George wondered if now might be the moment to reveal his real name, but lacked the strength. "Simon is fine with me."

"And I'm Joan."

While this was all better than his first visit, George was still uneasy. Friendly, yes. But her words weren't completely reassuring. It felt no less like a prison, and 'special to live in' didn't sound like it included the part-time plan he was nurturing. Doubts continued to grow as they drew closer.

As the car pulled up in front of the main door, the wheels crunching on the gravel courtyard, he was on the verge of asking to be taken straight back to the station. Only another cough prevented it. Maybe Joan sensed that too. "Right. That's enough travelling. Time for a coffee and a breather. How do you like it?"

Chapter 34

Sitting in a warm room, sunk into a comfortable sofa with a steaming cappuccino, George felt less stressed. From the outside it had looked like a headmaster's office and brought back memories of when he'd been caned for playing hooky from PE to do extra piano practice the day before a music exam. The inside was bright, informal, smelt of paint. On the wall, artwork. Not prints. Real paintings.

Sitting in an armchair opposite, coffee in hand, folder on her knee, Joan noticed George staring at the pictures. "Good, aren't they? They're by a local artist. We're changing them every few months to keep things fresh. And these," Joan pointed to a row that was vivid but with brushstrokes obviously clumsy and awkward, "these are the work of one of our guests. He's been exhibited at the Royal Academy's Summer Exhibition. Arthritis limits what he can do now, but he's still very talented. We're proud to have them. And him."

George nodded either side of another painful cough.

"Before we talk about Good Days, can I ask if you'll let my nurse check that cough of yours?"

'I've got enough tablets to sink a battleship. I didn't come here for more medicines. Don't patronise me.' That was the response George might have given had he not felt relaxed and engulfed by the sofa, or stifled by another bout of coughing. And anyway, she'd spoken in a way that he felt respected, reassured, not patronised. He simply raised a hand in apology that Joan took to be an acceptance of her offer.

"Good, we'll call in on her as we go round. But first, let me tell you about my plans."

She told him about the other guests, almost as if she already knew how lonely he'd become and how he craved company. He was comforted that it wasn't a sales pitch.

"But that's enough of my talking. Do you want to tell me about yourself?"

He skipped most of his life story. He told how he'd run a small grocery store, then worked in an office, that his wife had died suddenly and he lived with his granddaughter and a room full of records. "My wife, Evelyn, says they're the biggest collection that no one should have to listen to," he said, forgetting for a moment that the records had been stolen and she was no longer there to say it. And for the first time since she'd died, he started to talk about her. And Joan listened, sympathetically, nodding, prompting him when he felt he might choke as the memories flooded back.

"She sounds a wonderful woman," Joan said quietly when he finally stopped, his eyes close to tears.

"She was."

"On the phone, you said that you're a musician."

George nodded, grateful for the chance to compose himself and relieved that she'd said 'you're a musician', not, 'you were a musician.'

"That's right." He might have started on a name-dropping tour from the sixties, but there was a gentle knock on the door and another middle-aged lady stepped in.

"Sorry to disturb you, but did you want lunch?"

Joan addressed George. "I've booked you Sunday lunch, if you'd like one. Roast beef or turkey, whichever you fancy. You're not vegetarian are you?"

"Absolutely not. Sunday roast is my favourite." Confirmation at last. Today would be a good one after all.

* * *

Lunch didn't disappoint. It was the same room as Bernard's party on the previous, ill-fated visit, but transformed. Nothing like the canteen he expected, it was decorated and furnished like a restaurant, even down to a menu on the table and a wine list. Joan tempted him into a small glass of red.

"I'm hoping all this is sustainable." She smiled as she poured from the bottle. "It's just how I think it should be. Anything else would be just plain wrong." She caught George's eyes looking towards the centre of the room, where a glass fish tank stood empty. He remembered how last time it had contained two desultory fish. "Ah, I see you've spotted the tank. It's going. When we took over here, there were two goldfish in there and nothing much else. I say goldfish. They were nearly white with age." George nodded, picturing it in his mind. "We gave the tank a good clean and added some weed to make it look better – and probably better for the fish. But as I say, they were very old and one died. The other one seemed quite lost being on its own."

George looked surprised. "I didn't think goldfish had memories."

"Nor did I, but apparently they do. Then, a few days ago, the one that was left also died. I suppose they'd been together so long, it just gave up. Who knows? Anyway, there's old-fashioned rhubarb crumble for sweet if you fancy it."

After the lunch, it was time for the grand tour, as Joan called it. Although she was taking it slowly, George found he was struggling to keep up, his energy drained by the morning's journey combined with the warming effects of the wine and a full stomach. He was relieved when they arrived at a door with a discreet green cross.

"This is our medical facility." Joan's knock was answered by a 'Come in, please,' from inside. "This is Alice, our nurse. Alice, this is Simon who's having a look round."

Alice beamed at George and took his hand to shake. "Pleased to meet you, Simon."

"I suggested to Simon that you give him a quick check-up while he's here. He's got a rather nasty cough, if you don't mind my saying so." Joan looked at George who was yawning.

"No problem." Alice gestured for George to sit.

"I've some work to do so, if that's OK, I'll leave you to it." Joan turned to leave. "I'll be back in a while. We've got a birthday celebration and it'll be a good chance for you to meet everyone at once."

George was yawning again as he watched Alice prepare to strap a blood pressure monitor on his arm, humming to herself as she worked.

"That's 'Days' you're singing, isn't it?"

"Certainly is."

"How did you know that? Before your time, surely."

"My dad. He loved Kirsty MacColl."

"It was written by The Kinks. I played with them."

"That must have been really interesting." Alice was entering data into her computer. "I'm going to take a blood test now."

"Take as much as you like."

"I sometimes feel like I'm a vampire."

"What made you want to come here and look after old fogies?" He nearly added, 'like me', almost forgetting he was only there to suss out an occasional away day.

"You'll feel a little prick." She chuckled. "That doesn't sound very good, does it?" With a knowing look, she took the blood sample. "I love it here. I was in A&E and that was terrible. Then a ward nurse. But you never got to know anyone. Here, everyone's a friend. Joan, Mrs Tufnell, has such great ideas. And I'm not just saying that to get you to stay."

A good opportunity to test out his convalescence notion. "Do people just come for a few weeks, then…?"

"Sometimes, yes, sadly. We make them as comfortable as we can for their final days."

"I didn't actually mean that."

"Say 'ah', please." She tapped a stick on his tongue.

"Ahhhh."

"Sorry, you were telling me about The Kinks."

George didn't waste the chance while Alice continued busying herself with more tests and typing into her computer. He talked about himself, about the stars he'd met, the music they'd played, without fear of being contradicted or being told he was repeating the same old stories – and Alice appeared genuinely interested. Yet he couldn't help noticing her occasional double take at a reading or a look of concern – at least, that's how he interpreted it – as the tests progressed.

She typed a few more notes into her computer, then swung round and leaned in towards him.

"That's almost it. Is there anything else that you've not told me?"

"I used to play in folk clubs with Paul Simon." He realised as he said it that Alice might notice the similarity with his pseudonym. How he wished he'd picked a better one or come clean when he'd arrived. Luckily though, he couldn't see any reaction.

"What about you? Anything else about how you're feeling?"

"Since my wife died?" He wasn't sure he was ready to open up about Evelyn twice in a day.

"No, now. Your health."

"You've done all the tests."

"How about your hearing?"

"What about it?"

"I've noticed how you sometimes seem to strain to hear me. Turning your head to one side."

"I hadn't realised."

"It's my job to notice."

George knew that this was the moment to confess to his fears. There had been no further mention of it since the night with Tara in his room, and he had been frightened to raise it with his GP in case the news was bad.

"I've got tinnitus."

"You're a musician. They always have it. Industrial injury. The only remedy would have been ear defenders."

"That would have looked good on stage. Kids screaming at the big star and me at the back like a builder." He laughed at the thought.

"And perhaps a hi-viz jacket?"

"And hobnail boots." They laughed together. He hadn't laughed so much in ages.

"Didn't somebody actually do that?" Alice asked.

"Village People."

Alice began doing the 'YMCA' gestures so that the stethoscope she was holding swung in the air, narrowly missing George's left ear.

"Oops. Sorry. Note to self. Be more professional. I didn't catch you, did I?"

"Near miss, nothing more," George chuckled.

"So," Alice resumed in her professional voice, "anything else? Has the tinnitus got any louder recently? Or your hearing any worse?"

"Pardon?" He allowed himself the joke as it deflected from his worst fears.

Alice gave him a sympathetic smile. "Seriously, are you having trouble hearing?"

George gave a heavy sigh. "About two months ago, when I was listening to a record – The Kinks, funnily enough, 'Come Dancing', one of their later songs that I really like and people tend to forget."

Alice was still smiling. "And?"

"All the music was coming from one side. I thought there was something wrong with a loudspeaker. But it was my ears. One side had gone completely deaf."

"Is it like it now?"

"A bit."

"Let me take a look." Alice stood up, looked in George's ears, hummed a couple of times, and added some notes to her computer.

"Please tell me I'm not going deaf." All his joviality evaporated at the thought. A shiver passed through him as he imagined a life without music. What would be the point of his existence without it?

"I think you'll need some more tests. I'll have to let your GP know. He'll arrange things for you."

It wasn't the answer he wanted.

"In the meantime," Alice reached for a packet of pills from a cupboard and handed them to him, "try these. They might help."

"But you don't know what's wrong with my ears?"

"As I say, more tests." There was a knock at the door. "Don't worry. There's usually an answer."

George didn't question the word 'usually', though he wanted to. Nor did he interrogate her on what the answer might be. He couldn't explain just how important being able to hear was to him. Anyway, there wasn't time now. Joan had returned and was talking to him. He made a special effort not to look like he was straining to hear or cocking his good ear towards her.

"Do you fancy meeting everyone? It's Eddie's – Eddie McCann's – birthday. He's our artist I was telling you about. I think he also used to play in a band in the sixties too. Maybe you'll know him, though I think he was mainly in Ireland."

George could only think of Celtic music and drunken nights in the Irish pubs of North London.

"I'll only fall asleep if I stay here."

"I think we're having cake. If there's room for it after that lunch."

Joan helped him to his feet and they made their way to the lounge. George's heart sank. The space looked bright, newly decorated. But the people, in chairs lined up against the walls, looked grey and grim. They were prisoners, as they had been at Lastdays, and a world away from the picture Joan had described for Good Days. George looked around and immediately recognised Bernard. He waved, but there was no reaction, no response.

Joan gave George a brief introduction while the seated guests looked on in silence, staring blankly into the distance. A sponge cake with candles, with the name Eddie iced on the top, was presented without celebration. Everyone mumbled a rather feeble verse of 'Happy Birthday' before subsiding into obedient silence. It reminded George of how Hunter had looked when there were sweets that he wasn't allowed. Despite all the fine words, encouraging signs and smiles from Joan and Alice, here was *prima facie* evidence that nothing had really changed. Worse than that. He realised he just didn't like old people.

Joan must have sensed George's unease, maybe felt it herself.

"Don't judge us too much yet," she said gently. "We've lots to do. Work in progress." She pointed to an upright piano in the corner, camouflaged by books, magazines, pots and general bric-a-brac. "No one here plays the piano. Would you mind if I asked you to look at it? See if it's in tune?"

While everyone else was concentrating on the division of the cake, George obliged. Opening the dusty lid, he cracked his knuckles twice, then checked behind him to see no one was taking any notice of him. He tapped a few keys, then gently played a few scales. He was about to close the lid and report back to Joan that it certainly needed to be tuned, when he was struck by an idea. Without turning to see what else was happening in the room, he launched into 'Happy Birthday'. There was no response from the room. So he played it again, but this time in the rock'n'roll style of Jerry Lee Lewis that he thought some might remember. Giving the keyboard as much energy as he could muster, his illness evaporated, as it always seemed to do when he played. He'd managed a whole concert with the Beat Boys when he had flu without being sick, at least until after the adrenaline wore off. So he wasn't going to be defeated today by a cough or whatever Alice was diagnosing him with. With the eyes of Good Days suddenly on him, he hammered out the tune, almost shouting the lyrics, playing it twice before a final repeat of the last 'Happy birthday, dear Edd-ie, happy birthday to you,' and signing off with a 'cha cha cha' flourish.

At first there was jaw-dropped, open-mouthed, supine silence. Then a single clap that burst into a spontaneous round of applause. Eddie even raised his arthritic hands above his head and cried, "Thank you."

"Thank you, Worthing," George called back, imagining himself at Woodstock or the Winter Gardens.

"I think we need to give Simon a proper introduction. As you can see, he's a whiz at the keyboards." Joan was smiling, still clapping.

George nodded modestly.

"Simon was in a band – I'm right in saying that, aren't I, Simon?"

"Military band?" came a voice from a wheelchair.

"Brass band?" called another.

"Should be banned," came a weak voice from by the window. Was that Bernard?

"More like this." George gave what he hoped looked like a rock'n'roll swivel of the piano stool to face the keyboard and thumped the opening notes to 'Whole Lotta Shakin' Goin' On'. He looked over his shoulder to see if he should begin the vocals. One or two were gently tapping to the rhythm. One had his hand cupped behind his ear. Two ladies had clasped their hands over theirs. He stopped.

"What else do you know?" Joan asked.

"'Silence is Golden'?" called Eddie, to faint laughter.

"Can you play 'Far, Far Away'?" called the lady next to him. The ripple of laughter grew.

George wondered why he didn't stop there and then. Yet he felt encouraged that they felt confident enough to joke. He turned back to the keyboard, saying, "You might know this from 1959. This chap used to be on television."

He began playing a tune he knew as 'Side Saddle', a plinkety-plonk sort of melody that he'd not thought about, let alone played, for fifty years or more. Though it needed concentration and meant keeping his eyes on the keys, he could still hear comments from behind.

"Who used to play that?"

"Russ someone."

"Abbot?"

"Conway."

"I used to like his smile."

"Was missing a finger, you know."

"Didn't he used to drive a bus?"

"While he was playing? That would have been clever."

"You're thinking of someone else."

"Is he still with us?"

"What, the bus driver?"

"Russ Conway, silly."

Despite a few dud notes, someone started to clap along. By the end, they all were joining in. When he stopped, there was another round of applause and calls for different tunes. Alma Cogan, Winifred Atwell, Bing Crosby, The Beatles. George prepared himself for 'Twist and Shout'. But before he could start, a louder voice cut across the room.

"Isn't it time for *Escape to the Country*?"

All interest in George dissipated behind a chorus of, "*Escape to the Country*."

Joan came across to him and whispered something to him. It was his deaf ear and he made no sense of it, but nodded agreement nonetheless. As a result, he was offered a seat with a cushion, handed a cup of tea and a piece of cake and left to settle himself down with everyone else in front of the television.

* * *

When George awoke, it was because Joan was easing the plate from his hands. It was empty but for a few crumbs, most of the cake crushed beneath his feet. The room was now almost empty but for three sleeping figures slumped in armchairs of varying designs, age and degrees of wear.

"Simon, Simon. Sorry, I didn't mean to wake you but I thought you were about to drop the plate."

George was slow to respond, a combination of the haze of sleep and the unfamiliar name. "Sorry, how long have I been sitting here?"

"Nearly two hours."

"Crikey. I think all that walking around has worn me out."

"Well, time for a well-earned cuppa. If you've got room for another."

* * *

Back in her office, Joan poured tea using a real strainer, then passed him a plate of biscuits. "Jammy Dodger? I don't think you had much birthday cake."

He took one, and collapsed into a chair.

"I hope you liked what you saw."

George helped himself to a second Jammy Dodger. "Used to have these when I was younger."

"It's why I get them. Everyone remembers them. They love them."

"Though they're not as jammy as they used to be."

Joan nodded. "Can I just say that I thought what you did for Eddie's birthday was absolutely wonderful. The way you played the piano for them was terrific. I hope you didn't mind some of the things they called out."

"I used to get worse. Much worse."

"They didn't mean it. They loved it. They're still talking about it. I can tell you, some of those people who were joining in have barely spoken since I came here. You really helped bring some of them out of themselves. I can't thank you enough."

"Not me, the power of music. Don't underestimate it."

"I certainly don't."

"I just hope it's not too much for some of those old dears." He realised the 'old' was out of order given that he probably wasn't much younger, if at all, but he needed to make it clear to Joan that he was not one of them. She let it pass.

"So what have you made of Good Days?"

"You need to get that piano fixed."

"I will, don't worry. Apart from that?"

"I think it's very nice."

"Nurse Alice tells me that she thinks you'd benefit from some special care."

"She's probably right." This was the moment he was expecting; the sales pitch. He readied himself to reveal his own plan, the odd day or week to recuperate, to get himself back together.

"Unfortunately we can't offer short-term convalescence."

How had she guessed that was what he was after? "And might you have?"

"We're not really set up to be, you know, a convalescent home. Or a hotel." Joan laughed uneasily. "And no real plans to do it at the moment."

So all the effort and pain was to end in failure; nothing was going to be solved. After the euphoria of playing to a live audience – even if they were captive and barely alive – he felt tiredness, frailty, hopelessness and worthlessness sweep back through him. He shrunk into his chair and slowly screwed his eyes closed as he felt them swell with water.

Joan paused, took a deep breath, then said softly, "What I would like to do is offer you a job."

At first he didn't react, as if he hadn't heard; then he gradually eased himself forward, opening his eyes again.

Joan continued. "Not a big one or an arduous one, but one that's important to Good Days. It came to me while you were sleeping in there. We have a record and bookshop in the town, on the esplanade. It's meant to raise funds for us, but it's been closed for a few months. We've no one to run it. It's a bit of a mess. It needs someone who understands and loves music to help get it back into shape. Would you like to do it? It wouldn't be full time and we'll get some people to help and do the books. And only when you're well and feeling up to it." George had now sat back and closed his eyes again. She hesitated before adding, "We'd offer you an en suite apartment to live in. It's in a converted stable. We passed it on the way in. I don't suppose it's as big as the house you have in London, but more space than a standard guest room. That's something I want to improve for everyone. And we'd offer you full use of our care and medical services." She leaned forward and lightly touched his knee. "Just first thoughts but I'm sure we can make it work, if you like the idea. What do you think?"

He didn't know what to think. But Joan wasn't finished.

"I was also looking at the way everyone responded to you this afternoon. We need music here. Just having you here would be so perfect. If you're up for it, as well as looking after the records in the shop, I'd like to make a unique role for you here. To get people singing. Bring joy into their lives through song. I think we should call it," she paused to give emphasis to what was to follow, "Musician in Residence. How does that sound?"

He'd enjoyed the afternoon, of course. And here was Joan offering an alternative to living alone, to being ill, to being so lonely. Yet once again, here he was, faced with leaving his home and the memories of Evelyn and Hunter.

With no response, Joan withdrew her hand. "You remember Eddie, who you sang 'Happy Birthday' to and who did these paintings? He has a big, big record collection. I think he'd appreciate your help sorting them out."

George still didn't speak. He was looking down and just wanting to be home.

Chapter 35

Tara and Mark's weekend started badly. They were late leaving, each blaming the other, and roadworks on the motorway meant they arrived with only a few minutes before their first heat. It might have been a disaster but Tara had exercised her voice all journey and being thrown in almost on arrival left no time to be frozen by nerves. When the results were announced, the judges gushed that they were, 'an exciting and exhilarating mash-up of original sounds, melody and improvisation.'

The second heats in the afternoon didn't go so well. Maybe they'd had time to get nervous or just weren't as fresh. "I think we're out," Mark said gloomily as they packed up the kit. And they would have been but for one of the winners being disqualified for having already been signed by an agent. As next best losers, Mark and Tara made it to the finals on Sunday.

Saturday night was spent in frantic rehearsal, ironing out the flaws that had beset them in the afternoon and trying a few new ideas based on the judges' feedback. The only distraction was Tara checking her phone in dread of a message from Gramps.

"Stop keep doing that," Mark had groaned after the third time.

"I have to be sure Gramps isn't in any trouble." To her relief, there was nothing.

By Sunday, they felt they were ready.

"We meet at last." One of the finals' judges stepped over to them. "I'm Zak, by the way. Sorry we've not met up like I promised. But I'm excited to be able to hear you live after all this time. I hope you do yourselves justice."

The heats had been held in rehearsal rooms across the city in front of only the judges. The finals were in a large hall, packed with enthusiastic supporters, cheering and clapping the other contenders – a heavy metal band sporting the name Blade, three singer-songwriters, two four-piece rock bands, two folk duos and a choir. Tara and Mark were on last, following Blade.

"How can we compete with them?" Tara asked Mark as the band seemed to be refusing to leave the stage, reluctant to relinquish the adoration and rapturous applause given them by their fans.

"Come on, it's our cue. Be brave." Mark gave her hand a squeeze. Struggling with her microphone and stand, her route to centre stage was obstructed by Blade's drummer, deliberately she felt, then blocked by the lead singer, sweating and bare-chested, still waving and blowing kisses. He paused long enough to turn to her.

"I wouldn't bother, luv. Look at 'em," he gloated, before raising both arms in a salute to the baying mob below, releasing from his armpits pungent evidence of the energy and effort put into his performance.

'Blade, Blade, Blade,' they were chanting.

Tara might have responded but her mobile bleeped.

Blade's lead heard it through the cacophony. "That'll be the organisers. Telling you not to bother," he sneered, "though if you weren't so crap, you'd have turned that thing off." With a cackle, he swiped his mike stand up to gesture a triumphant farewell to the audience, catching Tara on the side of her head. For a second time she might have responded, but more important was the message. Muttering a profanity to herself, she checked the blow hadn't drawn blood, before tugging the mobile from her pocket.

It wasn't Gramps. It was a 'good luck' message from Jeff. Now she felt doubly sad and guilty.

"Come on, T. Put the phone down and let's get started. They're waiting." Mark's voice from behind her was urgent, his computer and keyboard set up and ready. The auditorium was emptying now Blade had left, leaving Zak and the other judges, notebooks in hand, watching from the stalls in anticipation. Now was her time. She clicked the cable Mark was offering into her microphone, took a deep breath and steadied herself.

* * *

"'There was such emotion in Mark and Tara's performance. Powerful and engaging,'" Zak read out before announcing the winners. "'The female singer, Tara, managed to combine joy with a deep sense of pain. The arrangements by Mark were really inventive and original – it was all so fresh. We especially liked the unique use of natural sounds to create percussion and accompaniment – what they called psychedelic rap – that melded with the softness and appeal of the female voice. Overall it was a very exciting performance. You really stood out. Well done.'"

They didn't win. But joint second, along with one of the singer-songwriters, entitled them to £250 and a place on a Best of the Bands tour in the New Year.

By the time they were ready to start the journey home, it was late and they were exhilarated and exhausted.

"Funny that metal band was last," Mark chortled. "Can't we stay another night and celebrate?"

"I wish we could, but I've got to get back to Gramps," Tara apologised, shaking her head. "How long do you think it'll take?"

"Hours."

"Do you mind if I sleep?" She yawned.

"So long as you don't mind if I do."

"You'd better not."

Chapter 36

As Joan's car hummed along, George sat in silence, drifting in and out of consciousness, running over and over in his head what he should do. Her offer was tempting. But would everything change as soon as he agreed? It always did.

Joan had driven him to the station. A problem with the engineering works meant it was still replacement buses and there was an hour wait for the next. With George doubled up through coughing and looking very pale, she said softly to him, "I know I told you we're not a hotel, but I really think you should stay with us tonight." She spoke with a concerned look. "In the morning, we can go through the medical report from Alice and see if we can get you some help. If you'll let us, we'll make up a bed for you in the Medical Room."

But he had no way of letting Tara know. She'd worry. And anyway, he could feel his body giving in. He didn't want to be in a strange place and especially not a hospital bed. He wanted to get back to his own bedroom, be in his own bed. "Thank you. But no. I want to go home."

Guided by the satnav, Joan drove him back to London, kept

awake by a discussion on the car radio about the role of the church sermon.

"There's never anything on the radio on a Sunday," he said as she turned the volume down to barely above a murmur, his only words all journey.

'You have reached your destination,' the satnav announced.

"Simon, I think we're here. Which door are you?"

George's eyelids felt glued to his eyes. "By the street light," he instructed wearily. When the car eased to a halt, he made no attempt to move. Joan's mobile bleeped. She checked it, then rang back.

"Yes, here now," she whispered. "I think he's asleep… Yes, all the way. He looks terrible. So frail. I'm really worried about him. I wish I'd made him stay… Well, if he doesn't look like he's able to get out of the car, I'm coming straight back. Can you get the bed in the medical suite made up? Yes, I'll let you know… See you in a couple of hours."

George was slowly easing himself up and felt for his seat belt. Joan reached across to help. "I'm OK," he said as he grappled it open. Seeing Joan unbuckling hers, he put an arm across to restrain her. "No. You stay where you are. I'm OK. I don't want any help." He knew he sounded grumpy, but he wanted to go in alone. It was his house, his and Evelyn's, and he felt closer to her than ever. He didn't want strangers in. Not tonight. "Please don't get out."

As he shuffled across the front of the car, she wound down the window. "You'll think about what I've said?" She gave him an affectionate smile.

He gestured wearily back at her. "I just want to get indoors."

"Of course."

"I don't mean to sound ungrateful."

"I understand."

"Thanks for the offers. I think things are clearer for me now."

"Let me know." Joan watched as he struggled up the path to his front door, not sure if he would make it, and wondered if she'd ever see him again.

* * *

Tara closed her eyes as Mark headed for the motorway, but she didn't sleep. Her mind was in turmoil, running continually over the whirlwind of the last few days and what might happen in the next few months. A tour could be the big breakthrough for them. Recognition. Success. But what of Gramps? If she went, what would happen to him? Was it wrong to hope her mum would take over caring for him? And would he let her? She expected Mark to ask her about it and was relieved he didn't. Perhaps he was too tired to raise it or was just biding his time.

That was when her mobile rang.

"Hello, is that Tara?"

"Yes, who's that?"

"Robin. Robin Brandon. You know, Uncle Robin."

It was as if a bucket of cold water had been thrown at her.

Mark noticed her jerk upright. "Everything alright?"

She flapped a hand at him to be quiet. "Why are you ringing me?"

"Your dad gave me your number. Told me everything."

"And?"

"I have some news for you."

"You're turning yourself in."

Robin grunted. "He told me you thought I'd broken into your grandfather's and stolen his records."

"And did you?"

"Of course I didn't."

"Who did, then?"

"If you let me speak, I'll tell you."

"What is it, T?" Mark asked again. Tara again waved to hush Mark. It was a long enough pause for Robin to seize his chance.

"I know where your grandfather's records are."

"Where?"

"In a lock-up."

"All of them?"

"I think so."

"So how do you know? If you didn't steal them."

"If you'd let me tell you without interruption." Robin paused, took the silence as affirmation, then carried on. "Out of order, what happened. Bang out of order. And nothing to do with me, before you say it again. Not directly, anyway."

Tara resisted the temptation to ask what that meant, but let him continue.

"Your dad told you I'd been in the house, yes?"

"Yes."

"And I did the wifi for you and stuff."

"Yes."

"And that I'd borrowed a few of your grandfather's records."

It was too much for Tara this time. "Borrowed?"

"Yes, borrowed. I took a few. I told your dad it was to have them valued. Which was true. Sort of. And I gave them back."

"Sort of?"

"Some of them are rare, worth money."

"Which is why you stole them."

"From family? Not me. I look for opportunities, give you that. But I'm not dishonest."

Tara let pass the history of the carriage clock and his family name. "So?"

"Your dad gave me a set of keys to check the wifi. Which I did. When you were all out."

"And?"

"And I also used them to let myself in to take a handful of records each time. Not so many that he'd notice." He paused for a moment. "I didn't tell your dad."

"So you stole them. To do what? Sell them?"

"Of course not. Anything that was worth money, I got made into bootlegs. You know…"

"I know what a bootleg is."

"Ron, the bloke at the studio your grandfather went to – he knows people who make pretty good copies. Limited edition. Coloured vinyl. Replica covers. Then I sold them online or traded them into shops. As they were rare, we got a good price. That was what I was borrowing your grandfather's records for. I took a few, got them copied, put them back."

"I suppose that might explain why Gramps thought things had been moved," she said, grudgingly.

"That'll be it. I wasn't stealing them."

"So when did you change your mind and take them all?"

"I didn't."

"Who did, then?"

"When your dad said the whole collection had gone, I knew straight away."

"Yes?"

"Ron."

Tara rolled her eyes as it dawned on her. "That bloke at the studio? Who made the bootlegs?"

"Yeah, Ron. I confronted him. Denied it at first. But I knew. A quick buck is what he was after. There's more money in originals than making copies. Thing is, though, we have history, so I laid it on the line to him. Said he had to give them back. In the end, he's told me where they are. All I've got to do now is get them back to your grandfather."

"But they got in using keys. And Dad gave you a set. He told me. And the car outside Gramps' house, Mark saw it, it was yours." Tara felt Robin's story unpicking like her dad's had. She was getting good at this sleuthing business.

At the sound of his name, Mark gestured at the approaching motorway services. Tara ignored him.

"The Beamer? Wasn't mine," Robin continued. "Ron's. I lent it from him, when I went looking for business. Made me look classy. It was his car. He had it the rest of the time."

"But the house keys…"

"If they were the ones I used… maybe I left them in the car or at his gaff. Or he found them, made copies. I don't know. But it wasn't me." He sighed. "I'd never have taken him for a tealeaf. Not from mates. Still, you live and learn. Even at my age. So there it is. I only called because I wanted you to know. Your grandfather's records are safe."

"Have you told the police?"

"I told you, I'm not a thief, nor am I a nark. So long as I get them all to give back to you, I said I'd say nothing. You must promise me you won't."

Tara didn't let on they'd already had a police message saying the case had been closed. "Maybe. Can I tell Gramps?"

"Why not. My word's my bond."

"Can I ask one more question?"

"If you make it quick."

"There were Gramps' records in Dad's house. How did they get there?"

"Were there?" He paused. "Can't say for sure. Maybe the ones I took first when I did the wifi. I gave them back to your dad and he said he'd drop them off. If that's them, I don't know why he never took them back. He said he would."

"I suppose that's possible." At least this corroborated her dad's version of events. "It all got a bit complicated at home."

"Yes, so your dad said. I hope they sort things out, your mum and dad. I know you don't think I like your mum and I can be a bit of a bastard but I'm a family man at heart. Family comes first for me. Believe me."

"I might if we get the records back."

"When. Not if. But I gotta go."

"OK."

"Bye now."

Tara let the phone drop.

"Anything wrong? That sounded really odd." Mark had slowed the car as if preparing to pull into the service area slip road.

"Keep going."

"Sure?"

"Sure. That was Uncle Robin. He's found Gramps' records. He's going to get them back."

"Wow. You mean he's a good guy, not a robbing bastard after all?"

Tara's shoulders slumped. "I don't know. Give me a minute. I need to think things out."

They drove on in silence.

***

"Are you awake?" Mark waited until they'd left the motorway before disturbing Tara.

"Just about. I think I've been asleep."

"You were."

"How's the road been?"

"OK mostly. We've made good time."

"Before I nodded off, I was thinking."

"What about?"

"Sshh. I'm calling Gramps." Tara, holding her mobile to her ear, let out a frustrated gasp. "Answerphone. Hi, Gramps. Sorry we're so late. We'll be with you in about twenty minutes. Hope you're OK. And I've some news for you. Love you."

"Does Uncle Robin have my hard drive, too?"

"How would I know? I expect so. I just hope Gramps is alright."

"It's late, he'll be in bed. Or on his piano. Wait until he hears what Robin's told you."

Tara let him chunter. Her mind was whirring over and over questions she couldn't answer. Mark didn't appear to notice, until they pulled into her grandfather's road.

"You OK, T?" he asked as the car drew to a halt.

"I've made a decision."

"What about?"

Tara drew a deep breath to prepare herself, but before she could answer, Mark's mobile rang.

"Hi, Zak," he answered. "Yeah, thanks." There was a pause while Mark listened and Tara fidgeted. "Wow. Yeah. I'll tell her. Great!" Mark let the mobile drop away. "Zak says there's a gig next weekend where someone's dropped out. Could we fill in?"

Tara heaved a sigh. "Tell him I can't do it."

"What do you mean, 'Can't do it'?"

"I was just about to tell you. I've made up my mind."

Mark lifted the mobile back to his mouth. "Sorry, Zak, can I ring you back?" He leaned in to Tara, looking her straight in the eyes. "I don't understand. What are you saying?"

"I'm saying I'm not going. I can't be part of Mark'n'Tara anymore."

Mark stared at her, uncomprehending. "I don't get it. The biggest thing that's happened to us and you say you're letting me down?"

"I know. I'm sorry."

"I thought you wanted this."

"I did. Just I've been thinking about it. Not just now but all the time."

"Thinking what? What's come over you?"

"It's Gramps. I can't just leave him."

Mark stared at her, expressionless.

"Thinking about what Robin said. Getting the records back." Her voice was soft, but quavering. "He said family comes first. That settled it." She ignored Mark's stifled snort. "Gramps is family. He's my grandfather. He's old, he's frail. He's depending on me. I can't just go swanning off and forget about him."

"It's not swanning off. It's an opportunity. And we don't even know if next weekend means we have to go anywhere. It could be local."

"Doesn't matter. If it's not this weekend, it'll happen eventually. I can't leave Gramps. I just can't."

"Is that what you call, 'doing your duty'?" Mark made the speech mark gesture to emphasise his disapproval.

"If you like. I know he'd do it for me."

"What about your mum? Can't she look after him?"

"He's my responsibility."

"You're giving up on your chance of success and fame."

She shrugged. "I've no choice."

"Think about it. Don't do this. Not now."

"I owe him. I can't help it. I couldn't live with myself if I abandoned him and something happened."

"But we're on the edge of something good."

"I don't care."

"We're a team."

"You'll be OK on your own." She saw Mark try to interrupt but gave him no space. "You won't change my mind. Sorry. You were going to go it alone anyway. Call Zak back and tell him. Mark'n'Tara is finished."

With that, she stepped out of the car and strode down the road. Last time she'd done this it'd been the night of the burglary. She hoped history wasn't going to repeat itself.

The house was in darkness. The streetlights glinted in the frosty air.

"He'd better be alright." Tara quickened her pace as she walked up the path.

Fumbling in her bag for the keys, she eased the door open. There was no sound from inside. No piano, no music, no radio, no TV.

"Gramps!"

Still no response. She could hear Mark's breathing behind her. "Please, T," he whispered.

"Shh." He was alongside her now. "Something's wrong." She stood, frozen in the doorway.

Mark pushed past her into the kitchen. "He's not in here." She steeled herself and followed. Neat rows of packets and tins were laid out on the worktop, unopened, Post-It notes intact, as she'd left them.

Turning, she opened the door to the living room. Empty. Her heart pounding, she ran up the stairs and burst into the music room, knocking as she pushed it open. "Gramps." Then, "He's not here either. I'll check he's not in my room." Passing his closed bedroom door, she raced, two at a time, up to her room. Empty too.

She walked slowly down to where Mark was waiting on the landing outside George's bedroom door. There was no light, no coughing from inside.

"He must be asleep," Mark whispered.

"He was coughing in his sleep all last week."

They looked at each other, hoping the other would have an answer.

"Perhaps a weekend in bed has cleared it." Mark did not sound convinced.

Tara knocked lightly on the door. "Gramps."

A shaft of moonlight streamed through the landing window on to the door handle. As if in slow motion, she put her hand on it, turning it gently, calling again, without conviction, "Gramps."

Mark put his hand to the door, nudging it gently. "Let me."

"No, he's my responsibility. If anything's happened, it's my fault. He depended on me. I left him." She took a deep breath, preparing for what she was going to find on the inside. Pushing with her fists clenched, the door swung open, the moonlight casting a gloomy pall across the floor. Face screwed up, eyes closed tightly, fearing the worst, she stepped in.

Chapter 37

Tara stood in front of the ticket barriers as suitcases, being wheeled, pushed and dragged, circled around her. There was no sign of her mum getting off the train or trailing along the platform.

"Tara!" Bridget materialised from nowhere.

A few teary embraces followed, then the usual questions about the journey and delays, before Tara pointed to a coffee shop.

"Tell me everything," Bridget said gently once they were settled. "I'm so sorry you had to cope on your own." It was only when the retreat ended that Tara had been able to reach her and break the news. Although they'd spoken on the phone during the journey, there was much to catch up on. Tara talked almost without breathing, while Bridget clutched her arm, listening intently.

When Tara paused, Bridget let go and slumped back to let it all sink in, sighing before saying, "And then there's clearing the house. What's left of it." She wiped a tear away.

"I know. I can't bear to think about it." Tara shook her head, blinking to prevent herself from crying.

"What about the piano? The magazines?"

"I know."

"And the records. Especially finding them now."

"I know."

"And the rest of the stuff? Did Robin have it all?"

"I think some of Nan's jewellery had already gone. But the big things are still there. In that bastard Ron's lock-up."

Bridget seemed to accept her daughter's description. "And it was really Robin who found it all?"

"So he says."

"How easy it is to misjudge someone. What I don't get is how they knew we were all in Basingstoke for your grandfather's birthday. Someone must have told them."

"We think it might have been Gramps, when he was trying to get hold of the studio. He says he left them a phone message."

"Not a robbin' bastard after all." Bridget lowered her voice, aware they were being overheard by a couple giving them shocked looks from a nearby table. "What are we going to do about the house? I know it's a bit early but we'll have to get a valuation done."

"I haven't had time, sorry."

"It shouldn't be yours to worry about." Bridget grimaced. "I'm just sorry it's landed on you like this." She sat back, blowing out her cheeks as she did. "So how's your grandfather taking it all?"

"I think he's OK with it. He's excited he's getting his records back, I know that."

"It's all happened so fast. Is he going to settle in, do you think?"

"He's not said that much."

"That's not good."

"I don't think it's bad. Mrs Tufnell's nurses are looking after him and I think he's just getting used to the idea of the move. He's still not well but he's already meeting people. Making friends. He even spoke about sorting out the record shop on the seafront. And he says he wants to start singing classes for the residents. So he's obviously feeling better in himself."

"The cough?"

"A bit better. He's on some pretty strong medication. It's making a difference. It didn't help that he was worrying about what he was going to do with himself. He was scared about going deaf."

"I thought something was wrong."

"They hope it's only linked to his cough, pneumonia, whatever it is. Just needs time and looking after. Mrs Tufnell is certainly doing that."

"Mrs Tufnell. Thank God for her."

"I'm not sure what would have happened if she hadn't been around. She was wonderful. And she really laughed when she discovered his name. His real name, that is."

"But is he happy?"

"It's a big change. I hope he will be. He's really excited about getting his records back, going through them, making sure they're all there."

"What about his piano?"

"Mrs Tufnell's arranging to get it moved down. She says it's much better than the one they already have. Gramps is really pleased about that."

"Will he know anyone, have any friends?"

"There's one guy there, Eddie I think Mrs Tufnell said his name is. He's also got records and they already seem to be getting on. When he's properly well, I think Gramps will be like a pig in muck going through them all. That's before he gets at the records in the shop. She says she's already heard them reminiscing about music and they even broke into song."

"I wished Toby had encouraged him to sing when he was with us. Remember how we all used to sing together when you were small?"

"How is it with you two?"

Bridget took a deep sigh and grasped her daughter's hand. "I think it's over. Before I went away, your dad called about meeting up. Asking forgiveness. Maybe getting back together. But I've had a week when they," she gestured over her shoulder back in the direction of Wales, "helped me think things over, about what I really want. And to tell the truth, I'm really not sure if I want to."

So they talked, Tara telling her mum about the Battle of the Bands, how their music was an online sensation and how it now had tens of thousands of hits.

"And tell me again, slowly this time, what happened, you know, when you got back."

"It was quite late on the Sunday evening when we found the house dark. Nothing had changed from when I'd left on the Saturday, and when I called out to Gramps and he didn't reply, I was scared shitless. Sorry, but I was." She looked apologetically at her mum for the language, but Bridget merely waved her to carry on. "I didn't know what to think when there was no one in his bedroom. But then there was an almighty crash from the hall, so Mark and I rushed down to find the front door open and him crumpled up on the floor. We got to him just as Mrs Tufnell rushed in."

"She'd brought him back from the rest home?"

"She said afterwards Gramps wouldn't let her help him, but she waited and, when she saw him fall, raced in. I'm glad she did. I wouldn't have known what to do."

"Who told you about the Resident Musician thing?"

"She did. After we got him into bed and waited for the emergency doctor, she told us about his visit, and her plan.

About the makeover of the home – it's called Good Days now, not Lastdays. And about the charity shop and the Musician in Residence."

"And Dad – Gramps?"

"You'll have to ask him, but he agreed for Mrs Tufnell to take him back. No one forced him. I think he knew something had to happen."

"I'm so sorry you couldn't get in touch with me."

Tara shrugged. "It's all worked out. Mrs Tufnell's great though."

"What about Mark and you?"

"We're OK."

"Really?"

"Really."

"And what did your grandfather say about you touring?"

"He insists I do it. Says he won't speak to me if I turn it down. I didn't want to make him make a decision about Good Days because of me. But he says he's going there because he wants to. When I told him about the Battle of the Bands, he couldn't have been more excited. I think he felt he'd been a part of it and that somehow made him feel better. I think if I'd not said I was going to do it, he'd have felt let down."

Tara could tell her mum wasn't quite sure what to make of this. But to explain would have meant breaking Gramps' confidence about his own missed opportunities and her mum's part in it, and she wasn't going to do that. So she went on to tell her mum that the reaction to her music was now so good, a tour of the States looked likely. There might even be a recording offer. She barely stopped for breath. It was like the old days.

* * *

When the story was finished, mother and daughter hugged. And the people on the other table, having listened to it all, took their trays to the disposal area and phoned all their friends about the odd couple in the station café.

Chapter 38

"'I Almost Lost My Mind'. Ready?" George ran his hands along the keyboard and began the introduction, raising his hand to cue in the vocals of the Good Days Choir.

It was the one, less familiar song that he had insisted on being in the repertoire when he came up with their set list. In the eleven months since he'd moved to Good Days, his music therapy sessions had proved to be so popular that they'd gained notoriety outside the home. They'd been photographed for the local paper and appeared on local TV news when the primary school nearby had asked them to perform at their community evening. There was even talk of a charity CD.

Some things hadn't changed. Rehearsals still had to stop for *Escape to the Country*. Except tonight, George had stopped them early to make sure they all watched the commercials on the other channel.

"Bloody adverts," moaned one of the other guests.

"Listen up, everybody." Joan didn't normally come to the communal room to watch TV, but she did tonight. "We have a celebrity in our ranks. The music for the next commercial was written by our very own George Turnbull."

And when the soap commercial began to a tinkling piano, instead of the usual 'What a rubbish tune', or 'That soap brings me out in a rash', tonight there was a round of applause.

The call from the advertising agency had come out of the blue, telling George that one of the songs he'd written years back had been picked up for a TV commercial. They told him it was premiering tonight and to look out for some royalties. What's more, they'd also said they planned to use it as part of a Christmas campaign. It might even get a download release and George would have a hit at last.

When he'd emailed Tara in America with the news, she'd told him hers – that she and Mark were now engaged. But more than that. They had a recording deal and were releasing a Christmas single too. They'd joked about whether his song would stop theirs from being Number One.

As he made his way back across to his new home, the only sadness was the call he'd had from Bridget saying she couldn't visit him for a couple of weekends as she was sorting out what would happen to the house in Basingstoke and finding somewhere new to live because of the divorce. *At least that's settled though,* he thought to himself as he opened the door to his new record room.

The walls were neatly racked with shelving, his records lined up alongside Eddie's. And there was a new section. This was where they were keeping the shared records that they had bought for themselves from the Good Days charity record shop. It had taken a while to get up and running but it was now making money. Joan joked that half the takings were coming from George and Eddie.

Some evenings, they would sit in the room together and sing along to each other's favourites. On Mondays, Thursdays and

Saturdays, they took a selection and played them to everyone at Good Days. There was talk of buying a vintage jukebox too, to put in the main lounge. And once a week, they'd put on a show, George on piano and vocals, Eddie on harmony. George made sure they always sang a Simon and Garfunkel song or two. 'Past Prime and Old Carbuncle', they became known as. And there were always requests for George to do 'Missing Evelyn'.

But the record room, on his own, was where George enjoyed most of his time. Like it had been in London, there seemed to be as many records on the floor as on the shelves. There was always a need to move, sort, re-sort. It was a never-ending delight.

Pulling up his rocking chair, he began riffling through a loose stack. He studied every sleeve – its colour, its design – before putting the record on the turntable and humming along to himself as it played. Sixth one down was a special one. He looked at his handwritten message, written over fifty years back.

'Shame about the grammar, Paul.'

Into his ears flooded the opening chords of 'Homeward Bound', the guitar and vocals wafting across the room. Closing his eyes, gently rocking back and forth, he sang along to himself until the rocking stopped and he was enveloped by blissful sleep.

 **Matador**